ON THE BLUFFS

A NOVEL

STEVEN SCHINDLER

THE ELEVATED PRESS
LOS ANGELES

Also by Steven Schindler

Sewer Balls

From the Block

From Here to Reality

The Elevated Press
PO Box 65218
Los Angeles, CA 90065
www.elevated.com

This book is a work of fiction. Names, characters, places and incidents are the products of the author's imagination or are used fictitiously. Any similarity to events, locales or persons, living or dead, is entirely coincidental.

ISBN-13: 978-0-9662408-1-8
ISBN-10: 0-9662408-1-2
Library of Congress Control Number: 2008938943

The Elevated Press Original Trade Paperback
First Edition September, 2009
Photography and cover design by Craig Wolf
www.craigwolf.com

In loving memory of Mom and Dad
We're forever thankful
They're forever in our hearts

Thank you to all the friends and family
who so graciously slogged through
the early versions
of this book
and a special thanks
to my wife, Sue,
for encouraging me
to always keep moving forward.

CHAPTER ONE

The "re-write" room, as the faded sign next to the doorway declared, wasn't that at all. It was a sorry excuse for a union-mandated coffee break lounge, with stained, worn carpeting and office furniture so old and decrepit, you wouldn't think there was a chance of anyone attempting to steal any of it for their office or home. But in fact, most office items, even personal possessions that weren't nailed down, were stolen from the studios and offices of Americana Radio System, or ARS as it was called by its loyal staff, supporters, and listeners. Its detractors simply referred to it as "the Arse."

There was a time when this really was a re-write room; years ago when the monstrous, peeling steel desk was new and the rusted teletype machine in the corner, now used as a base for a water cooler, noisily spat out headlines non-stop. At the very least, it was a room where a news writer could grab a cup of joe in a paper cup, read a copy of the *Washington Star* or the *Los Angeles Herald Examiner* or the *New York Herald Tribune* or any number of daily newspapers across the country that have long since sent their printing presses to the scrap iron yards, while listening to the incessant pounding of steel keys against rolls of paper in the teletype machine. And while reading a Washington Senators box score or the latest from *'Lil Abner,* you wouldn't even notice the news stories exploding letter by letter onto pulpy reams of paper just a few feet away unless a series of loud bells rang out. It was only then, that a person knew that something special was coming across "the wires." A news item preceded by bells meant, *Never mind what Frank Howard did against the Indians last night, put down that cup of coffee and pay attention to this story!* A news writer could glance at the breaking news story, and rush back to the news room to monitor the rest of the teletype machines that once lined a news room called "the bullpen." No matter how hard manufacturers tried to insulate those teletype machines, each one of them made a racket akin to a hardware store paint mixer mixing paint cans filled with ball bearings. There were a couple of dozen of them going at once; Associated Press, United Press International, Agence Francais-Presse, local news services, sports services, government services, and regional news services all spewing out information non-stop. That was all before ARS became a listener and foundation and grant-supported, self-described progressive-alternative news-talk radio network feeding over two hundred radio affiliates across America. Actually, if it wasn't supported by a couple of uber-rich Hollywood celebrities, it would have gone off the air years ago.

When Brian DeLouise first started in the news room fifteen years ago as a 135-pound, long-haired, ice hockey-playing desk assistant, the place was buzzing with activity. It doubled as the Washington bureau for the television and radio divisions of the Independent National News Service. Now the news "bullpen" is an eerily quiet cavernous space with cubicles extending from a darkened, round glass structure like the spokes of a wheel. The glass structure is the main studio for ARS where network radio programs originate.

Brian was pissed. Not because he's now a 175-pound, receding hair-lined, soft-bellied producer/production engineer. Or because he's just beginning his night shift as producer for *Night Hawks* and grabbing his first cup of coffee in the re-write room. He's pissed because he has once again lost at water cooler Russian roulette. Just as he pressed the blue plastic spigot on the water cooler sitting on the defunct teletype machine with the empty coffee pot underneath, he knew that once again he had the misfortune of having to go down the hall, to the storage room/slop sink closet where the heavy blue plastic bottles of water were stored.

"Shit! Why am I the only one who replaces the water bottles around here?" he exclaimed to no one, since he was the only person working the night shift, except for the host sitting in her hermetically sealed radio studio and another producer working the board, waiting to be relieved so she could go home.

Brian grabbed the only chair in the room with wheels on it and pushed it across the carpet, down the long hall. As he pushed the chair down the hall, he noticed there was another snot booger rubbed on the wall about six feet past where the other one has been for several weeks. He was convinced that the same person who drank the last drop of water from the cooler and didn't replace the empty five-gallon water bottle was most likely the same kind of person who would wipe snot on the wall.

He opened the slop sink closet door and was struck by the strong smell of ammonia as he grabbed hold of a large bottle of water and lifted it onto the chair. He pushed the chair loaded with forty pounds of water down the hall and into the re-write room. As he rolled close to the water cooler, the wheel of the chair got snagged on a hole in the carpeting. He gave an extra push, which opened up several more inches of the tear. Brian looked at the gaping hole and sighed before he removed the empty bottle and put the full one in its place, only spilling a few cups of water on the electrical outlet in the process.

Brian knew that he had exactly three minutes to get into position in the control room by the cue music playing on the speaker in the break room. He hated working overnights, but somehow, over the years, management decided that whenever someone was needed as a last minute replacement, he was called in. Maybe it was because he was the most competent or because they knew he never complained. Or maybe it was because they knew he didn't have a life.

Beth Keller hosted *Night Hawks.* Brian thought it ironic that the title of any show on the left-wing ARS radio network would have the word *Hawks* in it. Brian sat in his position in the control room, just opposite Beth, and inspected the rundown for that night's program, which included a telephone interview with the author of *Homeopathic Paradise.*

Beth looked up from her notes briefly and pressed a

button next to her microphone.

"Oh, hi Brain. Nice to see you again. Where's Sandra?"

Brian wanted the first thing out of his mouth to be, *Don't call me Brain, you dim-witted dolt.* Instead, he pushed a button on the console and replied, "Sandra's still sick."

Beth had no reaction and went back to her notes as she listened to the closing moments of a news program that preceded her show.

Brain is a moniker that irked Brian for years. It had nothing to do with his intelligence level, but rather to the fact that so many people who enter names into computers for everything from party invitations to Department of Motor Vehicle data transpose the *i* and *a* in *Brian* about 50 percent of the time, deeming him Brain DeLouise. And approximately 10% of the time the transposing of letters continues into his surname by incompetence and sloppiness, giving him the utterly ridiculous name, Brain DeLousie, or as it's pronounced, brain da lousy. Or worse yet, if a person is saying his last name first, da lousy brain, which was the inspiration for his nickname, Bad Brain, from the 1980s punk band from DC *Bad Brains*. In fact, the copy of *Bullsh*t Detector* magazine that he brought with him this evening to help pass the hours away is addressed to Brain DeLouise.

Brian thumbed through the magazine, looking for the article on homeopathic medicine, which of course was why he brought it this evening. One of the ways he entertained himself during the night was to read publications and articles on the Internet that totally debunked the whacked-out theories and conspiracies Beth and her guests espoused every night to the insomniacs, graveyard shift workers, and certified psychos who tuned in night after night and sometimes called in. Beth didn't take calls every show, but it was on the program rundown that the second half hour of the program would be call-ins.

Brian giggled as he read in *Bullsh*t Detector* that the active ingredients in homeopathic remedies are not measured in milligrams, but in molecules! And that the herbs and other substances which constitute the pills, powders, and liquids of homeopathic medicine are boiled and processed to the point of complete and total neutrality bordering on sterilization.

"Hello, America. This is *Night Hawks* on ARS. I'm your host, Beth Keller. With me tonight is the author of a new book that may just change your life the way it changed mine," Beth said in her radio show announcer voice, which was about an octave lower than her speaking voice and only slightly less breathy than Marilyn Monroe. "*Homeopathic Paradise*, from Nirvana Press, is Dr. Anibard Derk's fifth book on the homeopathic path to health and happiness. Welcome again, Dr. Derk."

Brian doodled in the margin of his rundown sheet and wondered if anyone ever transposed the letters of this doctor's name, as he wrote Dr. *Drek,* a Yiddish word for *shit,* under his cartoon drawing of a mad scientist eating a large tree. She could handle the show for the first half hour by herself, which meant Brian could pretty much read what a pile of horseshit homeopathic medicine is according to the article he was reading. That would be until about twenty-five minutes into the show, when she would announce to America that she would be taking phone calls. That's when the giggling stops and quickly turns into guffaws that must be hidden from Beth.

Brian didn't realize Beth made the announcement requesting listener phone calls until the lights on the multiple-line phone began flashing. Just before he picked up the first call to screen, he noticed that the private line was also flashing.

"Hello," Brian said into the receiver, hoping it wasn't his wife.

"Brian!"

It was.

"They're having another fight next door," Brian's wife lamented.

"What would you like me to do about it, Frances? I'm busy. Call the cops if it's so bad."

"Again? I'll be up all night. I have to sleep," Frances whined.

"I have to work. I'll call you. Good-bye," Brian said and waited for her reply. There wasn't one. Just the sound of the phone hanging up on the other end.

Every light on the phone console was flashing. Brian looked at the clock and saw he had about five minutes to set up the first call for Beth and Dr. Drek, but he didn't want to pick up a line from Anywhere, USA, and try to decipher whether or not the voice on the other end was some lunatic. Much like the call he just had.

Frances and Brian were going through what their friends called a "rough spot." Brian thought they would eventually get through the rough spot, until one of his friend's revealed to him that his wife said that Frances referred to her marriage with Brian as a "bottomless hell-hole of a marriage." Brian couldn't figure out why exactly their marriage was falling apart, but he had a pretty good idea. He and Frances hadn't had sex in almost two years, and what used to be conversations had deteriorated into two- or three-word sentences that usually involved him cleaning or moving something. They've even stopped going out together. Frances has a small group of work friends, whom he has never even met, that she spends all her free time with. Lately Brian has spent all of his time either at work or in the home office staring at his computer screen in the dark, listening to jazz.

Every one of the phone line lights was flashing at random intervals, creating a lighting effect in the room similar to sitting next to a large blinking Christmas tree. There were forty buttons flashing, five high and eight across, on the large industrial-sized telephone. Brian picked up a telephone headset with his right hand and reached into a drawer, retrieved a bottle of Windex, and began wiping it clean with a paper towel. He put the headset on, adjusted the microphone, made a large circle over the telephone, closed his eyes, and poked a flashing button.

"*Night Hawks*, what's your question?" Brian asked quickly.

"I'd like to talk to Beth," a high-pitched person on the other end of the line said. It was either a man with a high voice or a woman with a deep smoker's voice.

"What's your question?" Brian reiterated in the same brusque tone.

"I've been diagnosed with cancer, excuse me," the voice said before letting loose with a deep, hacking cough bringing up mucus. "I'm sorry. I've been diagnosed with cancer, and I'd like to know what homopathic can do for me."

"It's homeopathic. What's your first name, and where are you calling from?" Brian asked with both hands poised on his computer keyboard.

"Rhona. Schaumburg."

"Schaumburg? Illinois?"

"You've heard of Schaumburg?"

"Oh yeah. Turn down your radio, and when Beth says your name and city, you're on," Brian said as he pushed her button again and started typing her information in the computer.

Of course Brian knew Schaumburg. He grew up on Chicago's north side, and made fun of anybody who had the misfortune of growing up there. He and his college friends at Columbia College in downtown Chicago called it and the suburbs around there simply *the land beyond O'Hare*.

He waved to Beth, and pointed down to his computer screen, which signified that a call was ready to be taken. Beth gave the thumbs up sign and went back to her interview.

Brian pushed another button.

"*Night Hawks*. What's your question?"

"Okay. This homeopathic drugs thing; they're outside the mainstream of the global world domination new world order, right? The Carlyle Group, the Rockefellers, Skull and Bones, the Illuminati, the papists, the Jews…"

Brian laughed to himself. Usually *the Jews* are at the top of the rant. He pushed another button.

"*Night Hawks*. What's your question?"

"Who are you? I want Beth," a man drawled and possible drooled into the phone.

"Do you have a question?"

"Does she have a hairy cunt?"

Brian pushed another button.

"Night Hawks. What's your question?"

"I've been taking chelidonium ajus for my liver and gall bladder for four months now, and I'm wondering if I need to add anything else for my condition," an elderly woman said, with a heavy New York accent.

"First name and city, please?"

"Martha. Hollywood, Florida."

"Turn down your radio, and wait for Beth to say your name and city, thank you."

Brian watched the clock on the wall through the wee hours of the morning, jabbing his finger onto buttons that made voices come alive from across the country. He had long since stopped predicting what might be on the other end, just as he had long since stopped being shocked by the assorted psychos, morons, and pranksters who called throughout his shift. That, of course, was in addition to those desperately seeking help, the well informed enlightening others with pertinent information and the playful intellectuals just looking for some late night interaction who called in no matter what the evening's subject matter. All that mattered to Brian was whether or not the caller could add a few minutes of program time to the show without launching into the most dreaded of all infractions on live talk radio; using one of George Carlin's seven dirty words.

"And that's it for tonight," Beth whispered with her lips touching the windscreen on her microphone. "Please take flight with me tomorrow night, once again, for *Night Hawks*."

Brian took off his headset relieved he made it through another show, walked over to the studio door, and pulled it open.

"Everything go okay for you?" he asked Beth as she removed her headphones.

"Fine. Good callers tonight, don't you think?"

"Not too many psychos awake tonight," Brian said to Beth as he propped open the door. "Do you believe in homeopathic medicine?"

Beth turned to him with a suspicious look on her face. "Why do you ask?"

"Just wondering," Brian said, stepping inside the studio, letting the door close behind him.

"Yes, I do. Do you?" Beth asked with an accusatory tone.

"Uh, yeah, sure," Brian said as he turned and opened the door for Beth as she left the studio.

Beth smiled broadly as she passed him, and said "Good night. Nice job, Brain."

Brian held back his tongue again and was pleasantly surprised by her perfume as it lingered in the slight breeze she created as she passed him. He also noticed that for a slightly chubby woman, she had a nice ass and wondered if she liked guys. "Good night."

Although Beth's night was over, actually *morning* since it was just after five in the morning, Brian still had some production work to take care of before his replacement arrived at five thirty. He went to the position in the studio where Beth hosted the show. She had left behind a legal pad with some notes scribbled. One read, *check Amazon rankings on Derk's book later in day.* Brian knew that an author on a show was like an infomercial. And he assumed Beth would use the numbers on Amazon to convince other authors to come on her late night show; not exactly having morning or afternoon drive ratings.

Brian didn't mind working the overnight too much, because the station wonks weren't too strict about enforcing the eight-hour day. Starting at eleven thirty and leaving at five thirty wasn't bad. And since he was a member of C.O.W., the Communications Organized Workers, he received a nighttime differential pay of an extra 15 percent.

Brian decided not to take Rock Creek Parkway from the studios to his Adams Morgan home. The winding, narrow highway that cut through the park alongside Rock Creek could be treacherous in inclement weather. And although it hadn't rained for a several hours, with the temperature just about at freezing, it could create one of the most dangerous road conditions of the winter: black ice. Black ice is the most deadly manifestation of ice on the road. Most roads are paved with black asphalt, as is Rock Creek Parkway. When an otherwise harmless puddle of water sits on the road and the temperature suddenly drops, the shallow puddle forms an invisible patch of ice. And if it's on a sharp turn, you're screwed.

Taking side streets instead of the parkway also meant adding about fifteen minutes to his drive home. That was another reason he didn't mind doing it. Because then Frances would be just a few minutes away from leaving for her morning drive to work.

Parking in Adams Morgan was unbearable. Brian is lucky to have two parking spaces behind his attached brownstone town house on Lanier Place. When Brian and Frances bought the home ten years earlier, Adams Morgan was an affordable, diverse neighborhood with every ethnicity imaginable. In a stroke of luck, it became one of Washington D.C.'s most desirable areas once Dupont Circle became too gentrified and expensive. They were now sitting on several hundred thousand dollars of real estate equity, although they were also right next door to a hotbed of ethnic diversity gone terribly wrong.

The town house adjacent to theirs was converted into two apartments by the Venezuelan homeowner. But due to a rental applicant questionnaire that did not include the question, *Are you a supporter or opponent of Venezuelan President Hugo Chavez?* many hours of sleep have been lost in the DeLouise-Landry household. Not to mention the blood on the sidewalk, the calls to 911 and the broken windows they've endured by revolutionaries who either got their address wrong or didn't follow in Castro's footsteps as semi-pro commie-pinko baseball pitchers.

Just as Brian pulled into parking space, Frances exited the town house rear door, which opened onto the driveway. Her hair was still wet and her winter coat was slung over her arm as she struggled with a cardboard file box and a briefcase.

"What took you so long? I didn't get any sleep last night and I was hoping you could help me this morning with all this stuff."

Frances wore a suit that fit her nicely about six months ago. Now the buttons on the jacket were noticeably stretched to the limit. Brian knew he couldn't say anything. He wasn't exactly in fighting shape either, not having done anything more than pant heavily from running trying to catch an elevator at work. It wasn't totally unexpected that people in their forties would put on a few pounds. Just look around. Most of them are pretty chunky. But those are strangers with lots of clothes on. Yeah, it's a little disconcerting when you go to the beach and see people your own age with gobs of spotty flesh busting over and through their swimsuits, but that's nothing compared to the shock when one realizes while gazing nude in the mirror that you are one of those people and so is your spouse.

"Sorry. I got out late," Brian said to Frances as he helped her with her things as she got into her car.

"My hair is still wet. I'll have to put on my makeup while I drive. Good-bye," she said as she slammed her trunk and got into her car and drove away. She fishtailed slightly down the alley as she hit a small patch of black ice.

Brian stood in the alley and watched her as she bottomed out turning onto the street heading in the direction of Rock Creek Parkway just a few blocks away. Brian hated her in that moment. So much so he actually thought that if she hit a patch of black ice and got killed in a crash, maybe that would solve his problems. In that moment he knew something was wrong with *him*, not her.

"Yeah. Good-bye."

Frances would meander down Rock Creek Parkway and make her way to her job at the National Science Foundation in Arlington, Virginia. Normally it's about a twenty minute commute, but can be twice that or more depending on traffic conditions. When Brian met Frances, through a friend at work, she was a sales representative for IBM with clients all over Capitol Hill. Knowing how to work a good connection, she's now the head of IT Support at the NSF. A good Fed job with all the benefits and perks one would expect. At her job interview, the head of the department told her, *Anything short of shooting the president on the White House lawn, you've got this job for life.* That off-the-cuff comment has changed Frances' life. She uses every sick day, personal day, religious and government holiday, in addition to scheduling every possible medical, fitness, and grooming appointment right in the middle of her working day to her full advantage. Yet, she's rarely at home for more than fifteen minutes when Brian is there.

Brian entered the rear door of their town house and nearly tripped over a large cardboard shoe box on the floor. Frances had left a trail of rushing out the door from the back entrance up the stairs to the kitchen into the living room and upstairs to their bedroom. The bed was unmade, and her rejected outfits were draped over chairs, dropped haphazardly on the floor and there were even two bras, one black and one pink, left hanging on the shower door. There was a time when seeing one of Fran's amply sized bras meant instant sexual arousal for Brian. But now, even though the brassieres were several cup sizes larger than when they were dating, and the support systems that were embedded in them were designed for sails, he felt nothing but exasperation at the hanging undergarments.

Brian left the bras hanging, stepped over the towel and the skirts left on the floor, and went into his room. His office. His sanctuary. Of the three bedrooms on the upper floor of their home, this was the smallest. But it was his and his alone. One entire wall was an elaborate book shelf and drawer system from of those giant Scandinavian put-it-together-yourself stores. Those Scandinavians must have a lot of time on their hands, if they're putting all their furniture together with the tiny toy allen wrenches and screws they provide. Maybe they all have government jobs.

The other wall was an equally complex computer, audio, printing, and faxing setup. Another wall was entirely filled with a huge calendar, with dates already penciled in for the year. The fourth wall was filled with vinyl LPs, CDs, videos, DVDs, audio cassettes, and computer disks, all alphabetized, color coded, and not a single one out of place. Over the doorway was the only piece of "art"; a wall clock that was a tribute to the 1983 American League Western Division Champion Chicago White Sox.

The entire room, though chock full of every passion, interest, and hobby Brian had in life, was impeccably ordered, catalogued, and dusted. Brian walked over to a drawer under a book shelf, pulled out a folder, reached inside a notebook, and retrieved a DVD in a plain white paper DVD sleeve. He pulled out the DVD and read the label: *Playboy's 101 Best Kept Sex Secrets Volume 1.* Brian stared at the label, and he held the disk by the edge making sure not to touch the side that contains the digital signals that once put into his computer will bring to life the only sexual partners in his life lately. He knew each of them by heart and had even given them names, based on the slight resemblance of girlfriends past. He looked over to his computer, and the copy of *Baseball America* that was sitting next to it, having arrived in the mail the day before. He put the DVD back in its sleeve, into the notebook, into the folder, and back in the drawer. He then sat in the chair, turned on the computer, and picked up the *Baseball America* as the hard drive whirled into action and the screen began to flash to life.

Sure he was dead tired, and it was winter, and spring training was weeks away. But in a few moments, he would be plotting his road to victory for his Rotisserie Baseball teams. Not just one team owner, but three teams. And not only that, he was commissioner for three fantasy baseball leagues and responsible for the data keeping, dissemination of statistics, and budgets involving tens of thousands of dollars. Frances told him if he spent half as much time and energy in the stock market, they'd be living in Georgetown instead of Adams Morgan. She was probably right, and Brian told her he agreed with her. What he didn't tell her was that he much actually preferred their urban Adams Morgan neighborhood to the over sandblasted graystones of Georgetown-- both of the masonry and human variety. Every semblance of character and funkiness had long since been scrubbed clean from the streets of Georgetown in the fifteen or so years since Brian moved to Washington just after college. At least back then, there were still a few soul food greasy spoons and live blues joints on the backstreets of Georgetown. Blues bands were still manned with authentic middle-aged black bus drivers, postal workers, and railroad operators whose parents came from the Deep South and experienced Jim Crow first hand when they were young. They played the blues from their heart with calloused hands not from trying to perfect Clapton guitar runs, but from manual labor.

If you find a blues band these days playing in Georgetown, they're more than likely rich white lawyers and CPA weekend guitar warriors with bald patches and pony tails playing instruments worth more than the cars the old time blues guys drove. Even the tiniest Georgetown clapboard bungalow now costs what a mansion with a tennis court would cost in most parts of the country.

Adams Morgan reminded Brian of the neighborhood he grew up in on Chicago's near North side, called

Ravenswood. Although there weren't many Blacks in his old Chicago neighborhood, there was a strong presence of Deep South emigrants, only those drawling poor folk were white. They were Southerners called Okies if one was being polite and white trash or worse if not. There were also newly arrived foreigners in Ravenswood, mostly from Poland, Czechoslovakia, and Lithuania; whereas Adams Morgan consists mainly of newcomers from Central and Latin America and Africa. But just as the Eastern Europeans opened restaurants, secondhand stores, and shoe repair shops on Chicago's north side, so did the new immigrants in D.C.'s urban areas. You could eat in a different low-priced family run restaurant every night of the week in Adams Morgan and not repeat a country's cuisine. That was one reason Brian's belts were gaining in girth. Frances, on the other hand, seemed to be growing her mid-section from French eateries in Georgetown during her extended lunches.

As Brian stared at a summary of last year's results from the Loopy Loopers Rotisserie Baseball League on his computer screen, he wondered if he should start scouring the pages of *Baseball America* for some minor league standouts who might be available at this year's draft. And he thought about the hours that would turn into days and weeks of intense research, number crunching, and extrapolations of unproven high school graduates in the minor leagues for not one but three leagues.

It struck him at this same moment, that when he and Frances first fell in lust and used to spend more time in bed than any other activity, he would go through the entire 1983 White Sox roster in his head in order to prolong ejaculation. Thinking of baseball players was the one thing that could take his mind off sex. And here he was, in the middle of the winter, at seven in the morning, commissioner of three fantasy baseball leagues with several hundred computer files that demanded his attention to statistical minutia too trivial to interest even the most hard core baseball season ticket holder. His level of baseball knowledge had transcended the appreciation of the sport, and warped into an obsession that, above all, has helped him prolong ejaculating into Frances. It was working so well, he hasn't even been naked in bed with her for nearly two years.

CHAPTER TWO

Brian wasn't complaining, in fact, he welcomed all the overtime he was getting lately. Frances had taken to leaving notes around the house informing him of the duties she wished him to complete. Brian left Frances his mini-van so he could take her BMW in for an oil change. She hated driving his car. She thought it made her look dowdy. Brian knew it wasn't his white Quest that was doing it.

He didn't mind taking her Beamer in. The dealer was on the outskirts of Georgetown, and the cost of an oil change wasn't that much more than parking in a Georgetown parking lot for a few hours. It gave him the opportunity to spend a few hours walking around Georgetown on an unusually warm February afternoon. Since the last time he took a stroll down Wisconsin Avenue, which is the main commercial strip, there was yet another Starbucks and a Robek's Juice Bar. A boarded-up liquor store that had been there for fifty years had a sign in the window stating that a Victoria's Secret would soon be opening there.

As he passed the Café Milano, he was surprised to see his Quest parked at a meter, just off Wisconsin. Oh, he knew it had to be his by the White Sox license plate frame on the front plate. Brian thought it was a little funny that Frances didn't at least ask him to join her for lunch since she knew he was going to be in the area.

He approached the large side window of the restaurant and peeked inside the airy room busy with lunchtime diners. There she was at a table of six; just the number that can sit comfortably in a Quest. He studied the faces, recognizing four of them. The fifth person, a chubby-ish, baldish, middle-aged-ish fellow was sitting next to Frances and seemed to be the focus of the group at that minute.

Brian thought about entering to see what the reaction of Frances and her group would be. But he hadn't shaved, was wearing sweat pants and sneakers, and had a serious case of bed head, so decided against it. Instead he stood at the window surreptitiously studying the group. Frances and her unfamiliar dining partner were the only two drinking wine.

The group rose in unison and headed for the exit. Brian bolted across the street and took a position between a parked truck and a light post. Outside the restaurant, Frances and the four familiar people took position on the uphill side of Wisconsin, with the unfamiliar guy on the downhill side. As the familiar group turned and inched towards Brian's Quest, Frances took the unfamiliar one by the hand and planted a kiss right on his lips. Not on his cheek, as one might do on a public street with an old friend or co-worker, but smack dab on his pie hole. And although it wasn't a smooch it was a beat longer than a peck.

He watched as the five entered his Quest, and the unfamiliar one walked down Wisconsin with a little bit more bounce than your average chubby-ish, bald-ish, middle-aged-ish guy.

Brian's cell phone began playing *Take Me Out to the Ballgame*. He knew by the screen that it was the BMW service department.

"Hello. Yes. I'll be there in about twenty minutes," Brian said into his phone as he watched his van pull away and kept an eye on the unfamiliar one walking down Wisconsin Ave. He shoved his phone into his pocket and rushed across the street despite the lunch hour traffic buzzing by.

He picked up his pace in pursuit of the interloper still jauntily bouncing down the avenue. The man made a left onto M Street a block ahead of Brian, forcing Brian to break into a full jog trying not to lose sight of him. Fellow Georgetown pedestrians looked at him with suspicious eyes as he darted in and out of men in thousand-dollar overcoats and ladies in fur hats. He turned the corner on M Street and a half block down the suspect was opening the door of his 700 Series BMW parked at a meter. Brian kept a swift walking pace, and shot the car and its driver a quick glance as it pulled onto M Street.

He recognized a small sticker on the front windshield that was the National Science Foundation parking permit.

Brian pulled out his phone and hit the first saved speed dial number.

"Frances. It's me. Yeah, I was near Georgetown, and ah, I thought I'd give you a call to see if you happened to, er, be at a loose end, and maybe around or something. Oh, Okay. Just heading back from here with friends from work? Okay. See ya."

Brian turned back up M Street and made the turn up Wisconsin Avenue for the mile or so walk to the BMW dealer. It gave him a good half hour to stew over the possibilities. Confrontation? A sting? A private investigator? Spying?

"Take Me Out to the Ballgame" signaled another call. Brian saw it was work calling, which is never good news.

Could he be there in an hour to take a shift before his?

Sure. No problem. It wouldn't be the first time he showed up unshaven, in sweats, and with bed head.

Brian had just taken a step off the curb when screeching tires caused him to jump back in sheer terror as a car nearly ran into him. As a window rolled down, Brian guessed by the huge chrome search light on the driver's side that it was an unmarked law enforcement car. "Watch where you're going, asshole!" the driver shouted.

The sound of that immediately jolted Brian out of his funk.

"Hey George! How's it going? Great to see you! Opening day is just around the corner," Brian said as he shivered slightly while standing in a slushy puddle.

"You're standing in a slush puddle and talking about opening day? Hey, I'm on a call, what are you doing later?"

"I've got to pick up Fran's car, then go into work for a double."

"Shit, I'm working a double, too! I get off around six or seven in the morning. Call me and we'll have breakfast at the Taystee Diner!"

"You're on! I'll call your cell."

The car peeled away, fishtailing, and almost hit a parked school bus.

That was just what Brian needed. George was his oldest friend in DC. They were good buddies growing up in Chicago but lost touch somewhat in the college years, when Brian got busy studying communications at Columbia College in downtown Chicago and George took a course in Basic Security Officer Training in the neighborhood school, Truman College. But as luck would have it, their paths would cross again when George got accepted to the Department of Alcohol, Tobacco and Firearms, or ATF, and Brian got his first real job for minimum wage at a DC radio station. In the year they roomed together in a cheap walk-up apartment in Foggy Bottom, before that area was transformed into "Georgetown Adjacent," they rekindled their friendship and became tighter than ever. That was until Brian met Frances.

To say George and Frances didn't get along was an understatement. When Brian and Frances first started dating, George would tell Brian, "Bad Brain, she's too fucking hot for you!" She was.

Frances was trouble. She was built like a Playboy bunny, and liked to screw like a bunny, too. Her talents were wondrous and varied in the sexual performance area, but severely lacking in the honesty and integrity department. Before Brian and Frances were married, during many a night out, George would drop anvil sized hints on Brian trying to let him know that Frances was playing footsies under the table or grabbing more than just a smoke outside a bar, but Brian was oblivious. Frances knew George was an unpaid informant and frequently shot him a suspicious eye or the quick flash of a middle finger. But Brian thought Frances would settle down, which she did, as far as he could tell. And when her strawberry blonde hair had to be applied every month or so, and her body that used to kill, was merely taking the life out of sofa cushions, Brian thought her wild days were long gone.

Reporting for engineering duty at ARS, Brian went over the rundowns for his double shift. The first program would highlight space exploration. Under normal circumstances he would be thrilled to produce such a show. That was until he noticed that host Ben Stanton's in-studio guest would be Ted Crane. Crane's name has been the subject of more than one article in *Bullsh*t Detector* magazine and other reputable scientific publications. Crane and his scientific "foundation" have been riling up radio talk shows with theories that the government has been hiding photographs from Mars that "prove" there was an advanced civilization there. The so-called proof is a series of photographs of the Martian surface where a mountain range casts a shadow resembling a human-like face. Initially NASA issued several responses to Crane and his cronies explaining, in polite terms, that they were a bunch of hysterical ninnies. This of course gave Crane even more media exposure. Then, when NASA began ignoring Crane, the charges of a government cover-up took off like an Ed Wood flying saucer. And nothing rouses semi-sane and not so semi-sane space enthusiasts out of their La-Z-Boys and onto the phone more than a government conspiracy.

Brian had already gone through a dozen callers who were too nutty to put on the air, and combined with his anxiety at home it put him in a jumpy mood.

"What's your first name, city, and question?"

"Uh, my uh, name, is uh…"

Brian rejected the caller by punching the next flashing button.

"What's your first name, city, and question?"

"Yes, Charles from San Jose. In Dr. Crane's latest newsletter, in photograph five, I see another face that no one else is talking about."

"Turn down your radio and wait until you hear your name and your city."

Brian pushed the next button.

"What's your first name, city and question?"

"Harmony from Philmont, New York. I've taken Ted Crane's astral travel course and would like to report what I saw this evening?"

"Where?"

"On Mars."

"Hold on a second while I adjust my tin foil hat. You were on Mars this evening?"

"Yes."

"And you want to report what you saw?"

"Exactly."

Brian removed his headset and placed it on the console in front of him. He looked into the studio and saw Ted Crane and Bradley, the host, having a good laugh on the air. He began massaging his eyes, his forehead, his temples. Thinking he could push the tension out, he moved his jaw from side to side and pushed his fingers against the side of his face where the jawbone connected to his skull. He put the headset back on.

"Are you still there?" he asked, assuming the caller had long since hung up.

"Yes, I'm here," the male voice said pleasantly.

"Are you tired?"

"Of waiting, you mean?"

"No, no, no. Are you tired from your trip to Mars?"

"Oh yes, I'm mentally spent!"

"Mentally spent," Brian repeated.

"Yes. Are you familiar with Dr. Crane's astral travel system?"

"No, I'm not. Could you tell me about it?" Brian said calmly.

"I'd be glad to. Dr. Crane is a retired commander at the Pentagon and served for years in the CIA. He was part of a top secret plan at the Defense Department called Pysch Ops where a small group of telepathically gifted people explore mind control, future fact finding, and out-of-body espionage."

"Really," Brian said calmly. "Tell me about the out-of-body espionage."

"That is the most exciting part of the program. Through out of body, astral projections, people invisibly travel, undetected, to super top secret foreign outposts to gather intelligence or even venture to Mars."

Brian's calmness belied the fact that he was about to muster up enough rage to rip the headset from his head and smash it onto the phone console with all his might, breaking one of the earpieces off, which he did.

Brian began screaming at the headphone which had settled next to the phone, "Tell me about fucking astral travel. Tell me how you fucking flew to Mars and back and now you want to report it on the ARSE, you fucking asshole!

At that moment, Brian heard the sound that was the equivalent of hearing a clanging bell in a fire house; the dreaded music loop. The music loop was the sound that was broadcast when the host or producer hits the panic button. The panic button activates the dreaded music loop when a caller utters one of George Carlin's seven dirty words. And pushing the button utilizes the technology known as five-second delay. If a person utters an expletive, you have time to hit the panic button, which stops anything from going out on the air except for the music loop, which is broadcast in its stead.

Brian looked into the studio, where Bradley held up a large placard with a large red question mark on it. That was the panic button of studio placards. He scooped up the headset and replaced the ear phone. He pushed the intercom button which allowed him to be heard in the studio and said, "Sorry. Just a little accident."

Brian couldn't be sure if his profane tirade was broadcast, that was until he noticed the private line flashing on the phone console, and Ben quickly picking it up. A public service announcement called "Daddy's Smoke is Hurting Me" was being broadcast, and Brian hit a button that activated a microphone in the studio enabling him to hear the phone conversation.

"Jim, you'll have to ask him. I have no idea. He says it was an accident. What went out? Well, we got lucky there I guess."

Brian took his finger off the studio microphone switch and sunk in his chair. His head fell forward as the little girl in the PSA coughed and cried her story about her father's disgusting smoking habit. Maybe, he thought, his F-bombs didn't make air. Maybe Stanton pushed the panic button in time.

Ben hung up the phone, and announced on the intercom, "We need to talk."

Another PSA started playing. This one, called "Don't Judge," admonishes listeners who have the temerity to pass judgment on anyone for anything, except maybe smoking fathers. As Brian took off his headset, he wondered if it was for the last time. It would take him about ten seconds to make his way into the studio where Ben and his guest Ted Crane were, which was not enough time to come up with a brilliant excuse for going postal on the air.

Brian pushed the studio door open slightly and stuck his head in. "What's up?'

"You are lucky I'm an expert ping pong player. If it wasn't for my reflexes, and pushing the panic button on the first part of *fuckin*g instead of just after, you'd be out on your ass, right now," Ben blasted.

Brian paused. He looked at Ben, who was anxiously awaiting his response. Ted Crane was turned around in his chair, reading a magazine pretending he wasn't hearing a thing.

Probably on another day, Brian would have apologized politely. He considered telling Ben to fuck off and walk out, but instead he said, "Talk to my shop steward." He then turned calmly and went back to his production console.

That was the first time Brian ever uttered those words to anyone. He hadn't planned on saying that to Ben. He hated it when others who fucked up on the job resorted to hiding behind those words. He considered it a coward's way out of a situation. And he was glad he did it. He settled back into the show and produced the rest of the shift and the next one flawlessly.

There were a few railroad car diners left in the suburbs of Virginia and Maryland and more in the boonies, but the Taystee Diner was the only one left in DC. And with Starbucks, The Coffeebean, and Dunkin' Donuts all within five blocks, its days were surely numbered in months, not decades. As with most railroad car diners, the booths were cramped, the counters narrow, the grill small, the bathrooms tiny, and the kitchen nonexistent. The next stop for the fixtures in this railroad car was undoubtedly the Antiques Road Show. The stools were wobbly and the vinyl on each one was a different shade of red depending on what decade it was repaired or replaced. The exterior was stainless steel, but time was beginning to prove the stainless part wrong. The inside of the diner was holding up a little better where possible. Fighting decades of grease on back splashes and the ceiling was a losing battle. But the Taystee was open twenty-four hours, had grits as its standard side dish with eggs, and had an eclectic mix of servers consisting of black and white old-South senior citizens and pierced, punked-out Goths.

When Brian and George were single they used to hit the Taystee Diner at around this same time of the morning. Only then, it was after a night of drinking and carousing. Brian sat in a booth next to the window that looked out onto Columbia Road in Adams Morgan. It was a blustery morning, and there was some condensation on the window due to the steam heat radiators that were under the window sill. A pickup truck pulled next to the fire hydrant right in front. George hopped out, wearing an old Washington Bullets jacket, jeans, and sneakers. George was a few years older than Brian, but unlike Brian, maintained his high school weight and even started wearing his afro like he used to in senior year. He looked like he could jump back into the Ravenswood High varsity basketball team tomorrow.

One would never think George was an ATF agent in his street clothes. His mixed race roots gave him a dark complexion and Caucasian facial features topped off with a perfectly cool afro. It was a look that blessed him with an inclusive quality; not quite black or white with a personality to match. In the old neighborhood he moved among Blacks, Irish, Polish, Italian, and Latino circles with ease. He played basketball with the black guys, baseball with the Latinos, and hurling with the Irish. He was even on the front page of the *Tribune* sports section once, the only dark-skinned afroed dude on the state championship hurling team. He was dead center of the team photo; George Maldonado surrounded by O'Briens, O'Reillys, Callahans, Monahans, and the rest of what sounded like the Dublin phone book. Not many people outside of Ireland even heard of hurling. It could be described as ice hockey on grass. Players swing a long thick wooden paddle at a ball a little smaller than a baseball and just as hard and try to knock it into a goal. Unlike ice hockey, no one wears protective gear. And like hockey, there's lots of physical contact, frequent fighting, and bleeding.

It was George's street smarts and gangbanger appearance that helped him in his law enforcement career. Once on the ATF, he was immediately recruited to go undercover, which he excelled to the point of being the second youngest ever to make group supervisor.

Now an officer with a desk job, George claims to miss the old days of adrenaline fueled undercover gun and drug busts. And due to hundreds of answered prayers and amazing good luck for nearly ten years, the only visible scars-- from seven bullets fired in his direction, uncountable knives pulled, and one machete swung at his head-- are facial ticks and twitches.

"You can get a ticket for parking there," Brian said to George as the single bell on the front door rang as he entered.

"No. *You* can get a ticket for parking there. *I* get," George turned to the elderly black man wearing a white shirt, a black bow tie, and a pull-over v-neck sweater sitting next to the cash register, and gestured as if shooting a gun at him, "a free cup of coffee, black, extra sugar!"

"Isn't that illegal?" Brian asked holding out his fist for George to bump his fist into.

"So what! We're in the capitol of illegal. If it wasn't for illegal, I'd be back in Chicago doing this…" George slips behind the counter, picks up a push broom, and starts sweeping the floor behind the counter. "Hey, a quarter!" George said, as he disappeared behind the counter and bounced back up showing off his find. "Here Casey, this is a down payment for that coffee I might get when somebody gets off their butt and brings it to me," George said slapping the coin in front of Casey.

"Down payment my ass. Anything on the floor is mine," Casey said putting the coin in his shirt pocket. "Bob X will be right there, guys."

"Where have you been?" George said to Brian, as he took a seat across the table.

"Working. And, well, you know, other stuff. The leagues."

"The leagues? What the hell could you possibly be doing with the leagues. Draft day isn't for months!"

"Well, there's planning, studying, bookkeeping," Brian said as he stirred his coffee, even though it was black with no sugar.

"Bookkeeping? Is that what you call pushing the *update* button?" George said as Bob X placed a coffee stained mug in front of him.

Bob X was probably roughly the same age as Brian and George, but if his hair wasn't dyed jet black, his tattoos were hidden, and his nose and eyebrow hoops were removed, he probably would look like an undernourished, bony old man.

"I always forget you guys know each other," Bob X said as he put a knife, fork, spoon, and paper napkin in front of George. "I haven't seen you together in a damn long time. You're both from Chicago, right? I love Chicago. I played a gig there once. You ever hear of Kingston Mines?"

"Kingston Mines?" George and Brian said in unison.

"I played with Guitar Lefty there in…" Bob X paused and tugged on an ear hoop, deep in thought.

"Is that the brain switch you're tugging on there, Bob?" George asked earnestly while Brian laughed.

"Eighty-one!" Bob X said, pointing in the air. "I think. I was pretty fucked up in the early eighties. And come to think of it, the late eighties, too. Okay, that's enough about me. What about you?" Bob X asked holding a pencil to his pad.

"I think I was the most fucked up in the late seventies," George quipped.

"Very funny, G-man. What do you want for breakfast?"

As George ordered a grease-fest of breakfast foods, Brian wondered if he should be candid with him about Frances. He hadn't told anyone about his latest rough spot, and he hated to bring it up immediately with George, especially since they hadn't talked in so long. But at work, the only friends he ever confided in were long gone, as happens in radio jobs. And the seventy members of his three fantasy baseball leagues were more familiar to him by their goofy team names, than by their actual names. A typical phone call would start something like this: *Hi this is Thomas.* Then after a pause, *From the Alexandria's Ragtime Band.* The only time personalities from the seventy owners would emerge was on draft day. Each league of twenty-five owners would meet for a full day of arguing, bitching, whining, and conniving to get the best players available for the lowest price possible in a round robin auction. After that one day, virtually all the correspondence was via email or text messages from cell phones and Blackberries.

Although George loved sports, both as an athlete and as a spectator, he hated fantasy sports leagues.

"How are the geek leagues going?" George asked, buttering his charred toast.

"I'm already getting calls to send out the freeze lists," Brian said, scraping some of the burnt parts off his toast.

"What a freeze list?"

"It's the list of fifteen players protected by the owners going into the draft. That lets the others know which players are available to be drafted. It's a lot of work."

"Okay, mashed potato omelet with bacon, sausage, and peppers," Bob X said as he slid a plate the size of a cafeteria tray in front of George. "And two over easy with sausage and grits," Bob X said as he plopped the plate in front of Brian. "So, you guys know Kingston Mines?"

"Some of the best times of my life that I don't remember happened in Kingston Mines. I saw Muddy Waters play with the Stones there," George said shoveling a forkful of omelet and mashed potatoes in his mouth.

"I've thought about moving to Chicago. But I'm from Florida, so DC is about as far north as I think I want to get. This is way too frigid here, so I can't imagine what it would be like to have an entire winter of this," Bob X said as he used the tip of his pencil to massage the inside of his ear.

"You haven't felt cold until you get up at five in the morning, take a shower in freezing water, then have to go start your car and it's dark out and twenty-five below zero without any wind chill factor," Brian said picking up his coffee mug with both hands and absorbing its warmth. "*If* you can open the car door and get in, the seat is frozen solid. Doesn't give an inch…"

George slowly shook his head with his eyes closed as he relived the painful scenario.

"…you turn the key and if you're lucky, you hear *mmmMMMMmmmmMMMM* just that. Just a low, slow, groan that goes for a few seconds and dies. But at least you know you've got some juice in the battery."

George dropped his fork and opened his eyes. "You remember that old diesel Mercedes I had?" George laughed.

"That rusted old piece of shit," Brian concurred.

"I was going ice fishing in Pembine, up in northern Wisconsin, and it wouldn't start. But I had to get back to work. It had to be forty below without the wind chill. Everything was frozen solid. So I dug around the cabin, got some twigs and wood, some newspaper and started a fire under the fucker!"

"You're shitting me," Bob X said, his neck craned forward in disbelief.

"Diesel doesn't burn exactly like gasoline," George said authoritatively.

"Not *exactly*, but it *could* explode," Brian said as he popped half a breakfast link into his mouth

"It wouldn't be fun if there wasn't some risk involved, Bad Brain," George continued. "So I've got this bonfire going under my car, and a fire truck just happens to be going by, and these hickory heads jump out with fire extinguishers and start unrolling hoses, and I'm screaming, 'No, no, it's a diesel, it won't blow up,' George said, as he and the others laughed. "It was at that moment I knew I didn't want to be a fireman."

"Did they put it out?" Bob X asked.

"Not until I jumped in, started it, and drove off," George said with a look of satisfaction, either from the taste of his last forkful of mashed potato or the story's climax.

"I'll take this," Bob X said as he whisked away George's empty plate.

"What ever happened to that car?" Brian asked, sopping up last of his yolk with his toast.

"I totaled it. I was in Pembine going ice fishing another time, and a deer ran in front of me. I tried to swerve out of the way, but I hit it, and smashed into a tree. That deer saved me a DUI."

"How's that?"

"I was probably over the limit. But the trooper was so glad to have a month's worth of venison he didn't even give me a ticket. You know, if he nailed me for a DUI, I might not have gotten into the ATF. Here's to the little acts of kindness that total strangers do for you that can change your life," George said, holding his cup of coffee in a toast.

"I always wanted to try ice fishing with you guys," Brian said, as he pointed to Bob X for a refill on his coffee.

"Man, that was nuts," George said as Bob X poured into Brian's mug.

"What's nuts?" Bob X asked.

"We used to go ice fishing in Northern Wisconsin," George said holding his cup for Bob X, "on this humongous frozen lake, when it was thirty below outside and ninety-five inside."

"It was ninety-five in your hotel room?" Bob X asked.

"No!" George said, as the mere thought of the experience got him excited. "You have this wooden shack called a hot house. You assemble it in the middle of a frozen lake, put this portable blast furnace in there, cut a toilet-bowl-seat-sized hole in the middle, take your clothes off, and get wrecked the whole weekend. And one of you takes turns with a spear," George said, as he stood up, with hands stretched far apart, "and you sit there with a goddamm spear this freaking long waiting for this gigantic sturgeon to go by so you can stick the thing and pull it in."

"He's bullshitting, right?" Bob X asked Brian.

"Unfortunately, no. And now I remember why I never went with you guys."

"How many fish did you get?" Bob X asked, puzzled.

"Let's see, we went probably twenty five-times, and caught," George made motions in the air as thought he was adding up numbers, "Zero. None. Ever."

Bob X just shook his head and headed for the kitchen. George downed the rest of his coffee as he chuckled to himself.

"I think that the real reason I didn't go with you guys is that I just started dating Frances. We didn't spend much time apart during those days. Did any girls ever go with you guys?"

"Shit yeah! Remember Peggy and Maria? They came twice!"

"Did you have an orgy?"

"Well, not exactly. We were so nervous, we didn't even take our clothes off."

"You all just sat there in that ninety-five degree shed and didn't even get naked?"

"They weren't exactly the wild type; what can I say?"

"That's why I was spending so much time with Frances. She was the wild type, I'll tell you that."

George just nodded his head in agreement. He knew this was an area not to delve into if he wanted his renewed friendship with Brian to continue. Brian recognized George's lack of response immediately.

"I know, I was pussy whipped," Brian reluctantly admitted. He waited for a reaction from George, who just stared at his empty coffee cup. "Go ahead, say it."

"Say what?

"Go ahead."

"What?" George said, as he gestured his innocence with his hands held high.

"I know, what do you mean *was* pussy whipped?"

"I'm not saying a word," George said solemnly as he pulled out his wallet.

Brian watched as George pulled a twenty out and dropped it on the check. Morning commuters started streaming in, ordering coffees and bear's claws, filling the diner with small talk and chatter. Three telephone company workers sat in the booth next to them, and a cute young waitress began a new shift. Brian had hoped to talk to George about his marriage. He was really the only person Brian was still in touch with who knew Frances when she was a flirtatious wild woman just out of college and on the make, figuratively and literally.

At one time, Brian was pissed at George for dropping not-so-subtle hints that Frances was a playing him like a kazoo and handing out her phone number like a life insurance salesman. But in those days, when it came to Frances, Brian was blinded by three things: screwing, blow jobs, and lies. The sex was unbelievable. Long drives on country roads always included some kind of spontaneous sexual explosion; a visit to somebody's house for dinner invariably meant a quickie in the guest bathroom; and a long flight on a plane meant multiple memberships in the mile high club. Then there were the lies Frances told that Brian so readily accepted-- the weekends away to visit family, despite her rarely talking on the phone with them; the late-night business meetings; the sleepovers at girlfriends' houses. Brian thought one day she would change. And she did. She still left for weekends to visit phantom relatives, stayed out until three a.m. for business meetings, and slept at girlfriends' houses. What changed was she stopped having sex with him.

But only all these years later, had finally Brian realized that George was the only friend who tried to warn him what Frances was all about. Like a good friend, George not only stopped dropping hints once they were married, he stopped coming by. And Brian knew why.

"Frances and I are really having problems," Brian said softly, trying to exclude the phone company guys from the conversation.

George motioned to Bob X for a refill and rubbed his morning stubble. "You really don't want me to chime in on this, do you?"

"Yeah. I do. I mean, we haven't even had sex…"

"Whoah! Too much information!" George said holding his hands in the "T" for time out configuration.

Brian noticed one of the phone company guys looking toward their table. He leaned forward and spoke even softer.

"George, this is serious shit. Now that I look back, sex was all we had for years, and now that it's gone, we've got nothing. At least I'm getting nothing. I'm not so sure about her."

"You think she's screwing around?" George whispered, hip to the lineman sitting nearby.

"I'm almost positive. Just yesterday I spied on her at lunch with friends in Georgetown, and she kissed some bald guy."

"Like a shaved head stud, or a fatty bald guy?"

"Fatty bald guy."

"That's probably worse. Shaved head stud would've meant a sex conquest. Fatty bald guy means relationship."

Brian scrunched his face into a disgusted expression like he just tasted something awful, which George couldn't help notice.

"I should stop, right?" George said flatly.

"No. That's what I thought, too," Brian said as he lowered his head and his voice even more. "We haven't had sex in almost two years. She doesn't even undress in front of me anymore. Before we were married, she used to wake me up in the morning with a blow job, for chrissakes."

At this point the entire table of phone company guys got quiet and looked at Brian with smiles. Brian gave an awkward smile back.

"And the worst part is, I don't care," Brian said in a normal tone as he leaned back in his seat. "I just don't care. And I don't know what to do."

"Brian, I ain't never been married. And I sure as hell ain't no Dr. Phil, but what's keeping you there?"

Brian picked up a glass of water and took a small sip. He looked over the phone company guys who were arguing about the Redskins, and tried to think of an answer. He wanted to say *because I love her*, but he didn't. He gave a more truthful response which was, "I don't know."

"My advice to you is, you got to figure that one out--what's keeping you there," George said handing the check and his twenty to Bob X, no longer whispering. "Oh, check this out. You won't believe what happened to me yesterday. I'm in my car in Georgetown and I had to make a phone call, so I pull over next to a hydrant, right on Wisconsin. It's evening rush hour and it's getting dark, and there's people and traffic everywhere. So I'm sitting in my car, looking up a phone number, my engine's running, right? And I feel this thump," George said as he jerked forward slightly. "So I figure somebody's pulled in to park behind me and tapped my bumper. Then I look in my rear view mirror and my trunk is up."

"How'd that happen?" Bob X asked excitedly, smelling a good story brewing.

"That's what I wanted to know. Now my engine was still running, mind you,
my lights are on, I open my door, get out of the car, and there's this black dude in my trunk rifling through my stuff!"

The phone company guys have even stopped their haranguing over the faults of the Redskin's offensive linemen and are tuning in to George's story. Bob X smiled a grin so wide Brian noticed for the first time that he had a diamond chip in one of his front teeth.

"What the hell?" Bob X said sounding more like Gomer Pyle than the gothic punk bad boy he portends himself to be.

George knew he was the center of attention and became even more nonchalant in his demeanor. The elderly black cashier rose from his stool and inched closer to the table.

"That's what I'm thinking. He's got my gym bag, and he's going through it, and he pulls out my Ipod and my Bose headphones."

"Man, those are like two hundred bucks!" Bob X exclaimed sounding more and more like Gomer.

"Each!" George exclaimed. "So I'm standing there looking at this mother..." George caught himself before saying *fucker* and paused for a nanosecond as he scoped out the crowd for the closest female, child, or clergy member. The nearest woman was at the far end of the diner. He lowered his head and continued in a whisper "…fucker, about six feet from him and finally he notices me. Now I'm thinking to myself, H*mmmm, where's this going?* I say to him, what the," George whispered again, "fuck do you think you're doing?"

The elderly black cashier chuckled as he tugged on his bowtie. The table of phone company guys-- one burly black man, who probably was the foreman, a handsome black guy in his thirties who looked like he should be in an Armani suit instead of a Verizon uniform, and a red-haired white kid who looked too young to have a real job-- gave up pretending they weren't paying any attention and were tuned in just as everybody else was at this end of the railroad car diner.

Brian knew this was George at his best. He was a little black, a little white, a little Spanish, and could spin a story like a street-wise Garrison Keillor. Everybody wanted George on their team.

"So the puke looks at me, reaches into his jacket, and pulls out one of those Sears heavy duty screwdrivers that you could use to lift a house off its foundation if you had to, and then I think to myself…" George stopped cold. He stuck his lips as far out as far as they could go and nodded his head, in a facial expression that screamed *ain't I a schmuck.* "…my gun and my badge are under the seat, 'cause like a jerk I put them there in case I need them in a hurry. Now I'm freaked. This guy, who's bigger, blacker, and uglier than Ray Brown…"

George is sharp. He picked up earlier that the guys at the next table were big Redskins fan's so he mentioned Ray Brown, a veteran lineman on the team.

"…takes a step towards me. I don't know what made me think of this, but I put my hand like this..." George said as he stood up and slowly moved his right hand to the small of his back and reached under his jacket and into the back of his pants. "…I usually keep a gun in a holster right there as a back-up, which like a dolt I didn't do, but I put my hand there, looked him dead in the eye and said, 'You take one more step and I'll blow your motherfuckin' nigger brains out.'"

George froze in a theatrical pose and looked around. There was stunned silence in the Taystee Diner, that perhaps predated the fossilized grease on the ceiling. Oh, everyone had heard the word *motherfucker* in mixed diner company, but hurling an N-bomb in mixed race company, is always a risky proposition, even if the hurler is a large afroed mixed race dude himself. Once George knew he had the crowd he continued. "He threw the Ipod and the headphones in the trunk, turned and ran his ass off!"

Laughter, applause, and hoots from the cashier, Bob X, the phone company guys, and Brian caused such a stir everyone in the diner looked over and watched as George finished up his tale and soaked in the adulation.

Brian meekly asked, "Did you have to use the "N" word?"

Before George could answer, the old black waiter chimed in, "That's psychological warfare there, right, brother?"

"You got that right, but if you were a white dude, it would have been outright warfare!" the large African American phone company guy laughed.

"Let me pay for that," Brian said reaching for the bill.

"Nope. You get the next one, all right? Soon," George said, as he pointed at Brian with a scolding finger. "Don't be a stranger. I gotta run. I'm meeting some guys at the gym."

"You haven't slept yet," Brian said putting his jacket on.

"I can sleep when I'm dead. Later, gator," George said as he walked out the door as the every patron in the place watched him get into his car and take off.

CHAPTER THREE

When Brian wasn't at the Arse staring at his computer screens, he was in his home office staring at one. It didn't matter if Frances was home or not. He always seemed to have an excuse to sit on his ever growing ass and occupy his mind with something. And since Brian wasn't sleepy yet after his coffee klatch with George and Frances was already at work, he felt like using the computer for something other than pursuits of the mind.

Brian had explored pornography on the Internet in the past, but it only took one exploration and several clicks into a free XXX porn site to not only see things done with urine and excrement that he never wished to witness again in his lifetime, but cost him a couple of thousand dollars as well. After visiting those "free" sites, his computer was infected with enough explicit porno pop-ups, spywares, adwares, and viruses to render his computer worthless. He may have been able to have it repaired, but the thought of having some computer technician at Computers R Us witness the type of depravity and vile images infecting his computer, he thought he might actually be vulnerable to blackmail, or at the very least be humiliated by a tech geek in public.

Brian vowed he would never again risk visiting an Internet XXX porn site. He also made sure his new computer had a DVD player, and subsequently found a video store far enough from home with adult videos and bought *Playboy's 101 Sex Secrets* with cash, of course. He thought perhaps Frances had bought a DVD called *101 Excuses NOT to Have Sex With Your Husband* since he pretty much heard every one of them. And now, when he was sure Frances was away for hours, he popped in his only porno DVD. In the beginning, just seeing the first naked girl riding on top of a guy was enough stimulation for him to become aroused. But now he had gone through all thirteen chapters on the DVD and even used the montage at the closing credits to get his rocks off. He noticed it was taking longer and longer to get aroused and wondered if he should perhaps buy a new, more explicit DVD than a Playboy version, which really only simulated sex acts.

He shuttled through the chapters to find a new and arousing naked babe that perhaps he had overlooked before. There was a brief orgy scene in one, with four females and one effeminate looking guy. It seemed all the guys were effeminate looking. In order to get aroused Brian had taken to fantasizing about certain females based on whether they resembled ex-girlfriends. There was one redhead who reminded him of Frances, but even she stopped doing it for Brian.

The orgy scene was pretty tame, actually; lots of massages and lesbian kissing going on, with the gay-looking guy never getting an erection. Natch. As Brian slowed down the video to extend a naked lesbian make out session, a blonde girl turned her head and smiled at her playmate in a way that caught Brian's eye. He scanned back slowly and froze the video. He held the image on the screen and whispered to himself, *Portia*. This blonde female wasn't the typical Playboy bunny type. She had freckles, and her hair was a natural "dirty" blonde and curly to the point of being almost frizzy. Her breasts weren't especially large, and she didn't have the usual shaved pubic area or tiny "landing strip" that the other porn actresses sported.

He knew for certain that it wasn't actually his old girlfriend, Portia. He hadn't seen her in almost twenty years. But the resemblance was uncanny. And her naked, gleeful, frozen image made him long not for the girl on the screen, but for Portia herself. Where could she be? What did she look like? What ever happened to her? Why didn't they ever talk to each other again?

Brain pushed the eject button on the computer DVD button and the image of "Portia" lingered for a moment on the screen and then faded away. Brian clicked on his browser and placed his cursor in the blank Google search box. He watched the thin black line blink. It became mesmerizing in the darkened, quiet room. He slowly typed *Portia Smart.* He then moved the cursor to the search button and clicked it. In a flash, a page of websites appeared, nearly everyone with the name of Portia DiRossi, the actress, in bold letters. No mention of Portia Smart. He clicked to the next page of twenty or so website listings and still all Portia DiRossi sites. Several pages into his search he gave up. No Portia Smart listing.

He placed his cursor over the Google search box again and this time he typed *Beatrice Smart* and hit *search.* Another twenty or so websites appeared on the screen and about three quarters of the way down, a listing caught Brian's eye: "Beatrice Smart, Hampton North Theatre Tent, rooms to let."

Brian clicked on it. It was a newspaper article from *The Cape Cod Echo* dated July 4, 1995, featuring the home of Beatrice "Bea" Smart. Brian looked in awe at the one black-and-white photograph that showed Bea in her kitchen surrounded by a group of about a dozen attractive men and women in their twenties. The young people were the cast members of a national touring company of the musical *Chicago,* all of whom were staying for the two-week run of the show at Bea's ramshackle mansion on the bluffs of Hampton North, Massachusetts. It was a scene that thrust Brian back into a moment in time that has been seared in his mind for nearly twenty years.

The Hampton North Theatre Tent was, and for all Brian knew, may still be, the Cape's most famous summer theatre venue. Brian was in his senior year at Columbia College in downtown Chicago getting his degree in communications when an instructor told him about opportunities on the *straw hat circuit*, which was the anachronistic nickname for the Cape's vibrant summer theatre scene. Students from all over the country vied each spring to be accepted into the few apprentice theatre arts programs that were still in operation. And the Hampton North Theatre Tent was the ideal situation for him. Although The Tent wasn't the most highly regarded apprentice program for aspiring actors, writers, and directors, it was the program that had the most to offer students interested in the technical aspects of theatre.

The Tent was just that; a huge circus-type tent that was constructed each season to house a summer's worth of entertainment for Cape Cod vacationers. Due to the structure's temporary nature, each year they would lease the latest in lighting, sound, and theatrical staging equipment. Since most of their summer fare consisted of traveling companies of Broadway productions and top name musical and comedy acts, the sound systems had to be the most sophisticated in the business. And sound was what interested Brian the most. He applied, was accepted with ten other college students from across America, and opted to stay at the home of Beatrice Smart, since it was by far the cheapest way to go. He knew two other guys would be staying at the Smart house, but he wasn't told that the three of them would be sharing one small room. And that the rest of the large, decaying mansion on a bluff facing the rocky shores of the Atlantic Ocean would house Beatrice Smart, her ninety-nine-year old father-in-law, itinerant casts of several touring musicals, and her twenty-ish daughter, Portia.

The newspaper article was over ten years old, and Brian wondered if the Hampton North Theatre Tent and Mrs. Smart's mansion could still be in business. He went back to the Google search box and typed in Hampton North Theatre Tent. Immediately The Tent's official website was plastered across his plasma screen. The photo captured The Tent on an amazingly clear Cape Cod summer day; azure skies, white puffy clouds, a sliver of sea shore in the distance and the original green clapboard box office in the foreground. The Tent was still in operation, and advertised subscriptions to their "exciting 75th anniversary season."

There was no mention of the apprentice theatre arts program, but that wasn't something that a theatre wanted to boast about. Everyone in the business knew that apprentice programs were a way to circumvent union and labor laws and have talented young people operate the business for practically nothing. But since the apprentices weren't complaining the system continued. There was phone number listed for the offices of The Tent, which Brian wrote down.

He then moved his cursor to the *people searcher* box and typed in *Beatrice Smart, Hampton North, MA*. In an instant a phone number popped on the screen. Brian wrote that down as well. He then typed in *Portia Smart* and clicked on it. Still nothing.

Portia wasn't the first girl Brian ever had sex with, but she was the first girl he ever thought he might marry. He didn't care that she was probably a few years older than he was. Nor did he care that she didn't shave her armpits or her legs. Nor did he mind that her mother, Beatrice, was an avowed eccentric at best, and a certified nut at worst, as was her grandfather. Brian had never met a woman like Portia before and sensed he never would again. And sitting in his darkened office, nearly twenty years later, he still sensed he was right.

Brian clicked the *back* button on his computer, bringing Beatrice Smart's phone number onto the screen. He recalled the day he first arrived at Smart House, the name the locals gave it. The description offered by the head of the apprentice program of The Tent was factually accurate: a large Victorian home on an ocean bluff with an ocean-facing veranda, endless views, and lots of character. It was the *lots of character* part that should have been the tip-off. The home was barely visible from the street. Two cupolas protruded from decades of overgrowth that encapsulated the entire residence, transforming it into something resembling a hidden nest. The walkway to the house was a tunnel of shrubbery with an inch of dry leaves and branches underfoot. If standing in front of the front door, one couldn't see any of the house for the growth. Brian remembered how he almost turned back when he was about to drop the door knocker against the heavy red double front door. But when the door opened, with the wild haired, crazed, smiling Beatrice Smart standing in the foyer, any thoughts of checking into a Motel 6 for the summer were dropped. From the front door Brian saw a breathtaking panoramic view of the ocean, complete with a lighthouse-adorned island laid out right in front of him.

Having grown up in Chicago, the Lake Michigan shoreline was always an "L" ride away. But the thought of spending a Cape Cod summer, drinking morning coffee on the veranda with that view was the clincher. And that was even before he had met Beatrice's daughter, Portia, four weeks later.

Brian wrote Beatrice's phone number on a Post-it without including her name, and dropped it in his top desk drawer. He stared at the number on the screen and thought about calling that very moment. He then visualized Beatrice answering the phone in that home with twenty years of decay and deterioration surrounding her, not to mention the twenty years of decay and deterioration that Beatrice herself had undoubtedly undergone. Instead he swiveled around in his chair and studied the neatly printed labels on his file cabinet drawers. He knew there was only one photograph from that amazing summer, which his roommate, Fred, sent him a few years after they were apprentices at The Tent.

The color coded labels on the file cabinets were rather cryptic, so that only he would understand the filing system. Still sitting in his chair he wheeled himself over to the drawer marked *LBF* in small red letters. He assumed he had stashed the photo in there among other personal items that fell under the category *LBF*, i.e. *Life Before Frances.* If Frances had ever asked what *LBF* stood for his response would have been *Loose But Filed.* But Frances had never asked about his filing system or much else that went on in his home office. But that didn't stop Brian from creating excuses for things before they even happened. That was why he picked as his sole porno DVD *101 Sex Secrets.* If somehow Frances had ever stumbled onto it he would merely tell her that he purchased it as a guide to improve their sex life just in case they ever had sex again.

He pulled opened the *LBF* drawer and reached far into the back, behind the baseball scorecards and college papers that were merely placed in front as camouflage, and pulled out a manila envelope marked *photos*. He reached in and pulled out a handful of loose photographs. On top was a picture of his group's table taken on his high school prom night. He flipped through several other photos of girlfriends he had to think hard about to even remember their names, until he discovered the shot he was looking for. It was a black-and-white photo taken on the beach in front of Smart House. Nearly the entire frame of the photo was filled with the bottoms of Brian's feet, which were pointing outward in opposite directions. Slightly out of focus between his feet, Brian was laying on a straw mat in cut-off dungaree shorts, and Portia, in a two-piece bathing suit, had both arms around his neck. They were caught just a moment before their lips were about to touch.

Just as the photo was slightly out of focus, so was Brian's memory of Portia. The picture helped him to recall how beautiful she was, and how incredible that summer was, but in order to regenerate his memory cells fully he would have to dig deeper. He flipped through several more photos of friends and places from long ago, and stopped at a postcard of the Acropolis. He turned it over and read the inscription, *Dear Brian-- Greece is fantastic! It's everything I dreamed it would be. I've met some wonderful people. Love, Portia.* That was the last time he had ever heard from her, just a couple of weeks after she had left on her trip. An out-of-focus, feet-dominated photograph and a post card were all he had left from that summer with Portia. Brian smiled as he gazed on Portia's happy kiss about to be planted on his face, right between his two freak feet-- he had six toes on each foot-- which were a constant source of amusement for Portia.

Brian put the postcard and the photo into the envelope and placed it at the back of the drawer. He wheeled over to his computer screen, clicked on a map site, and began getting directions for a trip to the Cape.

Brian and Frances used to make trips to Chicago to visit his parents, until they passed away within weeks of each other five years ago. Since then, Brian made at least one trip a year to visit friends and attend a game or two at Comiskey, but without Frances. He hadn't figured out how he would explain a long weekend to Cape Cod without her, but he had a feeling she would welcome the idea. She was taking trips of her own. And some of those were under shady circumstances. Brian figured it was his turn to try and recapture some of his independence.

As he zoomed into the map of Cape Cod, he noted the sharp turns that led to Smart House. He remembered how dark the streets were at night, and how Portia and he would take long walks on the beach with only the moonlight to guide them. Nearly everything they did together on that moonlit beach was unforgettable. Skinny dipping and sex under the stars were all spectacularly daring firsts for Brian. He didn't care that it was with an older woman, who obviously had experience in those areas. Whatever Portia and he did seemed pure and joyous and never dirty or shameful. Even though they were performing things mere yards from the rear veranda of Smart House.

Brian closed his eyes and remembered the excitement of making love on a blanket under a starry Cape Cod night after skinny dipping in the cool ocean waters of the late summer. As he thought about Portia's sandy, nude body next to his, he flashed on his porn DVD with the girl who reminded him of Portia. He wheeled over to the file cabinet, retrieved *101 Sex Secrets*, and popped it into the computer. The DVD drive whirled and whizzed for a moment as the ersatz Portia popped onto the screen.

"What the hell are you doing?" Frances asked from the doorway.

Brian nearly fell out of his chair backwards.

"Shit, you scared the hell out of me," Brian said, as he tried to click off the nude girls from the screen.

"Are you watching…porn?" Frances said, placing her briefcase on the floor and taking a step toward Brian.

"No! It's a damn pop-up ad. Don't you ever get them?" Brian said nervously, as the DVD continued to make whirling and buzzing noises in the drive.

"Why is the drive spinning? Hey, that brings back memories," Frances giggled, as she looked at the orgy frozen on the screen.

Brian prayed that the image would disappear, as he tried to figure out how to react to Frances' comment about the orgy. He never had such a sexual escapade with Frances. Instead he just blurted out, "What are you doing home?"

"Um, I forgot something," Frances said as she picked up her bag and went into the bedroom. "I forgot some papers. I thought you'd be asleep."

Brian could hear Frances going through her desk drawers. Not just one desk drawer but several. "Here it is." Frances returned to the doorway of the office, with Brian fully composed facing her. "I have to get back for a meeting. Bye," Frances said as she turned and clomped down the stairs.

Brian waited a beat then ran over to a rear facing window in the guest room. He saw Frances get into her car in the driveway, and as she pulled out and turned, he thought perhaps there was somebody in the front seat, but he couldn't be positive. Frances always has so much extra clothes and crap in her car.

Brian went back into his room and hit the eject button on the DVD drive. He took *101 Sex Secrets* and bent it until it broke into two pieces. He then broke those pieces and subsequent pieces into smaller and smaller pieces until they were unidentifiable slivers and sprinkled them into his garbage can.

He sat in his chair, picked up his mouse, and hit his back button until the map of the Cape reappeared. He spun around went to the *LBF* drawer, reached into the envelope, and pulled out the photo of him and Portia on the beach. He opened the top desk drawer right in front of him and placed the photo on top, so that if he wanted to see the photo all he had to do was open the drawer, and there it was. And if anyone else opened the drawer, it would be right there for them to see as well.

Brian thought about calling Frances on her cell to see what her reaction would be, thinking that maybe there was a guy sitting next to her. Instead he moved his mouse to an icon marked *Rot Leagues*. Rot Leagues was short for Rotisserie Baseball Leagues. He clicked on the one marked Capitol Idea Baseball League and began to study the rosters of the twenty five teams. Each team had fifteen protected players, and clicking on any one of them would reveal a plethora of statistics that would make a Wall Street financial analyst's head spin. No other commissioner had this program, because Brian had designed it himself. Thanks to Frances, he had picked up enough advanced computer skills to design, program, and customize software programs. It was those skills that allowed him to be a commissioner for three separate baseball fantasy leagues. His predecessor in the Capitol Idea League nearly lost his mind trying to maintain the data necessary for the upkeep of a league that has to be updated almost on a daily basis.

Now that Frances was in management, she rarely delved into any hands-on computer work. Brian's current expertise with computers far outpaced Frances. The irony of the fact that he spent nearly every waking moment on the computer was not lost on either of them.

The columns of statistics began to wear on Brian, making his vision blur and his eyelids heavy. He looked at his watch and realized he had been studying the rosters, salaries, and projections for over an hour and it was time to try to get some sleep. He closed down his computer and sat watching as the screen went through its ritual of flashing screens and messages as it shut off and the screen went dark. Brian opened the top drawer and looked at the photo of him and Portia on the beach. He didn't remember his summer roommate, Fred, taking the photo or exactly when the picture was taken and if that particular kiss was a peck on the lips or a long French kiss. But as he slouched in his chair and closed his eyes, he most definitely remembered the many long kisses on the hot beach; the thrilling midnight nude swims followed by sensuous towel drying and making love by moonlight. Brian often thought what might have happened if Portia didn't go away on her European trek at the end of that summer. He wondered why he only received the one post card and never heard from her again. He wondered if he should have swallowed his pride and driven to the Cape years ago to confront Portia and win her back. But he didn't. Instead he moved to Washington and met Frances before he had even unpacked his boxes or had a bed. They screwed on an air mattress the first night they met in a bar, causing it to pop a leak and flatten out under them during their climax.

In the beginning, Frances made it easy to forget Portia. She was eager to perform sexually and had a beauty that was more supermodel sexy, bordering on slutty, than hippy earth mother, as Portia was. And when Frances announced she was pregnant, there was no question they would get married. The miscarriage three weeks after the engagement was traumatic, but they got through it and the wedding went on. But as the years wore on, and the sex wore off, they weren't left with much.

So Brian placed the photo of Portia back in the drawer and went to the bedroom. As he laid in bed, he thought of Portia and what might have been. He knew he didn't have the nerve to tell Frances he wanted a divorce. He would just wait and see what happened. Maybe things would just work out.

CHAPTER FOUR

Frances didn't like cheap hotels. In fact, she didn't like cheap anything. She knew that her drive to Tysons Corner with Raul wouldn't cause any suspicion. They had a satellite office there, and Raul worked closely with her on many of her projects, but stopping at a nice hotel in the Virginia suburbs was too risky. There could be a symposium, or lunch meeting or seminar, or maybe somebody else she might recognize from the countless government agencies and vendors she dealt with. So Frances took an exit off the Leesburg Pike and drove for a good fifteen minutes on a two-lane highway before pulling into the Triangle Motel for a brief dirty interlude before their meeting at the office with the regional managers.

"How did you even know about a place like this?" Raul asked as they sat in the nearly empty parking lot.

"I grew up in Virginia. I didn't fall off the turnip cart yesterday, you know," Frances said as she put her hand on Raul's briefcase, which he had on his lap. She thrust her other hand under the briefcases and grabbed at his crotch, making Raul jump back in his seat and hitting his head on the head restraint.

"Are you sure this is safe?" Raul whispered.

"I stopped off at the house and got all the safety we need. I already got the keys, we don't need to check in. That's our room right in front of us," Frances said, massaging Raul's crotch a little too hard.

"Ow," Raul blurted out.

"Grrrrr," Frances said, purring like a cat. "I'll go in first. You count to twenty and come in behind me. Wait! No! Don't come in behind me," she said in a soft little girl voice, "I'm not that kind of girl!"

Frances exited the car and entered the motel room just a few feet in front of her BMW. She closed the door behind her. Twenty seconds later, Raul followed.

This was the first time Frances and Raul had a quickie here. It wasn't the first time Frances had a quickie. This was one of the dozen or so out-of-the-way motels where she could take a business associate, acquaintance, or total stranger for a nooner or a night cap. Raul was different. She had been banging him on and off for six months. Raul wasn't married. That's what made him different.

Raul sat in a vinyl chair with his briefcase on his lap. The cheap hollow bathroom door swung open and Frances stood in the doorway wearing a pink negligee that skillfully hid her fat rolls and bulges. She slinked the three steps to the plaid bedspread and pulled it down.

"Put down that damn briefcase and let's go!" she said as she jumped in, causing the bed to make a creaking sound that made her think it might collapse.

Raul jumped up and began tearing his clothes off as quickly as possible down to his striped boxers and got into the bed a little more delicately than Frances did. She turned off the light and began doing things to Raul the way she used to do to Brian when they were still dating.

Frances was positive that Brian had suspicions about her playing around. He'd have to be an idiot not to. She just figured that he knew that was the way she was before she met, and that was the way she would always be. When she and Brian first started going out, Frances had three boyfriends she was sleeping with on a regular basis. Brian was even in bed with her one time, when at three in the morning, one of those drunk boyfriends showed up, demanding a blow job from behind a locked front door.. How could Brian not know that she liked to sleep around? She had even told Brian just a few days prior to that intrusion, on their second date, that he could ask for a blow job anywhere at anytime and she would gladly oblige. A service that Brian gleefully tested her on, from New Jersey Turnpike traffic jams to the nearly empty grandstands of the Oriole's old Baltimore Memorial Stadium. She just figured that once he stopped asking for them, he wasn't interested in her anymore.

Raul was hyperventilating and sweating profusely as Frances rode him from on top. As always, she kept her nightie on. In the darkened room, she could see that Raul had a grimace to go along with his difficult breathing pattern.

"Are you okay?" Frances asked with concern, as she continued to bounce on him like she was on an exercise ball.

Raul nodded his head in the affirmative with a look of terror across his face.

"Just keep it going a little bit longer," Frances demanded.

Raul grabbed his ears, concentrated, and whispered in gasps, "Focus, focus, focus."

"Okay, yes! Finally! Yes!" Frances rejoiced as she gave two extra forceful thrusts and then rolled over to the other side of the bed. "I told you half a Viagra would work fine. Oh, look! A pee pee tee pee!" She giggled as she pointed to Raul's erection pushing up the sheet he had pulled across his body.

"This thing better go down," Raul lamented.

"If it doesn't you'll be the most popular guy at this meeting. It's all women. I'm going to take a shower," Frances said as she got out of the bed, and straightened her nightie.

Frances always carried the same shampoo, perfume, conditioners, and everything else with her. She knew from experience that different smells were always the first signs of an affair. Not that she really cared if she got caught, but she knew if there was a divorce because she got caught, she'd get less in the settlement. At least that's what her friends told her. After Frances began flaunting her affairs in confidence with a couple of her close friends, she was pleasantly surprised to see that they too would soon be partaking in the thrills of extramarital dalliances. In fact, two of them had already gotten divorces, were getting a ton of alimony and child support, and screwing around like drunk college girls on spring break. Knowing that she would never get any child support, Frances knew she should be somewhat careful to not get caught in the act.

"Your turn," Frances said to Raul as she opened the bathroom door. He was sitting nude on the vinyl chair with his briefcase on his lap.

Frances walked over to her bag and picked up her cell phone. She scrolled through her missed calls, and saw a call from home. She thought for a moment about calling Brian at home, but then figured it would be safer to call from the office in Tysons Corner on a land line.

During the drive to the office, Raul still had a pained look on his face. Frances figured it might be her driving. She loved to drive fast. Especially on the kind of curvy country roads they were on.

"Don't you like to go fast?" Frances asked as the tires squealed slightly around a sharp turn.

"Why?"

"You look like you're in pain."

"My dick is killing me," Raul said meekly.

Frances smiled menacingly and took the next turn even faster.

Brian wasn't sleeping well. His mind raced from psycho call-ins at work to memories with George back in Chicago to lying with Portia on the beach to Frances busting him with porn and humiliating him with her comment.

He had called Frances earlier on her cell and was glad when she didn't answer. He didn't leave a message because he wasn't exactly sure why he called her. Now he was worried that she would call just as he was trying to get some sleep, so he reached over to the phone next to the bed and switched the ringer from low to off. He then remembered that the phone in his office was also on low, but thought he better switch that to off as well.

He walked down the hall, into his office, turned off the phone ringer, and sat in his desk chair. He was up. He knew he wouldn't be getting back to sleep. At least he had dozed on and off for a couple of hours, which was better than nothing. He switched on the computer and as the screen flashed strange technical messages which illuminated the room in colorful flashes, he opened the top drawer and gazed upon the picture of Portia and him. It would be stupid to end a marriage because of something one felt twenty years ago. He didn't even know if she was alive. She could be happily married with eight kids and maybe even a grandkid or two. But the grainy black and white image of lips just inches apart still haunted him for what might have been. There was just one way to find out. He picked up the phone and dialed the scheduling office at work.

"Hello, Jim? Yeah, Brian DeLouise here. Listen, any chance I could take off for a few days in the next few weeks? Like a Wednesday, Thursday, Friday so I could get a five-day weekend? Oh she's coming back, great! Next week is great. Thanks."

Brian couldn't believe how easy that was, which pleased him at first, then quickly turned to worry. Perhaps they were glad he would be taking some time off in light of all the commotion he had just caused. It was no secret that even though he was protected by a union contract, on-air hosts could keep anyone off their shows with due cause. Maybe he shouldn't take time off now. Maybe he should wait until his screw-up was long forgotten. Nope. He needed to take off as soon as possible. Next week would be perfect.

He went to a map site and began mapping his trip for the following Wednesday. He hadn't taken a road trip by himself for ages. Oh, there were journeys back to Chicago without Frances, but those were always races against time to get there as fast as possible without attracting a state trooper. Brian longed for a road trip where he could take his time and stop in a town for an hour or a day. Maybe play a game of eight ball in a run- down bar with a patron one would ordinarily try to avoid on a dark street. He might get to Hampton North in six hours or take three days. But he was going to find The Tent, visit some old haunts, and when the timing was right stop by Smart House.

Brian decided not to do another search on the Internet to hunt for clues about Portia or Beatrice. He would simply go to the town, poke around, and try to assess the situation before doing anything rash. Even if he didn't find the Smarts at all, at least he knew he made the effort, and at the very least, got a good road trip out of it.

"It's me, pick up!" the voice bellowed through the answering machine just inches away from Brian's head. With the ringer turned off, he didn't realize the phone was ringing, but Frances' voice was coming through the speaker loud and clear.

Brian instinctively reached for the phone, but stopped himself. Frances would just assume he was sleeping and hang up. He didn't feel like talking to her now. Especially now. Not with Portia's image peeking at him from the desk drawer and a red arrow on a computer screen pointing at Smart House on the bluffs in Hampton North, Massachusetts. Frances will just have to wait.

"I guess you're sleeping. Nothing up. I'm at the office in Tysons Corner. I might be home late tonight. Bye," Frances said through the answering machine speaker.

"Late again," Brian sighed to himself. Frances knew Brian would be leaving for work around eight this evening, so she was probably planning on being out at least until then. Looking at the photo again, he flashed on a moment when he was five years old on a family vacation in St. Joe's, Michigan. His family stayed at an Italian-themed resort on the shores of Lake Michigan, called Villa Lipani. It was a collection of austere bungalows nestled in mature pines available by the week, month, or summer. The proprietors, Gaetana and Giuseppe Lipani, could barely speak English and catered to the Italians of Chicago. There was Italian music, movies, and of course, food, food, and more food. He remembered he was exactly five, because that's how old he was when Grandpa DeLouise died at Villa Lipani. It was on the narrow, rocky beach by Lake Michigan that Brian's grandfather said to him when no one else was around, *The older you get, the lonelier you get.* Since his grandfather died the very next day, found dead on his cabin cot with a smile on his face and marinara sauce on his pajama top, Brian never forgot those words. He wondered why his grandfather would say such a thing. Now he was beginning to understand.

Brian closed his eyes and began to remember those summers at Villa Lipani. They never went back after grandpa died, but he had his memories and the old photos. He remembered the steep rocky path that led down to their private lake beach. He also figured that was one of the reasons he was so drawn to Smart House on the bluffs of the Atlantic. Thinking of the warm sun and the sound of the water splashing on the lake beach and crashing on the ocean bluffs gave him a peaceful, sleepy feeling.

He closed the drawer, turned off the computer, and went back to bed. Another hour or two of sleep would do him just fine for the rest of the day. As he lay his head on the pillow, pulled up the covers, and pulled his legs up into a fetal position, he thought more about the warmth of the sun, the spray of sea, the sounds of the birds and the kiss that almost was, forever frozen in a black-and-white photo.

"Pick up. Aren't you up yet?" Frances' voice again said through the answering machine speaker. Brian looked at the clock and was pleased to see he got another two hours of sleep. He picked up the phone on the nightstand.

"Yes, I'm up. What's up?"

"We're going out this Saturday, and I wanted to make sure you could come. It's a dinner party at Congressman Lutz's Georgetown town house. You can make it, right?"

"Uh, yeah, sure. I don't think I have to work. If I do, you can go without me, right?" Brian said, still groggy.

"Yes, but I want you to go. It's important to me. I was invited by Congressman Lutz's office, and he's taken an interest in our department. Wear that new blazer I bought you. You better bring it to the cleaners today. I'll talk to you later, bye."

"Bye."

Brian hung up, put his head back on the pillow, and began to mull all that over. He wondered why she said, *We're going out this Saturday, and I wanted to make sure you could come.* That made it sound like the *we* only included him as an afterthought. Maybe he should make an effort this time. Perhaps Frances was trying to make an effort to try harder. Or maybe she just wanted him to go along because it looked good. He searched for the blazer Frances bought him. He didn't like it. She said the stripes were slimming.

Brian almost had to work that weekend. The only reason being he had offered to fill in for anyone who cared to take off Saturday, but no one took him up on it. He gazed at the blazer still in its dry cleaner bag hanging on the chin-up bar he hadn't used since the week he installed it over five years ago. The gold buttons and the pin-stripes that were a little too bright for Brian's liking were visible through the plastic. He was afraid to try it on. He was always afraid to try on articles of clothing he hadn't worn in months. That was always a dead giveaway that his body fat was increasing by percentage and surface area. But judging by Frances' readiness, he guessed the moment of truth was less than an hour away.

After living with Frances for so long he could easily gauge stages of readiness by which phase of construction she was in. Presently she was in the foundation mode; panty hose, hair in curlers, bra and no makeup. Brian could tell that Frances was also concerned with her elastic bands being stretched to the limit, due to the fact that she now took to closing doors after she flitted through a room grabbing items from drawers and closets. Brian noticed that the bottom of her bra now pretty much touched the top of her industrial strength panty hose, allowing only a pencil-sized roll of fat to protrude. He nearly laughed when caught sight of the crack in her ass, which was actually a crooked zig zagged line due to the uneven distribution of her butt cheeks in the super support panty hose as she rushed by with her cosmetics. But he knew he had no right to laugh and secretly wished he could hide his expanding torso with tight undergarments.

Brian lifted the plastic on his blazer and sighed. It reminded him of the jackets Thurston Howell wore on Gilligan's Island. Somehow the style had returned to inside the beltway. He lifted it off the hanger and put it on. As he pulled the button closer to the button hole he sensed it felt a little tighter than last time, but not enough to attract attention. He undid the button and stepped into the bedroom. The bathroom door was slightly ajar, and he could see Frances heading into her final stages as she applied makeup to her face. He couldn't help noticing how huge her tits had become. As she was putting on weight, she seemed to be putting a disproportionate amount of extra flesh into her boobs. And as many larger-than-average women do, she was using it to her full advantage by exposing giant mounds of cleavage whenever possible. She really must want to make an impression this evening because as she wrestled with her dress it was evident that her boobs would be a featured attraction.

"God!" Frances gasped. "Help me zip this, please!"

Brian stepped into the bathroom with Frances in front of the full-length mirror. He stood behind her and marveled at how her tits were scrunched together and pushed up in the black cocktail dress. As he grabbed the tiny end of the zipper, he wondered if it was physically possible to pull it all the way up without the entire dress exploding.

"Okay, hold on," Frances said as she inhaled and sucked in her gut. "Now!"

Brian tugged on the zipper and inched his way up her spine as he pushed her skin into the dress. When he reached the top he was amazed, not only at the technical wizardry of the materials and design of the fabrics, but at how fantastic

Frances looked. For the first time in weeks, he thought about grabbing her from behind and maybe seeing if she might be interested in a little last minute action.

"Not bad, huh," Frances said as she rubbed her hands along her tight dress. "You're not wearing that tie!" she shrieked.

"I'm not?" Brian said, his moment of potential arousal dissipating, as he hung his head to look at the tiny white baseballs that adorned his red tie. "They just look like white polka dots."

"Exactly. Wear the one I bought you for Christmas."

Brian untied his baseball tie and went to retrieve the one Frances got him for Christmas. He knew he'd have no trouble finding it because it was at the bottom of his closet, still in the box it came in.

As usual, when Brian and Frances went out together they took her brand new BMW. It was the only time Brian ever got to drive it, which irked him since he was the one paying the monthly bill. Brian thought it was ostentatious, but he enjoyed how it handled the curves of Rock Creek Parkway as they headed to the party at Congressman Lutz's home on Capitol Hill. He only hoped that there was secure parking there, since some areas of the Hill could be pretty rough.

"Will I know anyone at this party?" Brian asked as he exited Rock Creek and headed for Pennsylvania Avenue.

"Um, let's see. You know Patricia, my boss Ted, Raul, and I think you've met the Congressman's aide Ebony and her husband, Lance."

"Oh yeah, Ebony and Lance. We met at the jazz fest on the mall that time. That was ages ago. I think Raul was there, too."

"Ebony used to be in our office, and now she's a congressional aide with Lutz. This party could be good for me. They may be re-doing all the computers in Congress and they're looking for a director."

"Now I get it."

"Get what?"

"Why we're going. Why I'm going."

"Yeah, well, we're going," Frances said, adjusting her boobs.

As Brian pulled in front of the town house where the party was being held, he passed the valet, who had set up on the sidewalk.

"Where are you going?" Frances asked.

"I hate valet parking. If I can't find something around the corner I'll use the valet."

"Drop me off here then. I'm not walking through the streets in my *CMFM* heels."

Brian stopped the car and let Frances out a few cars past the door. *CMFM heels*? She hasn't used that term since they first met. It means *chase me fuck me*. He wondered who was doing the chasing this evening. He doubted he'd be doing any fucking. He made a right turn and at the end of the block he found a parking spot in front of a town house with a *for sale* sign in front. He knew that just a block or two down, the town houses weren't sandblasted, remodeled homes, but dilapidated homes for the urban poor. Some town houses waiting for renovation became crack houses overnight as they sat abandoned for weeks or months as real estate speculators waited for their deals to come together.

George had told Brian about his days of posing as an illegal gun buyer in these row houses in the shadows of the halls of Congress. But he figured this block looked okay to park on. Besides, it was just around the corner from a Congressman's home. There was bound to be extra security.

Whereas Frances thrived in these parties, Brian dreaded them. On more than one occasion he had made the mistake of talking politics among Frances' circle of government supported coworkers and friends. Brian considered himself a libertarian rather than a pure conservative, but he soon learned that the mere hint of not conforming to the talking points of an NPR news commentary or the current democratic platform meant immediate name calling and abrupt endings of conversations. He had more open-minded exchanges of ideas having breakfast at three in the morning with cops, construction workers, and hookers at the Taystee Diner. He knew to when to bite his lip, take a sip from his glass, and excuse himself to go get another shrimp.

This was a livelier affair than most of the parties Frances would drag him to. The music was loud enough so that people needed to talk above it, which made the scene seem rather boisterous. A rap song was thumping from file cabinet-sized speakers next to a professional DJ, a young black kid wearing an oversized Washington Wizards jersey and a backward baseball cap. The main room was not very large, and it took some maneuvering to squeeze through groups.

Brian scanned the room trying to find Frances. Since half the people there were African American, she should be easy to locate. Well, that and the fact that she probably will be surrounded by a group of men laughing at one of her off - colored jokes. There was an adjoining room, not lit as brightly as the main room, with a handful of couples dancing to Ludikris. There was Frances, drink in hand, dancing with a guy. Brian stepped inside the room a little further and was relatively sure the guy was her coworker, Raul. The same guy he had seen her kiss in Georgetown. Frances' boobs were jiggling to the music, and Raul kept looking off to the side as if he was trying to avoid looking at her bouncing boobage. The same couldn't be said for the other men and women dancing, who would take turns jumping in front of Frances, give an extra thrust to a dance move, just to see what kind of inventive gyration she could come up with to make her cleavage almost come out of her outfit. And this was after being at the party for less than ten minutes.

Most of the parties Frances dragged him to were in the suburbs, with low volume New Age jazz, the crowd 99 percent white, and the dancing nonexistent. Brian thought he could actually have a good time here, regardless of what kind of antics Frances got into on the dance floor. He had long since gotten used to her flirting, handing out business cards, and getting the hairy eyeball from spouses witnessing her act for the first time. Or for that matter, the second, third, fourth, or fifth time.

Brian was pleased as he overheard conversations about music, sports, and last night's Leno monologue as he squeezed through the crowd to grab some finger food and a cocktail. He may have gotten used to Frances' exhibitionist tendencies, but he doubted he could ever get used to nodding his head in silence as government and media wonks went on and on as they bashed the *gun-toting, NASCAR, Bible-thumping retards* who they believed were trying to take over the country and the world. Oh, these self described progressives were fine as long as you agreed with them. But if you injected any amount of skepticism into any one of their sacred cow causes of the month, such as global warming, you'd think *they* were the gun-toting retards.

Brian thought he recognized Ebony and Lance laughing with another couple by the food table. He sauntered closer to eavesdrop and once he heard Lance go on about Thelonius Monk, he knew that was him. Lance was about Brian's age, but where Brian had gone pale and soft, Lance was deep black and solid. He didn't get to talk much with him when they met at an outdoor jazz festival a few years ago, but he remembered that in a few sentences of small talk, where he mentioned Louis Jordan and Jackie Robinson, he instantly liked him. His wife, Ebony is an aide to Congressman Lutz, whose house the party was in, although he was nowhere to be seen. She used to work with Frances at the National Science Foundation where she got dialed in to where the money was going and who was getting it.

There was a lull in the conversation, so Brian stepped in and smiled.

"Excuse me, aren't you Lance and Ebony? I'm Frances's husband, Brian. We met at the DC Jazzfest a couple of years ago."

"Yes! Great to see you," Lance said as he extended his hand to Brian.

"I was wondering if you were here when I saw Frances flit by," Ebony said as she exchanged a friendly peck on the cheek.

"She's tearing up the dance floor as usual," Lance laughed. "This is Ed Lee and his wife, Beverly," Lance said as he gracefully swept his hand to the others. Ed and Beverly were an older, well-dressed African American couple; Ed in a conservative pinstriped suit and Beverly in a full- length floral print evening dress. "And this is Chaz and Ronald," Lance said, motioning toward two middle-aged white men with matching fashionably oversized eyewear, whom Brian assumed to be a couple. "We were just talking about the music."

Brian stopped himself. He knew from past experience he should just shut his mouth and let the others opine on whether or not the rap music currently blasting was good or bad.

"It's not music!" Ed said in a serious deep voice. "That's what bothers me about it."

Just then, the word *niggaz* could be heard in the rap song that was being played by the DJ.

"Not to mention the language," his wife Beverly added indignantly. "We risked life and limb to get rid of that word, and now I hear it more than ever. I'm going to have a word with that young DJ man."

Brian waited again to see where the direction of the conversation would lead. Lance glanced at Ebony, took a sip of red wine, and shook his head.

"I know, but just think of what we listened to when we were kids. Our parent's thought the same about Little Richard. Youth is rebellion. Hopefully, they grow out of it," Lance said, calmly.

"Damn right, I've grown out of it, but how come I got to still listen to that crap at a party filled with old people!" Ed bellowed, causing laughter all around.

The rap song ended and Billie Holiday began singing *Strange Fruit.*

"See! That's what I'm talking about!" Lance said holding one hand to his ear. "This song, *Strange Fruit* caused a ruckus in the forties because it was a song about a taboo subject-- lynching of blacks in the South. Not everybody understood the message, but when the media covered the controversy all hell broke loose. At least a dialogue began."

"But that's just it," Brian said, wondering if he had just made a huge mistake by interjecting his opinion. "It was artfully told with metaphors. And by somewhat conforming with the mores of the times, they got their message out to more people than if they just blurted out a protest song."

"That's right," Chaz said, "Sometimes a little nudge goes a long way compared to shove in the shnozz."

"How is Frances doing?" Ebony asked Brian, tilting her wine glass toward the dance floor where Frances was in the center of a circle with everyone clapping to the beat at her.

"She appears to be doing great," Brian deadpanned.

"I have to corner her. I've got some stuff we need to talk about," Ebony said to Brian as the others continued to talk about Billie Holliday. "You know, business things," she said, reassuring Brian it wasn't anything more than that. Brian of course picked up on the qualification of her comment, wondering what she may have might have been alluding to. But more importantly, he was trying to keep an ear on the conversation with Lance, Chaz, Ronald, Ed, and Beverly, which was honing in on their jazz heroes. They were still on Billie Holliday, but began talking about sidemen, producers, and influences, which demonstrated an acute interest and knowledge from each of them.

In his day-to-day experience as a talk radio screener, Brian had become very perceptive to a person's intelligence level just a few words into a sentence. A good screener has a great bullshit detector. His livelihood depended on it.

"Ed, tell them about your foray into the music biz," Lance said tapping Ed on the shoulder.

"Well, before I moved to Washington, I worked in Detroit for Soul Tower Music with Abel Washington."

Brian was riveted to Ed upon hearing that, as were Chaz and Ronald. Obviously Lance, Ebony, and Beverly, who returned from talking to the DJ, had heard this story before.

"Wow! *The* Abel Washington?" Brian asked in awe. "He wrote and produced almost everything that came out of Soul Tower in the sixties and seventies!"

Chaz and Arnold struck a pose as if in a sixties soul group, with their hands on their gyrating hips and sang, "Don't say it's nothing when you mean it's something, bay yay yay beeee," to the delight of the group.

"You boys nailed it!" Ed laughed. "It was while I was still in law school, and I was kind of an office manager slash legal consultant, so I saw pretty much *everything* that was going down in the summer of sixty-eight. So I'm in Abel's office one day, and this scruffy, skinny little white boy no more that eighteen years old comes in with a guitar, no case, wearing cut-off shorts and a tattered tee, and hair down to his ass," he looks at his wife Beverly for a moment, "I mean, down to his butt, sits in front of Abel. So, Abel has this big ugly fake plant in front of him, which is where he hides his microphone hooked up to a tape recorder in his desk drawer. So the kid sits down, and Abel just goes, *Let's hear it.* Man, if that kid didn't start singing like an angel! Man alive! And it had rhythm too! I mean you just knew it was a hit. So Abel sits there with a big 'ol cheap, smelly cigar in his mouth, choking us out-- I think even that fake plant of his was gasping for air-- with a disgusted look on his face like he's listening to Elmer Fudd sing *I Pagliacci*! So the kid finishes, I almost broke into applause, but thank goodness I didn't, and Abel just taps his ash into his fake plant and says, *I know I'm making a big mistake, kid, but*... and he opens his top drawer and pulls out a roll of twenties and begins laying them out in front of the kid on his desk...*I'll give you three hundred dollars right now for that song.* Needless to say, that kid's eyes almost popped out of his head looking at those fifteen twenties laid out in front of him. Then Abel opens another drawer and pulls out a single piece of paper and says, *Sign here.* That kid reached for the pen so fast I thought he was going to throw out his shoulder."

"So which song was it?" Chaz eagerly asked.

Ed paused, looked Chaz in the eye and said "Been Dreamin' On You."

"But Abel Washington wrote that," Chaz said crestfallen.

"After that kid signed that piece of paper he did," Ed said shaking his head.

Chaz and Ronald looked at each other in mock sadness and started to sing, "I tried and I tried. I cried and I cried. You lied and you lied. And since you been gone, I've been dreamin' on yooooooo."

The group applauded with fervor, and when they stopped, Brian chimed in, "We had Don King on one of our shows once, and he was commenting on a tour he once promoted and produced for Michael Jackson, and he said that he thought the fight business was tough until he got into the music business."

"What kind of show do you work for?" Ed asked guardedly.

"Radio. ARS talk radio," Brian responded

"Now tell me you're not going to be letting out my little story on the airwaves! I still have family in Detroit!" Ed said only half kidding.

"No need to worry. My shift is more concerned with pulling chicken guts out of people."

"What's up with that?" Lance asked.

"Most of the overnight shifts deal with the fringes of science. And I do mean fringes; like psychic surgery."

"I've heard about that!" Ebony said inquisitively. "What is it?"

"Oh, these *quote* psychic surgeons sucker people into thinking they're pulling these tumors and growths out them, when in reality, they're just slight-of-hand magicians pulling chicken guts from what looks like their insides," Brian stated matter-of-factly.

"I hate to sound stupid," Ronald asked, "but how could they do that on a radio show?"

"Believe it or not, the host did play by play of the procedure, live on the air."

"Let me get this," Ed said with a look of bewilderment on his face, "the host does play by play, and describes this on the air? Is that…ethical?"

The group looked at each other, and all together said, "No!" followed by laughter.

"What's going on here?" Frances said excitedly as she squeezed into the group right next to Brian.

"Frances! Finally!" Ebony said. "Where've you been! We're having some fun here just conversatin' with your hubby!"

"Oh," Frances said with a look of mild surprise creeping across her face.

"Frances, before I lose you, come with me to the little girl's room, would you?" Ebony asked Frances as she took her by the arm.

"That's the best offer I've had all night," Frances said as she sexily slithered away arm in arm with Ebony.

Chaz and Ronald excused themselves, as did the rest of the group, one by one, leaving Brian there alone. He was on his second glass of wine and just starting to get a buzz. He knew he was driving this evening, because Frances almost always got sloshed at these things. There was a time when he enjoyed that part of it, because it almost always meant a wild night of sex from the moment they got in the car, into the hall of the house, the shower and then in bed. But lately it just meant making sure Frances didn't throw up on anything. He decided one more glass of one wouldn't hurt, so he grabbed a glass from the bar.

The deejay must have gotten some complaints about the music, because he ditched the rap music and was playing classic disco and sixties R&B. Brian liked the sounds, and the third glass of wine made him extra relaxed as he sat in a corner chair and simply watched the party transpire in front of him.

He watched Frances go back to the dance floor and sweat it up with Raul, Ed, Chaz, Ronald, and a score of other eager males. He sat in the same chair for over an hour, as the music segued into slow R&B and people started picking up their coats and begin leaving.

Brian was almost nodding off, when he saw Frances, Beverly, and Ed coming toward him with their coats on.

"I told Ed and Beverly we can give them a lift back to Dupont Circle," Frances declared.

"That's if it's no trouble," Ed added.

"Not at all. Are we ready to go?" Brian asked as he shook some cobwebs loose and stood up. "The car's a couple of blocks away. Do you want me to go get it and pick you up in front?"

"No, I could use a walk in some fresh air," Beverly said, nodding at Ed.

"After you," Brian said, pointing toward the front door.

It didn't seem as cool out as it did the past few nights. It wasn't quite balmy but one could sense that the first signs of spring weren't too far off. Brian walked a few steps in front of Frances, Ed, and Beverly, who were doing post-party analysis of who was wearing what and who was about to do who as they walked arm in arm.

As they turned the corner on the narrow sidewalk, the street lights were a little farther apart and one light halfway down the block was out. As they reached the broken lamp, which created a pool of darkness, a small flash of light in a doorway caught Brian's attention. About twenty yards ahead, a dark figure lit a cigarette, and in that brief moment of illumination, Brian saw a black man's face. Brian became a little concerned, seeing a black man in a doorway, and felt a tinge of guilt for feeling fear. Was it because he was black? Would he feel fear if it was a white face he saw? He didn't want to alarm Frances, Ed, and Beverly, who had dropped a little farther behind him, so he just continued down the sidewalk, keeping an eye on the dark doorway where the cigarette was lit.

As Brian studied the doorways on his right, he wasn't quite sure exactly where the man had been standing. Maybe he went inside the building.

Suddenly a dark figure with a black ski mask completely covering his face, except for two eye holes and a mouth hole, stepped in front of them. Brian immediately stopped dead in his tracks, causing the three to bump into him.

"Don't make a sound, don't move, just give me all your jewelry and money, wallets everything or I'll stick you! Fast. Everything."

Brian heard gasps from the two women, and Ed whispered, "Shit." The robber sounded young. He was over six feet tall and weighed maybe a hundred twenty-five pounds. But in his hand was a knife that was just as long, lean, and lethal.

Brian's mind raced. Ed, Beverly, and Frances were behind him, and the mugger was about five steps in front of them. The mugger lifted his knife, making sure they saw it, and took a step forward. "Everything. Fast!" the thief said through his ski mask.

Just as the mugger took a step forward, so did Brian. Brian then motioned for the others to stay back, and lifted his right arm high so the thief could see it. Brian slowly and deliberately moved his arm behind him and went under his jacket, placing his hand exactly where an ATF agent might keep a gun if he kept one in a holster in the small of his back.

In a monotone voice, Brian said loudly, "You take one more fucking step, and I'll blow your motherfucking nigger brains out."

The thief twitched slightly for a moment, turned, and ran full speed in the opposite direction, speeding around the next corner.

Brian turned around and saw Beverly collapse. Ed stopped her from hitting the pavement, and said "Here, call 911," as he managed to toss Brian his cell. Frances tended to Beverly, as she knelt to assist her.

"Yes, we've just been attacked by a male in a ski mask on…where are we?" Brian asked Ed.

"Thirteenth and E, southeast!" Ed yelled.

"Thirteenth and E, southeast. Do we need an ambulance?" Brian said, turning to see Beverly getting back on her feet.

"No, I don't think so. Just send the police," Ed said as he comforted Beverly.

"Just send the police. We think we're okay. Yes. Thanks," Brian said as he handed the phone back to Ed.

Two men from the party ran full speed up to them. "Are you okay? What happened?"

"We were almost assaulted. Dude had a knife as long as a sword," Ed said as he used a handkerchief to wipe the tears from Beverly's face. Three more men from the party turned the corner, and began to assist them.

Brian was wondering if anyone could see him shaking. He hadn't planned on using George's strategy. It just popped into his head.

"Let's get Beverly back to the house. Here come the cops, now," Ed said with a siren getting closer. Frances and two friends escorted Beverly back to Congressman Lutz's.

Once the police arrived, Brian and Ed went over everything in great detail, including Brian noticing the man in the doorway when he lit a cigarette and using the "N" word in his bold bluff.

A half hour later, Brian's adrenaline was still coursing through his system as he and Frances approached their car at the end of the block. He opened the door for Frances and she entered. He walked around and got into his seat, and Frances yanked her head toward him.

"I am humiliated!" Frances seethed.

"Excuse me?" Brian asked in disbelief.

"I can't believe what you did," Frances said, still seething.

"You just better cut to the chase on this because with my adrenaline level right now, I might shoot through the sun roof any second. What in God's name are you talking about?"

Frances narrowed her eyes into fierce slits. "You said the 'N' word."

"This is a joke, right?" Brian said as he banged the steering wheel with both hands. "Am I being punked? This isn't happening, is it? Are you serious?"

"You didn't have to say the 'N' word in front of Beverly and Ed."

"Wait a minute. I just saved the three of you from getting stabbed to death, and you're worried I offended your friends by saying the word *nigger*, which we heard all night long at the party in assorted rap songs?"

"Why did you have to say it then? Why?"

"What's the difference? I probably saved our lives!"

"Don't pull that hero shit. You don't know he was going to stab us."

"I'm not hearing this. I'm not. I'm not."

Brian starts the engine, and pushes the sun roof button, opening it. He stands on his seat, putting most of his body outside, and screams, "My wife is insane! Can you hear me, world? She is out of her mind." He sits down, pushes the button again, which closes the sun roof.

A police officer appeared at his window and tapped on it softly. Brian opened it.

"What's the problem, sir? Do you need assistance, ma'am?" The young black officer asked Frances.

"No."

"Sir, were you with the party that was assaulted?"

"Yes. We were."

"Are you the person who scared off the perpetrator?"

"Yes. I believe that I managed to do that," Brian said, as he turned to Frances, who turned away, looking out her window.

The officer reached in the open window and held his hand out to shake hands with Brain. "Good job, sir."

Frances turned and saw the officer's hand clasping Brian's. The cop walked away and Brian closed his window.

"Let's just go home, okay," Frances said buckling her seat belt.

The ride home was dead silent. Not a word was spoken the entire half hour it took them to wind through the streets of Washington, Rock Creek Park, and into their driveway.

Frances leapt out of the car as soon as it stopped. Brian followed her into the house and up the stairs. Brian stopped just at the doorway to the bedroom and watched Frances as she began to drop her clothes on the floor. He turned, walked into his office and switched on his computer in the dark room. Just as the screen illuminated, Frances stomped in and took a stance behind him, wearing a robe that accentuated her unsupported fat.

Brian slowly turned to see Frances, who in the time it took to boot up his computer had transformed from a sexy party girl to an enraged water buffalo.

"When did you become such a redneck?"

Brian didn't get up from his chair. He just stared at her in disbelief.

"Why am I a redneck?" Brian asked her, trying to contain his anger.

"You used the 'N' word, didn't you?"

"Here it goes again. Yes, I used the 'N' word to save our asses from getting stabbed to death."

"My friends are African American. And the mugger was, too."

"Oh, God forbid I should insult a street thug who's about to stab me to death. The mugger was African American? Who's being racist now?"

"What are you talking about?" Frances said, shocked.

"How do you know he was African American? Oh, you just assumed he was because he was a thief? Right? Didn't you?"

"Yeah, well, you…you…you voted for Bush!"

Brian rose out of his chair and covered his face in astonishment. He paced across the room and turned to Frances and screamed, "Yes! Yes, I voted for Bush in '04! We were at war! For the last time, I voted for him for one reason! I'm not an isolationist!"

"You're not an isolationist? Ha! Then why the fuck are you in this goddammed room in the dark by yourself jerking off for twelve hours a day?" Frances shrieked. She turned, grabbed the door, and slammed it behind her with such force that the White Sox wall clock crashed to the floor and smashed into pieces.

CHAPTER FIVE

It was as though some kind of fog machine capable of spewing dread and anger blew through the central heating and air conditioning system of their home. Brian had requested double shifts right up until Wednesday, the day he was scheduled to take off on his trip. If Frances happened to bump into him in the driveway, or on the way to the kitchen, she pretended she didn't even see him.

Brian wondered how he was going to break the news to her that he was leaving on a trip to the Cape. Frances knew of just about every one of Brian's ex-girlfriends, and even most of his one night stands. Before they were married and sex was as much a part of the day as going to the bathroom, Frances loved to grill Brian on his ex-lovers during foreplay. She seemed to revel in the fact that it made Brian uncomfortable, but more obvious was that Brian's reluctant admission of sexual escapades got her even hotter and hornier than usual. He wasn't sure when he might have last done it, but he was certain that he had on more than one occasion mentioned that there was a summer romance while working at a theatre on the Cape. And that it was an older woman with hairy armpits and legs, and an appetite for sex that was only second to Frances herself in her prime.

It didn't work the other way for Brian. If Frances so much as mentioned an old boyfriend's name, his woody turned to silly putty. Although Frances tried for years to get Brian to partake in her foreplay name game, it wasn't until he totally lost his cool and threw a pillow across the room, which knocked over a candle and briefly set the curtains on fire, that she finally stopped trying.

Tuesday morning at six a.m. he was going to tell Frances that he was going by himself to the Cape for a few days. He figured morning would be the best time to tell her because she would have to leave for work. After his overnight shift ended, he picked up a cup of coffee and a bagel and sat in the driveway until it was exactly six a.m. He downed the last gulp and went into the house. Much to his surprise, Frances was already fully dressed and made up, sitting in the kitchen. Brian noticed that her coat was on the table, and a suitcase was next to her chair.

"You're up and ready early," Brian said, breaking the ice.

"I've been waiting for you," Frances said coldly. "I'm going away for a couple of days,"

"But..." Brian tried to interrupt.

"Let me finish. I've had it. I want a divorce. I'm going to stay with a friend for a couple of days."

"A friend? Who might that be?"

"Never you mind," Frances announced sternly, as though she was daring him to do battle.

Brian wasn't pissed off or enraged or even surprised, really. He felt stupid.

"You don't have to leave," he said defeated. "I'm going on a trip tomorrow. I was going to tell you this morning. I'll just get my stuff out when I get back next week, and we can talk then."

Frances looked stunned, as though she had been gearing up for the fight of her life and she was the one shocked that no blowout followed. "Where are *you* going?"

"I'm going to the Cape."

"With who?"

"No one. Just me. We'll talk when I get back. You just stay here. Invite Raul for all I care. Maybe he can talk politics with the people next door. I'm going to bed, bye," Brian said, his voice filled with sadness. He wasn't sad that it was over. He was sad that he had waited so long for an end. And he was mad at himself for letting Frances decide when the end would be. He went into the guest room, kicked off his shoes and plopped down on the unmade bed. He was tired, but couldn't sleep because of the coffee. He heard the back door close and Frances leave in her car.

Brian hadn't even thought about what exactly he would do when he got back after his trip. Where would he stay? Should he cancel his trip and find an apartment? Should he stay in a motel for a while? What about George? He had a decent-sized place and was living alone. He picked up the phone and called him. His answering machine came on: *Leave it after you hear it*, George said on the machine.

"George, Brian here. Listen, I'm leaving tomorrow morning for the Cape for a long weekend. I need to talk to you. I might need a place to stay for a few days…"

The phone was picked up. It was George. "What? I was taking a dump. I only heard part of your message. You need a place to stay?"

"Frances and I are done. For real."

"What's his name?"

"Raul, I think."

"My place is a disaster area. When do you need to crash?"

"I'll be back either Sunday or Monday morning."

"Good, that'll give me time to scrape the funk off!" George paused, and said quietly, "Are you okay?"

"Yeah, I'm still going on my trip to the Cape. This works out great. Thanks."

"No problem, Bad Brain. Just give me a call to let me know when you're arriving. You know, in case I got an orgy going, I'll want to air the place out before you get here," George kidded.

Frances had no idea what Brian was up to, and it made her nervous. She knew she took a huge chance by implying she was staying with Raul. It could affect their divorce settlement, merely by the fact that Brian might be pissed off. But she had a master plan involving deception, intimidation, and superior thinking. The exact same strategy she used to snag Brian when they first met and she was unemployed.

The Capitol City Hotel, wasn't either. It was in College Park, Maryland, and it could hardly be classified as a hotel. It was a three-story motel, but the owners thought it should be deemed a hotel because the hallways were on the inside. The red sign read *vacancy* continuously for so many years it was a wonder of neon technology. Frances noticed Raul's Jaguar parked on the street as she instructed him to. Frances didn't like the fact that it wasn't a top of the line Jaguar, but the X-type that looks like a glorified Taurus designed, no doubt, after Ford bought them out. She parked, took her suitcase out of the trunk, and headed to the room where she knew Raul would be waiting.

"Well, it's done. No more sneaking around for us," Frances said as she walked over to the windows and jerked the curtains closed.

"What did he say?" Raul said from his chair next to the bolted down table. "Was he mad?"

"Mad? The only time he's mad is if his stupid Patisserie baseball team, or whatever the hell it is, goes into a slump. He just slithered away as usual," Frances said opening her suitcase on the bed, and holding up a black nightie. "Ain't this precious?"

"You didn't mention me, did you?"

"Not exactly…"

"What do you mean?" Raul shouted, leaning straight forward and extending his neck as far out as physically possible.

"Relax. I think he already knew, the sneak," Frances said as she unclipped her heavy duty bra and her huge tits collapsed down nearly to the top of her panty hose.

"He won't come after me, will he?" Raul said, sliding over to the curtains and peeking out.

Frances was dismayed that Raul was looking out the window and ignoring her display of naked boobage.

"He doesn't have the nerve," Frances said as she reeled Raul closer to her, putting his face between her bare breasts. "Don't worry, mama will make sure everything works out."

"Hmmm. Good. I want everything to work out," Raul said, his words barely audible from inside her cleavage.

"You can move in on Thursday."

Raul's head popped up, making her tits reverberate. "Move in Thursday? Where?"

"To my house. Just for a few days. It'll be fun."

"We never discussed that," Raul said his voice fraught with terror.

"Well, we will. No rush. Let's take it nice and easy," Frances said as she tugged hard on his belt trying to undo it. Raul let her remove his belt and trousers and laid down on the bed as Frances took her nightie into the bathroom.

After screwing until Raul came, which occurred after about ninety seconds of grimacing and grunting, Frances thought about how different her life would be. She was sure that Brian would fall into line with her plan to sell the house, making sure she got the better end of a huge settlement. That should translate into at least an eight hundred thousand-dollar bonanza. It was her idea to buy the place. Even dumpier houses in the neighborhood have sold for over a million bucks. And in addition to the car-- the BMW, of course-- her savings and half of his savings would set her up pretty good. She was sure that Raul wouldn't expect her to contribute anything to his monthly bills. Quite sure. Her future was finally going the way she wanted it to.

Frances had long ago promised herself that she would not wind up like her mother-- widowed and alone at forty, without a pot to piss in. Her father committed suicide by Seagrams, and she wasn't going to let any man leave her hanging in the balance. She still had her mother to help support, along with her brother and sister, back in West Virginia. She never expected to be sitting on hundreds of thousands of dollars in equity, but now that it was hers for the taking, it was time to cash out. If she had listened to Brian, they would still be renting some crappy apartment.

There was a time when Frances couldn't imagine life without Brian. He was everything she wanted in a man. He was agreeable-- okay, easily manipulated; he was sexy-- well, he was horny; and he had a career. Granted, she assumed a career in radio meant a rise up the corporate ladder to a future position of wealth and prestige, which in Washington goes a hell of a long way. She never expected him to stagnate the way he did. She still didn't understand what a radio producer did anyway. All she knew was that her friend Gail Paccione's husband worked in sales at the radio station that carried the *Morning Zoo* and they lived in a Georgetown mansion.

As Frances watched Raul dry his flabby body off after showering, she wondered if he could keep up with her bold dash to the toppermost of the poppermost. Or at the very least, let her lead the way and hold onto her skirt. She liked Raul just fine. He wasn't the best-looking guy she ever banged, but he seemed appreciative and complied with nearly all of her wishes. And that would do just fine.

Brian awoke refreshed for the first time in days. For that brief moment when he opened his eyes in mid-afternoon, he forgot where his life was headed. When he realized in that nanosecond where electric impulses of thought travel from the unconscious mind of sleep into the forefront of awareness, he was panicked. And a split-second later, once his conscious mind could compute the data, he was relieved. Frances made her move to end their relationship, just as she had made the first move to bed him the first time they met.

He knew that night's shift would be easy because he was working on the only night of the week when the format was music. The host was a Deadhead who only played music that, in his mind, had some sort of six degrees of separation from the Grateful Dead. Brian enjoyed the Dead's studio albums, but naturally, those cuts were never played. Instead, there were six continuous hours of psychedelic jams, atonal sax solos, amateur Dead wannabe bands, awful live recordings of the Dead in concert, and of course, the brief interludes of poetry readings by people who no doubt dropped acid like Tic Tacs.

But fortunately for Brian, most of the cuts played were between ten and twenty minutes in duration, which gave him plenty of time to surf the Internet and prepare for his trip later that day. The most difficult part of the job was keeping the broadcast's volume in the studio monitors low enough so he wouldn't want to blow his brains out from the monotony and loud enough so he could hear his cues for station breaks and PSAs.

The last strains of an interminable Ornette Coleman solo was being faded out by Danny Freeworld, the host, and Brian's replacement was already there, ready to take over. Brian wasn't a bit tired, and couldn't wait to get home, load the car, and begin his journey.

Just as he was going over the evening's station log with the next producer, Jason, his boss appeared outside the glass door to the studio. Brian knew something was up, because he usually doesn't arrive until ten.

Brian went to exit the studio, and as soon as he reached for the handle on the door Jason grabbed the other side of the door, opening it for him.

"Brian, may I have a word with you in my office."

"Sure," Brian said, trying to hide the fear. He thought this could be the life changes trifecta-- divorce, kicked out of your own house, and getting fired-- all within twenty four hours.

Brian knew it was trouble as soon as he saw the union shop steward, Gus, already in the room. Gus was the last holdover from the old school union guys. He wasn't that old, maybe in his mid-fifties, and he probably would have been fired years ago for being a hard line pain in the ass. Brian assumed that the only reason he was kept on was that the company could not fire him because of his union stature. He was a burnt-out old hippie radical, with thin gray hair worn in a pony tail, despite the ever-growing bald spot. He spent most of his time walking around the building and tacking up articles he had gleaned from obscure conspiracy theory Web sites that quoted Noam Chomsky as if it was the New Testament. Probably, they also thought they couldn't mess with him, or he'd blow the place up.

Brian sat down across from Jason and knew by the expression on his face and the fact that a file folder was already on his desk, he wasn't about to receive an award for employee of the month. Even Gus looked solemn.

"Brian, as you know, we had to investigate a recent incident where a serious lapse in judgment on your part resulted in the broadcast of the emergency broadcast interruption loop," Jason said, never looking up from his notes laid out in front of him.

Brian paused, hoping Gus would jump to his support and yell, *Fuck the pigs,* or *Off the man,* or *We're mad as hell and we're not going to take it anymore.* Instead he just took a sip of tea from a mug that had the caption *For those of us left* printed on it.

"Gus and I have had preliminary negotiations regarding what type of disciplinary action should be taken..."

"Nobody said anything about disciplinary action before," Brian said, interrupting.

Jason looked at Gus, who subtly nodded his head in approval.

"According to the bylaws of the collective bargaining agreement, it must be referred to as disciplinary action, Brian," Jason added firmly, which was difficult.

"We've got to stick to the CBA, Brian. It's cool," Gus said winking.

"Due to the seriousness of the situation, we've negotiated a deal. You will be suspended with pay for the period of ten days," Jason said, still avoiding eye contact with Brain.

Brain looked at Gus, who raised his mug as if in a toast. "It's the system, Brian."

"But, I'm already taking off the rest of this week," Brian said, confused.

"We know that," Jason said, his voice cracking.

"And now, you don't want me to come in all of next week either, but I get paid."

"That is the agreement," Jason added as sternly as he could muster.

"But," Gus said, "and this is a big but. But you have a year to challenge the disciplinary action notation in your file and have it expunged."

Brian looked at both of them in dumbfounded amazement. "But I don't have to give back the money?"

"No," they said in unison.

"I'm sorry, Brian," Jason said rising as he folded the folder to demonstrate just how closed the situation was.

"Yeah, me too," Brian said as he shook hands with both of them and left the room.

Brian preferred the mini-van over the BMW, especially now. With another week added to his trip, he was utilizing every inch of space inside and on the roof rack. In the unlikely event that there was a warm spell, he even took a tent and sleeping bag. He loved camping out, but hadn't camped since before he was married. The front seat was reserved for the essentials; a small cooler and his laptop. With wi-fi hot spots all over he could keep tabs on his email, check maps, and even update any roster moves or stats updates in his three baseball leagues.

He thought about calling Frances, but instead left a note on the kitchen table; *Back in 10 days on Sunday. I'll call before I show up. –Brian.* As he finished the note, he thought this could be the last time he looked at the place as his own. And as he scanned each room, he realized there really wasn't anything that *was* his in any room-- the furnishing, paintings, knick-knacks, rugs, pillows, lamps, even the books that Frances never read-- were all picked out by her. The only room that contained his stuff was his office. And except for the wall unit, everything in that room could fit in the mini-van when he moved out.

The broken White Sox wall clock was still on his desk in pieces. The hands were stuck on the exact moment when Frances slammed the door on their marriage. Then Brian remembered a phrase his mother used to tell him when she tried to warn him about questionable friend: *Even a broken clock is right twice a day.*

CHAPTER SIX

Brian exited the Beltway, turned onto 295 going north, and his mind flashed on a line Groucho Marx frequently used on male contestants on his game show, "You Bet Your Life." He'd take the cigar out of his mouth and ask, *Are you married or happy?* Brian wasn't quite sure what his answer would be.

Heading north, he noticed the slight traces of spring that had begun to emerge in Washington were fading. The trees were bare, allowing for the view to extend to the horizon of the bright winter morning. Brian thought of stopping in Aberdeen for breakfast, but then realized that the old railroad car diner there had been demolished a few years earlier. He thought he could hold out for a while longer, perhaps all the way to Baltimore.

In that space where DC radio stations faded and the stations from Baltimore began to dominate the airwaves, Brian switched off the radio. He was in the midst of an American no-man's land: a place equidistant between two major cities. It wasn't quite rural, not quite suburban. It's where friends, families, and neighbors were divided between which city they aligned themselves with. Are you a Ravens or a Redskins fan? An Orioles or a Nationals fan? A blue collar Baltimoron or a Washington asshole?

Brian knew his trip to the Cape would be about seven hours if he drove straight through, but he was in no hurry, especially in light of the fact that his "punishment" gave his an extra week off with pay. So, he decided not to head north on 95, but instead took an exit that would put him in downtown Baltimore for a late breakfast.

Baltimore's touristy Inner Harbor is pretty much like every other planned consumer mall in any other American city, except that it's on the water. But nearby is Fell's Point, a collection of restaurants and bars that predates not only the Inner Harbor complex, but most of America itself. Since colonial times, sailing ships would pull up there to unload cargo while sailors got loaded at the dockside saloons. As Brian enjoyed an omelet and a cup of coffee while gazing on the waterfront, the importance of his journey began to truly sink in.

Not a soul on earth knew where he was at this moment. Sure, George and Frances knew Brian was headed to the Cape for a week or so, but no one knew exactly where he was at any particular moment or where he was headed. And as Brian asked for a refill, he realized he didn't, either.

As Brian walked off his hearty breakfast, he realized Baltimore must have a terrible identity complex. Just two blocks away from the marvelous ballpark, Camden Yards, is the Babe Ruth Museum. He wondered what kind of civic mentality would allow a tribute to the most famous Yankee in history just two home run lengths from the home of the team the Yanks have been killing for decades. He couldn't imagine Chicago allowing a similar tribute to such an interloper; okay, except maybe for the statue of Goethe in Lincoln Park.

From where he was standing, Brian could see the empty grandstands of the idle ballpark and imagined the seats being filled and the roar of the crowd being heard from exactly where he stood. He was certain that just weeks from that moment, when the season opened, that would be the case. Where he would be standing in several weeks was an entirely different matter of certainty. It also reminded him how far behind he was with his responsibilities as commissioner of three fantasy baseball leagues.

Continuing north on 95, Brian noted the scenery looking more and more as though winter was just a little bit farther in the distance than in DC. He even began to see patches of snow in the hills through the empty trees. He had decided not to listen to any of his CDs on the way north. He didn't want to rely on familiar tunes to get him through his journey. Instead Brian went for hours without listening to anything except for that voice in his head.

Like a road traveled long ago with a fork in it, Brian intended to backtrack to that fork and take the other way. He realized the green road sign with white lettering that read *Frances* pointed one way; a road he had been traveling for almost fifteen years. Brian wanted to go back to that exact point, and follow the sign that pointed in the other direction, but only had a large white question mark on it.

It seemed like just a few minutes had passed since Brian had pushed the button on his dashboard to prevent any more of the outside air in Elizabeth, New Jersey, from being sucked into the vehicle. The stench of the refineries and the burning fireballs of excess gasses escaping from the many smokestacks make Elizabeth look and smell like the gateway to hell. After getting off the George Washington Bridge, which connects Jersey with New York, he decided to take a detour south on the Major Deegan Expressway in the Bronx.

He followed the exit to Yankee Stadium, and after passing through an ugly industrial area he found himself under an “L”. Brian was no stranger to elevated subway trains, having grown up by one in Chicago. He knew that in New York, it was abbreviated as an “el,” and in Chicago it was simply the “L,” just to be contrarian. And he also knew that there wasn’t a chance in hell that a museum and statue of Ted Williams or Hank Aaron or Sandy Koufax was within walking distance of the ballpark. It was bizarre to see two Yankee Stadiums, the old and the new, next to each other. The grand old cathedral waiting to be torn down, adjacent to its billion-dollar facsimile next door-- like the two human clones in *Invasion of the Body Snatchers*-- one with a soul and one without. It was obvious which was which. With the ballpark closed and most of the satellite businesses dependent on the baseball season also shut tight, the neighborhood looked surprisingly dull. The only things open were a few Yankee-themed restaurants and bars, and fast food joints. He didn’t even get out of his car, but got back on the highway and followed the signs to the New England Thruway.

Brian looked at the clock on the dash and realized he had been on the road for nearly ten hours, and he felt it. As he approached the Boston metropolitan area the traffic was heavy, and he wondered if he would be able to find his way to Hampton North in the dark. Although it had been years since he was there, he doubted they had improved the signage in the area. He had heard from the locals that the lack of signs was no accident; it helped keep tourists away. Instead, he figured he'd set a record for himself by visiting four major league ballparks in one day and followed the signs to the Fenway district of Boston. Once he got off the highway and made his way to Fenway Park, it was even more desolate than the neigborhood around Yankee Stadium, especially in the darkness. So, just another loop around the park in his van would have to do.

Rather than stay in Boston, Brian decided to get at least close to Hampton North. He remembered some restaurants and motels just off the highway exit, which was only ten or so miles from the Cape, so he headed there hoping things were as they were when he was last there.

It took him more time to find the entrance back on to the highway in Boston than it took him to get to the Hampton North exit. He was surprised to see how tacky and developed it had become just beyond the exit, identical to every other over commercialized suburban and exurban village, town, and city in America. Huge parking lots lined both sides of the wide street, with alternating mega box hardware stores, fast food drive-thrus, Gaps, Starbucks, Bed Bath and Beyonds, Pier Ones, and cheap motel chains. Brian held out hope that Hampton North, being a good ten miles away and part of a different township, hadn't succumbed to such crass consumerism.

He drove about five miles from the highway and noticed that the businesses were becoming fewer and farther between. He pulled into the Hampton North Motor Inn, a small motel that he remembered staying at once before he moved into his room at Smart House. The owners of the Hampton North Motor Inn had been cashing in on the proximity to Hampton North since the sixties, even though it was a good five miles from there. But, as Brian recalled, the rates pretty much quadrupled once you entered the exclusive environs of the Hampton North Township.

The young man at the front desk wore a name tag that read Larry Olivier and a flash of recognition shot through Brian's brain.

"Are you Larry the owner's son?" Brian asked the clean-cut young man wearing a blue polo shirt with the motel's logo embroidered on it.

"Yes. He passed away a few years ago. Did you know him?"

"I'm sorry. No, I just remember him when I stayed here a long time ago. That's a name you don't easily forget."

"Larry?"

"No, I mean Lawrence, as in Lawrence Olivier."

The young man stared at him blankly. "We pronounce it Oliv-ah," he said in a New England accent thicker than condensed canned clam chowder.

"The famous English actor? Did a lot of Shakespeare?" Brian added.

"Never heard of him," the young man said, handing him his room key. "Your room's just a few doors over, and there's coffee in here starting at seven a.m. Checkout is at ten. Any questions?"

"To be or not to be? That is the question. Just kidding. No, thanks."

The room was cold, so Brian scanned the walls for the thermostat. Not seeing one, he examined what appeared to be an air conditioner beneath the window. It had a switch on it for *heat,* which he pushed, and an immediate blast of loud hot air belched from the machine.

Once in bed, Brian turned on his laptop on the outside chance he could be in a wi-fi hot spot, but to no avail. Instead he called up his files for each of his three Rotisserie Baseball Leagues, grabbed a yellow pad and his latest copy of *Baseball America,* and began to formulate his strategies for the coming baseball season. But after staring at statistical minutiae for five minutes, he could barely keep his eyes open, powered down, and was fast asleep.

After a morning cup of motel hell coffee, Brian hit the road and soon discovered the map he downloaded from the Internet was pretty much useless because street signs were either nonexistent, barely visible on various sized poles, or nailed to trees. And the fact that it was now pouring rain didn't help matters either. At checkout, Larry had given him additional directions that were also proving to be futile since they mostly consisted of instructions like, *make a left by a rusty wagon wheel next to a red mail box.*

A road sign that was clearly visible was one that probably had been in that location for at least a hundred years. It boldly announced in forged iron with brightly painted white letters to all who passed, *Entering the Township of Hampton North, Established 1670*. Somehow Brian had made it. From there he could at least find the town center, and once there he was sure someone could steer him in the general direction of Smart House on the bluffs. The house was a landmark all those years ago, and if there's a Smart still living there, it surely still is.

Even though Brian couldn't see the water from the town center, he knew the rain was blasting in from the North Atlantic Ocean, less than a mile from the hills that were at the end of the street. Fortunately, the storm had discouraged shoppers and there was a parking space available right in front of The Laughing Gull, a restaurant and bar that had been untouched by time for the better part of two centuries. Brian was comforted by the sight of The Laughing Gull looking exactly as he remembered it. It gave him hope that maybe things hadn't changed all that much in Hampton North.

As he entered the vestibule, which at one time was a mud room where dirt road travelers would clean the mud off their boots, Brian stopped to study a familiar framed poster on the wall. There wasn't an apprentice at the Hampton North Theater Tent who dropped into The Gull for a meal or a beer that didn't stare in awe at the sight of it. It was a simple black-and-white poster from the old Hampton North Theater, which was a converted old barn that blew down in the hurricane of 1938. In bold letters across the top it read, *MURDER MOST DEADLY*. And underneath the title, in lettering nearly as big, it read, *Starring Frederick O'Reilly*. But what stuck in everyone's mind was the credit listed below the producer, the writer, and the director, which was a line about one-fifth the size of the star's lettering that read *Featuring Humphrey Bogart*. The O'Reilly family had owned The Laughing Gull for five generations, and Frederick had star billing over Bogie in the late twenties. But, as the legend goes, Frederick didn't want to leave Hampton North for the bright lights or Broadway or Hollywood. Perhaps it was fear of failure that made Freddy resist stardom, or maybe it was just the fact that he was an alcoholic. And when Brian was a regular at The Gull around twenty years ago, it wasn't just the poster that was so unforgettable to the Hampton North Theater Tent apprentices, it was the sight of old drunken Freddy still tending behind the bar.

"Just sit anywhere, the server will be right with you," an attractive, dark-haired woman wearing a full-length white apron said from behind the bar. She had a friendly face, but at the same time there was an air about her signifying she didn't take crap from anyone.

"Is there a newspaper around?" Brian asked as he pulled a chair out by a table next to the front window.

"Here, take mine. I'm done with it," the woman said with a polite half smile. She plopped the paper onto the bar and continued going over what must have been the receipts from the night before.

Brian walked over to the bar to retrieve the paper.

"Hell of a storm. If this was a couple of weeks back, this would be about a foot of snow," she said as Brian picked up the paper.

"Lucky I didn't come up here a couple of weeks ago, then," Brian said as he paused in front of her. He immediately noticed that she was a beauty. Maybe late thirties, no makeup, traces of freckles, and cheek and jawbone structure that could make someone with similar characteristics and different ambitions a movie star.

"Oh, a traveler," she said in an accent that gave away the fact that she was born and bred in the area.

"Yeah, just visiting…some friends." Brian paused, hoping she wouldn't follow up with too many inquisitive questions.

"Well, I hope the weather clears up for you," she said, making it clear she wasn't digging any deeper into his story.

Brian picked up the *Boston Globe* and sat at his table. He scanned the front page for the headlines, then immediately searched for the sports section to see if there was any baseball news, which there wasn't.

The rain continued to come down in slanted sheets, making it difficult to take in the view from the window. But a fire was crackling in the fireplace, and the aroma of bacon and onions wafted through the air from the kitchen, whetting Brian's appetite for his breakfast and what lay ahead for him over the next ten days.

"Looks like your server is having trouble getting out of bed this morning, so I'll take your order," the dark-haired beauty said, surprising Brian as he read the paper.

"Great. I'll have two over easy, bacon, whole wheat toast, and grits."

"Grits? You're up north now, pilgrim. Home fries or potatoes O'Brien?"

Brian felt foolish, partly because he couldn't remember what potatoes O'Brien were and partly because he usually felt that way in front of really attractive women.

"What are potatoes O'Brien, again?" he asked sheepishly.

"See, you've been down south for too long. That's with onions and peppers mixed into the home fries."

"Yeah, the O'Briens, please. And coffee," he said handing her the menu.

"So where down south?"

"Oh, it's not really the south. Washington, DC."

"Anything below Connecticut is too far south for me," she said smiling and headed for the kitchen.

Brian went back to the newspaper, and absentmindedly started turning the pages as he wondered if she was coming on to him. Having been faithful to Frances their entire marriage, he always dismissed any come-on from women out of hand. Oh, he had been tempted, but he was such a lousy liar, he knew he'd never be able to deceive Frances. And although his marriage wasn't officially over, it was like the White Sox being up by ten runs over the Kansas City Royals in the top of the ninth. Well, the Sox always did have a problem finding a closer since Bobby Thigpen. Why would a beautiful woman come on to an out-of-shape, middle-aged guy? He knew the answer to that-- she wouldn't. He picked up his baseball guide and read an article about the nation's top high school prospects. He wondered if there were any on the Cape.

"Here you go," she said placing the plates in front of Brian. "Oh, reading about baseball in the off -season. Are you a Sox fan?"

"You bet!" Brian then caught himself making the mistake he made that entire summer in Hampton North. "Oh, you mean Red Sox fan. No, I'm a White Sox fan."

"Gee, that's right! You forget that there's more than one Sox out there. Especially around here. Well, at least you're not a Yankee fan."

Brian watched her return to the kitchen, and still wondered if she was *friendly* flirting, or *come-on* flirting. Nah.

Had to be friendly flirting. He couldn't be that lucky. He bolted down his meal, particularly enjoying the O'Briens, and killed time reading his magazine and getting refills on his coffee.

"Can I get you anything else?" she asked, exhibiting warmth.

"Just a check. By the way…" Brian paused. He wanted to ask her if she had any information on the Smarts, but nearly blurted out something silly, like, *Can I take you dinner?* "Do you, by any chance, know the Smarts, from out on the bluffs?"

"The Smarts? Oh yeah. I've lived in this town my whole life. How could I not know the Smarts? What is it you want to know? You're not from some collection agency or something, are you?"

"No. I'm er, in the area on some business, and well, I stayed there one summer. I was working at the Theater Tent, and I boarded there one summer, and thought I might stop by there, if they were still there."

"From what I understand, yeah, they're still there. I don't know who or how many or what on God's green earth goes on up there, but yeah, somebody's out there. I think the old lady is still renting rooms in the summer to the kids at The Tent. When did you work there?"

"Around twenty years ago."

"That's a little before my time. But not my brother's. He probably knows more about the Smarts than I do. The daughter was closer to his age."

"Is your brother still in the area?" Brian asked as he glanced at the bill, and left a twenty on top of it.

"You'll find him right here. He works nights. Do you need change?"

Brian almost said *yes*, but decided to leave her a large tip. "No, keep it. Thanks. Do you mind if I sit here for a few more minutes and finish my coffee?"

"Not at all. Enjoy," she said, smiling.

"Oh, by the way. What's your brother's name?" Brian asked, wondering if he should also ask for her name.

"Terry. I'm Katie," she said offering her hand. "Nice to meet you."

"Nice to meet you, too. I'm Brian," Brian said, shaking her tiny hand.

"No wonder you liked the potatoes."

"Uh... Oh yeah, Oh-Brian," Brian said chuckling. "Could you give me directions to the Smart house? I might want to drive by there later."

"You know, I'm not good at directions," she said. Brian interpreted this as a clever way to avoid giving directions to a stranger, just in case that stranger had no business finding the Smart house.

"Can you tell me how to get to the ocean, then?"

"Follow that road right there," she said pointing, out the front window, "and take it until your hat floats," smiling broadly and walked away.

The rain let up slightly, and the smell of the wet street and sidewalk mixed with the salty sea air gave the air an amazing fresh fragrance. Despite the cool temperature and the bare trees, there was a wisp of spring in this rainfall. Brian figured he could find the Smart house once he reached the water.

He was stopped at the last traffic light in the small town center before the road traveled up-hill and then wound down to the rocky coast when he glanced into his rear view mirror. With all the baggage he could only see through a small space out the back window, but what he saw shocked him.

A man in the car behind him was reaching behind his seat and punching something with considerable force. Brian thought for sure that he was hitting a dog in the back seat. Brian swung his door open and jumped out even though the light had just turned green, and stepped to the rear of his car to confirm his fear. But what Brian saw was even more disturbing. The man was not punching a dog, as he had feared. He was beating a young boy strapped into a child's seat.

"What the hell are you doing?" Brian yelled at the maniac, who whipped his head around, surprised to be caught in the act. Brian stooped down to get a better look at what was going on, and as he did he noticed a strong stench of cheap cologne.

The driver of the car was a chunky, bald man in his fifties. His puffy, piggy eyes had the watery red tinge of a recent alcohol binge. In the front passenger seat was an Asian woman who appeared at least twenty years younger than he, and sat frozen staring at Brian. The driver rolled his window down.

"Who are you? he asked, enraged.

"I have a good mind to report you to the authorities."

"It's none of your goddamned business. Who are you, the fucking Gestapo?" the driver shouted at Brian.

"*I'm* the Gestapo? You're the one looking like the Gestapo right now."

"Get the hell out of here! Mind your own goddamned business."

"Don't do that again or I'll call the cops. Hear me?" Brian shouted at the driver as he got back into his car, not turning back, but listening to hear if the nut's car door swung open. The light had turned red, and as he waited he could see the man screaming at his wife and the kid, but not hitting anyone. Yet.

Brian was a little freaked out, and still pumped with adrenaline once the light turned green, so as they passed through the intersection he pulled over to calm down. Just as he did, the red beater car pulled along side him. The Asian, or maybe Philipina-looking, woman rolled down her window, and sheepishly said, as if by rote, "We have every right as parents to discipline our child." The mad driver gripped the steering wheel and said nothing, as they awaited Brian's response.

In that split second, Brian thought about picking up his cell phone and dialing 911, but instead said, "Keep going and just watch it," glaring at the driver.

They sped away, and Brian tried to get their license plate, but could only make out a couple of letters, maybe an L or a 1 and VP. He jotted them down and took a few deep breaths. After a minute or two he continued on the road to the water. He wondered if he should have called the police. Maybe just the confrontation would be enough to make the asshole think twice about hitting his kid in public. Or maybe not. And by the cowering expression of his wife, he guessed she was used to his abuse.

The road to the ocean was a circuitous one. At the edge of town, the homes were modest with short driveways and chain link fences, but during the ascent the driveways became longer, the chain link fences changed to high walls of shrubbery, and the homes became majestic. There was a stop sign at the apex of the hill, which allowed a driver to take in and enjoy the splendid panoramic coastline view for at least a moment.

Brian instantly remembered the stop sign and the breathtaking view. The rocky coast was laid out before him. At the horizon, he saw a break in the clouds and noticed that the rain had subsided. As if by muscle memory, Brian began to circumnavigate down the hill, taking turns intuitively. As he did so, flashes of memory began to come alive, creating a narrative for his drive.

He was sure the Smart house was a good mile or so to the north, but instead, he made a right turn going south at an iron girder bridge, passing over one of the many water channels that created a wetland rich with wildlife. He noticed the Little League field had built a higher fence behind home plate, and a rickety old wooden staircase that led to the only beach that had public access had been rebuilt, but everything else was exactly as they were when he last saw them. The road signs were as hard to read as ever, but he made lefts and rights for a while, with almost every turn revealing another vista that had him wondering why he had never returned in all those years.

A quick left toward the coast at the only small coffee shop outside of the town center put him on a wider road that in a few minutes put him in the parking lot of the Hampton North Theater Tent. Brian was initially shocked by the sight of only the skeleton of the tent structure being there. But of course, it was the off-season and the tent wouldn't be put up for weeks. The center mast, with its circular support rings surrounded by the other permanent poles, resembled a network of antennas that could be monitoring the cosmos for alien communications. In the center of the circle of support poles was the theatre pit, which contained the stage's foundation and terraced platforms without the seats.

Brian parked his car, walked to the perimeter of the theater and recalled the hardest day of work the new recruits ever had. That first day was orientation, when the theater directors and staff wowed the new arrivals with tales of show business rich with the excitement of summer theater. He remembered checking out the others, wondering who was gay and who was straight, and began fantasizing immediately about a few of the females. But the next three days were the worst of the summer. That was when the apprentice actors, carpenters, technicians, writers and directors nailed every one of the 750 chairs to the floor of the theatre. It was an awful job; fingers banged with hammers, nails stepped on, splinters in knees, and pretty much erasing whatever illusions he had about the glitz and glamour of the theater.

The white clapboard buildings that housed the offices, rehearsal halls, and box office looked freshly painted and well maintained. As Brian made a circle around the structure, he was surprised there wasn't another soul to be seen. He peeked in the window of a rehearsal hall, and saw the same ancient upright piano next to the small stage. He cringed when he recalled how all of the apprentices, whether signed on as performers or technicians, were required to sing a song in front of the group in case there was any hidden talent to be mined. It was a moment that forever cured Brian of any aspirations to be a performer of any kind.

It was hard to imagine this pit of concrete and wood would come to life in just a few months and patrons from hundreds of miles around would pack this place to gaze in awe at the rinky-dink round wooden platform positioned in the middle of this theater in the round. Top names from Broadway, Hollywood, and even Nashville would be performing right there, and getting paid tens of thousands, if not hundreds of thousands of dollars, on that rain-soaked, oversized soap box.

"May I help you?" A female voice startled Brian from behind.

Brian turned around to find a female figure in a long trench coat whose face was hidden by an umbrella adorned with *the* scene in *Singing in the Rain* where Gene Kelly is swinging around a lamp post.

"This is private property, you know," the female stated with a voice possibly seasoned with Virginia Slims and apple martinis. She raised the umbrella slightly, revealing red lipsticked lips bordered with the lines of late middle age.

"I'm sorry. I was just observing. I worked here one summer. Things haven't changed much."

The woman lifted the umbrella, exposing her face. She was middle aged, but a looker. And topped off with a red beret at a jaunty angle. "When?" she asked, with a playful look on her face.

"About twenty years ago," Brian answered. He picked up on the fact that she was studying him, and assumed she was trying to imagine his middle-aged face without any pudginess or lines and with more hair.

"I've been here for over twenty years," she said closing her umbrella and holding its handle as if it were a cane.

"Are you…I mean, were you the box office girl? Uh, let me see, ah…" Brian had to be careful. There were two box office workers; one was a loose local girl who was known for getting blind drunk, screwing whoever was next to her at last call, and conveniently forgetting everything about the experience the next day. The other girl was as prim and proper as a southern charm school graduate from the 1950s and auditioned for every play the apprentice actors put on, but never got a part. Not because of lack of talent, but because she was too valuable to the theater running the box office. "Kerry?"

"No!"

Damn, Brian thought to himself, hoping she was the slutty one. "I remember you. You were a very talented…actress."

"Well, I tried," she said extending her hand to Brian. "Margaret Branton. I'm the executive director now."

"Brian DeLouise…"

"Mid-'80s, right? You were a techie, weren't you?"

"I still am. I work in radio."

"Radio! That's exciting. What brings you here?"

"Oh, uh, a little business and a little pleasure."

"Well, I have to open up. Stop by when you're done with the business part and ready start the pleasure part. Oops. That didn't sound right, did it?" she said, smiling and walking toward the office.

Brian thought perhaps he was wrong in deeming her as the prim and proper one. He went back to his car and sat wondering whether or not he should go into the office and start picking Margaret's brain for information on the Smarts. He didn't want to raise too many red flags in a small town where gossip is the main channel of communication. Instead he started his car, pulled out of the parking lot, and drove north up the long and winding coastal road where, eventually, he would come upon the Smart House.

The clouds were breaking apart and streaks of sun light were dancing on the ocean waters below the road that wound along the jagged coast. Sometimes the road was just a few feet from a sheer cliff. But wherever the land between the road and the beach was wide enough, there was a magnificent house sitting on the bluffs or occasionally precariously perched at the bluff's edge with the support of stilts. Brian could tell there were a few newly constructed homes wedged into available spaces, but most of the homes were old mainstays of the area. Except of course for those that were lost during a hurricane and sucked into the sea.

After a sharp uphill curve that turned toward the water, there were three small white crosses with dirty plastic Christmas wreaths hanging on them on the side of the road. No doubt they were a memorial to a fatal car accident. Brian recalled how he recklessly drove drunk on many occasions that summer, and thanked God he didn't wind up with a white cross of his own at that very spot. And there it was-- Smart House.

Brian had only seen the place in the midst of summer growth when the trees, shrubs, and weeds were in full bloom and the house was barely visible from the street. It always had the feel of a secret hideaway. Visitors were constantly driving right by, never even noticing that a house was even there. But on this wet, late winter morning, with trees and shrubs bare, the old Smart house stood naked and exposed. He drove past the house and pulled over just before the driveway next door. He pushed the remote button on his right side rear view mirror, angling it so he could see the front entrance of the house. He wondered if this was a good idea after all. Obviously he didn't really have to make contact with the Smarts. The whole thing could be a huge mistake. No one on the planet knows he's even there. No one would know if he just continued heading north, got back on the interstate, and drove to, well...Montreal! He hadn't been there since his fifteen-hour bus ride to see the Canadiens play the Black Hawks with the Black Hawks fan club back when he was in high school.

Cars were swerving to avoid him on the wet road, which made Brian eager to make a decision, when a taxi cab pulled right in front of the Smart house. Brian adjusted his left side view mirror to get a better angle and watched as an elderly woman was helped out of the cab by a younger woman who was carrying a couple of grocery bags. The cab driver went to the trunk and grabbed several more bags and assisted the woman with the old lady, slowly, to the front door.

Brian felt bad, sitting there spying on them, rather than helping them. He opened the car windows a little more to try and eavesdrop, but couldn't make anything out. The cabbie sped past him, and Brian could hear the front door of the Smart House slam shut.

"Well, there they are and here I am," he muttered to himself. He began to imagine different scenarios that may occur if he actually knocked on the door. In his mind he was certain the elderly lady was Beatrice Smart. But he had his doubts about the other woman. Could it be Portia? Or might it be just hired help. Or perhaps just a boarder who helps Beatrice with her shopping. "Fuck it," Brian said out loud as he closed the windows and exited the car. Just as he did, a car honked loudly and swerved away from his open car door, narrowly missing it. "Shit. That's a hell of a start," he said to himself as he walked toward their front door.

In the summer, the walkway to the door is a tunnel of green. Now it resembled a tunnel of pointy sticks and bony branches guarding the entrance. Brian walked along the path, leaves and branches crackling under his feet, and he noticed a curtain being pulled back on the window to the right of the front door. The window was either dirty or had condensation on it, which made it impossible to see the figure peering out briefly at him.

The large double door entrance was in dire need of a paint job, its red paint faded and peeling. He reached for the door knocker and banged it against the door three times. He listened for a response behind the door, but there was only silence. Suddenly the door swung open, and there she was--Beatrice Smart, twenty years later. Her straw-like gray hair was wild. Her head and shoulders slumped forward, and she strained to keep her face aimed high at Brain. She did not look friendly and kept one arm on the door as she held it open just enough to see who was there.

"Please go away, we're not in need of anything. Good day," she said as she slammed the door shut.

Brian stared at the door and pondered the situation. He certainly wasn't welcome, and he didn't want to cause a scene. But he had traveled all this way and thought this was his only shot to make contact with Portia. He reached again for the door knocker, and just as his fingers touched it the door swung open, revealing something that he was not prepared for-- Portia! But it can't be. Because in front of him was Portia from about twenty years ago. The face, the eyes, the hair, but the only thing different was the expression. This Portia did not have the warm earth-mother aura that Brian remembered so well. She had more in common with Beatrice in that department. But the resemblance was uncanny.

"Can I help you?" she asked, foot against the door, her arms folded tightly across her chest.

"Uh, yes. Um, I, er, spent a summer here about twenty years ago. In the back room facing the ocean…"

"You and about two hundred other people," she said cutting him off. "What can I do for you?"

"I was in the area, on business, and wondering if perhaps I could maybe stop by and say hello…"

"Well you just did, didn't you? Is there anything else? I've got groceries sitting on the table."

"Oh, yeah. I understand. Thanks," Brian said turning slightly away, then swinging back toward the door just before it closed. "Is Portia around?"

The young woman stopped the door from closing and cocked her head slightly. "Who wants to know?"

"My name if Brian DeLouise, and I was…friends with Portia, and wondering if it would be possible to see her while I was in town?"

She scanned him and inched toward him slightly. "I'll tell her you called. Do you have a number?" she asked, slightly less abrasively.

"Here's my cell number," Brian said as he pulled out a business card from his wallet.

"That always sounds strange to me," she said quietly.

"Excuse me?"

"You said you wanted to give me your cell number. You know, like a prison cell number."

"Oh, yeah," Brian said and wrote his number on the back of the card. "I'll be around the area for a few days. If she could call me, that would be great."

"I'll tell her. What year were you here?"

"Late '80s."

"I'll tell her you called. Good-bye," she said, closing the door.

Brian thought it was at least a good sign that she didn't slam it.

He got back into his car and continued on the road headed north. He drove about a half mile, where the road jutted to the right, into an overlook. He remembered that from this vantage point, he could see the Smart house and the entire coastline south of there. He took his binoculars out of a bag and fixed his eyes on the rear of the house. The veranda in the back was far away, but he could see several figures out there, and it looked like they were…exercising. He put his binoculars away and headed back to his motel room.

CHAPTER SEVEN

Brian had seen more of Massachusetts in the past three days than he had seen the entire summer of 1989. He drove to Lowell, the home of Jack Kerouac, and visited his memorial and gravesite. He even checked out the stadium where the Lowell Spinners minor league baseball team played. The name *Spinners* wasn't derived from a sect of whirling dervishes, but from the textile industry that once dominated Lowell and the surrounding communities. He drove to Provincetown and was shocked at how empty it seemed. In the summer the town is known as a hotbed of shoulder to shoulder revelry, catering to gay clientele from all over the world. But, except for a few restaurants and art galleries, it seemed almost lifeless in the late winter haze.

His cheap motel room on the outskirts of town was nothing more than a place to sleep and charge his phone. He was so concerned that he might miss the call from Portia that he made a habit of calling his voice mail whenever he lost service for a little while. But there were no calls from Portia.

The Laughing Gull became a home base for him before he went back to the motel. He had breakfast there twice since he first met Katie, but the regular waitress was on time both days, so the only interaction he had with her was a polite hello. When Brian entered this evening, he was glad to see Katie at the bar talking with the bartender who, perhaps, was her brother.

Although Brian could use a hearty hot meal, he decided to take a seat at the bar a few stools over from Katie. It worked. As soon as he ordered a Sam Adams she glanced over.

"Oh, hi," she said with a smile as she turned on her stool toward him.

Brian took that as a good sign.

"Hi, Katie. Undercover? Or off duty?

"Off duty, thank God. I'm sorry, I've forgotten you name."

"Brian as in O'Brien, like the potatoes," he said as the bartender tossed a Red Sox coaster in front of him and put his pint of Sam Adams on it.

"Oh yes! And this is my brother, Terry," Katie said, as she motioned to the sturdy bartender. Broad-shouldered and barrel-chested, he looked like he could take care of any barroom situation in or out of season. His crisp white shirt and striped tie gave him an air of class, and his gray mustache, which framed a broad grin, beamed friendliness.

"Nice to meet you, Brian. Terry," he said, as he wiped his hands on a towel just before shaking hands.

"Is this the guy you told me about who was looking for the Smarts?" he asked Katie.

"Yup. He's from Washington, so I wouldn't cough up too much info," she said with a half-smile.

"Portia was in my class in grammar school," Terry said, his arms folded across his chest.

"Really," Brian said. "I haven't seen her in close to twenty years, when I lived at the Smart house for the summer. I was an apprentice at The Tent."

"Oh, you're one of those, huh? That explains a lot," Terry said, walking away to tend to another customer at the end of the bar.

"One of those?" Brian asked Katie, who looked slightly embarrassed by her brother's remark.

"A lot of people come back, years later, to town after spending a summer at The Tent. Most come back in-season, so that makes you a little different. That, and the fact that it's been almost twenty years. Isn't that what you said?"

Brian took a sip of a beer and laughed to himself. His adventure did sound a little goofy when put so simply. "Yeah, it is a little unusual. But timing is everything."

"I remember Portia. Like I said, she was my brother's age, about seven years older than me. She was of the older crowd," Katie said taking a sip from a glass of water. "But she wasn't really of any crowd," she said, glancing over to Brian to gauge his reaction. Brian raised his eyebrows slightly, showing interest in her lead-in. "She wasn't exactly one of the gang. You know. The whole family… kept to themselves. In fact, we've always been curious as to what really went on in there," Katie said pulling her stool closer to Brian. "What was it like?"

"It was a long time ago," Brian said, stalling for time. He took a drink from his glass, put it down, and looked at Katie. He noticed that she wasn't wearing a ring on her left hand, and picked up his beer again, this time finishing it off. Just as he placed the empty glass on his coaster, Terry appeared.

"Another?"

"Sure," Brian said as he waited for the pint glass to be filled and plunked in front of him, and waited for Terry to walk to the end of the bar.

"It was strange, living there for a summer," he said to Katie, who was focused on him like he was about to unravel an ancient mystery. "I didn't know anything about the place. The theater people just asked whether I wanted to stay in a nearby motel, or in a home located on the bluffs that was cheaper."

"That was a no brainer," Katie said smiling, and taking a sip of ice water.

"They didn't tell me I'd be sharing a tiny room with two other guys."

"Nice. What were they like?"

"Actually, that worked out great. One guy was really gay. But I think because me and the other guy were straight, he went way out of his way to be extra accommodating, and you know, share his food, offer to give us a lift, and stuff."

"So no hanky panky there, huh?" she asked coyly.

"Not there, no. The other guy was great, too. He was from Scituate, so there were a lot of nights he didn't even spend the night there. But I'll never forget the night I arrived there for the summer. I drove straight from Chicago, so I was totally spaced. It was about two in the morning, so I thought

I'd just sneak in and go immediately to bed. It took me about a half hour of driving up and down the bluffs just to find the place, it was so hidden from the road."

"When we were kids we thought it was a haunted house," Katie said, inching her stool a little closer.

"I walked through the tunnel of shrubs; the front door was unlocked so I just walked in. There was thick dust everywhere, hammers banging away, and people yelling at each other."

"At two in the morning?"

"Two in the morning. So I enter, walk to the right, and here's Beatrice…"

"The mother."

"Yeah. And this guy, older than dirt, is standing there with his hands on his hips, yelling at Beatrice, who has a hammer in her hand, standing on a kitchen chair, holding onto this huge dining room cabinet that was attached to the wall, and my future roommate on the other side of this monstrosity, holding onto it so it won't crash to the floor. There's holes in the wall where the thing was attached, the old man is yelling 'You fool, I told you to leave well enough alone!' and there's an old lady in a recliner with a blanket on her snoring like a sailor."

"Welcome to Smart House," Katie said, holding her water glass in a toast.

"Exactly," Brian responded, clinking his beer glass to her water glass. We got that thing off the wall, and Harry and I, he was my roommate, moved it to another room, where it sat, propped up against a wall for the rest of the summer."

"Why?"

"We never found out the answer to that. All we knew was that the entire chorus from *42nd Street* was arriving the next day, to stay for two weeks, and she needed the room."

"Was Portia there?"

"She didn't arrive until the middle of the summer," Brian said, trying to hide the real reason for his sentimental journey.

"What about the weird older brother?"

"You know, I heard about him, but I never saw him once the entire time I was there."

"You're lucky. Excuse me," Katie said as she got up and slipped behind the bar to help Terry with a matter at the cash register.

Not having eaten dinner, Brian was feeling a little lightheaded from his two beers. He picked up a menu, and decided on some chowder and fish and chips.

"Are you going to eat at the bar, or would you like to sit at a table?" Katie asked, pencil and pad in hand.

"I thought you were off-duty?"

"Emergency workers are never off-duty."

"Are you sitting at the bar for a while? Can I buy you a drink?" Brian asked, his eyes shyly scanning the menu.

"I don't drink."

"Oh. I'll have a cup of chowder and fish and chips."

Katie disappeared into the kitchen. Brian ordered another beer from Terry, who squirted some soda from a dispenser and parked himself in front of him.

"Yeah, that Portia was something else," Terry said after taking a sip of soda. "She was one of those brainiac girls. You know, didn't hang out with the kids much. We were all down at the beach drinking beers and playing spin the bottle in eighth grade, but not Portia. But we sure hoped she would've stopped by some time. She was stacked in the eighth grade, I swear to God! So did you and her have a little summer romance?" Terry asked with a gleam in his eye.

Brian tried his best poker face and raised his glass, but didn't drink. "You could say that."

"Well, congratulations! You're the first I've ever heard of," Terry said, clinking his glass of soda against Brian's beer glass.

"Are you serious?"

"Serious as a heart attack. Once we went to high school, Portia became even more scarce. Plus she kind of went off into that hippie thing, you know, the long dresses, no makeup, didn't shave her legs. Then by the time college came around, that was it. No one ever heard from her again. I feel for her, though. It had to be tough for her."

"In what way?"

Brian felt he knew about Portia's rough family life, but not everything. She had told him about her father, who abandoned the family when she was just a year old, barely giving them enough money to maintain the home. The house was once the jewel of the bluffs. A classic Cape Cod, bordering on being called a mansion at one time; but by the time Brian came along, it had deteriorated to the point of being an eyesore. Even a laughing stock. Beatrice started taking in borders when Portia was in grade school. She hinted at abuse when she was young, but said she learned to fight them off at an early age. She even told of a story where Beatrice hit one guy over the head with a cast iron frying pan at the breakfast table after a tawdry comment. But as soon as he came to, he was shoved out the front door never to return.

Brian remembered holding Portia so close on warm summer nights on the beach during those stories, with tears in his eyes; he never wanted to let her go. He wanted to save her from her secret past.

"Oh, looking back, it had to be rough," Terry said shaking his head. "The old man was a big exec at John Hancock, and I heard he left them with nothing. Two kids and he runs off with his secretary. Bastard. He got his, anyway."

"What happened?"

"Committed suicide. In fact, it must have been right about the time you were staying there. About twenty years ago, right?"

"Yeah."

Brian was puzzled. He didn't know about that. Perhaps it was just after he left that summer and lost touch with Portia. Maybe that's why she didn't want to get in touch with him, he thought to himself.

"An ugly one, too," Terry said leaning in and whispering. "Bullet straight through the eyeball and into the brain. Right here in town."

"Where?"

"At the Hampton North Motor Inn."

"That's where I'm staying."

"Room thirteen, I heard," Terry said as he shuffled to the other end of the bar.

"Here you go," Katie said, plopping a bowl of chowder in front of Brian. "Did you talk to Terry about the Smarts?"

"Yeah. It's always interesting to fill in the missing pieces of the puzzle. Even twenty years later."

"She was a beauty, that Portia. I remember that much. Must be tough being a single mom in that place."

"So she lives there?"

"As far as I know. With her mom, her daughter, and whoever else is renting a room over there. Gosh, her daughter must be around twenty! Hard to believe."

Brian lifted a spoonful of chowder, blew on it, and then it dawned on him. If Portia's daughter is about twenty, she must've been born just after he spent the summer there.

"Are you okay?" Katie asked, concerned.

"Huh? Oh, yeah. The chowder looks hot. I don't want to get surprised with scalding chowder."

"Nobody likes those kinds of surprises."

From the mountains of the Berkshires, to the sand dunes of Provincetown, to the Revolutionary War plaques, memorials and buildings of Boston, he had enough of Massachusetts. He told himself he would wait one more day for Portia's call. He had driven by the Smart's at least once a day, but didn't want to arouse suspicion and come off like some kind of stalker. Each time he slowly drove by, he thought he might see Portia coming or going, or maybe doing some yard work in front.

The weather had finally improved, and although it was still in the forties, the sky was bright blue with puffy white clouds and you could see for miles along the coastline. Brian decided to institute a plan he was saving as a last resort. A walk on the beach.

He parked just south of the Smart house in a parking lot next to a public access to the beach. It was the only such parking lot around, which the city fathers intended as a way to exclude too many out-of-towners. He stashed his compact binoculars in the pocket of his White Sox jacket and took the staircase down to the rocky beach. He was surprised at the amount of debris that apparently washed ashore, and how narrow the beach had become. That was usually the case in the winter months when the coastal areas take a beating.

There was a tidal pool just a few yards from the staircase, and as he approached he saw little crabs scurrying away from him. He also noticed what remained of a dead sea gull, first by its stench and then its eaten-away carcass.

From a hundred or so yards away, Smart House looked like a stately home, perched on one of the best locations on the entire Hampton North coastline. A half mile or so out in the ocean there's a small island with an unmanned lighthouse, which was visible through the window when you sat on the toilet in the upstairs bathroom. They say that the lighthouse was manned up until the early seventies. There was a small apartment in the base of the tall structure where attendants worked two weeks on and two weeks off. It was a job conducive to alcoholism but not much else, the story goes.

Brian picked up a piece of driftwood, which made a nice walking stick, and continued up the beach. It was a glorious morning and the sights, sounds, and smells reminded Brian why he was there. His summer of love with Portia on this very spot was probably the happiest time of his life. It was the most passionate love affair at that point and she was the last girlfriend he had before he met Frances. That says it all.

He picked up a long string of seaweed with his makeshift walking stick, twirled it over his head, and flung it into a wave. That reminded him of the time he covered himself with seaweed and came out of the water like the Creature from the Black Lagoon, purely for the amusement of Portia. It got a lot of laughs and gave him a rash that lasted three days. Just as Brian stopped to retrieve a large clam shell, he heard a noise from the back veranda of Smart House, which was now just ahead of him. The back door opened, and out came three figures. Brian dropped the clam shell and reached into his pocket to retrieve his binoculars. He sat on a rock that was dry because the tide was out and hoped he wouldn't be noticed as he focused on the rear of the house.

Three women. One elderly, one young, and yes, one in the middle. He wasn't positive if it was Portia, but pretty sure. She was wearing a knit cap pulled down quite far, and was bundled up in what appeared to be a Scandinavian wool sweater with a belt around the waist. The three of them were walking around the deck pointing and seemed to be discussing the state of things at the rear of casa del Smart.

Brian wondered if he should approach them. Would it be too weird for him to walk up the stairway onto the veranda uninvited? Then the elderly woman and the younger woman opened the back door and went inside the house, leaving the other one alone. She closed the door behind them, tightened the belt around her sweater, and walked to the stairs that led to the beach. Brian figured that if he paced himself properly, their paths would intersect in about fifty yards.

He could feel his pulse racing and hear his heart pumping in his inner ear as he watched Portia stop at the bottom of her staircase and take off her shoes, even though it was far from summer. Just as she did all those years ago, she placed them neatly on the bottom step pointed at the ocean. He walked at a medium clip, on a slight angle toward the water, and noticed that Portia glanced his way. Brian was certain she knew she wasn't alone on her beach, and hoped she didn't panic and head back up the stairs.

He was only twenty or so feet from her when he smiled slightly and waved with his left hand while he held the walking stick in his right.

"Excuse me," Brian said, his heart pounding uncontrollably.

Portia stopped and turned towards him. She squinted at him. Brian could see her face now. It was indeed Portia. Her thick hair was sticking out the back of her hat, and of course, there were the lines of age. But she was still a beauty. Her thick eyebrows were touching the bottom of her hat, but her almost-Asian eyes seemed to be already twinkling.

"Yes," Portia said her feet planted firmly.

Brian walked slowly, directly toward her, wondering if his chest was going to explode and his heart just splatter all over Portia like a scene from *Alien*. He stopped about two steps from her and whispered, "Portia?"

Portia's eyes widened. Her lips parted slightly and she gasped as she sucked in a gallon of sea air. Brian stood motionless as Portia raised her right hand and placed her fingers to her lips. More than anything, Portia looked puzzled. Brian wasn't certain if she was going to run away, or yell, *Fuck off*.

Portia snapped her head around and took off at a clip that left no doubt that she was getting away from Brian in a mad dash down the beach. She took no more than three steps and Brian watched in horror as she shrieked in pain, yelled "Shit" and fell to the sand in a lump.

Brian rushed over as Portia grabbed her toes on her right foot; the jagged piece of driftwood she tripped over sat innocently nearby. She looked more pissed off than merely suffering in pain.

"I've got extra toes if you need one," Brian said as he knelt next to her.

As she rubbed her bare pinky toe she looked up and smiled. “It is you, isn’t it?”

Brian saw the creases next to her eyes and the marionette lines that went from her nose to her chin; but still, she was gorgeous. Her blue eyes were clear and bright, and a smile began to widen, revealing straight white teeth with a small gap between the two front teeth. She held her hands out with palms facing outward and said softly, “Brian.”

Brian knew he was heavier, had less hair, and probably looked like a goofball in his White Sox jacket. But he also knew he wasn’t so hot to begin with. And what he and Portia had went beyond looks.

Brian dropped his stick and grabbed Portia’s hands. She pulled him toward her until he was leaning against her thick Scandinavian sweater. They dropped each other’s hands and embraced awkwardly as they sat on the sand. Brian closed his eyes and went into sensory overload; the smell of her hair, the ocean air, the gulls, the waves crashing, the feeling of her breasts pressed against his chest.

Portia whispered, so quietly he could barely hear her, “I missed you.”

Brian pulled back so he could look into her eyes and said, “I missed you, too,” as he helped her up stand up.

“Let’s go for a walk,” Portia said as she turned up the beach and led Brian by the hand.

“Why did you run?”

“Just a habit, I guess. Are you married…or happy?”

Brian stopped dead in his tracks. He had forgotten that it was Portia who often repeated that Groucho line.

“Funny you should ask,” Brian said as they continued their walk. “Right now I’m in between. What about you?”

“Happy,” she said turning her head, smiling broadly. “I thought this day would come, sooner or later.”

“I guess it was later.”

“Yes. Much later.”

They walked for about ten paces without saying anything. Brian walked on the left and held his walking stick in his right hand. Portia looked out to sea and back at him and chuckled to herself.

"So, what have you been doing… for the past twenty or so years?" Portia said, her hands in her sweater pockets.

"I got a radio job in DC. Met a girl. Got married. And now, here I am."

"And where is that?"

"Well, just before I left, I got suspended at my job and my wife essentially kicked me out of our house."

Portia stopped and picked up what looked like a misshapen green marble. "I call this sea glass. It was once a shard of broken glass. But after years of being tossed and turned in the ocean, its edges are smooth and rounded. It looks almost like a jewel now. But it took a long time," she said as she dropped it back onto the sand.

Brian picked it up. "And what about you?"

Portia turned to him and smiled. "I still paint and do photography. I work designing signs, I have a daughter. I take care of my mother."

"Does your mother need to be taken care of?"

"It's not too bad. Yet. What brings you to town--besides the rebound, I mean."

Brian wasn't sure how to react. The way she said *besides the rebound* made him feel defensive, but he decided to ignore it. "To be honest…"

"I don't like when a sentence begins with *to be honest.* It's usually followed by a lie," Portia said, smiling.

Brian remembered that side of Portia. She didn't suffer fools gladly, and she didn't take shit from anyone. Not all her edges were worn smooth. "I came to town to…" Brian pushed his stick into the sand, using it as a brake. "I came to look for you. When you didn't call, I figured you didn't want to see me…"

"Didn't call? You mean, twenty years ago?"

"No, I mean this week. I stopped by your house five days ago and gave my number to your daughter at the front door."

"That little rat," Portia said as she kicked Brian's walking stick and they started walking again. "She's very protective of her mother and her mema. To be honest…" Portia caught herself and laughed, "You're not the first… to come by searching for their past."

Brian got the message. His heart sank a little. He was a fool to think it would be all pizza and fairy tales from the get-go. "And probably not the last."

"That remains to be seen," Portia said coyly. "Let's head back."

They walked to the stairs of Smart House without speaking. Portia sat on the bottom step and began to put on her shoes. Brian removed his shoes and began shaking the sand out.

"Why did you come by if you knew, or I should say, assumed, that I didn't want to see you?" Portia asked, looking up to him as she tied her shoelace.

"I don't give up so easily. I didn't give up so easily twenty years ago either. But eventually, I do take a hint. I'm leaving tomorrow. Can I take you to dinner this evening?" Brian asked, standing in the sand in his socks.

"If you show me your feet. Just so I know you're who you really say you are," Portia said with a twinkle in her eye.

My fee…? Oh yeah, you always were fascinated with my freak feet. You know, feet with six toes are not that uncommon," he said as he pulled off his socks and revealed his bare feet. "Okay, are you happy?" he asked twinkling his twelve toes.

"Yes, I'm happy," Portia said as she stood up and darted up the stairs. "Pick me up at eight," she said, blowing a kiss with two fingers.

Brian sat on the bottom step and looked out to the lighthouse. He knew those lips. Those were the last lips he kissed before he met Frances. He hadn't kissed any other lips besides Frances' since. And as he gazed on the lighthouse, at the exact spot since he last kissed those lips he couldn't help but feel anything short of total exhilaration. But the rush of the moment that flooded Brian with memories of Portia wasn't without pain. At the end of that summer, when the tent was lowered and the seats were again torn from the planks with the same hammers, the scraped knuckles and knees of that last day of hard labor were only a hint of what was to follow.

Brian knew Portia was leaving on a trip to Greece the day after the tent was struck and the season ended with the cool late night breezes of early September. She told Brian she didn't know how long she would be gone; maybe a few weeks or maybe several months. Portia had a friend in Greece, and they had plans to travel Europe together. She was very secretive about her friend, and wouldn't reveal if it was a male or female. Portia said it shouldn't matter, but it did to Brian. Saying good-bye to the crew at the theatre was difficult enough, but saying good-bye to Portia knowing she was venturing off to another world made it sting more than the hydrogen peroxide he had poured over his bloody knees and knuckles after a day of working on his knees at the theatre. Although long good-bye kisses and making love one last time under the moonlight seemed unbearably bittersweet, it was nothing compared to the panicked pain Brian felt in the months ahead.

Things moved quickly after Brian returned to Chicago after that summer. Out of the blue he received a job offer in Washington, DC at ARS radio, loaded up his car, and was living there before fall had officially arrived. In the coming months, he wrote to Portia, called her at Smart House, even drove there hoping to find her. But Portia would not respond. No letter, no phone call, no reply. And when Frances burst into his life, with her insatiable sexual appetite predating her appetite for rich foods by years, Portia became just another ex-girlfriend.

Brian had no choice but to compartmentalize Portia's memory into a neatly ordered file folder. Frances was unlike any woman he had ever been with. She was a partying, dirty joke-telling extrovert with huge tits, strawberry blonde hair, and a fashion sense just a notch down from a thousand-dollar-a-night call girl. In those early years, Frances certainly acted as if she loved him. She was out of work, moved in with him, and before they knew it, she was pregnant. Plans were made for a wedding, and she had a miscarriage three weeks later. They went ahead with the wedding and the marriage, but Brian always wondered what would have happened if she never got pregnant, or what their life would be like if they were able to have a child. But he stopped wondering about Portia. Or rather, he stopped for almost twenty years.

Brian turned the shower faucet an imperceptible amount to the right, which made the water go from lukewarm to scalding. He jumped back and turned it the other way slightly. Lukewarm would have to do. After shaving, he remembered that Portia didn't like smelly cologne or after shave, so he stopped himself just before he splashed some on. He also recalled that she didn't like the phony fragrances of deodorant, which is probably why he buys the unscented variety to this very day. He thought about wearing his White Sox jacket, but thought better of it. He walked over to the front door of his room and stuck his head outside. It seemed almost balmy; just about warm enough to wear the blazer he brought along, just in case.

He stood in front of the mirror that was attached to the wall above the dresser. It didn't show his lower body, which was just as well. Brian kept putting off getting back into shape with each stressful event that seemed to be forever popping up. He thought he might get an urge to start an exercise program on this trip, so packed his ice skates, running shoes, jump rope, and hand weights. He hadn't touched any of them. But from the neck up, he was fairly comfortable in his appearance. His hair was thinning-- okay, receding-- and the gray was creeping in, but many his age were already totally bald. He had all his teeth, and they were straight and relatively white. He had to concentrate a little harder to find attributes below his neck.

As he drove the dark winding road to Smart House, he forced himself to think of worst case scenarios; Portia is a lunatic who has been plotting to get revenge against him all these years, or maybe she's a pathetically desperate and lonely old maid who's about to throw herself at him and never let him go, or perhaps she's going to demand large amounts of money or scream rape.

He stopped in front of the walkway, and the front door opened. Portia's hair glowed from the lights behind her, cascading down like the Virgin Mary's veil. She was wearing a short black leather jacket, over a long gauze white dress that for a brief moment in the light revealed the outline of her legs straight up to her crotch. She kissed her daughter and her mother at the door and walked down the dark tunnel of winter dead shrubs and weeds. Brian jumped out of the van and met her at the other side, and opened the door for her. As she sat in the front seat, he could smell her hair and her light, sweet perfume. As he paused at the back of the van as a car speeded by on the sharp turn, he flashed on a best case scenario; falling in love again.

CHAPTER EIGHT

Cape Cod in the winter is beautiful in its desolation. The full moon glistened off the ocean and the many inlets, marinas, and lagoons that they passed on the way to a small restaurant that Portia recommended in Provincetown, over a half hour away.

"This road will be bumper to bumper before you know it," Portia said as they drove past a closed restaurant next to a picturesque bridge.

"Even at night?"

"All day long. I love it this time of year. Just before the tourists invade. The quiet before the storm," Portia said looking out the front window.

"Doesn't it get bleak during the winter with the blizzards and the bitter cold? Plus there's hardly anyone out here."

Portia smiled with glee. "That's absolutely the best time. Seeing snow on the sand, the light in the lighthouse, the sky thick with fat snowflakes…it's what I imagine when I'm stressed. Do you do that?"

"What's that?"

"Whenever I get overwhelmed, no matter where I am, I just close my eyes and imagine that scene; a mid-winter white-out, gazing out the rear window at home, seeing the lighthouse, the wood burning and crackling in the fireplace. Christmas lights on the windows."

"Do you put up Christmas lights?"

"Yes. Don't you?"

"We used to. We haven't in years."

Brian sensed that Portia was looking at him. He momentarily took his eyes off the road and saw she was, indeed. He had trouble gauging her expression in the darkness, but sensed it was a serious, squinting one. "Are you okay?"

"Do you mind if I put on my glasses?"

"Why would I mind? Not at all."

Portia took a pair of glasses out of her purse.

"That's better. What is your wife like?" Portia asked quietly.

"You mean now?" Brian laughed.

"Okay, now."

Brian made a half-groan, half-laugh, as he parted his lips. "I think right now she's probably banging a guy named Raul in my own bed." Brian glanced at Portia. She wasn't laughing. "I'm sorry. That was rude of me to have said that."

"Is that what you really think?"

Brian nodded his head without looking at her.

"If that's what you think, it's okay to say. I'm a big girl."

Brian bit the inside of his cheek, a device he used since he was a kid to hide his emotions.

"Breaking up is funny. It doesn't happen overnight. It's a long process of…change, I think," Brian said, gripping the steering wheel a little bit harder with both hands. "The really funny thing is that now, she's probably closer to what she was when we first met. So maybe I'm the one who changed."

"Or maybe she just changed for you temporarily."

"Nearly two decades is a long time for temporarily," Brian chuckled.

"Not necessarily," Portia said as she placed her hand on Brian's thigh and squeezed lightly for a moment. "Turn left at the light just ahead. I want to take a little detour before we get into town. It's the perfect night for it."

Brian followed her directions down a sandy road and through a broken gate that read *No Trespassing* and stopped at a dune with a mangled fence at the foot of it.

"Let's get out," Portia said as she opened the door.

Brian buttoned his blazer and Portia zipped her leather jacket up, as the wind picked up considerably. She took him by the hand and walked next to the dune, where there was a partially hidden wooden walkway that led right to the ocean.

"In the summer, this is a nude beach."

"I have to remember those directions," Brian said, following Portia down the path.

"A gay nude beach."

"Yeah, well, my sense of direction isn't that good anyway."

They came to the end of the wooden walkway and came upon a horseshoe-shaped alcove. The full moon was so bright that the sand seemed to glow. High waves crashed and the white of the surf exploded onto the beach. City lights could be seen off to the right, and to the left nothing but bluffs.

"If it wasn't for zoning, this would be all condos and hotels," Portia said as she removed her shoes.

"Are you telling me that government can actually do something beneficial?"

"I never thought of it like that, but yes, I guess so. Rules can guide us for good," Portia said as she led Brian closer to the surf.

"I've been pretty good with rules," Brian said stopping Portia and turning her toward him. "You, know like, wedding vows."

"I've heard of those. They make you say them in public," Portia said, inching closer to Brian.

"And in front of God."

Brian took both hands and placed them on Portia's cheeks next to her lips. "There's an old saying, my buddy George always said to me when I was dating Frances. He'd say, *You're either married or you're single.*"

"You mean as opposed to married or happy?"

"I guess," Brian said as he gently pulled Portia toward him and placed his lips against hers for a brief kiss. "But I intend to be happy soon."

"I always liked rules," Portia said turning them back toward the van. "I think that's why I got into sign design."

"I thought that was purely an artistic decision."

"Not at all. The most important part of my job is going into large building complexes and designing signs so the public can find what they need. You have to imagine yourself being totally ignorant of the environment, and then be as simplistic as humanly possible to guide folks through illogical paths to reach their goals."

"Are you a guru or a sign maker?" Brian asked as he opened the van door for Portia.

She smiled slyly. "You tell me," she said, getting into the vehicle.

The main street in Provincetown was desolate, although many of the restaurants, coffee shops, boutiques, antique stores, and bars were open for business. Portia directed Brian down a side street and down another toward the water. At the end of a dark street with every business closed, except one, there was a group of cars parked by an establishment at the end of the block. The handpainted, simple wooden sign in front read *Provincetown Café and Gallery, Est. 1919.*

"Do you remember coming here?" Portia said as they parked and walked toward the café.

"Yes, I do. But wasn't it just a fisherman's breakfast joint?"

"It was. It opened at four a.m. and closed at noon. A couple from New York bought it in the nineties. They made a killing on Wall Street and got out just before the dot com bust," Portia said as Brian held the door open for her.

It was a large room with paintings illuminated by dramatic overhead lights covering every inch of wall space. Off to the right was a horseshoe-shaped counter, which Brian remembered sitting at with Portia early one morning after staying up all night. Each of the stools now had a bust on it; Beethoven, Lizst, Einstein, Kerouac, Jefferson.

A woman wearing a full-length apron adorned with a paisley print was loading a CD player behind the counter. Her untamed frizzy hair was bunched with a barrette. In profile,

Brian assumed her to be either Italian or Jewish. She pushed a button and a Mose Allison song began playing softly. She turned around, and a smile quickly transformed her face. "Portia! How are you? Sean and I were just talking about you! How are you?"

"I'm great. This is an old friend, Brian. He's in from Washington.This is Heddy."

"State or DC?" Heddy asked, wiping her hands on her apron to shake hands.

"DC." Brian responded. "I get the same with the Sox. Red or White?"

"I get that with the chowder," Heddy said, waiting for a response from Brian, who looked puzzled, and then she added, "Chowder. Red or white."

"Brian and I met when he was an apprentice at the Theatre Tent almost twenty years ago. He's in town. Visiting."

"That's wonderful. Let me get Sean," Heddy said as she walked through a swinging door.

"They're the owners. Amazing people," Portia whispered to Brian.

"Portia! How the hell are you?" A thin man with a chef hat said in a heavy New York accent. "Get the hell over here, would ya!"

He lifted a hinged panel of the counter, jumped to Portia, and gave her a warm bear hug.

"You look fantastic! Really! You look just...dynamite! Sean said, as he looked Portia up and down in a caring, long-lost relative kind of way. "Hey, I was going to call you!" He exclaimed, pulling Portia by the hand across the room to a painting on the wall. It was average sized, about two feet by two feet, and was an ultra realistic image of a lizard without a tail on sand. Underneath the painting there was an index card, and written in black marker was *"Soul Survivor" Portia Smart. $750.00-unframed.* "Sold! Just this afternoon. A real estate agent said it would go great in her office. The color of the lizard matched her sofa."

Portia looked embarrassed by the attention.

"That's awesome," Brian said, reaching down and squeezing Portia's hand. "That is truly an amazing piece. I forgot what an amazing artist you are. Um, can I ask a stupid question?" Portia nodded. "Why doesn't the lizard have a tail?"

"If a bird snatches a lizard by the tail, it just falls off, allowing the lizard to escape, sans tail," Portia answered somberly.

"You're staying for dinner, right?" Heddy said waving them to a table by a side window that looked out to a pier. "You've got to celebrate!"

"You bet we're having dinner!" Portia said following Heddy and Sean. "What's cooking tonight, Sean?"

"We just got in some flounder, right off the boat an hour ago," Sean said excitedly. "We'll let you look over the menu for a few minutes. Take your time. You really, really look great!"

Brian and Portia studied their menus in silence. Brian thought about asking Portia if there was anything to Heddy and Sean's obvious emphasis on her appearance, but decided against it. He didn't want to screw up the evening before the appetizer even arrived.

"If you're wondering why they were asking about… how I was feeling, I just haven't been here for a while," Portia said peering over her menu.

"You don't have to explain anything to me…"

"Let's celebrate. It's not every day I sell a painting," Portia said, holding a glass of water for a toast.

He put on a brave, smiling face and clinked her glass.

Old friends really are like a comfortable pair of old sneakers. No need to step gingerly because of hard edges. The familiarity is all- encompassing. One is free to approach a conversation any way you like: hike, explore, run, jump, or just relax. Brian and Portia talked as though they had never parted. They didn't need to re-live the past, doing play-by-plays of what happened and what almost happened. There wasn't much *why didn't you?* or *why did you?* or *when will you?* Instead there was conversation as if yesterday was that day nearly twenty years ago, when Brian and Portia said good-bye under the moonlight. And today was the very next day.

"The only new music I listen to is over forty years old," Brian said between chews of fried calamari. "They call Fall Out Boy and Nickelback new? To me every pop act for the past thirty years is a rehash of music that was invented from 1964-'79. And that includes rap. Thelonius Monk. That's new even though he died in '82. It takes a brain to listen to Monk, Dizz, Miles, and Bird."

"I find that I used to listen to music to rile me up. Now I want music that will help me calm down," Portia said as she continued her intricate pattern of eating her salad; several deliberate fork stabs into various veggies, then she dips her forkful into a small bowl of salad dressing. "My favorite piece right now is *St. Francis Preaches to the Animals*, by Lizst."

"Do you have any animals?"

"I'm down to one cat."

"What's his name?"

"Puck. We wanted consistency in the lineage."

"There's a lineage to hockey references in your family?"

"Shakespearean names. Feline and human alike."

"I feel even more stupid. I never realized that. You're Portia, your mother is Beatrice, your daughter is…"

"Juliette."

"And don't tell me! Your brother's name is Macbeth."

"Oh no! Get out!" Portia said her face stretched in mock terror.

"What?" Brian asked, looking behind him expecting to see an ax-wielding maniac approaching.

"Get out, get out!" Portia demanded as she stood up, grabbed him by the hand and shoved him toward the door that led out to the deck.

"What did I do?" Brian asked as he was dragged through the door onto the darkened deck in the cool night.

"You said the word, Mac-you-know-what so you must leave the room, spin three times to the right, spit over both shoulders, then knock on the door and ask for permission to go back into the room!" Portia said excitedly, holding him by the shoulders.

"For real?"

"Yes!"

"Um, why?"

Portia inched forward, lowered her chin, and looked Brian dead in the eyes. "To break the curse."

Brian considered laughing, but was beyond knowing whether or not Portia was serious. He spun three times to the right, spit over each shoulder, and walked to the doorway. Portia motioned for him to stop as she opened the door and went inside the restaurant. Brian knocked and Portia opened the door.

"May I come in?"

Without smiling, Portia said, "Yes."

They sat at their places and Brian waited for Portia to speak. She didn't.

"What curse?"

"The curse of Mr. M."

"Mr. M, as in Mac…"

"No!" Portia said, terrified, holding up both hands to stop him.

"Okay. Got it. There's a lot of murder, violence, and betrayal in…that play, isn't there?" Brian asked, and quickly added, "So what's your brother's name?"

"Richard."

"That was your mother's idea, the Shakespeare monikers?"

"Yes, she always felt her life was Shakespearean."

"Tragedy or comedy?"

"We're still working on it. I think we're in Act III now."

Seafood is sensual enough, but Brian couldn't help notice how much baked mussels on the half shell resembled female genitalia. He wondered if Portia noticed, but didn't dare ask. It was merely urban legend that seafood, especially shellfish, made one horny, right? Portia was making sucking sounds as she got the last bit of crab meat out of a thin spiny leg that was inserted in her mouth. Since he was driving, Brian limited himself to two glasses of red wine from the bottle they had ordered. Noticing the bottle was nearly empty meant Portia must be sloshed, but she didn't show it.

Brian studied Portia as she methodically dissected her meal with the precision of a surgeon. He felt like he had half his meals on his hands or on his clothing, but Portia was immaculate. She smiled as she chewed slowly with her lips sealed and dabbed her mouth with the white linen napkin. Brian looked at her and the panorama of the view out the window behind her; the pier, the sailboats, the buoys in the distance. He felt incredibly blessed and lucky. He doubted he'd be where he was at this very moment if Frances hadn't dropped the bomb on him before he left. He hoped there weren't any bombs on timers.

Portia was tipsy, not drunk. She laughed at Brian's jokes, even the one about the grasshopper that walked into a bar and the bartender says, *Hey, we have a drink named after you,* and the grasshopper says, *You have a drink named Myron Finkelstein?* Once they were back on the dark road home, there was a silence that said too much. The silence before the good-bye when things would have to be said. It couldn't be another good-bye where they both hoped for the best. It was too late for them to hope. Brian wondered what he would say when he kissed Portia good-bye again.

Portia turned on the radio and quickly dialed in a classical station that wasn't a very strong signal, but good enough.

"Radio. Couldn't live without it," Brian said while he concentrated on the dark curvy road.

"That's right. It's your livelihood. Is that exciting?"

"It was. Now it just riles me up. Let's stop at The Laughing Gull for a nightcap."

"I don't know. I don't like going there, really."

"Oh. Okay. That's fine," Brian said softly, not wanting to pressure Portia in any way. The Gull was a local place. And there would be locals there on a Saturday night. Maybe she didn't want to meet any locals.

"No, on second thought, let's go. Turn left at the next intersection."

Terry the affable bartender was busy attending to the Saturday night crowd. Katie wasn't in sight. Brian and Portia took the last seats available at a table for two next to the kitchen door. A basketball game was on the television with the sound muted.

"Oh, the Celtics are playing the Bulls," Brian said, sipping from a glass of water that a busboy had just placed in front of them.

"Why aren't they called the *keltic*s?" Portia asked, using the hard *K* sound instead of the *S* sound for Celtics.

"What do you mean?"

"It should be pronounced Celtic with a hard *C*, like a *K*, not a soft *C* with an *S* sound. I assume they're named after the Celts of Ireland?"

"Yeah, their logo is a potbellied leprechaun in a bowler hat, smoking a pipe and wearing a vest with shamrocks all over it, holding up a basketball on one finger."

"Maybe it's just as well, then. But there must be a lot of embarrassed Sallahans, O'Sonnells, and Sassidy's living on Sape Sod," Portia said, as she and Brian laughed together.

"Do you recognize the bartender?" Brian asked Portia, pointing to Terry who was pouring a drink at their end of the bar.

"Oh, that's Terry, isn't it? He was one of the nice ones. He looks well."

"I guess there were some not-so-nice ones."

"There still are."

Bursting through the kitchen door, Katie emerged balancing two trays of food. "I'll be right with…Oh hi, Brian. And Portia! I'll be right back," she said rushing to the other end of the restaurant.

"Aw. She's still so pretty," Portia said fondly. "She was so adorable. I remember when she was in first or second grade, she used to ask me why I was named after a sports car."

"I don't think I even heard of a Porsche until I was in college," Brian added.

"That's because you didn't grow up in Hampton North."

Katie rushed past the table again in the opposite direction. "I'll be right with you, I swear."

"We knew the O'Reilly's were one of the richest families around, but they were also the nicest, so the old clichés didn't always hold true. Although they certainly did hold true for some other blue bloods."

"That must've been hard…" Brian stopped himself, not wanting to offend Portia.

"It was hard for us. There were no secrets in this town. And to suddenly have your father run away with his secretary, and…worse…and lose whatever security and money your family had…. Let's just say kids can be terribly cruel," Portia said with a weak smile.

"Hello, Portia! How are you? I see Brian finally found you!" Katie said warmly as she gave Portia a peck on the cheek. "I was hoping you two would hook up eventually. When are you leaving, Brian?"

"Tomorrow."

"You cut it close, didn't you? How's everybody…at home, Portia?" Katie asked as she scanned the crowd with a look of concern across her face.

"Oh, fine, thank you," Portia said politely, but obviously not wanting to divulge any personal information.

"What can I get you?"

"Actually, two coffees would be great," Brian said to Katie as she headed for the kitchen.

"I'll be right back," Portia said excusing herself and heading for the ladies room.

Brian suddenly felt guilty that his idea to hit The Laughing Gull last thing might cheer her up had backfired.

A loud crash of dishes disrupted the barroom chatter across the room and a male voice could be heard complaining, "I said I want to speak to the manager! Not a waitress!"

"I said, I am the manager. As if you didn't know!" Katie said in a stern voice.

Brian looked across the room as a large man stood up from a table and threw his napkin down on the table.

"Oh shit. That asshole!" Brian said to himself, recognizing him as the brute who had beat his kid at the red light.

"I'll never come back here again!" the irate customer announced to all.

"I wish you'd keep your word on that promise for once," Terry the bartender said after stepping out from the bar and standing in front of his sister, Katie.

The loudmouthed moron took a look at Terry first, then glanced over at Brian sitting there and obviously decided it was not in his game plan to pick on somebody his own size and huffed out. Brian wondered if he possibly could have recognized him from across the restaurant.

Portia returned from the rest room with a puzzled look on her face. "Did I hear something?"

"Oh, you heard something all right," Brian said, shaking his head in disbelief. "I just saw the only other person I know in these parts."

"Who's that?"

"Oh, just some crazy asshole who I confronted after I saw him beating his kid at a red light."

"Oh my God. He was in here? Making a scene?"

"Yeah, a show stopper."

Katie and Terry sheepishly approached the table together and stood awkwardly next to each other.

"We're sorry for the commotion," Katie said looking toward Portia, smiling weakly.

"We hope we didn't embarrass you," Terry added.

"Embarrass us? Why? Portia asked.

"Wasn't that your brother?" Terry asked gingerly.

"I didn't see him, actually."

"The coffee's on us," Katie said, walking away with Terry.

Brian studied Portia as they both fiddled with their coffee cups, water glasses, and napkins. During the summer of their love, Portia referred to her brother only remotely, as if he was far away and out of touch. He seemed much older than she, and there was no family resemblance as far as he could perceive at this point, anyway. As far as Brian knew he never appeared for a single moment at Smart House that summer. And Portia's mom never once mentioned him, ever. Brian assumed he was estranged and left it at that. But it wouldn't be so easy for him to ignore him now.

"Is he dangerous?" Brian said, interrupting the silence.

Portia looked as though she was going to laugh hysterically, but stopped herself. "That's an apt if understated description. You said you saw him beating a child?"

"When I arrived I was stopped at a red light, and I happened to look in my rear view mirror and saw someone beating something in the back seat. I thought he was hitting a dog. I stepped out of my car and was ready to admonish him for hitting an animal. When I saw he was hitting a little kid, I almost lost it. Seeing his pathetic wife in the front seat was the only thing that stopped me."

"What did she look like?"

"Asian or maybe a Filipina lady."

"We heard he had a mail order bride. We didn't dream she came with accessories. Can we leave?"

Brian nodded, dropped a tip onto the table, and waved to Katie and Terry at the register.

It had turned quite chilly, and Brian pulled Portia close to him as they slowly walked around the corner to the van.

"He was away for years. He was already on his own when Father left Mother. We had absolutely no contact with him until a few years ago. We had heard rumors of a mail order bride. He knows Mother isn't doing well."

"What does he want?"

Portia snickered. "Money, of course. He thinks we have this hidden stash. Buried treasure. And he wants it. We barely have enough to live on."

"Money seems to bring out the worst of humanity," Brian said as he opened the door for Portia. Brian entered the driver's side. "Tell me if I'm prying…"

Portia softly stroked his hand on the steering wheel.

"Can't you sell the house?"

"That would kill Mother. That house is Mother. She's a fighter. She protects Juliette and me like a mad lioness."

Brian started the car and drove through the fog that had descended on the dark coastal roads. He could hardly see twenty feet in front of him and concentrated on the yellow line. He tried his brights but it seemed to make the fog glow and the visibility even worse.

He pulled over next to the walkway of the house, which was shrouded in fog and barely visible from the road.

"Should I go in with you?"

"I don't think so. It's late."

"Is it *too* late?"

Portia looked at Brian as though she read his mind. "It's not too late for us. I'm not going anywhere. You know where to find me...now."

Brian undid his shoulder belt, and hers, leaned across the console, and kissed her gently at first; then sensing a surging passion, they began a long, hard kiss. The soft moaning, groaning kind of tongue-in-the-mouth kiss that one never wants to end.

"This isn't good-bye this time," Brian said, his face next to Portia's. "I'll just walk you to the door," he said, opening the car door.

As he opened the door and stepped outside, out of nowhere two bright beams of light came ripping through the fog, blinding Brian. He squinted his eyes and held his hands up to try and block the light.

"Look out!" Portia screamed from the passenger seat.

Tires squealed on the curving, damp street and a loud, sickening thud could be heard as the van filled with light and Brian let out a guttural "Fuck!"

The car sped away. Portia ran to the other side of the van, and Brian was lying in the road, face-down in the darkness.

"Brian! Brian! Help! Help!" Portia yelled into the dark fog. She knelt down and put her face next to his, and although he was motionless, she could tell he was breathing. "Help goddammit, help!"

Brian stirred slightly. Blood was streaming across his face, but she couldn't tell where it was coming from.

The front door of the house opened and out came Portia's daughter, in a robe, with a flashlight and a phone. "Oh my God! I called 911!" she said as she turned on the van's emergency flashers. "Let's move him over here."

"Should we move him? They say you shouldn't move someone," Portia said, now sobbing uncontrollably.

"You'll both get killed if another car comes around the corner," Juliette said reassuringly. "Come on, we'll just slide him out of the road."

They grabbed his shoulders and slid him across the blacktop to the front of the van, leaving him face-down, with Portia placing her jacket under his face.

A siren could be heard in the distance, and red flashing lights lit up the white fog in a surreal flash, like a red cloud was surrounding them.

Brian opened his eyes and asked, "Where am I?"

"You're okay. Help is here, don't move," Portia said, stroking his bloody face and crying softly, her face next to his on the damp street.

A police car turned the corner and stopped next to them. A young female officer with a two-way radio in one hand and a flashlight in the other approached. "How does he look? Was he struck by a vehicle?" she asked, kneeling next to Brian.

"A car swerved into us. I couldn't tell how badly he was hit,"

"What's your name?" the officer asked.

"Brian DeLouise," Brian said without hesitation.

"Do you know what happened to you?" she asked loudly.

"I think a car swerved into us. My head…"

"Stay still, sir. The ambulance will be here shortly," the officer looked up to Portia. "He's going to be fine. He's got a crack on the head, which is always bloody, but he's fine. Just banged up a bit," she said smiling.

An ambulance rounded the corner, stopped immediately in front of them, and two attendants sprang into action. Brian was rolled onto his back, a brace was put on his neck, and within a few minutes he was placed on a gurney and lifted into the ambulance.

An EMT guy came over to Portia, who was giving details to the cop, "He's fine. We're taking him to Memorial."

"We'll meet you there," the officer replied. "Do you want to come with me, or do you want to drive yourself?" the cop asked Portia.

Portia knew she was in no condition to drive, either emotionally or blood alcohol-wise. "Can I go with you?"

"Sure, we'll go as soon as the backup comes and we get some information. It'll take a few minutes, being a hit-and-run and all."

It wasn't until the officer said it that Portia took in what the totality of what had just happened. It was a hit-and-run. Someone plowed into them, knew they did it, and didn't stop; in fact, they sped away. *What kind of sociopath would do such an awful thing?* she asked herself, hoping to God she the answer she came up with was wrong.

CHAPTER NINE

Portia was not unfamiliar with Northeastern Memorial Hospital. A nurse took her through the emergency room to Brian's bed, behind a curtain in the corner. His head was wrapped in a bandage, but he was sitting up and looking much better than she anticipated.

"It's a good thing I fell on my head, otherwise I could've gotten really hurt," Brian joked.

Portia didn't say anything, but rushed to hug him.

"I'm fine. Just a nasty headache, that's all. I'm a little sore in here, too" Brian said sweeping his hand across his chest.

"I was scared to death. When I saw you lying there on the road, I thought…" Portia's voice morphed into sobs.

"I'm fine. They took me to x-ray, and if everything's okay, I can leave here tonight."

"Leave? I don't know. After what you've been through? It could be serious."

A small Indian man with a file folder, obviously the doctor, pulled back the curtain. "Thankfully, no. We looked at the pictures. Just a slight concussion. Nothing to worry about. You're very lucky. A few inches and you could have been a goner. The car did not hit you," he said, pulling back the covers on Brian. "We believe the car grazed your van door, and it whip-lashed back striking you, forcefully, knocking the wind out of you, causing a contusion here, and then you struck something on your vehicle on the way down when you collapsed unconscious onto the road."

"Am I being released?"

"Oh yes. You can leave. But take it easy for at least three days; no driving, no activity. We're giving you some Vicodin, but don't take them unless you need to. Just take aspirin in the meantime, and get plenty of rest."

The doctor turned to Portia. "Make sure he doesn't try and do too much! Keep an eye on him. You know how boys are!" he said, laughing and pointing at Brian. "The nurse will be here to check you out. Call me if you have any problems. Good-bye and good luck," he said as he left and closed the curtain behind him.

"I guess I have to keep an eye on you, and I sure as hell am not doing it from that no-tell motel where you've been staying," Portia said leaning in to Brian, finally looking relaxed.

"And where will you be watching me?"

"It just so happens your old room is vacant."

"I hoped to get a look at that room on this trip, but this isn't exactly the way I thought it would happen."

"Life's funny that way," Portia said, as she gave him a soft kiss on his bandaged forehead.

The next morning Brian had forgotten where he was when he first opened his eyes and gazed out onto the lighthouse on its rocky island with the sun rising next to it. But as he lifted his head, and the pain shot through from the back of his head through his spine, the events of the night before became painfully self-evident. He often thought of this spectacular view; the ocean crashing onto the rocks, the sun rising amidst red-streaked clouds. It seemed so utterly beautiful in his memory, he wondered if perhaps its beauty was enhanced by nostalgia. But seeing it again, from the very bed he slept in for that entire summer, it was even more spectacular now.

He reached for his wristwatch on the night stand and a pain zapped him immediately. He pulled up his t-shirt and saw that he had a nice thick black-and-blue line diagonally across his chest. It was just after seven, and he wondered if others would be already up.

"Come, Mr. Dawson! Don't be obstructionist," the familiar voice of Beatrice Smart bellowed from downstairs. "Mrs. Pangborne is entitled to sit and read the paper if she pleases."

"Good morning!" Portia said, as she entered the room holding a breakfast tray loaded with goodies. "How's the pain?"

"Not too bad," Brian said.

Portia placed the tray on the bed and tucked the blankets tightly along Brian's side. She then extended the legs on the tray and placed it over his midsection. Despite the throbbing pain, he absorbed the aromas in front of him; the dark, steaming coffee, the butter melting into the nooks and crannies of the English muffins, the sweet citrus smell of a sliced orange, the fragrance of the open jar of fruit preserves. Portia walked to the left side of the window and gazed out. The red tint of the sunshine almost made her look like she had a summer tan.

"I think this room has the best view in the house," she said, staring into the distance.

"That's how it looks to me," Brian said, admiring Portia from behind.

Portia turned and smiled.

"With you standing there, it is," he said enjoying Portia's sunny profile. Do you want to share any of this? It looks fantastic!"

"No thanks, I already had something. Go ahead. Eat," Portia said, pulling a small wooden chair next to the bed. "You'll have to stay here for a few days, you know. Mother said it's fine. But listen…"

"No, I'll pay! Really! I don't expect to be waited on…"

"That's very sweet of you. Mother didn't ask for anything, but frankly, that would be a nice gesture on your part. But what I wanted to tell you is that there are some things I should prepare you for."

"Prepare me for? You're not about to bring in your lifelong female companion, are you? Not that there's anything wrong with that…"

"I'm serious. We have two borders staying here, as I'm sure you've picked up on. Mr. Dawson is in his nineties, demanding, usually in a foul mood, sex obsessed, and it seems every other word is a profanity."

"Sounds like a charmer."

"He's also one of the country's leading mathematicians, and he doesn't like to be disturbed when he's working, which he prefers to do in the late afternoon in the sun room." Portia looked at Brian, expecting a smartass comment. Instead he took a large bite of his muffin and nodded his head.

"Continue."

"Mrs. Pangborne has Alzheimers. She's incontinent, which you will be able to tell by her…smell…and the dampness of the sofa cushions if she forgets to sit on her plastic pad. She's also as sweet and gentle as a kitten, and will want to talk with you, even though her language skills are shot and she'll make about as much sense as cut-up poetry, which it sometimes sounds like."

Brian took a sip of coffee.

"Mother looks fine, but she's not one hundred percent. We think she's had some mini-strokes, infarctions they're called, and as of six months ago has vowed never to visit a doctor again. She's also…somewhat incontinent."

Brian took a bite from a slice of orange, clearly trying very hard not to show any kind of negative reaction to the domestic situation described. He was a guest, and would behave as such, he thought to himself.

"You'll be getting up soon, and I just didn't want any surprises," Portia said holding Brian's hand, looking up at him from his bedside.

"What's life without a surprise every now and then?" Brian said, sipping his coffee.

Portia lifted herself up to Brian's level, leaned over, and kissed him on the tip of his nose.

"You know, that's the only part of my body above my waist not wracked with pain."

Portia left the room with Brian's tray. He slid down his pillow a few inches to get comfortable and scratched under the front of his bandage. The sky wasn't nearly as red as it had been just minutes ago. A fishing vessel passed behind the lighthouse toward the sunrise. Brian wanted to make a phone call, but his cell was on the other side of the room inside his jacket. The thought of getting out of bed made Brian just a tiny bit nervous. He wondered if the pain would increase, or if he might lose his balance and fall, requiring to be rescued again by Portia or someone else from the unusual household. He sat up straight, and did feel a pang of pain in his neck, but nothing to worry about.

He slowly removed the covers and moved his legs over the side of the old-fashioned bed, which was unusually high. He stood straight up with his feet planted firmly on the floor...and felt fine. He took the few steps over to his jacket and felt a tiny bit of pain, much like a hangover, when he leaned over to retrieve his phone from the pocket. He sat on the side of his bed and sighed as he looked out the window, where the fishing boat was now just a tiny dot on the horizon. It was time to call Frances.

Brian knew he would also have to call work, and tell them he wouldn't be back for a few days on doctor's orders. That would be easy. But he wasn't quite sure exactly what to tell Frances. She would probably be feeling her own headache, from an actual hangover this early Sunday morning, which could mean two things: either she'd rush him off the phone, not wanting to be bothered, or she might give him holy hell.

Brian scrolled through his speed dial numbers, stopped on *home* and wondered how much longer it would remain with that title on his phone. What would he call it, *the house I pay for but don't own?* He pushed the button and waited.

Frances was awakened from a deep alcohol-induced sleep when the phone rang. She assumed it was Brian calling, letting her know he was on his way back to Washington. She had everything all planned. She would invite him over this evening, for a very brief encounter. The place was immaculate. There would be a few clues lying around that, yes, Raul was indeed there, but nothing too obvious. She would be aloof, unemotional, professional. She would inform him of their meeting the next morning. And then she would drop her bunker buster on him-- she wanted it all! Just like in business, she knew she had to be cutthroat to get what she wanted. Ask for the sun, the moon, and the stars, and settle for the moon.

"Hello," Frances mumbled into the receiver.

"Did I wake you?"

"Oh, it's you. When are you coming home? What the hell time is it?"

"It's just after seven. Listen, I have to tell you something…"

"Where are you? Are you on the road already?"

"I'm not coming back for a few days. I've been in an accident…"

"A few days? Are you kidding me? I have…arrangements!" Frances said sitting up.

Brian didn't respond, stunned that the fact that he was in an accident didn't even register a blip on her radar screen.

"Hello? Are you there?" Frances said sarcastically.

"I'm here."

"When will you be back?"

Brian wanted to push the little red button that would disconnect the conversation, but didn't. He would have liked to have said that he'd never be back, but extenuating circumstances, namely a paycheck, prevented him from doing that as well. "I'll probably be back in three or four days. I'll call you. Bye," he said, punctuated by punching the little red button with the phone icon on it. He shook his head, forgetting that he had a slight concussion, which brought on another twinge of pain. His cell rang while still in his hand.

"Did you say you were in an accident?" Frances said, sounding somewhat concerned.

"Yes. I was in a minor traffic accident, but I'm okay. Just a slight concussion. I'm staying…at a motel for a few days."

"You're okay, though?"

"Yes. Thanks for asking," Brian said with mock gratitude.

"Okay. See you in a few days."

Frances hung up the phone, sat straight up and said softly to herself, "I just better go make sure his life insurance is paid up. He's such a goddammed martyr he wouldn't even tell me if he was on life support."

Portia appeared in the doorway with a newspaper. "Want to read the Sunday paper?"

Brian looked at Portia and a wave of bliss went from his battered head down his achy torso and settled in the pit of his stomach. "Yeah, that would be great."

"Think you can make it down to the sun room?"

"Do I have to fight Mr. Dawson for a space on the couch?"

"In your condition he'd probably win. Let's go," Portia said pulling the blanket down and offering her hand in assistance.

The sun room was the largest room in the house, situated on the southeast corner, offering a spectacular 180-degree view of the rocky coast. There were no draperies or blinds on the windows, which went from a foot above the floor to nearly the top of the ten foot ceilings, which made the room as bright as sitting on the beach. There were storm windows on the outside of every window except one. That allowed the one window to be opened slightly, which created a whistling sound of sea air as it rushed into the room.

Mr. Dawson sat next to the entrance to the room, rigid and erect in a sturdy wooden chair, his arms stretched out on the unpadded wooden arm rest. In front of him were a series of three snack trays, each one with neat piles of loose leaf pages. A fourth snack tray was to his immediate right, and on it was a thick math textbook. He sat there motionless for several moments, then picked up a red pencil and leaned forward from the waist with his back remaining straight as if he were on hinges. He then began writing furiously on one of the pages.

Brian and Portia sat on the rattan sofa next to the southern wall of windows, placing the Sunday *Boston Globe* between them.

"What is he writing?" Brian whispered.

"Mathematics. See that thick book off to the side?" Portia asked softly. "He wrote it."

Brian bugged his eyes open in amazement and began leafing through the paper in search of the sports section.

"Why, we have a guest!" Beatrice announced in voice that would have easily projected to the last row in a large theater. "It is so nice to see you again!" Beatrice said, gliding across the large room.

Brian put down the paper so he could rise to greet her. It became hard to concentrate as his movement caused self-conscious awareness of his condition, which he hoped he was able to suppress as he forced himself to smile. He hadn't seen Beatrice in over twenty years, and although time had chiseled lines in the usual places, caused a mole or two to darken and made her still shoulder-length hair appear thick and wild, she still somehow carried herself elegantly. She raised her hand in a royal kind of way, expecting it to be held briefly, and looked down her nose. But it didn't seem put on. It seemed genetic and natural.

"No, don't get up! Save your strength, you poor thing!" Beatrice said, warmly waiting for Brian to grasp or kiss her hand.

"Thank you so much for letting me stay for a couple of days, Mrs. Smart. It's very gracious of you," Brian said, shaking her hand.

"It's my pleasure," Beatrice said. "And Portia's, of course."

Just then, Juliette appeared in the doorway and stood silently, with a large black garbage bag at her side, filled with something heavy.

"Oh, it's Juliette!" Beatrice said noticing her. "Come here, sweetheart, and say hello."

Juliette dragged her heavy load across the floor. "Hello. I think we've met," she said, standing awkwardly next to Beatrice.

Brian was again amazed at the resemblance of Juliette to her mother at that age, and suddenly was also reminded of the fact that someone in the household was incontinent by a smell coming from the bag at Juliette's side. "It's amazing how much you look like your mother," Brian said, holding his hand out to shake hands with her. "You're just as beautiful and charming," he said, glancing at Portia briefly.

Portia sighed deeply, and then made a soft sound, like a whimper as she brought her hand to her neck. She then closed her eyes, as though she was going to weep, but didn't, abruptly changing her expression. "She's such an angel."

"Mom," Juliette said, drawing out the single vowel into three or four syllables.

"I was just so worried about Brian. Thank you for responding the way you did. You really kept a level head."

"All I did was make a phone call," Juliette said, still sounding annoyed at the attention.

"All's well that ends well," Beatrice said happily.

In the doorway, Mrs. Pangborne appeared in a robe and a worried look on her face. "My, my, my, what a strong group of…dogs! I'm okay, right?"

"Yes, Mrs. Pangborne, I'll be right with you," Beatrice said politely. "Make yourself at home," Beatrice said, walking away and taking Mrs. Pangborne by the arm.

"Juliette, why don't you dispose of that and come join us?" Portia said to Juliette, who seemed to be gazing into the horizon through the windows.

"Okay. I'll be back in a few minutes."

"Do you need any help?" Portia asked.

"No. I'm fine," Juliette answered firmly as she dragged her bag back across the room and out the front door.

"Woof, woof," Mr. Dawson said, not looking up from his equations.

"This is a friend of mine, Mr. Dawson," Portia said loudly, as if talking to someone who is hard of hearing. "His name is…"

"…Brian! I'm not deaf," Mr. Dawson said, looking up from his work. "Nice to have some damned testosterone around here for once," he said with a straight face.

"Nice to meet you, too," Brian said, chuckling a bit. Mr. Dawson dropped his head down and continued to wiggle his red pencil across some pages.

Brian returned to the couch, picked up the sports section and Portia turned the pages of the arts section. The sound of the waves crashing on the shore was mixed with the whooshing of the air rushing through the one-inch slot of the opened window. A tinny radio speaker in the kitchen played baroque organ music and occasionally lost its reception to static. It was easy to tell where someone was in the house, because of the hardwood floors throughout.

Brian tried to remember one instance where he and Portia sat on this sofa on a Sunday afternoon reading the paper, although he did recall this exact sofa being in the same location. Perhaps it was because Sundays were usually extremely busy at the theater tent. That was the day that the apprentice actors put on their own productions in the afternoon. Being the technical wizard, he was always the first to arrive and last to leave for any show.

But maybe that wasn't why he had never sat so comfortably in this room with Portia doing something so homey and comfy as thumbing through the Sunday paper. Perhaps it was because back then, he wouldn't think that sitting in this room with his head bandaged, silently with Portia, while an elderly man wrote math equations and occasionally farted loudly, was his idea of bliss. And as he skipped the news about basketball and hunted for the slightest bit of new baseball information, and smelled the salt air rush into the room, watching Portia intensely read an article, it was indeed his newfound definition of bliss.

"Are you feeling okay?" Portia asked, turning to him.

"Yes, I'm fine," he said smiling.

"I hope you and I and Juliette get a chance to spend some time together. She's so special."

"I hope so, too."

"Maybe later, if you're feeling strong, we could perhaps just sit on the veranda and chat."

"Absolutely. She seems like a great kid."

Portia beamed with pride. "Do you really think so?"

"Yeah. Definitely," Brian said, reassuring her.

Portia dropped her paper, and reached over hugging Brian. Her head leaned against his. "That's good. That's good."

"Somebody open the door, I'm locked out!" Juliette shouted from under the window.

"I'll be right there," Portia said as she rushed to the front door.

As soon as she stepped outside, Mr. Dawson looked over to Brian. "Psssst."

Brian looked at him quizzically.

Mr. Dawson leaned forward, surveyed the room to see if anyone was around and said, "I'll give you five thousand bucks if you fuck Beatrice."

Brian's mouth dropped open and no words came out. He cleared his throat and stared at Mr. Dawson, thinking he would follow up with a *just kidding*. He didn't.

"The offer's on the table," Mr. Dawson said, with all the warmth of a used car salesman trying to seal a deal on a used Yugo.

The front door opened, and Portia and Juliette could be heard having words in the foyer. Hushed words that more than likely were an argument in progress. Juliette ran past the sun room doorway and up the stairs. An upstairs door slammed shut.

Portia walked sheepishly into the room and took her place next to Brian. A strange wave of emotion brought on some pangs of pain under his bandage.

"Is everything okay?" Brian asked, masking his own mixed emotions of the moment.

Portia put on her own brave face. "Oh, it's nothing to speak of. Just teenage angst."

Brian remembered Katie in The Gull telling him about Juliette's age, which puzzled him.

"How old is Juliette?" Brian asked, nonchalantly.

Portia looked at Brian solemnly. The bright sunlight in the room cast a sharp shadow across her face, making one side almost invisible like the cover of *Meet the Beatles.* The harsh light also accentuated the lines on her face and for the first time made her look her age.

"She'll be twenty in September."

While Mr. Dawson scribbled his complex equations that stretched across pages, Brian struggled to do the simple math of that in his head. He last made love with Portia in August of 1989…so add nine months…May. Portia must have gotten pregnant on her trip. At first he felt relieved that there was no way that Juliette could be his love child according to the math, which quickly morphed into guilt.

"She seems mature for her age," Brian said, hoping that Portia couldn't detect the intense emotions bouncing in his post- concussion brain.

"At times. Other times she cries just like a little girl," she said rhythmically.

"Were you doing Dylan?"

"You caught me. I told her we're having lunch on the veranda this afternoon if it's warm enough."

"Sounds like fun."

Mr. Dawson ripped a loud fart, startling Portia and Brian briefly, but not phasing Mr. Dawson in the slightest.

"He's a character," Portia whispered.

"I'll say," Brian said, as he momentarily flashed on Mrs. Smart nude in his mind.

Portia, Beatrice, and Juliette had been fluttering around the kitchen all afternoon in preparation for the first outdoor meal in months. Brian's assignment was to take the tarp off the deck furniture to ready it for the occasion, which seemed like an easy enough task for someone convalescing. He was instructed he need only prepare four chairs since Mr. Dawson and Mrs. Pangborne would be dining indoors.

Portia seemed almost as nervous as Beatrice as she poked her head through the door every few minutes to check on Brian. Beatrice could be heard through the one open window shouting orders and admonitions to her kitchen staff. She had even put Mrs. Pangborne to work folding the same four paper grocery bags over and over, which made her feel like she was contributing to the effort. Brian knew that Beatrice's meals could be unforgettable, both as successes and failures. She never used a cookbook and concocted dishes merely on instinct, sometimes throwing the most unlikely combinations together. But today, a delicious aroma was making its way to the back veranda, probably due to Portia.

The afternoon wind had picked up, but not enough to deter them from enjoying a festive Sunday afternoon meal with the exquisite rocky coast of New England surrounding them, despite temperatures in the mid-fifties, at best.

"At least there are no bugs this time of year," Beatrice said as she carried a large blue oriental casserole dish and placed it in the center of the table.

Portia and Juliette were right behind with trays loaded with other covered dishes, which they placed on the table. Within a matter of minutes, each had a large plate full of fragrant, colorful foods; green beans with almonds, crab cakes, mashed potatoes, baked mussels, and salad.

"Enjoy!" Beatrice said proudly. "Does this remind you of the time you spent here twenty years ago, Brian?"

"Absolutely," Brian said, remembering a meal Beatrice had served on the veranda consisting of a stew made of chicken necks and gizzards, carrots a day or two past their prime, and overripe bananas. Seeing Juliette in this setting looking so much like her mother brought Brian back. She had her mother's coloring, hair, facial features, physique, but not her personality. Juliette seemed hard and bitter for someone so young.

"I wonder what would have happened if we had gotten together earlier in the week, instead of the day before I was scheduled to leave," Brian said as he placed some butter on his beans. "I guess everything happens for a reason, even if somebody forgets to give somebody a message," Brian said joking.

Eyeballs started darting. Portia, then Juliette, then Beatrice.

"Did you tell Brian I forgot to tell you?" Juliette said, looking at Portia in astonishment. "I didn't forget anything."

Portia's look of embarrassment was followed by a long pause. "She's right, Brian. That wasn't fair of me to use that as an excuse. Juliette is very responsible. She gave me the message and your number. I…just…I was afraid to call, that's all."

"What's done is done," Beatrice cheerfully announced.

Brian sensed a subtle tension brewing at the table. Every family has secrets, and the Smarts were famous in Hampton North for that very reason. Some secrets are kept from outsiders. Some secrets are kept from one's self. "No biggie. I'm just glad we're able to do this today. It's not very often you get to pick up exactly where you left off twenty years ago. It's like a dream where one minute you're floating over the White House and the next you're naked in second grade class taking a math test, but when you wake up it all kind of makes sense." As Brian looked at his dining partners, he realized he wasn't making any. "If you know what I mean."

"I'm just thankful we were all able to get together. Finally," Portia said, beaming at her daughter.

"This is just so stupid!" Juliette blurted out as she pushed her chair back forcefully. She spun around and rushed to the doorway.

"Watch out!" Portia yelled. But it was too late.

Juliette tripped over the tarp that Brian had left in a pile, thoughtlessly thinking it was far enough out of the way. She went face-first onto the deck, managing only at the last second to break her fall with her hands.

"Motherfucker! Who left that there? Shit!" Juliette yelled in anger as she turned over and sat on the deck.

Beatrice, Portia, and Brian rushed to her aid.

"Oh sweetie, are you okay?" Portia said, holding her close and examining her hands and face for injuries.

"I'm fine. I hate it when people are careless. I'm okay, but what if Mema or you tripped over it? With your vision, it could have been really bad!"

Brian was silent as he knelt next to Portia. Beatrice stood there, her face twitching and contorted with fear. They helped her get to her feet.

"I think I have a splinter," she whimpered.

"Oh poor baby," Portia said, comforting her while she examined her hand more with her sense of feeling than of sight.

The three generations of women morphed together in an embrace of strokes and comfort. As they clung together, Brian could tell this was how they kept it together. This was how they survived life's rough seas. He felt very much an outsider watching their sympathy scrum. They needed each other like they needed oxygen.

Brian and Portia didn't talk much as they cleaned up after the meal. Juliette and Beatrice were off taking naps. Mr. Dawson was back in his chair trying to outdo Einstein, and Mrs. Pangborne stood off to the side in the kitchen still folding and unfolding the same four brown paper grocery bags. Portia was washing and Brian was drying.

"I think I'm ready to go home now," Brian said, putting a dry dish into a cabinet. "I mean, in the morning."

Portia kept her eyes on the knife she was washing under the running water. "Are you well enough? You are my personal responsibility, according to the doctor."

A shriek could be heard from another part of the house, undoubtedly coming from Mrs. Pangborne.

"Put that away, Mr. Dawson!" Beatrice shouted.

"Oh, you silly bitches! Get the hell out of my way and let me take a damn piss! You'd think you never saw one before," Mr. Dawson replied angrily.

"That's very rude, Mr. Dawson!" Beatrice scolded him.

"Aw raspberries!" he snarled.

Portia continued washing the silverware, ignoring the commotion.

"Do you want me to intervene?" Brian asked cautiously.

"Hmm? Oh, Mother and Mr. Dawson? That's nothing."

A loud crash came from that same part of the house, sounding like a large metal pan bouncing off a tile floor.

"I refuse to pee in a damn bed pan! I'm not an invalid, dammit!" Mr. Dawson screeched.

"Was that also nothing?" Brian asked Portia.

"Yes. Nothing."

A clicking sound could be heard approaching from down the hall. Brian looked to the doorway and saw Mr. Dawson, who had stopped there holding a classic Raleigh three-speed bicycle, complete with a front basket, front light, and an oversized handlebar bell. He was wearing a white cap, white jacket, and khaki pants.

"The offer still stands," Mr. Dawson said to Brian. He then pushed the bike past the doorway, continuing through the house and out the front door.

"What was that?" Brian asked Portia, still dumbfounded.

"He's going for his nightcap."

"He goes for a bike ride before bed?"

"No, he goes to the tavern. Remember the Terminal Tavern, down by the old ferry station?"

"Sure. He goes there? At night? How does he get back?"

"It's all downhill going. He has his single malt scotch and gets a lift home."

"What about the bike?"

"He usually just leaves it at the bar, and somebody brings it back the next day."

"How old is he?"

"He'll be ninety on the fourth of July."

"Must be plenty of fireworks around here on that day."

Portia smiled sweetly and motioned for Brian to catch up with his drying duties. "We have fireworks all year 'round. How can you even contemplate leaving all this?"

"I'm not sure I can," Brian leaned over kissed Portia softly on her cheek. "Why did Juliette say you can't see well?"

"Oh, that's nothing," Portia said, trying desperately to look unconcerned.

"What is it, then?"

"Oh, just my vision is bad. Getting worse all the time."

"How bad?"

"They say in ten years, I could lose my sight. But right now, I'm not nearly as blind as Mr. Magoo, so I do okay."

Brian didn't want to push it, so he just dropped it. They completed the cleanup in silence.

The crystal clear skies of the afternoon had transformed into a spectacular evening with stars strewn in every direction. It was a new moon, so the absence of any moonlight made their sparkle seem almost artificial. The house was finally quiet, with Mr. Dawson presumably getting plastered at the Terminal, and Beatrice, Juliette, and Mrs. Pangborne having retired to their rooms.

Brian sat on the veranda's padded patio sofa waiting for Portia, who had gone inside to get a blanket. As he gazed at the sky, he wondered what the future might hold. His mind raced, going from best to worst case scenarios as he thought about including Portia in his future. His stress caused a slight pang of head pain, which reminded him that he just had a concussion. He thought about Frances and their failed marriage. But that didn't seem to bother him. The only thing that troubled him about the pending divorce was that Frances had no need for him anymore.

He looked into the heavens and for the first time in months, he prayed. Not a prayer he had memorized in grade school, but a prayer to God. He didn't really know what he was praying for. Was it happiness? Strength? A sign?

Just then Portia came through the door with a blanket and sat down next to him. She placed the blanket across both their laps, and just as they both settled in to enjoy the view, a shooting star shot across the sky.

"Did you see that?" Brian asked.

"My God, I think so…yes!" Portia said, adjusting her thick glasses.

Brian removed Portia's glasses, pulled the blanket up to their necks, and they began make out in the sweet dark night. Brian was aroused so quickly he became embarrassed. Timing was everything, and the timing just wasn't right and both of them sensed it. Brian stood up, got down on one knee, kissed her hand, said goodnight, and went to bed. He couldn't believe what he just did.

CHAPTER TEN

Brian tried to block what lay ahead of him as he packed his bag. A low fog had rolled in, which blanketed the coast. Only the tip of the lighthouse out his window was poking through what looked like a giant cloud had fallen to earth and flattened out. He felt he no longer needed his bandage, but any sharp movement of his head would still rattle his brain a bit. The thought of what lay ahead had the same effect.

His call to Frances earlier that morning was characteristically mysterious and ominous. Brian knew she had something brewing, and it wasn't his favorite ale. No one was in the office at the Arse just yet, so he figured he'd just leave that call until he was on the road. His shop steward left him a voice mail reminding him that if he was sick on any of his vacation days he could use sick days instead of vacation days.

He had been warned that he could blackout at any time in the few days following his concussion, so he was a little nervous about doing so while driving seventy miles an hour on I-95. A soft knock on his bedroom door brought him back to the one good thing that could be in his future: Portia.

"May I come in?" She had a small tray with two cups of tea and two biscottis balanced on one hand as she entered the room.

Brian racked his brain to think of the last time Frances had been as thoughtful, and he thought maybe it was on their honeymoon but then remembered that was room service. "That's very nice of you. I'll grab some breakfast on the road. I don't want to get too late of a start."

"I'm sorry about your accident. I'm afraid I feel somewhat responsible," Portia said, taking a seat next to the window, looking solemn.

"This is very Edward Hopperish. The lighthouse poking through the cloud, your teacup, the lighting…you."

"There's always a certain sadness to Hopper. Even his landscapes. There's a melancholy, inner spirit." Portia turned toward the window, her face illuminated softly by the hazy morning sunshine. "The ocean is just so powerful," she said, squinting with her left eye to the point that it appeared to be entirely shut tight. "All these years of looking at it and listening to it in every sort of weather; I never tire of it."

"I'm going to miss it," Brian said as he zipped his bag closed. "Is your eye all right?

"Of course, why do you ask?"

"You had it entirely closed."

"No, it's fine, just something in it, that's all." She rose from her chair. "Do you remember that poem from Mason Williams, of all people?"

"Right, the *Classical Gas* guy. In fact, I remember you quoting it; *Never go to the ocean...with a notion...of what you will find*. It's funny the things that stick in your brain after all these years."

"You learned a lot about what sticks in your brain on this trip," Portia said, tapping her own head where Brian had his injury. "I'll see you downstairs," she said exiting.

Brian shoved his last remaining bathroom items into his bag's side pouch and zipped the final zipper for his trip home. He sat on the bed and reached down for his Indian moccasins. As he slid in his foot, he felt sand under his thin sock. He removed his foot and pulled over a garbage can to empty it out, but just as he was about to turn the shoe over he stopped himself. He looked at the grains of white sand on his inner sole, shook them around a little, and placed the shoe on the floor. He slipped his foot in the moccasin and felt the gritty reminder underfoot. He picked up his bags, looked out at the lighthouse from the bedroom for the last time of this trip and hoped it wasn't the last.

Mr. Dawson and Mrs. Pangborne were sitting in the sun room eating breakfast from snack tables with large plastic bibs on. Mrs. Smart was in the kitchen closely examining fruits and vegetables that were stored in the bottom drawer of the refrigerator.

"I don't know why the call this drawer a *crisper*. They should call it a *wilter,*" Mrs. Smart said as she carefully peeled a leaf or two off a browning head of iceberg lettuce and placed it in the trash.

"Wilter weep for me. Wilting willow tree," Portia sang sadly beautiful as she entered the kitchen.

Brian was standing in the foyer, just outside the kitchen, where he could see the sun room off to the right, and dead ahead the picturesque and ever-changing, fog-shrouded lighthouse. "I forgot what a lovely voice you have, Portia. You didn't sing for me once."

"That's something we can save until your next visit," Portia said, winking.

Brian took a step toward Portia with the intention of grabbing a quick hug, and his phone rang. He looked at the number displayed. It was Frances. "Excuse me," Brian said as he walked to the back veranda for some privacy.

"Hello," Brian said as neutrally as he could muster.

"What's that sound in the background?" Frances said as though annoyed.

"The ocean."

"When will you be back? I have some things for you to sign."

"You want me to do my interpretive song signing at Gallaudet? That's great!"

"Don't be a wise ass. When?"

"If I drive straight through, between six and seven."

"I'll have it set up for eight p.m. in my kitchen. And you should know my lawyer will be there, too."

"*Your* kitchen? I haven't signed anything *yet*."

"Eight o'clock."

Brian turned off his phone and breathed in the sea air, so thick he could taste it. As he turned to go back into the house, he noticed Juliette leaning out of an upstairs window, topless. Their eyes met briefly, then she retreated into her room, closing the window quickly. Brian wasn't quite sure what to make of it. Was she giving him a cheap going-away thrill? Pulling a *Woody Allen* wasn't in his moral universe. When he was single and on the prowl, he wouldn't even date a friend's sister. More than likely she sleeps in the nude and was just getting some air. Oddly, Brian wasn't a bit aroused by her youthful, perky boobs.

"Anything urgent?" Portia said as he entered the foyer.

"Oh, just my life, I mean, my wife."

A handful of silverware hit the floor, and Beatrice tip toed to the doorway. "Are you…married?"

Brian and Portia exchanged panicked looks.

"I'm in the final throes of marriage. My wife and I are getting divorced," Brian said flatly as he looked at his watch, "oh, in about ten hours, I think."

"Oh," Beatrice said bewildered, as she returned to the kitchen.

"Mother's rather sensitive when it comes to marriage and divorce and…men," Portia said, trying to comfort Brian.

"Good-bye, Mrs. Smart. I'm leaving now."

Mrs. Smart shuffled into foyer. "It was so nice to see you. I do hope you come back, after you're…settled."

"Thanks," Brian said, giving her a soft peck on the cheek. He stuck his head into the sun room and announced, "See you soon, Mrs. Pangborne!"

"I'm running to blazes!" Mrs. Pangborne said cheerfully, waving her pink paper napkin.

"See ya, Mr. Dawson."

"I've doubled my offer if you do it in the next three months!" Mr. Dawson said with his mouth full of oatmeal.

Brian looked at Beatrice, who luckily didn't react. Portia had a puzzled look on her face and said, "What does that mean?"

"Oh, he made me a…bet about the Red Sox and White Sox."

"I don't believe you, but okay."

"Should I say good-bye to Juliette?"

"Oh, my goodness, yes! Let me get her," Portia said, rushing off down the hall and up the stairs to Juliette's room. The door opened, whispers could be heard, and then footsteps down the stairs.

Juliette was wearing a night dress that looked like it could be a hippie wedding gown. Mother and daughter side by side descending the stairs looked like some kind of baffling time space mix up. Two ages of the same being.

But as Brian saw them both together, resplendent in their beauty, he realized he had such different emotions for both. Even though he had just seen Juliette's naked breasts, and she was a dead ringer for Portia twenty years ago when he loved and lusted for her like only a man his twenties can, he had a warm, tender fondness for her. And seeing Portia, beaming with pride as she strode in step with her daughter down the stairs, he was experiencing an intense desire to hold, to care for, to make love to Portia.

"Juliette wanted to say good-bye," Portia said tenderly.

Brian held his hand out. "Good-bye."

Juliette looked at her mother, and a soft smile crept across her face for the first time. "Good-bye. I hope to see you again," she said taking his hand and softly kissing him on the cheek.

No words were spoken as Brian and Portia departed, until Brian had placed his bags in the van and went around the van to enter the driver's door.

"Be careful over there!" Portia said chuckling.

Brian got in and lowered the passenger window where Portia was standing. "I made it this time, unscathed!"

"I'm so glad," Portia said as she reached in to touch Brian's hand one last time. She turned and went back into the house without turning around.

Brian started the van and made his way back into town. He thought he'd grab a bite to eat just before he got on the freeway. He was tempted to stop into The Laughing Gull to say good-bye to Katie, but decided against it at the last moment.

Just as he was passing the Gull, he noticed the shitty red car pulling out, being driven not by Portia's brother, Richard, but by his Filipina wife with Richard in the passenger seat. He craned his neck to get a good look at it, which triggered a bolt of head pain, and noticed that on the passenger side, there was a long gash along the side of it that he didn't remember seeing before. It was hard to tell, but it looked fresh.

A tank of gas, a cellophane-wrapped bear's claw, and a super-sized cup of gas station mud-coffee would have to do, to make some time on the road. In order to not allow his thoughts to drift into an endless monkey-mind of worry about what Frances had cooking in her kitchen, Brian blasted his favorite sing-along CDs as he drove ten miles an hour above the speed limit south on I-95. By the time he sang every song on *Rubber Soul*, Mose Allison's *The Earth Wants You*, Tom Petty's *Echo* and *The Best of the Temptations*, his voice was hoarse and he was nearly halfway to Washington. And after a Dylan's *Greatest Hits* and two Sinatra CDs, he was sick of singing and driving, and enraged that Frances was going to ambush him in his own house.

It was rush hour traffic from Baltimore into DC, which added to Brian's mad ride to the end of his marriage. Out of songs to occupy his mind, he decided he needed some last minute advice. George had never been married, but in his line of work, he was used to getting out of some tight jams, so he punched him up on speed dial.

"Hello."

"George!"

"Where the hell have you been?" George asked, breathing heavily.

"Are you shtooping?"

"No, just shvitzing. I'm on the treadmill. Where are you?"

"I'm on the Beltway. I've been on the Cape chasing down a dream for a few days."

"Did you find her?"

"Yes. More on that later. Listen, can we meet at the diner? I need a quick Knute Rockne talk before I get my clock cleaned by Frances and some Georgetown lawyer."

"Meet me at Taystee in an hour."

"Okay, mah bruthah!"

When Brian entered, George was already holding court with Bob X and a new jet black hair-dyed, pierced nose, eye brow and lower-lipped gothed-out waitress. He was famished from his long journey with only bear's claws and over-sugared coffee for nourishment. George was just finishing a work story, "So she comes from around the door, stark naked, bends over, and says, *kiss my black ass*."

"What did you do?" the heavily eye-linered waitress asked in amazement.

"I didn't do nothing, but let's just say my partner complied with the citizen's request. Hey, here he is! The prodigal son has returned!" George said, motioning for Brian to take a seat at their usual window booth.

"I am beat," Brian said, his voice heavy with exhaustion, but still glad to see George.

"Coke, meat, and potatoes, please."

"Got it!" Bob X said, rushing into the kitchen with his new apprentice in tow.

Brian slumped in his red pleather booth. "I am so freakin' tired. I don't know how I'm going to deal with Frances."

"Not to worry. You're going in with reinforcements," George said reassuringly.

"I am? Who?"

"You're looking at him."

"Really? Why?"

"Are you kidding me? You think you have a chance against Frances *and* a sleazebag lawyer? I wouldn't give you odds against Frances alone. It's my job to deal with scumbags. I don't even have to say anything. All you have to do is say I'm there as an eyewitness. Then when they ask who I am, I'll just tell them who I am; Federal Agent George Maldonado. Then watch them sweat."

Brian held his head in his hands with his elbows on the table while he watched George reveal his strategy. Dealing with Frances was the last thing he wanted to do. "I just want to pull the plug on this thing."

"See? That's what they want. They know you want out. What do you think, Frances is stupid? She's trying to sucker punch you. I'll have your back, that's all. I have a saying I live by…don't be a prick. But don't be a pussy, either."

Bob X arrived carrying plates of hot food and cold drinks and started laying them out in front of them. "How do you guys like our new waitress? She's in a band. The Sores."

"Just make sure she doesn't ooze anything in my chili," George said dumping Tobasco sauce onto his chili and elbow macaroni.

Both of the parking spaces behind the house were taken; Frances' BMW and a brand new Mercedes with the plates *ISUE4U,* so Brian had to drive around the block and look for a spot in front. Brian and George walked side by side down the block quietly, then stood in front of the front door.

"Should I use my key or ring the bell?" Brian said as he held the key to the front door out.

"Five bucks says your key doesn't even work."

"I didn't even think of that. You're on!"

Brian slowly pushed his key to the door and inserted it into the lock. He smiled wryly as he turned to George. The smile disappeared when he realized he couldn't turn it.

"Shit," Brian said, pulling the key out. "The bitch works fast."

"You ain't seen nothing yet," George said as he pushed the doorbell.

Frances opened the door wearing a dark blue pin-striped business suit, which she saved for important business meetings at work. "Oh," Frances said doing a double take, obviously surprised to see George with Brian. "I thought you'd be alone."

"I try never to be alone," Brian sarcastically said entering. "You remember George."

"Of course. This way," Frances said leading the way to the kitchen.

Already sitting at the kitchen table was an attractive blonde woman in her thirties wearing a black pinstriped suit similar to the one Frances was wearing.

"Dressed to kill," George whispered in Brian's ear.

"This is a dear, dear friend of mine, Kimberly Cunningham," Frances said waving her hand across the table, which was covered with piles of papers and pens.

"Pleased to meet you." Kimberly said as she shook hands vigorously with Brian.

"I don't recall you mentioning Kimberly ever before, Frances." Brian said with mock puzzlement.

"I don't mention every person I know."

"Oh, that's right! That's one of the reasons why we're here."

"Nice to meet you," George said, leaning forward to shake Kimberly's hand. As he finished he whispered to Brian, "Down, boy."

"And who is this?" Kimberly said, smiling broadly as she looked at George.

"I'm sorry. George Maldonado. Well, Agent George Maldonado, ATF. I'm just another dear, dear friend," George said, patting Brian on the back.

Kimberly managed to stretch her broad smile even broader and she tilted her head and glanced at Frances. "A pleasure. Let's get right to it. Frances and I have done some number crunching while you were…on vacation, Brian. And we've come up with some numbers that I think you'll find quite agreeable."

"I've never been one to find numbers disagreeable. Have you, George?"

"Not I. I like numbers."

"Don't start, Brian. This is serious," Frances snarled.

"I am a lawyer, and as you know, this is just an informal, preliminary, non-binding exploratory discussion. If we can agree to terms, we can avoid the cost and aggravation of going through the courts and file a non-contested divorce," Kimberly said as she began to pull documents from piles on the table.

"The last thing we would want is cost and aggravation!" Brian chuckled.

"Stop it, Brian," Frances said through her teeth.

"Brian, here's a list, with bullet points, outlining what we feel is a fair and balanced settlement."

"Fair and balanced? Just like Fox news! I love that, you know, with me having voted for Bush and all," Brian said dripping with sarcasm.

"Take it easy," George said softly in his ear.

Brian sat down opposite Kimberly and began to look at the document. "This is an overview. Okay. Hmmmm...We sell the house for around a million; she gets an $800,000 payoff, I get the left overs, yada yada yada...We divide the other stuff; she gets sixty-five, I get thirty-five more, yada yada yada. Uh, gee where do I sign? Oh wait! Maybe not."

Kimberly and Frances exchanged worried looks.

"And who has already admitted to defiling and desecrating our sacred marriage vows? George, what do you think?"

"I'm no lawyer. But, let me just say this. My dear, dear friend, Brian, has asked me to, you know, just keep an eye on, er, Frances so to speak."

"What? Why ,you sneaky bastard!" Frances said, half coming out her chair and popping a button on her blazer.

"Frances! No," Kimberly sternly said. "Continue..."

"Let's just say, clandestine photography is a hobby of mine. Stills and video, that is."

"Everything fifty-fifty, and I'll sign right now," Brian coyly said.

Frances heaved heavily as the color drained from her face. "We'll talk."

"It's been a pleasure," Brian said, standing up and then bowing to the ladies.

"Oh, how's your head?" Frances asked just as Brian and George exited the kitchen.

"My head? Clearer than ever. Thanks for asking," he said, waving gleefully as they exited.

It didn't take long for Brian to realize that living with George was not much different than living with Frances: They worked different shifts so they barely saw each other; George was sloppy, drunk a lot of the time, and they didn't have sex. The only difficult part was that George's apartment was much smaller than the home Frances was trying to steal from him. Whereas Brian found comfort in his office; it was hard to have any privacy in the living room, where he was sleeping on a pull-out bed.

It had been five days since Brian returned from the Cape, and probably the only thing that was keeping him grounded was the fact that he was living with his old buddy George. Work was a worry, and he sensed something was up at the Arse. He was training a Dartmouth graduate, essentially, to do his job, and not only were coworkers not talking much to him, they gave him that awkward, forced smile people put on while passing in the hallway when they are trying to hide the fact that they heard some awful gossip about you in the re-write room. And all the overtime suddenly disappeared.

He was scheduled to have another confab with Frances and her lawyer Saturday afternoon, which had him trying to prepare himself for every worst case scenario he could come up with. But more disturbing was the fact that he hadn't heard from Portia the entire week, despite the fact that he had left two messages. In all his worst case scenarios, no matter how devastating, he almost always included Portia as the solution. And the fact that she hadn't returned his two messages meant that his worst case scenarios began to sink even lower into desperation. As his options for happiness decreased in Washington, he held out hope that his fantasy of building a new life with Portia on the Cape would be his salvation.

Brian was experimenting with a new approach to his job: not screwing up. Fearing Frances and her lawyer were cooking up a bitch's brew of financial disaster, he was vying for employee of the month as far as he was concerned. He showed up early, stayed late without submitting overtime, and was all smiles as he trained Mr. Ivy Leaguer. He had gotten through his first week back without a hitch until Friday, when he received a phone call on Friday afternoon at four thirty p.m. from his boss asking him if he could come in early for a meeting. Late Friday meetings are never about good news.

When Brian opened the door to his boss's office and saw his shop steward, Gus, his boss Larry, and the vice president of human resources, Dennis, he wanted to jump through the glass of the closed window into the parking lot. Instead, he smiled and shook each of their hands and calmly took a seat.

"Brian," Gus started, his voice fraught with sympathy, "as you know, the union is behind you one thousand percent. We will fight for you. But, the company does have the right to lay off the person with the least seniority."

Brian felt the air escape through every pore of his body. He closed his eyes and saw Frances and her lawyer laughing hysterically at him. He knew that when he switched from being a non-union producer to a union producer/engineer that he would have the least seniority in his union at the station. But Gus assured him it wouldn't make a difference. They hadn't laid anyone off in years.

"We hate to do this to anyone, especially a dedicated employee such as you," Dennis, the V.P. of human resources said without emotion.

Brian thought about grabbing the large glass snow globe off the table and smashing it, then picking up a large shard of glass and holding it to someone's throat-- perhaps his own-- and threatening them with a violent death, but instead he asked Gus, "What's the deal?"

"You get two weeks' severance for each year you've been a union employee…"

"Great, two weeks' salary," Brian said, sarcastically.

"…and one week severance for every year as a non-union employee," Gus said as if reading a death sentence.

Dennis, the HR VP wagged a finger. "We're under no legal obligation to offer severance at all in the state of Virginia."

"Don't forget, Brian," Gus said as if he were about to reveal a spectacular silver lining around Brian's black cloud of disaster, "if someone quits, you're the first on the list to be rehired."

"That's it, then? Do I do my shift tonight?"

"Actually, no…" Gus said, "we have a replacement for tonight. You'll be paid in full for today, though."

The door to the office opened momentarily, and the Dartmouth grad poked his head in briefly and said, "Oh, I'll come back later."

Brian figured that was his replacement, but kept didn't say anything as the three others shared embarrassed glances. He stood up quickly, and said, "You'll be hearing from my lawyer. I'll go get my things and be gone."

He walked out without turning, but heard them rustling together silently, waiting for the door to close behind him. Brian wondered if maybe getting a lawyer might actually be a good idea. Then shook his head…*nah.*

Kimberly and Frances sat in the kitchen with towers of white file folder boxes surrounding the table. They were well aware that the next afternoon could change the quality of Frances' life forever. The front door bell rang, and Frances jumped out of her chair.

"Thank God! You'd think they had to churn the cheese themselves in the time it takes them to deliver!" Frances exclaimed, wasting no time to get the pizza at the front door.

Kimberly was amazed to see Frances return while carrying two pizza boxes, a large paper bag, and a half-eaten slice dangling out of her mouth.

"I couldn't wait," Frances garbled.

She put the cardboard pizza boxes with a caricature of a mustached Italian wearing a chef's hat on the granite counter and ripped open the brown paper bag revealing two Styrofoam salad containers. "Help yourself."

Kimberly finished banging away on her calculator, then pulled the footlong paper from the machine and began to study it for errors. "I'll be right there. Good," she triumphantly said.

"What's good?"

"With this new formula, even if he's being aggressive, you're payoff will still be just under a million over five years easy, with him bearing most of the tax burden."

"Ooh, that would be nice!" Frances said dropping a gooey glob of mozzarella cheese into her grinning mouth. "What can we do to make him go for it? He's usually such a pussy, I don't how he's gotten balls all of a sudden."

"He doesn't have balls. It's his G-man friend. I deal with those macho dicks all the time. You just smile and show some tit, and they're like Silly Putty," Kimberly said as she picked the black olives from her salad and dropped them in the trash.

"What if he tries to stick it to us?"

"Well, does he have the goods on you or not?" Kimberly said sternly. "Don't lie to me. I do it for a living."

"I guess he…could," Frances said sheepishly as she shoved three quarters of a slice into her mouth. "I haven't been too…discreet lately."

"That's why we have to get him to agree to this uncontested divorce with mutually agreeable numbers. A judge is not going to look favorably on triple x porno pictures of some triple-D bosomed, bleached blonde, slutty wife with no kids, screwing half the office softball team when making a judgment."

"Well, thanks for that vote of confidence!" Frances said, slamming down the crust of her slice into the box.

"If it goes to court, that's the way his lawyer will portray you, that's all. Get real, Frances!"

"And who the fuck told you about the softball team?"

"Oh shit. That was just a guess. Let's crunch some more numbers."

Brian was closing up the sofa bed and as he bent forward to replace the cushions, he was reminded of the iron bar that stuck in his back all night from under the two inch pad. You couldn't really call it a mattress.

"How do I look?" George said as he entered the room wearing a black suit, white tie, and black tie.

"All you need is hat and a harmonica, and you can go as one of the Blues Brothers."

"All right, I won't wear the glasses."

"Why do you even have such a get-up?"

"Every ATF agent at work has this outfit. There's a funeral home down the block and we all work there as pall bearers and drivers when we're off duty," George said, walking into kitchen. "Where do you think all those pall bearers come from at funerals? You think everybody has six good- looking guys with the same black suit in their family?" George said as he twirled around with a banana in his hand, showcasing his duds.

Brian grabbed a banana from the bowl and sat on a chrome kitchen chair. "What I want to know is, why do you have to look like a pall bearer for the meeting with Frances and Kimberly? It's not my funeral…yet."

"Where's your sense of drama? I've got to dress the part of a hard-working, no bullshit, private dick."

"Maybe just dick."

"This is like going in there wearing a sign that says *I'm cheap, I'm hungry, I'm angry, don't fuck with me!*"

"In that case you should wear it all the time," Brian said as he finished his banana and threw the peel across the room and right into the garbage can.

"My turn," George said as he turned his back to the can, threw his peel, missing the can by a mile, and knocked a glass off the counter and into the sink, shattering it.

"I hope your judgment improves once the meeting starts."

"How do you know what to ask for in this meeting? This is some complicated shit. You could get screwed for life."

Brian looked at George and dropped his head. He could feel the after-effects of a mild concussion, getting laid off, and getting divorced.

"Well, you know what I mean," George said, trying to comfort Brian.

"I looked on the Internet and found the guidelines for the District of Columbia in divorce settlements. They know just as well as I do what they are. So our job today is just to intimidate them, like the other day. Make them think we're a little crazy, we've got the goods on her, and…"

"You've got your back up against the wall!" George gleefully shouted. "It always works!"

"She will not want to go to court. I'm going to lay some numbers on her, and say we sign the uncontested divorce papers with our numbers and get out nice and clean."

"I love going undercover!" George said, putting his dark sunglasses on. He talked into his sleeve and whispered, "We've got a visual on the perpetrator. Five-foot-four, blonde hair, huge tits, possibly double Ds…"

"All right Kojak, simmer down. Let's go," Brian said, pointing towards the front door.

Being around sixty degrees, it had to be the warmest day of the year. The ride through the park with the windows open and slight tinges of green on the trees gave Brian a carefree feeling. He knew that even if Frances took him to the cleaners and he never got his job back, he was beginning a new life. A life he let slip away from him, ever so slowly. Small concessions in his marriage gave way to capitulation and ultimately, unconditional surrender. He wasn't even sure what he wanted from his new life, except that he wanted to feel at least useful.

They pulled up to his driveway, and Brian was again annoyed that both parking spaces were occupied. He rang the front door bell, and Frances answered wearing a pink sweat suit. The kind of outfit that was probably originally worn to hide fat, but over time only accentuates it.

"Nice day," Frances said flatly, as she waved them into the home.

Kimberly was at the kitchen table, wearing a running outfit of long pants and a zip up jacket, with her piles of papers neatly laid out in front of her like an elaborate last meal.

"I'm so glad winter is finally over," Kimberly cheerfully said.

"There's still some chill left in the air," Brian said taking his seat next to George, "but I expect that to be gone soon."

"Let's get down to the brass tacks," Kimberly sternly said. "We've gone over the numbers, and I think we've reached a place I think that is mutually agreeable."

"Can I say something here?" George said innocently, looking at Kimberly and Frances for their approval. The two looked at each other, rolling their eyes. "We're all friends here, right? I mean, nobody wants to hurt anybody else, right?" George stood up, took a position behind Brian, and placed his hands on his shoulders. "Brian doesn't want anything but the best for Frances."

Brian strained to keep a poker face. He couldn't believe the poise George was exhibiting.

"We've talked long and hard. Oh yeah, we started out thinking how we could nail Frances with what we've got on her, but we also, we also thought about the good times. About how much in love these two were...and we...cried."

Brian didn't know if he could keep a straight face any longer. He started biting on the inside of his lower lip rapidly. But more important was the expression on Kimberly and Frances' faces. They seemed to be buying it. Go figure.

"We cried and we cried. And we vowed we would be open minded and willing to sacrifice," George said as he took his seat again. "To a point. A point that is fair to both parties. Two parties who have no children, and in fact, one party has a great job with the federal government, and the other just got...officially laid off."

A tiny, high-pitched gasp was heard, almost a whimper, coming from Frances.

"You're laid off or fired?" Kimberly quickly asked.

"Laid off. Cutbacks. Last to join the union, first to be let go," Brian said dejectedly.

"Here's what we suggest," George said, rising again out of his chair. "We're going to get a cup of coffee. I suggest you look at your numbers one more time. We'll be back in one hour. Come on, Brian."

Brian got up and followed George out the front door onto the sidewalk. “Where the hell did you come up with that line of bullshit? I thought I was going to bust a gut.”

“I feel like sneaking back in there and watching them squirm. Right is might, mah bruthah!” George said, doing an end zone dance next to the van.

“We haven’t scored yet, so no flagrant celebrations,” George said, starting up the Quest.

CHAPTER ELEVEN

Over coffee, Brian and George didn't dream they'd get anything near a fifty-fifty split. But they expected at least a few percentage points as a starting point for negotiations. So when they returned to the kitchen table and were greeted by a curt "Take it or leave it, girly-man! Nothing changes. Eight hundred K and a sixty-five thirty-five split is it!" as Frances sat there drinking a glass of red wine from a tall-stemmed glass, they were stunned.

"That's it. You want out? Then sign or forever hold your piece. That's p-i-e-c-e," Frances said smugly as she spilled a couple of drops of wine that went down her chin and dripped into her cleavage.

Brian looked at George, hoping for a quick comeback line about catching Frances in bed with a mule or something that would scare the bejesus out of Frances and her lawyer, but a shrug was all the George could muster.

"Let me think about it," Brian said, knowing full well there wasn't much to think about. He *did* want out, but he wanted at least a safety net. He knew friends and relatives who had been drawn and quartered by ugly, public divorces, and he didn't want to go through that. Not now. So Brian and George quietly exited without a whimper of protest and their tails between their legs.

"I could probably get fifty grand out of this, if I sign," Brian said, raising a glass of beer in the Argentinean restaurant around the block from George's apartment.

"It's better than a poke in the eye with a hot poker," George said earnestly.

"I'll spend it on hookers, gambling, and partying and the rest I'll just piss away," Brian joked. I think I might do some traveling," Brian said just as his phone vibrated in his pocket. He looked at the caller ID hoping it was Portia, but it was a number he didn't recognize, so he let his voice mail pick it up. The very thought of Portia changed his mood.

Although the disbursement of funds would take a while, an uncontested divorce could become official in six months as long as they weren't cohabitating and in total agreement on the numbers.

He closed his eyes and imagined Portia and he sitting on the back veranda on a balmy summer evening. He wondered if he would have ratcheted up the timeline of his divorce with such urgency if Portia wasn't in the picture. But was she?

"So what are you going to do?"

"When?" Brian asked, his daydream interrupted.

"*When*. Now! Do you want to go out somewhere? Have a few drinks. You'll have your freedom. Wasn't that the whole point?"

"Oh, yeah, that," Brian said solemnly.

"Isn't this what you wanted? Isn't this a best case scenario?"

"Would you mind if I went back to the apartment and got some sleep?"

"Dude, you gotta buck up. You get some cash, freedom, and the time to use it. Ninety-nine percent of the world would kill for what you got. If that's not floating your boat, you've got to figure out what that is and do *that,*" George earnestly said.

"You piss me off when you're this right."

"Come on, we'll pick up a six pack on the way home and watch TV. I Tivoed *Dog the Bounty Hunter*, brah," George said, giving Brian the Hawaiian extended thumb and pinky hand gesture for *hang loose.*

It took a week for Brian to go through the house and salvage whatever bits and pieces he could recover before the truck came from Goodwill to take away the things he and Frances decided weren't worth keeping. Amazingly there were two entire rooms stacked from floor to ceiling full of things that neither of them liked or wanted, yet they both had assumed the other person found them precious. Everything that Brian decided was worth keeping fit into a six-by-six storage locker at the Silver Spring U-Store. As he pushed in the rasp of the lock, he wondered where these items would wind up next. Would they go from here into a Goodwill truck like the other stuff that lost their worth over time? The only things Brian kept at George's were his laptop, a few books, his MP3 player, some clothes, and a couple of boxes of papers and files, which easily fit into a small corner of the living room. Yet, for years he had the impression that all that…stuff…was important. He couldn't leave all that stuff. And now, he didn't want any of it.

Brian had a schedule in his head for Portia, and his self-imposed deadline was at hand. He told himself he would give her two weeks to answer the couple of messages he left in the first day or so after he returned to DC, and two weeks was up. During the drive back to George's he mulled over the reasons that may have prevented Portia from calling him. He also went through many excuses. He didn't like to think of them as excuses, because they more than likely would be lies. And he had hoped that his new relationship with her would be based on truth this time. He parked in front of the brownstone where George's apartment was and decided the time had come. He dialed Portia's number.

There was no answer, so he decided to leave a message; "Portia. Hi. This is Brian… Listen, er, ah, I've got to talk to you. I've got an emergency, and I might have to leave the country…"

"Hello, hello! Brian! Are you okay?" Portia asked, obviously after monitoring his message.

"Portia," Brian said with duplicitous feelings; at once relieved he finally got her and at the same time hurt that she probably has been monitoring his calls all the time and not responding. "I've been trying to reach you…"

"Are you okay, Brian? Do you have to leave the country?"

"I'm sorry. That was a lie. I just wanted to emphasize my need to find you. Did you know I've called you several times?"

Silence.

"No. I didn't know you called," Portia whispered, sounding disheartened. "Mother's very ill. She..." Portia couldn't continue.

"What? What's wrong?"

"Mother had a stroke. She's still in the hospital. I just came home to get some things," Portia weakly said. "I miss you."

"I'll be there in ten hours."

"No, don't, it's too much. I can handle it...alone."

"Do you want to?"

"No."

"I'll be at the house in ten hours. Bye."

"Good-bye."

Brian grabbed his things and wrote a note for George--*Needed on the Cape. Will call.*-- and dropped it on the kitchen table. His van wasn't as loaded as it was when he left on his previous trip. Although he was hungry, about to jump on I-95 during rush hour for a ten-hour journey and was about to leap headfirst into a family crisis, he felt a strange mix of sadness and purposefulness. He didn't know what he would be doing, but for the first time in ages, he felt like he was needed. And on a much deeper level, doing something that boys are trained for from their earliest sense of awareness: coming to the rescue. There's a powerful place deep in every male's brain that was nurtured from the first time he was plopped in front of the television that taps into the concept of coming to the rescue. Whether it was watching Superman, Scooby-Doo, Popeye, or Underdog, boys could be sucking their thumb and pooping into Pampers and understand that the greatest deed a person could perform is come to the aid and assistance of someone in need. And of course, when the rescuing somehow involves a female with a romantic link, there's nothing more primal.

Brian gauged the time remaining as he subtracted the miles to Hampton North from his trip counter and wondered if this feeling was something that an ATF agent, like George, experienced on a daily basis. Was there a focused pursuit of truth, justice, and the American way, like on Superman? Or did it merely become a job, even if one actually is helping society fight bad guys on a daily basis? He wondered if he hadn't been laid off, and still stuck in a quagmire of a marriage, if he would be so quick to take this journey. He didn't really know. All Brian knew was that Portia needed help and he was on his way to help her.

Brian didn't know a lot about strokes. He did have an uncle who died a few weeks after one hit him, never regaining consciousness. Then again he remembered a coworker who had a stroke when she was forty-five, and after a few months made a full recovery with no noticeable after- effects. He knew Beatrice was a strong matriarch, but if she wasn't able to fully recover, he wasn't certain that Portia would have the strength to go it alone. Then Brian had a thought that caused him to grip the steering wheel white-knuckled: *What about Richard*? Portia's scumbag brother would probably see this as an opening for him to weasel his way into the picture. Without trying to prejudge too harshly, somebody who has a mail order bride, beats a kid in public, and is known as the town psycho, probably will not suddenly be a source of compassion and strength in light of the current circumstances in the Smart household. Brian thought that Richard is probably already calculating how to grab whatever he can as quickly as possible, which caused Brian to turn off his cruise control and go ten miles an hour faster than it was set.

As Brian watched the signs that counted down the mileage to Boston whiz by, he couldn't help but contemplate how much evil just might lurk inside Richard. He even racked his brain to recall the last time he had been in a fistfight. It was probably when he was in high school and playing pick-up ice hockey on the frozen over softball fields in Lincoln Park by the lakefront. He remembered the feeling of getting an elbow in the teeth, seeing the blood on the sleeve of the white Blackhawk's home jersey he was wearing, and the feeling of satisfaction after dropping his gloves and feeling his fist smack against the jaw of the asshole who elbowed him. His hand hurt like hell afterwards, but it was well worth it. He didn't think Richard would be the type to allow himself to be physically challenged in person. Someone who gets his jollies by beating the crap out of a toddler is most likely too devious for that. He'd probably devise some covert cowardly violent act, the bastard. The thing about sociopaths is you never know how they will act or when. They have no moral compass. Just a strident, focused notion that they are entitled to something and nothing should stand in their way.

"Goddammed potholes!" Brian yelled to no one as his front wheel hit a pothole so deep and jagged on the highway that it sounded like his axle broke in two. It didn't. But it did give him a reminder of the concussion he had just after his head banged against the headrest. And the pain also jolted him into an awful realization.

"That fucker," Brian whispered. The jarring of his brain brought him back to the moment that night when a car swerved into him, which could have been fatal. And just then he flashed on Richard's car with the gash on the side that his wife was driving as he left town. *Of course,* he thought to himself. In his twisted, not-so-passive, but possibly criminally motivated mind, Richard followed them, waited for the perfect moment and swerved into him; possibly in a fit of rage or maybe in a cruelly calculated act to scare him off. Or worse. The miles couldn't pass fast enough. Now that it was dark and the rush hour traffic long gone, he set his cruise control to fourteen miles over the speed limit and zipped through New England, cutting an hour or possibly more off his trip. That also meant he had to constantly check his rear view mirror and the traffic ahead for state troopers. The radio was off, the heater was on low, and the only sound was the thumpety thump every few seconds of the seams in the road marking the distance every twenty feet or so.

Brian couldn't help himself. He kept seeing Richard in his mind, plotting against Portia to abscond with everything. It was merely Bea's strength and iron will that kept Richard at bay, and everyone knew it. Portia didn't have the stomach or the kick-in-the-balls gene that was needed to battle him. Was that the reason Brian was so possessed in his determination to save the damsels in distress? Was it purely caveman instinct? No. It was love. The mere thought that Portia and her daughter might be in harm's way brought out a rage in Brian he hadn't felt since he was a confused teenager, a rebel without a clue, and felt that his family, his classmates, even his best friends were against him. He soon learned it was merely his imagination, cooked up in a hormone-saturated brain. Was it the same now? He didn't care.

Seeing red flashing lights up ahead on the shoulder, he tapped on the brake pedal, disengaging the cruise control. He slowed down to the speed limit as he got closer to the scene and pressed the brake again, slowing to looky-loo speed as he passed the accident site. An SUV was in a drainage ditch, and a team of emergency workers were extricating someone with the Jaws of Life. He didn't stop, but was going slow enough to see a person in excruciating pain, their face bloody and screaming in agony. *At least they were conscious*, he thought to himself.

He sped up to fourteen miles over the speed limit and set the cruise control again. A sign read *Boston 40 miles*, which meant his turnoff was in twenty. He could be at the Smart's in less than half an hour. He held the wheel with both hands and thought of George Reeves as Superman, Lois Lane and Jimmy Olsen cowering behind him as the bullets bounced off his chest. Superman didn't look angry that a crook was trying to kill him, Lois, and Jimmy; he looked *annoyed*. He gazed upon the stupidity of the inferior human being thinking he could bring harm to Superman. What a fool! Brian wasn't afraid. And his back was just about against the wall.

It was well after midnight when Brian pulled in front of the Smart's house. There were still a few lights emanating from some windows, upstairs and down. Brian opened his window, and it was dead quiet except for the ever present sound of waves crashing on the rocks just beyond the Smart's veranda. Being so late, he wasn't sure if he should knock on the door, call on the phone, or check back into the motel. But after sitting in his vehicle for the past nine or so hours, he decided to stretch his legs and left his car in front.

Brian took the path around the house to walk on the beach. It was overcast with no stars visible and a sliver of the moon barely discernible as the clouds passed each other. The sky looking north, up the coast, was pink from the city lights from the South Boston suburbs. But looking south, the sky was nearly black. There was just enough light being thrown from the solitary street lamp to light Brian's way to the water's edge. The tide was out, so there were flotsam and jetsam left from the high tide. He reached down and picked up what looked like an interesting piece of driftwood. But as soon as he touched it, he realized it was covered with some kind of black gooey tar. He looked at his fingers on his right hand and noticed they were stained, and stunk like street tar.

A flood light from the back veranda of the Smart's was switched on, illuminating much of the beach just to his left. He walked toward the back stairs to see if Portia or Juliette were perhaps outside getting some air.

He stepped across the damp seaweed and onto small, round beach stones that squished down into the soft sand below his running shoes. He paused on a large, flat rock several yards from the back stairs and closed his eyes. He thought about what lay ahead. He knew he was ready to take on whatever domestic strife that would come his way. He might get annoyed, but he vowed not to get angry.

"Portia?" he asked the shadowy figure in the dark corner of the deck.

The dark figure leaned into the light, and Brian could see it was, indeed, her. She put her hand over her eyes to shade the bright light. "Brian! You made it!" she said happily, then reached inside the door and switched off the light.

Brian was momentarily blinded by the loss of light and slightly tripped as he bounded up the stairs to meet Portia. They both groped for each other in the darkness and were relieved when they grasped onto each in comfort.

"I wanted to call you. But I know you have so much going on in your own life," Portia said softly into Brian's ear.

"I'm glad I finally got you," Brian said relieved. "I was worried. I took care of everything back home."

Portia leaned back. Their eyes had adjusted to the darkness and they could see each other now. Portia squinted her left eye shut and studied Brian's face up close. "Mother would've been happy to hear that, as she spied on us from one of the windows."

"Is your left eye okay? You seem to be squinting with it even more."

"Nothing wrong. Just a nervous tick."

"How is Beatrice?" Brian asked, studying Portia's tired face, which revealed the lack of sleep and stresses of the past few days.

"We have to decide by tomorrow whether or not to do brain surgery to take care of a clot in her brain," Portia said, her hands firmly grasping Brian's.

"Is she conscious?"

"Not since the stroke. Funny, it was Mrs. Pangborne who found her collapsed in the kitchen. Mrs. Pangborne came into my room in a panic, screaming that the dog needed a bath. She led me to Mother. It's chilly. Let's go inside."

Brian and Portia walked in the darkness to the sun porch. Mr. Dawson's books and notes were still piled neatly on his tables, and the same window was still slightly open the same amount it was when he left. Brian could hear and feel a slight bit of sand underfoot as he walked across the wooden peg-and-groove floor.

"Should I turn on a light?" Portia said as they sat on the love seat-sized rattan couch.

"Nah. I've had lights shining in my face for the past nine hours. How is Mrs. Pangborne?" Brian said, settling in nicely next to Portia.

"Fine. As is Mr. Dawson."

"And Juliette?"

Portia lowered her head. "She's holding up okay."

"And you?"

Portia slowly lifted her head, giving the impression it weighed too much for her neck. "I'm okay. We hired an aide. A nice Filipina lady named Reyna. I don't know how we'll pay for her, but we will manage."

Brian thought to himself about mentioning that fucker, Richard, but decided against it. "So everyone is about as well as can be expected?"

"Yes. I'm tired," Portia said, gazing out the windows facing south. "Are you separated?"

Brian began patting from his chest down to his ankles, "I don't think so. Not since I last checked."

Portia looked at him and smiled a crooked smile. "I don't think I've laughed since you left. There's finally a break in the clouds. There's the first star of the night."

"We're not officially separated. But unofficially, we're galaxies apart," Brian said, leaning closer to Portia and placing his hand behind her neck.

Their lips met and they kissed a long, slow kiss. Portia's tongue softly slipped into Brian's mouth, which elevated Brian's sexual desire to a level he hadn't felt in a long, long time. They stopped kissing, and Portia collapsed against Brian as she kicked off her shoes and put her legs on the couch. The moon peeked from behind a cloud, and a few more stars emerged.

"I prepared your room for you," Portia said into Brian's chest.

Brian didn't respond. He just pulled Portia even closer to him. He stroked her hair and leaned closer to smell its fragrance.

"We should probably get some sleep," Brian said, tenderly squeezing the muscle that connects the shoulder and the neck.

"I'm going to stay here for a while. You go up to your room. I'll see you in the morning," Portia said with her eyes closed and her face revealing the joy she felt from Brian rubbing her neck and shoulders. He kissed her neck one last time and headed for his room. He looked back just before he exited the room and saw Portia curled up like a cat on the small couch. Brian slowly tiptoed over to her, leaned over, and whispered in her ear.

"Care to spoon in my room?"

They walked hand in hand into Brian's room, quietly closed the door, and tiptoed to the bed like teenagers in love.

CHAPTER TWELVE

Brian awakened with a pain that rivaled getting smashed by a swerving car and planting his skull on the pavement. It only took him a moment to realize he had forgotten to flatten his pillow out and had a crook in his neck. But wait! Where's Portia? He scanned the room for clues, and on the top of his *Sporting News* was a handwritten note-- *Went to hospital early. Here's address. Come when you get up. We might bring Mother home today. We'll need you. Ask Juliette if you need anything.*

Brian looked at his watch and saw it was just after nine. He could hear voices downstairs, assuming it was Juliette, Mrs. Pangborne, and Mr. Dawson having breakfast. He pulled open the curtains and opened the window fully. The cloudy evening had given way to a superb spring morning, with dog walkers on the beach and even a wetsuit-clad surfer waiting for a swell.

After a quick shower and shave, Brian bounded down the stairs to greet Juliette briefly before he hit the hospital. He looked in the sun room where Mr. Dawson and Mrs. Pangborne were gumming their oatmeal from folding snack trays. He then peeked around the doorway and saw Juliette sitting at the kitchen table drinking a cup of tea.

"Hello?" Brian said, and no sooner did the word leave his lips than Juliette dropped her cup and reached for a large knife that was on the table.

"Christ!" Juliette said, firmly gripping the knife handle then realizing it was him.

"Sorry I startled you," he said, stepping softly into the room.

"Don't sneak up on me like that," Juliette said, releasing her grip from the knife and wiping up the spilled tea. "Mom told me you arrived. Did you sleep all right?"

"Actually, I slept a little crooked and have a stiff neck."

"Want me to work it out for you?"

Brian wasn't sure what to say. Recalling the time she looked out the window topless had him thinking twice about accepting her offer. *There's nothing sexual about someone rubbing someone's neck*, he thought to himself. Then he remembered rubbing Portia's neck the night before and where that led. The very thought of something even hinting of sexuality where Juliette was concerned gave him a deep, disturbing feeling.

"Uh, no thanks. I'll just hit the road. I have the address to the hospital. Bye," Brian said haltingly as he backed out of the room. He exited the front door and stopped halfway down the path. He walked back several steps and separated a few branches that blocked the view into the kitchen. From where he was he could see Juliette still sitting at the kitchen table, holding her tea cup with both hands just under her nose, with a huge ear-to-ear grin.

Brian knew the hospital well, since he had been there just a short while ago, but he would trade that pain for the pain he now felt as he waited for the elevator.

The nurse's station was busy with activity on the third floor, and Brian felt awkward standing there, not wanting to be obtrusive by asking where Room 3004 was. Instead he figured he'd find it on his own, walking down the hall. He immediately recalled the hospital sounds of that night he was admitted; the groans, the shouts, the family members whispering outside doorways, and the occasional weeping.

He stood outside 3004 looking through the open door, and in the bed closest to the door there was an elderly thin man fast asleep in the sunny room. Beyond the curtain next to his bed, Portia sat in a chair by the window reading a dog-eared paperback book. Being silhouetted against the bright window, she appeared to be just a shadow. Brian stepped past the sleeping man, who looked quite dead, except for the beeping EKG he was hooked up to.

"Did you order a pizza?"

Portia stood up and turned toward her mother lying in the bed, whose eyes were open and seemed to be looking at the television, which happened to have *The Price is Right* on.

Portia looked at her mother and smiled slightly. "She's been a little more alert this morning." She turned her head to Brian. "I decided not to do the surgery. I don't think she'd survive. She's just too hard-headed."

"How long is she staying here?" Brian asked as he stroked Portia's cheek.

"She can go home."

"When?"

"Now."

"I'm ready when you are."

Checking out of a hospital turned out to be even more complicated than checking in. They're quick to get you out of the bed and into a wheelchair, but once you are in the wheelchair and out of the room, you feel like a lone piece of luggage on an airport baggage carousel going around and around waiting to be claimed.

As Mrs. Smart sat in her wheelchair just yards from the Plexiglass-encased booth that was her last stop before heading home, Brian thought that she didn't actually look that bad. Her eyes were open, she had color in her face, and her wrinkles seemed to have disappeared. But there was a vacant look in her eyes that belied the fact that she had a full sea bag, but it wasn't stenciled right.

Portia hadn't taken her hand off the wheelchair handle for the entire half hour they stood in line. She was constantly touching her mother tenderly and whispering in her ear.

"The doctors gave me a list of some items we'll need for mother's sick bed, Brian. They also want to give me some documentation of her condition in case we need it. Why don't you go pick up the supplies and meet us back at home," Portia said as she brushed Beatrice's hair.

"Are you sure you'll be okay?"

"Yes. Someone will help me get her into the car, and Juliette can help me if we arrive home before you do. Reyna starts tomorrow."

Brian gave Portia a kiss and took the list from her. "I'll be quick," he said, sticking the list in his pocket and heading for the medical supply department.

Smart House felt different now, and everyone knew it. Probably even Mrs. Pangborne, who stood and stared as Bea was wheeled through the front door. Beatrice sat quietly as Portia gave Brian instructions on where to put the supplies in the bedroom closet. The sadness mixed with the sea air and the soft sound of the ocean as Portia and Brian tended to their tasks. A deep vertical line had invaded the space between Portia's eyebrows, just above the bridge of her nose. Brian wondered if perhaps he just didn't notice it before or it had appeared as suddenly as the clot in Beatrice's head.

"Did the doctor's have anything to say about how long her recovery would be?" Brian asked as he tightened the screws on a bed railing that would now be part of the bed.

"They didn't give her much hope for a full recovery," Portia said, unpacking a few Depends and putting them in a dresser drawer. "There are a lot of unanswered questions rolling in with the day's tide. We'll get mother settled in and have some lunch," Portia said smiling, which made the tension line between her eyes disappear.

The moment came when bed liners were on the mattress, the bed pan stored under the bed, and the television was turned to face Beatrice from the position she was likely to be in for a long period of time. Portia and Brian lifted Beatrice out of her wheelchair and placed her in the bed.

"I think she wet herself," Portia said. "Brian, I truly appreciate you helping us out. But I just want to reassure you that I don't expect you to change Mother's Depends."

"I'll be in the sun room if you need me," Brian said, taking the hint.

Brian stood by the door that led out to the veranda, where he could see Mr. Dawson in his usual location writing furiously on a yellow legal pad.

Mr. Dawson lifted his head and squinted at Brian. "I was ready to up it to ten grand. That's a crying shame."

The thought crossed Brian's mind to expose the evil old geezer to Portia, but thought he could be a source of much needed income and wasn't worth the risk. But now that Beatrice was incapacitated, who would do all the work needed to keep two geriatric boarders? He couldn't imagine how much money they charged to care for Mr. Dawson and Mrs. Pangborne but assumed it provided the lion's share of their income. Why else would anyone put up with that mean old bastard?

At that moment, Beatrice made a sharp guttural sound for the first time since she had been placed in the bed. It was so loud that it caused Brian to go back upstairs and into the room. The three of them looked at Bea in stunned silence as Bob Barker's voice on the television described a matching pair of jet skis.

"Do you think she can hear us?" Juliette whispered.

Portia muted the television and bent over, getting within inches of Bea's ear. "Can you hear me, Mother? Can you hear me?" Portia studied Bea's face for any sign of a response, but there was none. "Is that a tear?" Portia asked, staring intently and wiping a bit of moisture from below her mother's eye. Bea seemed to be watching the two models on the television screen as each mounted a jet ski and waved to the audience.

"What were you talking about when she made the sound?" Brian asked.

Portia inched toward Bea and said "We mentioned dinner, Mr. Dawson, and…"

"Richard." Portia and Juliette said in unison.

"They say that sometimes stroke victims can hear and understand what's going on around them, even though they can't communicate," Juliette said, stepping closer to Bea. "Maybe she reacted to Richard."

"I'll sit with Mom for a while," Portia said, pulling a chair close to the bedside.

"I'll stay, too," Juliette said as she sat next her mother.

Brian left them by Bea's bedside and stepped into the doorway of the sun room, where Mrs. Pangborne and Mr. Dawson sat in silence on opposite sides of the bright room. Neither Mrs. Pangborne nor Mr. Dawson even noticed he was standing there. He realized there were five other people in the house and the only human voice that could be heard was Bob Barker's. A gull laughed on the veranda, and Brian stepped to the window. The bird was in the process of noisily tearing apart some kind of flesh. He surmised it was probably either from a fish or possibly the remains of a sandwich. Gulls were scavengers. Opportunists. And they weren't quiet about it. He opened to door to the veranda, and the gull flew off. Brian stepped over to the grisly remains and gasped. It was Puck. The poor kitty was dead, smashed by a large rock, and the gull was tugging on its exposed intestines like a vulture. He picked up the rock and was so shocked a jolt of fear zapped his nervous system, causing him to jump backward. The kitty was decapitated and the head was nowhere to be found. Instead of screaming bloody hell like he wanted to, he discreetly grabbed a garbage bag from under the barbeque, picked the dead animal up in it, then inverted the bag so the poor thing was hidden inside the black trash bag.

"I wondered what Richard had been up to?" Brian asked the screeching gulls on the beach as he tried to think of a way to break the news of the tragic demise of the Smart's only pet.

"Brian!" Portia said from the veranda door. "We found some things we want you to look at."

Brian held the bag tightly. "Portia!" he said in a stage whisper. She sensed something was wrong and walked to him.

"What is it?"

"I'm afraid I have some very bad news."

Portia grabbed at her ears and closed her eyes.

"I'm afraid that Puck is dead. He's in the bag. I…found him just a minute ago right here."

"Oh no," Portia quietly sobbed.

"How did he die?"

"I can't be sure, but he may have…"

"What?" Portia asked, eyes ablaze.

"He may have been killed. By a sea gull or…something."

"Sea gulls don't kill cats. An owl might, but only at night, and Puck was in the house last night."

"So it's the *or something*, then?" Brian asked, sensing that they both had the same fear.

"Or some *one*."

"He was killed. With a big rock," Brian said, withholding the fact that his head was missing.

"Richard left his calling card," Portia said strangely numb, then slumped into whimpering, quivering pile of weeping flesh.

Brian tried to console her but knew it was hopeless so just hugged and hugged and hugged her, joining in the sad crying jag. Then Portia shot straight up so fast her feet were briefly an inch or so off the planet. A seething rage emanated from her eyes and radiated outward enveloping her entire body and everything within ten feet, including Brian.

"Are you all right?" Brian asked, reaching out to touch her shoulder, but she instinctively jerked away. She stood rigid, vibrating almost imperceptibly.

"He's coming for Juliette now, I know it. He is…he is…" Portia said in a scary Linda Blair-as-the-devil voice.

"What? Richard?" Brian said standing eyeball to eyeball, trying to connect with her far-away eyes.

"He did the same thing to my kitty, Banquo, and said if I ever told he'd do it to…Mother."

Brian was shocked into terrible mental calculations; *Richard killed her cat and said he'd do it to their mother? What the fuck?!* "Tell me, Portia. Why?"

Portia's quick vibrations slowed to trembling from head to toe. "He made me *do something*…don't ask me what! And the next day, Banquo was dead. Smashed. No head. I was nine. Richard told me if I told anyone, he'd do the same to Mother. Smash her head and kill her."

Brian tried to stop her trembling with an embrace but it was too powerful. He held her close anyway. Suddenly her trembling stopped cold and she looked at Brian, fiercely.

"Mother somehow kept him away from us. From me. And later, from Juliette," Portia said, composing herself, smoothing her hair, wiping her tears. "And when Father was found dead, they said it was suicide. But we weren't so sure." She put her hand on the bag that held Puck. "I think I'll have him cremated. Puck, I mean. Give me ten minutes to tell Juliette and meet me in Bea's room." Portia said in full control of her senses and the situation now.

Brian kissed Portia on the lips, walked to the high water mark on the beach and just stared out at the lazy, powerful ocean. He battled with his thoughts as horrific scenes of Portia's abuse flashed. He then heard a scream. He knew Portia had just told Juliette.

After Brian walked the beach alone for a half hour, he went up to Bea's bedroom. Portia sat silently next to Beatrice with an old White Owl cigar box on her lap. Brian stood in the doorway and waited. He could see the redness still in their eyes.

"I looked at Puck," Juliette seethed.

Brian and Portia exchanged helpless looks.

"I won't let this go on," Juliette added matter-of-factly.

Brian and Portia exchanged worried looks. They both sensed Juliette meant it.

"Look at this," Portia said, adjusting her glasses on the bridge of her nose, changing the topic of conversation as she lifted the lid on the box.

A slight smell of cigars became apparent as Brian leaned to examine the contents of the box. "Where did you find this?"

"Juliette was going through Mother's things. It was inside a hat box on the top shelf of her closet behind some things."

"It was hidden?" Brian asked, lifting a small key with a round metal tag attached. "First Massachusetts Savings," Brian read from the tag.

"I didn't know Mother had a safety deposit box," Portia said, picking up a handful of rusty jacks from the box.

"Do you know what these are, Juliette?" Portia asked, offering them to her.

"They smell old," Juliette said, squinting as she studied them closely. "Are they some sort of baking thing, like to put holes in the top of pies before you bake them?"

"They're jacks. Those were mine. From a game little girls used to play. You would bounce a little ball, and have to pick those up from the ground before the ball bounced. I can't believe she kept these," Portia said as she lifted a dried, cracked, red ball from the box. "Look! I wrote my name on it!"

"What about this?" Brian said, holding up the key.

"Are we allowed to open it?" Portia asked sheepishly.

"Let's call the bank and find out," Juliette said, leaving the room. "I'll get the phone."

"What documentation did the doctor give you? Anything to do with being incapacitated?"

"Yes, but I didn't really look," Portia said, reaching for her hand bag. "Here, what do they say?"

"Basically, that someone will have to take care of Beatrice for a long time and she isn't capable of handling her own affairs, from a doctor's perspective," Brian said, perusing the medical papers.

Juliette returned to the room with the phone in her hand. "I already called the bank; they looked up Grandma's files and they said only Grandma can open the box unless you go to court for permission. *Wheel of Fortune* is coming on. Grandma likes that," Juliette said as she turned to glance out the window.

"Does Richard know about the stroke?" Brian asked. Juliette and Portia looked at each other as though Brian announced a forbidden secret.

"In light of recent…events, I think the answer is yes," Portia said, stroking her mother's hair.

Vanna turned over several letters on *Wheel of Fortune* before another word was spoken.

"If we go to the bank to look into this, can you handle everything here?" Portia said to Juliette, rising off the bed.

"No worries! The thrill of victory and the agony of defeat, you idiots!" Juliette shouted.

Portia and Brian grabbed each other's hand and held tight. Maybe Juliette was losing it. In the silence, a contestant on *Wheel of Fortune* shouted *the thrill of victory and the agony of defeat* to much ballyhoo and fanfare.

"We'll see you later, Juliette," Portia said, smiling as they left the room.

A wind was blowing in from the ocean and sweeping dark clouds with it. The road to Falmouth, where the bank was, was a two-lane highway, and every few minutes afforded a peak at the rough coast as the waves crashed on the rocks.

"It looks like a storm may be brewing," Portia said, squeezing the safe deposit box key in her hand.

"I hope we can get there and back before it starts," Brian said without taking his eyes off the winding road. "I don't relish the idea of driving this road in a nor'easter. Isn't Falmouth where there was another theatre tent?"

"That's long gone. The one in Hampton North is the only one to survive. Did you think you would work in theatre as a career?"

"No, I wanted to be a mixing engineer in a recording studio. I only took the Tent gig because they had top of the line audio gear."

"Do you enjoy working in radio?"

"It's a job. Pays the bills, or should I say paid."

Portia hesitated before she spoke. "I wish I could have worked in something really creative."

"It's better to do something useful, I think. Tell me when to turn."

"Make a left at the second light," Portia said, squinting through her thick glasses and then motioning with her hand.

From the outside, the bank looked exactly as it would have in the early 1900s when it probably opened. It was a sturdy, two-story brick structure that reeked of stability without a trace of extravagance. The interior was a different matter entirely, with its modern corporate color scheme and décor.

Brian stopped to inspect a photo display next to the entrance that had large photos of the town from the early days of the twentieth century. The bank was in each photograph, beginning with horse drawn carriages, through model-Ts, 1940s sedans, 1950s hot rods, and station wagons from the sixties and seventies. In one photo from 1929, tellers were behind heavily fortified bars and a mustachioed security guard held a rifle.

"I remember looking at this display when I was a little girl," Portia said, standing next to Brian. "My father would take Richard and me and lift us up to look at each photo."

Brian thought better of asking about her father or Richard. "I guess we should talk to someone sitting at one of those desks."

They approached a desk where a young Middle-Eastern looking female was typing away on her keyboard. Without taking her eyes off the computer screen she said, "May I help you?"

"I'd like information about opening a safe deposit box."

"Fill this out, please," the woman said, passing a small card to Portia as she continued to concentrate on her computer work.

"This is an application to open a new box. We'd like information on opening my mother's box. She's out of town for a bit. "

The banker stopped her banging on the noisy plastic keyboard.

"Oh. You want permission to open your mother's box. Sorry, I'm a little crazed this morning," she said as she reached into a drawer pulling out a file. "No, only she can open it, unless you are on her list she filed with us. Here's the information on how to add a name and other rules and procedures. What's your mother's name, and do you have her box number?"

Portia looked at the small tag and the key, "2612. Mrs. Beatrice Smart."

The banker put the papers down in front of Portia. "Mrs. Smart? Hold on a second." She picked up the phone and dialed an extension. "Ryan? This is Yvonne. Wasn't someone in earlier today inquiring about the safety deposit box of Mrs. Beatrice Smart? That's what I thought. Thanks." She placed the phone in its cradle. "Yes. A man was in this morning as soon as we opened. I believe he said he was her son. Should I check with Ryan?"

"No. No need to. Thanks for your help," Portia said, gathering up the forms.

The air was thick with mist as Brian and Portia got back into the van and began the drive back on dark, damp roads. Although the sun hadn't yet set, it wasn't visible through the charcoal clouds.

"Is there a light I can use?" Portia said as she opened her hand bag.

Brian reached up a pushed a button above the rear view mirror, illuminating Portia's purse perfectly.

"So, Richard has a head start on us," Brian said flatly.

"Yes. Money always brings him out of his hole."

"This isn't the first time?"

"When father died, mother had to file a restraining order to keep Richard away. That's when I came back home to live for good. Mother and I fought off Richard for several months until he suddenly disappeared. But like a zombie movie he keeps coming back to haunt you."

Mist turned to a hard rain as the invisible sun dropped behind the horizon, plunging the road into darkness, and the windshield wipers laid down a beat that Brian began to count as he tried to think of a way to get back into conversation. There was a challenging stretch of road ahead with street lights few and far between and curves that required total concentration. He decided to be silent.

The sharp turns, almost like switchbacks, seemed deadly in the rain-soaked night, the only protection from oncoming traffic being a yellow line in the road. They sat quietly anticipating what lied around the curve ahead. The interior of the van was cloaked in darkness until another vehicle came around a bend in the road, usually blasting its high beams into their faces, and sometime momentarily blinding Brian, who just white knuckled the steering wheel and hoped for the best.

All seemed quiet back at Smart House. Only the kitchen light was on and the sitting room was empty, except for the pile of books and papers at Mr. Dawson's position.

Brian followed Portia to Bea's room, where Juliette was fast asleep in the chair, next to the bed with the television, still on, turned to a channel with an infomercial featuring The Who's Roger Daltrey hawking hits from the sixties.

"I don't know what's sadder; Juliette asleep in that Ikea torture chair, or Roger Daltrey in an infomercial," Brian whispered.

They roused Juliette from her sleep and the three of them went their own ways toward bed, leaving Bea to watch Roger Daltrey introduce The Monkees doing "Daydream Believer."

Sun shined through the bank of windows in the sun room with not a trace of a rain cloud left behind. Portia had assumed the role of Bea without discussion. Breakfast was being prepared for everyone while Brian and Juliette still slept. Mr. Dawson and Mrs. Pangborne were already in the sun room, and Mr. Dawson was deep into his papers and books with a *Boston Globe* in one hand and a red pencil in the other.

"Thank you, Mrs. Smart," Mrs. Pangborne said cheerfully as Portia placed a bowl of breakfast mush in front of her. Portia worried that perhaps she looked too much like her mother or was it Mrs. Pangborne letting her Alzheimers show. Mr. Dawson didn't flinch when his mush was plopped on his snack table, yet Portia apologized for her clumsiness. She was preoccupied with the morning's assignments; it was time to connect the dots and find out all there was to know about Bea's finances.

Ever since her father died while she was away, Portia observed how her mother ferociously guarded every cent she had in total secrecy. Bills that were local were paid in cash, and although Bea used checks, Portia never actually saw her write one or saw her balance a checkbook. That was her mother's domain, and Portia just accepted it like so many other things when she returned to Smart House, unmarried with a child in tow. It was just another unspoken family secret that Beatrice preferred that way. But now that it seemed likely that

Beatrice's secrets would be locked forever in her brain, Portia knew she had to unlock them herself.

Over the years, Portia had observed her mother stashing papers in drawers, jars, and boxes. She knew Beatrice spent time in the attic when she was out, or caught her coming up from the basement with a calculator in her hand. So the scavenger hunt for the Smart fortune or lack thereof would begin this morning.

Reyna, the nurse's aide Portia hired through an agency for Beatrice, arrived that morning. She was a tiny lady, probably under five feet tall, had a man's haircut and dressed like one too, with neatly pressed black pants and a white button-down collar dress shirt. She spoke in a lilting Filipina accent, and from the first minute she arrived, everyone knew she took her duties as Beatrice's aide dead seriously.

While Juliette cleaned up the breakfast dishes and Brian went to the market, Portia began digging; closets, drawers, cabinets, sideboards, and bookshelves contained manila envelopes, shoe boxes, old candy tins, and wads of receipts held together with rubber bands. She knew the attic and the basement more than likely held the vast majority of secrets, but she wanted the flotsam and jetsam of stashed odds and ends first.

In a matter of an hour and a half she managed to fill two shopping bags with paper that would eventually have to be examined and filed. She carried the bags to the basement and placed them in front of an armoire that extended across an entire wall. She had no idea how that enormous piece of furniture could have been moved into the basement, and just assumed it had been built there. She put her hand on top of the unit and felt around for a key that would unlock the doors. She assumed that the debris up there was insect and mouse poop or worse, and when she looked up there she was startled to see an entire mouse skeleton.

The key did unlock the door, but it required a strong jerk to open it. The doors creaked open and revealed four columns of assorted old boxes which were once loaded with bananas, automobile oil, Kotex and eggs. They were stacked from top to bottom so tightly that is was difficult to remove one from the top. Portia tugged on one, once, twice, and then unexpectedly, it popped out of its position and spilled its contents all over the gritty linoleum-covered basement floor. But as Portia looked at the mess of papers, she knew she had hit pay dirt. There were cancelled checks, statements, and checkbooks scattered everywhere. Portia took her magnifying glass from her pocket, sat on the floor, and began her search.

This box, she discovered, was from three years ago. She began to sort items in piles; bank statements, cancelled checks, checkbooks, receipts, etc. And as the categories began to grow, she discovered something that required her to use the little circle of extra magnification in the corner of her magnifying glass.

"Damn it!" she said to no one. She knew what it meant. Richard had been getting paid off by check for years, and Beatrice didn't say a word. "That fucker." Every month a check made out to "cash" in the amount of one thousand dollars was cashed with Richard's signature on the back. "So that's how she kept him away," she said to herself glumly. And using the magnifying glass, Portia could see that some of her mother's signatures were more than likely forged by Richard.

Portia continued to build the piles, which she started putting into shoe boxes. A smaller box inside a larger box in the column had her more concerned. It was a statement from a large Boston stock brokerage. It couldn't be true. Could it? A portfolio with over $500,000.00 in stocks and bonds in Beatrice's name? But it was from five years ago!

Portia became frantic. *What if Richard got his hands on this?* She began tearing through boxes searching for the most recent documents. Apparently the top boxes, which were from two years ago, were the most recent. She had to find the most recent documents fast. She bolted up the stairs and jumped back in momentary fear when the door swung open just as she reached for it.

"Sorry, I just can't do it," Juliette said, holding her hands palm up, which had plastic gloves on them. "I just can't do this. Grandma made a mess in the bed, and I can't do it."

"Where's Reyna?"

"She went to the store for supplies."

Portia paused at the top of the stairs and instantly knew that searching for a half million dollars in stocks and bonds would have to wait until Beatrice's poop was cleaned up.

"Should we wait for Reyna to return? Juliette asked as she followed Portia into Bea's bedroom.

"That sounds like a good idea, but no," Portia said as she entered the room and immediately began scanning for possible hiding places for the missing documents as she pulled the sheets off of Beatrice, ignoring the smell of fresh excrement and urine. Portia watched as Juliette rushed out of the room with a worried look of imminent vomit.

"You'd be amazed what you can get used to," Portia whispered to herself. She gently shifted her mother in the bed, while skillfully dumping the soiled clothes and linens into a large plastic garbage bag. She went into the bathroom, ran some hot water into a basin and then began cleaning her mother's body. As she put a pair of adult diapers on her, she flashed back on the days of putting diapers on Juliette. She often wished those baby diaper days could have been shared with a husband. And then as now, she was alone putting on a diaper.

"Can I come in?" Brian asked as he poked his head into the room.

"Do you mean, is it safe to come in?"

"Well, yeah. I guess. Sorry," he said, taking three baby steps closer to the bed. "I'll help. When I get used to it a little. I thought that was Reyna's job."

"She stepped out. Some things can't wait. Did you ever change a diaper?"

"No, but I cleaned up lots of drunken vomit off my ex. Does that count?"

"Yes. That counts," Portia said as she fluffed the pillows and placed a clean sheet over Beatrice. "I started looking through the papers and discovered a couple of shockers." Portia waited for a reaction from Brian, who just raised his eyebrows in anticipation. "Somebody has been forging checks, Mother has been paying off Richard for years, and I found some...information that Mother *may have* over a half million dollars in stocks and bonds."

"May have? Why *may have*?"

"The statements were from a few years ago, and I can't find the most recent documentation."

Portia held up the garbage bag that contained the soiled linens and clothing. "Exactly. Come with me to the basement while I dump this in the wash and show you what I found."

"It all comes out in the wash," Brian said as he took the bag from Portia and followed her to the basement.

"Hopefully it isn't all down the drain," Portia said icily.

CHAPTER THIRTEEN

Portia had to buy a two-drawer filing cabinet just to store the items of sentimental value she unearthed while trying to locate the elusive documents. Days and days of searching the nooks and crannies of the hundred year-old home even uncovered stashes of the original owner of the home, including an advertisement for the lot itself, with drawings of homes that would be "built to suit."

It was the quiet time of the late afternoon. Mrs. Pangborne and Mr. Dawson were taking their afternoon naps. Brian was in the basement assembling the two file cabinets, and Portia was sipping tea at the kitchen table trying not to ponder the consequences of losing a fortune to a maniacal brother.

"I can't believe how dumb we were," Juliette said, holding something behind her back as she posed proudly in front of Portia. "Guess what I have?"

"What?" Portia said rattling her cup onto its saucer.

"The mail. Duh." Juliette said revealing the day's mail high above her head.

"Brian!" Portia shouted towards the basement doorway. "Come here!"

"Keep it down out there! I'm trying to masturbate in here!" Mr. Dawson yelled from behind his closed bedroom door.

"We'll keep it down," Portia responded.

Brian bounded into the kitchen, "That'll keep him busy 'til dinner."

"Stop! He'll hear you," Portia laughed. "Believe it or not, our search is over thanks to the due diligence of one very important party."

"The FBI? The CIA? The EPA? What?"

"Nope. A neighbor," Juliette said, holding up several envelopes. "The new owner in the house just up the road had some mis-addressed mail delivered. He said he usually just drops them in the mailbox, but this time he was driving by and thought he'd deliver them himself," she said, dropping two envelopes on the table.

"Of course! The post office!" Portia said, smacking herself in the head with the envelopes. "I'll bet you dollars to clamshells that Richard has been stealing our mail from our mail box out front, or snatching it from the post office where he used to work. These were delivered to the wrong address as sometimes happens, only usually you just give them back to your mail carrier or you drop them in the mail box. So he'd have another chance to grab them."

"Is Richard retired from the post office?" Brian asked.

"He's out on permanent disability."

"He didn't look permanently disabled when he was throwing left jabs at that kid,"

"He doesn't work there anymore, so why would he have access to our mail?" Portia asked as she picked up the bank envelope.

"Come on, Mom! Who's gonna stop a nut at the post office?"

Portia picked up a knife and slit open the envelope from the bank with surgical precision. "Mother always did it like this. Then she'd just disappear with the paperwork. I never gave it a second thought."

"What does it say?" Portia asked.

"Well, there's twelve hundred left in checking. Here are the cancelled checks, including probably the last one that Richard will be able to cash," Portia said, holding the checks and examining them through her magnifying glass.

"Are you sure?" Brian said, leaning in to get a look at them.

"I'm sure. Here's the second one from the bank. This must be savings," she said, slicing into the envelope. "Eight thousand with no withdrawals, thank God," she said with a sigh of relief. "Here comes the biggie," she said as she stuck the knife completely inside the envelope slit and cut the top open in one swift motion.

"Oh no. God, no," Portia said, deflating and almost collapsing in her chair.

"What?" Brian said, reaching for the statement from the brokerage company and examining it. "Fuck! We have to call the police now. We have to!"

"What is it?" Juliette seethed.

"Two days before Grandma's stroke, I think all the stocks and bonds were cashed in. The balance is zero," Portia droned.

"How much?" Juliette said angrily.

Brian read the numbers, "Five hundred seventeen thousand, one dollar and thirty two cents."

"Holy jumping shit!" Juliette whispered. "Do we call the police or what?"

"Well, we don't know if he actually took the money," Portia said glumly.

"True. But, since we don't see any five hundred thousand-dollar deposits in checking or saving accounts, where the hell is it? This may sound stupid, but let's look in Grandma's mattress."

Juliette suddenly looked worried. "That's just silly."

"So what?" Portia said, shaking her head in unison with Brian. "Let's go."

The three of them walked quickly up the stairs into Bea's bedroom. Reyna was sitting in the chair next to the bed reading *Reader's Digest.* The television was turned to *Jeopardy,* and Bea seemed to be watching it. Each of them took to the sides and foot of her bed and began poking under the bedding and into the mattress.

"Don't mind us, Reyna." Portia said as she began to search between the mattress and the box spring under her mother. "This is insane," she said as she pushed deeper into the mattress side. "Wait a minute," she said pulling out some papers. "Guess what? Here's where grandma has been stashing some papers."

"Let me know if you pull out a half-million bucks," Brian said as he continued to poke and prod the bed as Juliette and Portia looked at the papers.

"You know where it could be?" Portia said as the TV audience erupted in applause, causing Reyna to glance at the TV screen momentarily.

"Excuse me, while I go downstairs for a moment," Reyna stated politely as she left the room.

Brian and Juliette's eyes widened and Beatrice gurgled.

"I think Grandma's hungry," Juliette announced. "Six months is a long time to wait," Juliette said matter-of-factly as she held up the key to the bank safe deposit box. "All that money could be in the safe deposit box. And I've been thinking about how we can get into it right away without waiting for the legal stuff."

"Yeah, and while we're at it, let's just empty the vault, too," Brian chortled as he sat next to the television set.

"Sarcasm is the lowest form of wit," Juliette scoffed at Brian.

"We're listening, Juliette," Portia said, stroking Juliette's hair and throwing a scowl in Brian's direction.

"Do I need to remind you both what my talent is at The Tent has been every summer for the past three years?"

"Okay, hair and makeup," Portia said, sitting on Brian's lap.

"Mom, don't take this wrong, but you're a dead wringer for Grandma. I could easily make you up to look just like her. You saw what I did last summer for *Arsenic and Old Lace*. Those girls in the lead weren't old enough to drink, and the audience bought it.

"But that's from thirty, forty feet away," Brian scoffed, stroking Portia's cheek.

"I must admit, I sat in the third row and they looked great," Portia said. "And it's not like she would have to add that many years to get up to Grandma's age. I'm sure they haven't seen Grandma in ages."

"Are you kidding me?" Brian asked incredulously. "What if you get caught? That's got to be a felony."

"We just want to look in the box; we don't necessarily have to take anything out of it," Portia said as Juliette nodded her approval. "If there's cash or something else in there, we know it's safe. If there's nothing in there, we can figure out how to have Richard investigated. We're just looking, right?"

"Okay, I guess I'll be your escort and driver. If one of us gets locked up, we all get locked up," Brian said, giving in.

Portia planted a kiss on his cheek. "Make a list, sweetie, of what equipment you'll need, and we'll go into Boston for it. Is this a caper?" she asked, excitedly skipping out of the room.

"On television it's a caper. In real life, it's just called crime," Juliette laughed.

"I'll take over, thank you," Reyna said, smiling as she nudged Brian aside. She began to feed Beatrice, and he was amazed that as soon as the food touched her tongue, she reflexively made a chewing motion and swallowed. How could it be, he wondered, that a part of her brain understood how to eat, breathe, urinate, and defecate, but couldn't hear or understand what was going on around her? But as the woman on *Jeopardy* jumped and screamed after winning thousands of dollars, Brian thought he noticed Bea's eye's widen, which made him wonder even more.

With Mr. Dawson and Mrs. Pangborne taking naps in their rooms, Beatrice asleep in her room, and Juliette and Portia on the way to Boston, Brian relished the idea of having the sun room all to himself. During the entire summer he spent at the house, never once did he have a quiet, empty house at his disposal.

He picked up the day's sports section and sat on the rattan sofa next to the open window, where a salty ocean breeze whistled through the one-inch opening. As Brian turned the pages of the paper, he realized his eyes were in a competition. It seemed every time a word in a headline such as "grapefruit league" caught his attention, a sound, like the laugh of a gull, would distract him and he would search the scenery for the source of the commotion. This went on for several pages until Brian realized what was happening, and put the paper down. He pushed open the window wide, letting all the sounds and smells of the beach into the room.

In the distance, he could see something red and blue bobbing in the water, beyond the lighthouse in the distance. He reached into the drawer of the end table and pulled out the huge black binoculars that probably were purchased and placed there decades ago by the long since departed Mr. Smart. He focused on the object, thinking it could be someone in distress, but once he focused he could see it was a red sea kayak with someone in a blue wetsuit happily battling the swells. He watched as the hardy paddler rounded the lighthouse island and headed south.

He glanced down at the sports page, which featured on the front page, above the fold, four shirtless morons approaching middleage who had painted their paunchy bodies red and white with poorly drawn red socks on the bellies beyond the outfield fence of the Red Sox spring training ballpark in Florida. A feeling of embarrassment blew over him like the gust of ocean wind that whipped through the window. The baseball fans in the photo looked silly to him. Not just because they were Red Sox fans, because he knew that at every outfield of every spring training ballpark that day there were similar fans with their paunchy bodies painted and exposed for all to see. But looking at the red and blue object bobbing in the surf, he knew that was a real sports fan. There was someone battling the elements all alone, for no reason other than the challenge it presented him in his own soul.

Brian knew that's why he played sports from early childhood through college. It had nothing to do with making it to the pros. It was all about competition and pitting yourself against…something. He remembered the times all alone at the basketball court trying to outdo himself by hitting as many foul shots as possible in a row. Or even walking down the street seeing how many times he could consecutively spit exactly into a crack in the sidewalk. But somehow sports morphed into sitting in front of computers, crunching numbers and trying to get the most points in a ridiculous competition that has nothing to do with sports. In his mind he began writing his resignation letter as commissioner of his fantasy baseball leagues.

He watched as the kayaker became a small red dot in the distance, and longed to have the balls to accomplish such a feat. Or for that matter, do anything physically challenging again.

Brian grabbed the binoculars and went out to the back deck to get a better view of the kayaker before he disappeared entirely. He focused far down the coast line and saw the kayak crash through the surf onto the beach. A guy pulled the kayak across the sand and pushed it onto the roof of a station wagon that also had a bicycle on its roof. Brian focused on the guy as he removed his life jacket and squirmed out of his blue wetsuit, and Brian was stunned to see it wasn't a guy at all, but a woman. She was in a one-piece bathing suit under the wetsuit, and her long hair fell down her back when she removed her cap. In a matter of seconds, she was in her vehicle and exiting the parking lot.

Brian laughed to himself as he lowered the binoculars and wondered what a woman like that was made of, and how she had the balls for kayaking alone in the ocean and he didn't.

"Why don't you quit spying on people and get me a goddammed cup of tea," Mr. Dawson grunted out the window at him.

Brian knew his flirt with peace and quiet was over as he went back inside, placed the binoculars in the drawer, and Mr. Dawson began reviewing his papers with red pencil in hand. Tea was easy. He just hoped Portia and Juliette could make it back from Boston before Dawson started clamoring for dinner. As he prepared the tea, Brian watched Mr. Dawson shift the heavy textbook from one side of the table to the other and wondered if he really was doing mathematics or just busying himself in some elaborate obsessive-compulsive behavioral ruse. The book did have his name on it, but that didn't mean that he was still formulating equations.

"Here you go, Mr. Dawson," Brian said, placing the teacup and saucer by him.

"Are you banging any of the Smarts?"

"Excuse me?"

"You heard me."

Brian wondered if a noogie could be considered elder abuse. "Mr. Dawson, you're quite an ornery son of a bitch, aren't you?"

Mr. Dawson didn't react for a moment. Then he slowly picked up his teacup and held it high as if in a toast. "Cheers," he said through a menacing smile, put his cup back on the saucer, and started writing equations on a new page of his spiral notebook.

As darkness descended on the coast, Brian became concerned that Portia and Juliette were taking longer than expected, but knew that Boston rush hour should be called Boston rush three hour. More and more people were moving farther and farther away from downtown and even commuting from the outer edges of the Cape; a factor that contributed to the suburbanization of the landscape and attitudes of the townspeople.

Fortunately, he was able to placate Mr. Dawson and Mrs. Pangborne with excuses as to why dinner was tardy, but knew he couldn't hold them off for much longer. His kitchen table solitude was interrupted, however, by a knock on the door. Without hesitation, he rushed to the door and swung it open, and upon doing so he let out with a loud "Shit!" at the sight of a horrible faced creature, which he soon realized was Portia in a cheap rubber witch mask.

"Trick or treat?" Portia said meekly, as she peeled off the mask.

"Very funny. Did you get everything you need?" Brian asked, kissing her on the cheek. "You taste like Hong Kong rubber."

"Yes, Juliette will be right in with everything. The shop owner let us practice with some items, and I think this will work," Portia said heading up the stairs. "Has Mother been behaving?"

"Yes, but I didn't change her or anything," Brian said, following right behind.

"I told you, you don't have to worry about that."

Beatrice was almost exactly as they had left her hours ago; eyes seemingly transfixed on the television, covers just slightly askew.

"As one gets older," Portia said as she straightened the blanket, "one always wonders if one is becoming your own parent. Sometimes I say a word or see myself in the mirror and see Mother. And now I have to become Mother in a way I never imagined."

"You don't *have to*," Brian said gently touching Portia's hand.

Juliette entered with two shopping bags in her arms. "When do we start?"

Portia stroked Bea's face. "In the morning. I'm going to check Mother and then start dinner."

Juliette and Brian left the room, and Portia closed the door behind them. Portia changed the television channel from Jerry Springer to the public television station which was airing a program about some high school students who started their own blog.

"How was your day, Mother?" Portia asked as she positioned Bea to change her adult diapers. "I don't know if you heard what we're up to...what I'm up to...but it's the only way I can think of to do this quickly. If you wanted to give Richard something, or everything, that would be fine by me. It would. Really. But I don't think that's what you want, and the only way is to see what's in that box at the bank. Quickly. Now. And whatever we discover...shall be," she said, softly kissing her mother on the forehead.

The next morning Juliette wore very short shorts and a half t-shirt as she placed Mr. Dawson's morning mush on his snack tray. Brian stood in the doorway and watched as Dawson stared at her ass when she bent over to pick up a napkin next to Mrs. Pangborne's table and then gave Brian a lecherous, gleeful smile. Brian was becoming a roving centerfielder in his duties around the house; picking up the slack between Juliette and Portia as they did most of the important jobs. Brian did the heavy lifting, operated the household appliances, and cleaned up the messiest messes--except for changing Bea's diapers. Thankfully, Reyna was adept at the tasks that demanded the most tolerance of substances and smells most humans prefer not to deal with. But that didn't exclude him from cleaning the toilets and the immediate areas around them.

Once food was served, dishes washed, and the morning bathroom visits were completed, Brian, Portia, and Juliette met next to Beatrice's bed for the masquerade that was anything but a trick-or-treat gag. They had decided that each of them had veto power over the charade once the makeup and wardrobe were complete.

Portia sat in the chair, which was placed as close to Beatrice as possible. The room was bright with morning sunshine, which would hopefully magnify any imperfections in the job at hand.

Brian stood in the doorway so he could hear if Mr. Dawson or Mrs. Pangborne needed any assistance during the hour or so procedure. Portia lowered her blouse, exposing her bare shoulders and a good portion of the upper part of her breasts so that Juliette could apply the makeup base there as well.

It was certainly a surreal sight for Brian, as Beatrice seemed to stare blankly at the TV while Drew Carey issued calm directions to frantic women on *The Price Is Right* and Juliette spread makeup on Portia's partially naked upper body, which he found strangely erotic in light of the present circumstances.

"Why exactly are you going so…low…with the make-up?" Brian asked, hoping that by talking he would distract himself from becoming aroused.

"In case any skin is exposed under the clothing, of course. You don't realize that elderly people have a very light, almost opaque quality to their skin. Portia's skin tone is rich," Juliette said, applying the makeup with a brush. Brian could see the artistic flair of Juliette's makeup brush strokes she inherited from her mother. Brian imagined the artistic genes flowing from Beatrice to Portia to Juliette and back through Juliette's brush strokes onto Portia's skin. Three generations of Smart women in an intense, symbiotic swirl of hormones, sensuality, and devotion.

"What about my hair?" Portia asked as she raised her arms to tighten the elastic band that held her hair, which made her loose blouse slip even lower, which exposed both her breasts entirely. "Oops," she said coyly as she pulled her blouse back up.

"Mommmmm," Juliette whined, which caused Portia to giggle uncontrollably.

"Don't mind me!" Brian said gleefully.

Juliette turned to scowl at Brian.

"I think I'll check on our guests," Brian said, as he exited the room.

Juliette continued applying the makeup. "Do you want to marry him and be taken away from…all this? What happened to *Are you married or happy*?"

"I don't want to be taken away from anything. What makes you think we want to get married, anyway?"

Juliette just shook her head and poked her upper lip with the brush. "Are you kidding? It's like you the two of you have been married for years. Quiet. Don't move your lips anymore."

Juliette applied the base, then peeled layers of latex off of a palette and applied them to Portia's face, neck, and upper chest. Portia sat as motionless as her mother, watching the television, and had no idea how Juliette was progressing. After fifteen or so minutes, she began to feel a little woozy from the smells of the ingredients being plastered on her. That, and the fact that her pores were being clogged with Lord knows what kind of petroleum by-products.

"I'm not feeling so hot," Portia whispered like an amateur ventriloquist trying not to move her lips. "I mean, I'm feeling very hot and woozy from the chemicals."

"I'll open the window a little more."

She placed her brush on the table and made a mental note of where she left off, then raised the window a few more inches. "I see you!" Juliette sang to Portia.

Portia had reached for a hand mirror to sneak a peek of herself.

"Don't move, turn, talk, or anything until I'm done and this stuff has a chance to settle and dry," Juliette scolded her as she sat back down.

Portia thought that if she could see how she looked now, halfway through, it wouldn't be such a shock later. Actually, she was downright scared she would look too much like Beatrice.

"There's something beautiful about aging," Juliette said, glancing back and forth between Beatrice and Portia.

"Oh thanks," Portia said through motionless lips and a clenched jaw.

"Don't speak. Have you noticed how grandma's wrinkles seem to be disappearing? I mean, it probably has something to do with lying in bed all the time, or the concoctions we've been feeding her. But there's a quality to her skin, which I'm am meticulously trying to recreate on you, I may add, that's almost like mother of pearl. I remember in high school when we wanted to look old for a play we'd just paint these awful black lines on our faces, and it always looked so bad. It's not the black lines; it's the skin's texture and shading. I wonder if I'll look like you when I'm your age. God, I hope so."

A cool ocean breeze helped Portia feel less woozy, but Juliette's voice and soothing strokes from her brush had put her in a light day-dreamy state. Her eyelids were closed, and she was a little bit frightened when the brush went across them at first. And when the hairs of the brush hit her eyelash, it reminded her of the angel kisses she shared in first grade with little boys, and also with Brian in their summer of love. She hadn't had an angel kiss since Brian did it to her one morning after spending the night together in a sleeping bag on the beach. She thought that the feeling of someone fluttering their eyelashes on your own eyelashes first thing in the morning is the only way anyone should have to wake up in their lives.

Juliette put her brush down. "Don't open your eyes or move. I'm not done. I just need to step back a little bit and observe from a distance." She stood and began backing up slowly in small steps and gasped softly when she bumped into someone.

"It's me," Brian whispered in her ear. "This is freaky."

Brian and Juliette stood in the doorway, maybe five feet away from Beatrice and Portia side by side looking like identical, silent, napping twins.

"This reminds me of that scene in *The Invasion of the Body Snatchers* when they open the pod for the first time and it reveals the identical twin of the guy," Brian said softly.

"I can hear you," Portia said through motionless lips.

"Oh my God! It's alive! Alive!" Brian said loudly.

"Don't make me laugh," Portia managed to say without cracking her mouth open.

"Sshhh!" Brian and Juliette said in unison.

"How much longer?" Brian asked bent over and moving forward as he inspected Portia's face until he was just a few inches from her.

"I know that's you, Brian," Portia muttered, eyes closed, still trying not to move her lips.

Juliette switched on the overhead light briefly, and back off again, several times.

"Are you signaling someone in the lighthouse?" Brian asked Juliette.

"Just watching how this small amount of overhead light might affect her face. I'll be done in ten minutes. Then ten minutes to dry, and twenty or so to get dressed, so come back in half an hour," Juliette said, pushing Brian out the door and closing it behind him.

"I can't imagine him being a dad," Juliette said as she blended colors on Portia's face.

A smile formed across Portia's face and her eyes turned up at the ends, revealing more laugh lines.

"That's good, I can use those laugh lines," Juliette said, attacking the lines with a dark pencil.

"Can I talk?"

"I guess so."

"Why did you say that?"

"If I exaggerate the *laugh lines* it will be a more natural way to age you."

"Why did you say you couldn't imagine Brian as a dad?"

"I don't know. He doesn't seem like a…dad. You know, like a…overbearing, authoritative, pain in the ass."

"Is that what dads are like?"

"Wasn't yours?"

"Not all dads are like that," Portia said, opening her eyes to make eye contact with her daughter.

"Not *all* dads. Just most."

"I can imagine Brian as a father," Portia said, closing her eyes again. "A wonderful father."

"That's love talking."

Portia's *laugh lines* extended a little farther.

Brian was sitting in the kitchen, observing the few tiny leaves on the bottom of the cup that had escaped from his silver tea ball, and wondered if they could portend the future. Not the far-away future, but merely that afternoon. He knew they were taking a chance, but the real chance was being taken by Portia. He didn't even want to think of what would happen to her if their plan backfired. He looked up and was stunned at what stood before him. There stood Beatrice, but of course he knew it was actually Portia, makeup complete and wearing Beatrice's clothing.

"Her clothes still smell like her," Portia whispered. "Is Mr. Dawson in the sun room?"

Brian placed his cup down and peeked through the other kitchen doorway and observed Mr. Dawson in his usual spot, reading a copy of a decades old *National Geographic*.

"Let's do a little test," Portia said as she walked toward the sun room and over to Mr. Dawson. "I'm going into town. Do you need anything, Mr. Dawson?"

Mr. Dawson raised his eyes from the magazine and squinted as he looked at Portia, who whisked past him and picked up a tea cup from the end table on the opposite end of the room. Mr. Dawson kept his eyes on her, and as she walked past he said, "Where the hell have you been?"

Portia tried not to laugh and pushed Brian away as he tried to kiss her on the cheek. "No, don't smudge anything. I'll go tell Juliette it worked, then we'll go."

Brian poked his head into the sun room. "Do you need anything, Mr. Dawson?"

"I just told the old battle axe, no. By the way, my offer is back on. Ten grand."

"I just might take you up on that offer this time," Brian said, winking.

Portia stood about six feet from the mirror in her bedroom as she adjusted her wig and kerchief. She found it curious that she had no butterflies or shakes. From the moment they decided to go ahead with the masquerade, she assumed she would back out from fear of being caught. The hours spent in preparation added to her anxiety as she patiently sat immobile next to her incapacitated mother.

No doubt about it. She now felt good. Instead of nervousness, she felt emboldened by her appearance. As she ever so slightly touched the aging makeup on her face, admiring the intricacy of the artistic detailing, she felt as though it was Beatrice who was going to the bank. She flashed on her daydreams during the long transforming session and realized that as the minutes and hours passed, she felt her mother's energy entering her with each stroke of Juliette's brush. Portia always wondered if she could ever be as strong as her mother in the face of extreme adversity, and now the ultimate test was at hand.

"Can I come in?" Juliette said from behind the door.

"Yes."

Juliette stood behind Portia, and they both gazed into the looking glass. Juliette studied Portia's face, neck, and hair in the mirror, but Portia was studying Juliette's reflection. Since Portia's face was disguised as Beatrice's, Portia studied Juliette in the mirror, trying to decipher bits of herself in her daughter. Yes, there were the eyes, so close to her own, the slight widow's peak, and the small ear lobes. But she studied the cheekbones and imagined that was from her father.

"You look amazing," Juliette said as she tucked strands of hair under her kerchief. "Is the kerchief too much?"

"You know Grandmother wore it quite often," Portia said adjusting it slightly.

"It's so *old world*. But somehow it does suit you. You will be careful," Juliette said, her voice trembling.

"It's a little late for that. Let's go."

As Portia and Juliette walked through the tunnel of shrubbery toward the van, Brian remembered how Juliette opened the front door not too long ago and he thought it was, in fact, Portia standing there. And there was Portia playing the role of her mother, and Juliette a dead ringer for Portia, yet again.

Once in the van, Portia placed her hand on Brian's thigh as they drove off and Brian noticed that even her hands looked aged, but was afraid to ask in case he was mistaken and that was merely the way Portia's hands looked.

"Well?" Portia asked, her hand squeezing Brian's thigh as he accelerated away. "Didn't you notice my hand?"

"How could I not notice a hand squeezing my thigh near the intersection of pleasure and arousal?"

"She even aged my hands. Juliette is amazing. I don't know where she gets all her talent."

Brian glanced at Portia. "No mystery there as far as I'm concerned."

Portia stroked Brian's hand on the steering wheel and smiled softly. "Want to try another experiment?"

"Such as?"

"Want to stop at The Laughing Gull for a cup of coffee?"

Brian switched on his right turn signal and turned toward town.

"Might as well," Brian said brightly, trying to reveal the fear that began to infiltrate his casual demeanor.

They parked a few doors down from The Gull, and Portia looked into the mirror on the back of her windshield visor. "Do I need to adjust anything?" Portia said in a raspy whisper.

"I can barely hear you."

"But you can hear me. Good. That's the voice I'm using. Just say I've got laryngitis."

"This is getting deep," Brian said, exiting the van to assist Portia. After he closed the door and walked around the front of the vehicle he mumbled to himself, "Hope it's not deep shit."

Portia worked on her elderly lady shuffle while she held onto Brian's arm. They paused in the doorway, looked at each other, and entered.

Katie was behind the bar going through some papers and heard the door open. She did a double take, which made Brian tighten up with anxiety.

"Brian?" Katie said, as she put down the papers and smiled. "Good to see you. Table for two?"

"Yes, thank you. Anywhere is fine."

"Sit here, I'll clean it up for you," Katie said as she ushered them to a table by the door that wasn't quite ready yet.

Katie smiled broadly as she wiped a wet rag across the table and placed a set up in front of them. "I'll be right back."

"Is there perspiration dripping down my face?" Portia whispered.

"No. How about me?"

Katie returned with two menus. "Aren't you Mrs. Smart?" Katie said respectfully.

Portia nodded while she smiled slightly.

"She's not feeling well. I'm taking her to Falmouth...for an...appointment."

"It's lovely to see you, Mrs. Smart," Katie said sweetly.

"Actually, we'll just have two cups of tea," Brian said, handing the menus back to Katie.

"Certainly," Katie said as she backed away.

"She was always one of the good ones," Portia said softly. Suddenly Portia's eyes widened in horror. "Fuck. I'll be right back. Stay here and don't move," as she swiftly headed for the ladies room.

A loud male voice boomed from the register. "I want the manager! This is a goddammed disgrace! Cockroaches in my food! I'm calling the health department!"

"Just leave. Go. Now," Katie said pointing toward the door. "I don't want your money."

Brian knew that face, that voice. That's why Portia ran to the ladies room. Richard. The door slammed shut as the maniac left in a huff. Ten seconds later, Portia returned from the ladies room.

"You missed all the excitement. You're not going to believe this…" Brian said, still stunned

"I saw him. Let's go out the back way."

Katie returned with two cups of tea, only to find a five dollar bill on the table as she heard the back door by the restrooms slam shut.

"What do we do now?" Brian asked flatly, getting into the van.

"Continue as planned," Portia said firmly, in her regular voice.

"What about him? Do you think he saw you?"

"At this point I could care less."

There wasn't much conversation on the drive to the bank in Falmouth. Portia spent most of the time nervously fiddling with the finer points of her makeup that needed some touching up. Occasionally Brian would comment on a boat at sea or a bird on a sign as they drove the half hour to the final climax of their risky plan. He didn't want to share with Portia the many scenarios that were running through his mind faster than the white lines in the road. Everything could go flawlessly and the box may be filled with cash. That would be a happy ending. Or the box could be empty. Or Lord knows how disastrously it could wind up. But he knew, whatever the outcome, he'd stick with Portia.

"Should I park right in front?" Brian asked, just a block away from the bank.

"Certainly. That's where you'd park with an elderly woman in the van."

Brian pulled into the parking spot right next to the bank door and turned off the engine. "I'm not sure if it's good or bad that it looks so empty in there."

"Makes no difference," Portia said in her normal, firm voice. She grabbed the door handle, cleared her throat, and whispered weakly, "Help me out, please."

Brian knew this was his cue to go into character and follow Portia's lead. They shuffled through the doorway into the nearly empty bank. Brian escorted her to the lone person sitting at a desk across from the bank of teller positions. Thankfully it was a different person from the last time they were there.

"Can I help you?" a young African-American woman said, still staring at her computer screen.

"Yes, I'd like to open my safe deposit box," Portia said in a raspy whisper.

"Just fill out this form, please, ma'am," the young woman said, pushing a card toward where they would be sitting.

Brian and Portia sat down, and she slowly filled out the few lines of information in the handwriting she had been perfecting all week. Brian quickly glanced at her card and admired how flawless the forgery was. Portia pushed the card across the desk and smiled weakly.

"Very good, let's go to the vault," the banker said politely.

Portia walked slowly with Brian just behind the young woman and into the box area. The banker led them to the box and inserted her key. "Now put your key in and turn."

Portia turned the key, and the banker pulled out a long rectangular box.

"You can examine the contents in the privacy booth," she said, leading them to a small, well-lit room where customers could open their boxes in private. "You step inside here, and I'll be right with you. I just have to do one more thing."

Brian and Portia sat in silence, both thinking that the room could have a hidden microphone or camera.

The door opened and the young woman stood there holding a small white container that fit in the palm of her hand. She opened the lid, revealing a black substance inside.

"This is just routine," the young banker said, standing with the other banker who dealt with them the other day and a middle-aged man in a dark pinstriped suit stood together in the doorway. "We just need your fingerprint on this card."

Brian felt as though all of his internal organs were being squeezed in a vice. He heard Portia gasp almost imperceptibly. The man in the suit stared at Portia intently, not moving a muscle. Portia watched the fingerprint jar as it was placed on the counter in front of her. She made a fist with her right hand and stuck her thumb straight up and smiled awkwardly, then slowly rotated the thumb downwards into an obvious *thumbs down* gesture.

"What do they say here?" Portia said in her normal voice. "The jug is up."

"Jig," Brian said flatly.

"Please both come with me," the man said, gesturing firmly with his hand to lead them out of the room, down the hall, and into a small office. "Sit down, please. I'm the branch manager. I already know your family has been coming to this bank since before I was born. Let's talk, and maybe we can avoid having to get the police involved."

The woman entered with some paperwork and handed them to the man. "Here's everything."

"Did I look that bad?" Portia said to the young banker.

"I never would have known, but we do try to watch out for each other in these cases. These things happen with siblings…" the young woman said, but stopped herself when the man held up his palm and waved her off. She held her mouth to her hand in embarrassment, and left the room.

As the man examined the papers and began typing on his computer keyboard, Portia turned to Brian and mouthed silently, *Richard.*

"Let's go into my office," the branch manager said, waving his arm toward the door as he stood. Portia instinctively stood, as if at attention and said, "Oh, God" softly, almost in the voice she used when she was pretending to be her mother. Suddenly she collapsed forward and crashed with her full force of weight, with her head striking the corner of the desk and fell limp to the floor, with blood gushing from her face.

The manager immediately got down to assist her and barked, "Call 911!"

Brian lost all sense of time and place as he saw awful, red blood overwhelming Portia's extra pale makeupped face at the end of a swirling black tunnel. Her eyes were closed, lazily, not shut tight, and drool was running from the corner of her mouth as he tried to straighten her head to comfort her.

"Don't move her," the branch manager said softly, joining Brian on the floor and holding her head so it was straight. "We've just got to keep her air passageways straight and open,"

Brian barely heard her. He was concentrating on Portia, hoping, praying, demanding silently that she would make a sound, any sound, any sign of life. He used his handkerchief to wipe the blood from her face, and as he did so the layers of makeup came off as well.

"What the hell is going on there?" the manager asked, his eyebrows and ears rising slightly in surprise.

"It's makeup. We were on a…caper," Brian said, slowly shaking his in disbelief at the awful absurdity of the moment.

"How old is she?"

"Forty, I think," Brian's voice trailed off as the sound of an ambulance's siren turned off and the rush of emergency workers and equipment could be heard approaching. Brian stood up and watched as a whirlwind of activity unfolded in front of him with the speed, strength, and precision of an Indy 500 pit crew. Within seconds she was hooked up, strapped, belted and rolling to the ambulance.

"Can I go with her?" Brian asked as they walked briskly behind the gurney.

"Okay, let's go."

Brian sat in the front of the ambulance.

"Put your seat belt on, sir," the female paramedic said calmly and turned on the whoop whoop siren.

He watched at the people in the street as they stopped and stared as the ambulance blasted through the town, then onto a highway, then through a smaller town, and then whisked into a hospital driveway.

"Wait in the regular waiting area until they need you for something," the paramedic said to Brian as he watched Portia's gurney go through a door and disappear.

He wasn't sure if he felt nauseous or hungry or angry, and he thought of a line that his buddy George used to say: *I didn't know whether to shit or go blind.*

Brian couldn't sit still as he watched the digital clock over the heavily protected bulletproof glass booth where a sleepy-eyed male nurse sat in a nurse's coat festooned with mini baseballs and footballs. He paced around the room, trying not to notice the others there also waiting or what might be happening to Portia.

Suddenly, a man who he assumed to be a doctor appeared. He was extremely tall and middle aged, with thick black glasses and thinning blonde hair, but looked like he could still play a killer game of half court.

"Anyone with Portia Smart?"

Brian weakly waved.

"And you are…"

"I'm Brian De Louise," Brian said nervously.

"Any relation?"

"Um, boyfriend?" Brian said feeling like a total moron as the words left his mouth.

"I'm sorry. I can only give information to an immediate family member."

Brian stood there paralyzed with stupidity.

"Is there an immediate family member I can talk to?" the doctor asked as if talking to a first grader.

"I'll call…her daughter. Right now!" Brian said snapping out of his dumb funk as he dialed his phone.

The doctor shook his head, punched a code word onto a pad and exited through a door.

"Juliette! I'm at the hospital. Portia fainted and hit her head. She's okay, but you've got to come quickly. They won't tell me anything…"

Brian paused as he listened, closed his eyes and whispered, "Because I'm not an immediate family member. Bye."

He slowly snap-closed his flip phone, shoved it into his pocket, and slunk into the molded green plastic chair, watched the red numbers click away on the clock, and made three trips to the bathroom to urinate. Only one was successful.

The attendant behind the bulletproof glass pushed a button, which caused a brief blast of feedback, then said, "Are you with Portia Smart?"

"Yes," Brian shouted at the booth.

"See the doctor through that door," he said pointing to the security door, which started to buzz.

Brian rushed through, and standing in another mini waiting area was the doctor whom he had spoken with, now talking to Juliette.

"Hi," Brian said softly.

Juliette looked at Brian, eyes red and swollen and tried to smile.

The doctor motioned with his chart for him to get closer. "I've told Juliette what we know, and she has given me the authority to include you while she's present. Sorry, but those are the HIPPA rules. "Are you the father?"

"Um, no, I'm not Juliette's father. I guess I'm just a boyfriend," Brian said, wondering why the doctor was asking the question.

"I mean," the doctor said with a slight sense of befuddlement in his voice, "are you the father of the baby?"

"What?" Brian said stunned.

"The fetus."

"There's a fetus?" Brian said, holding onto the back of a chair.

"You didn't know?"

"No."

"Sit down, Mr. De Louise."

Brian obeyed promptly, like a schoolboy in the vice principal's office, and stared up at the long, lean doctor.

"Portia is pregnant," the doctor said, trying to gauge Brian's reaction.

Brian closed his eyes and the words *shit or go blind* flashed yet again. He opened them and found Juliette's red swollen eyes. She wasn't trying to smile.

"Are you aware of any other medical conditions, Mr. De Louise?"

"Other? No. Well, just that her eyesight isn't so good anymore?"

The doctor looked to Juliette and waited for a reaction. She nodded.

"Mr. De Louise, Portia has a growth very close to her brain. We decided to do a CT Scan because of the circumstances and discovered it."

"I'll bet Mom didn't know either. She refused to go to the doctor for a while now," Juliette said quietly, as if in defeat.

Brian slumped forward and felt as though the air he was breathing had no oxygen. Black dots with white ragged edges appeared from behind his eyeballs whether his eyes were opened or closed, blurring his vision.

"Are you all right?"

Brian straightened up in the chair and clenched his fists at his side.

"Yes. Can we see her?"

The doctor led Brian and Juliette through the maze of beds, mostly enclosed by curtains, but a few had openings that revealed patients in varying degrees of emergency care. Brian focused on staying right behind the doctor.

Portia laid there, eyes closed, a bandage wound across her head. A single IV was in her arm, but other than that, no beeping machines or strange equipment was connected to her.

"What's the IV?"

"Basically, we're just hydrating her," the doctor said, picking up her chart.

"What's next?" Brian asked.

"We're not sure if the nasty bump on the head-- we gave her twelve stitches, by the way-- has her semi-conscious or if that growth is perhaps pressing on something, which may be why she collapsed. Or…" the doctor said as he felt her pulse.

"Or what?" Juliette asked leaning in.

"Or perhaps she fainted due to something related to her pregnancy."

"Mommmm!" Juliette whimpered softly "Oh, Mom…" her voice trailing into sobs as she knelt on one knee beside the bedside. She turned toward the doctor, "Is she in a coma?"

"She's just sleeping."

"I'm so sorry, Juliette," Brian said, standing behind her and placing his hand on her shoulder. Juliette placed her hand on top of his, and Brian immediately felt better.

"Is everything all right back at the house?" Brian asked, placing his other hand on Portia's arm.

"Yes, the aide, Reyna, is there."

"I'll be back in a minute," the doctor said as he exited.

"Her eyes were just open a little," Juliette said excitedly, "and I think she smiled when she realized it was me."

Brian rushed to the other side of the bed and stroked Portia's face with the back of his hand.

"You love her dearly, don't you?" Juliette asked, still looking at her mother.

Brian tried to answer, but choked up. He tried to hold back the tears but couldn't. "Yes," was all he could manage.

Juliette tried to smile but it turned into look of worry as she put her face against Portia's breast and also wept.

"Did it happen just before you went back to DC the last time?" Juliette asked aloud.

Brian didn't understand the question at first, then realized Juliette was referring to the moment of conception.

"Yeah."

"She changed when you left…"

Brian braced himself as Juliette paused and looked deep into his eyes.

"…I hadn't seen her that happy in years," Juliette said, completing the thought and settling on a broad smile.

Brian pulled a chair next to the bed, sat, and held Portia's hand. Juliette did the same on her side. They sat next to Portia for the next hour, waiting for her to open her eyes again, interspersed with small talk, eyes fixed on Portia. Nurses came and went as did the doctor, who agreed that was all they could do right now. In fact, it was the best thing they could do.

Portia moaned slightly and her fingers began to move. Then the moan became a weak "Oh."

"Mom? Can you hear me?"

Portia strained as she pushed her heavy eyelids open, revealing one eye that was red with blood. It was the eye that was on the same side as her injury.

"Where am I?" Portia managed to say in a raspy whisper.

"Everything's fine. You fell and hit your head," Brian said calmly still holding her hand.

"How do I look?" she asked, straining.

"Beautiful," Brian said, touching her hand gently.

Portia smiled and closed her eyes.

"You've got a nasty bump and stitches," Juliette said, "you just need to rest. You're getting a low level pain killer, but you'll be fine."

Portia nodded and appeared to fall back into semi-consciousness again.

Brian and Juliette didn't realize it, but a nurse was standing in the doorway. "That was good," she said as she approached the bed. "She'll be fine. We'll let her get a good night's sleep here, and she'll more than likely be released in the morning. I suggest the two of you get some rest, too."

"Do you mind if I stay here?" Brian asked, looking at the nurse and Juliette for their approval.

"Fine by me," the nurse said.

"I'm glad you'll stay. I'll go home and get things ready," Juliette said as she bent over and kissed Portia on her cheek.

The nurse and Juliette left, and Brian adjusted his chair so that he could lean his head against the side of Portia's pillow. He put his head down and over and over said every prayer he remembered from childhood. And with the sounds from nearby beds, where assorted moans, groans, and occasional shrieks of pain emanated, he slowly sank into a state that was about as close to sleep as possible in an emergency room bed area and wondered what the morning would bring.

CHAPTER FOURTEEN

After a day of rest at home, Portia knew she wasn't right in her dizzy, pain-racked head. She put on what she thought was her brave face as she laid there, but what Brian saw was a black-and-blue face on one side and an eye still red with blood. He also caught a glimpse of her as she struggled with a magnifying glass trying to read the newspaper, just before she dropped them onto the bed and dozed off.

Brian didn't know it, but he and Juliette were silently repeating the same mantra in their heads as they sat for afternoon tea in the kitchen; *It was only the first day back. Surely Portia would recover from her bump on the head.*

"The doctor said the first forty-eight hours will tell a lot," Brian said. He thought his tone of voice was too obvious in its optimism after he spoke.

Juliette tried to smile, but realized she couldn't and put her hot tea to her lips too quickly, which hurt slightly. "Yes," she said after blowing on her teacup, "we'll see."

It crossed Brian's mind to tell Juliette that people lived full lives with tumors and sometimes tumors disappear. And he was going to tell her he was going to propose marriage to Portia and they would have the baby and face whatever the future threw at them together.

But he couldn't tell Juliette. First he had to tell Portia.

Forty-eight hours came and went, and Brian and Juliette accepted the fact that Portia didn't make a sudden miraculous recovery. She managed to go to the bathroom without assistance and stayed awake for a couple of hours at a time and ate some soft food, but miraculous recovery? No. Her left eye was almost always closed when she tried to focus, but no one dared mention it anymore.

Snores were heard from all over the house as Brian tiptoed from his bedroom at two in the morning to Portia's room. He pushed the door open slowly and Portia was still awake, illuminated by an unusually bright full moon. She stared out the window motionless.

"Can I come in?" Brian said softly.

"Of course," Portia said, sounding the strongest she had in the two days since she had come home from the hospital.

Brian picked up a chair and put it next to the bed between Portia and the window. "You look beautiful in moonlight."

Portia smiled a real smile and chuckled. "You're such a good liar. Almost as good as me. You know, right?"

"That you're a good liar?"

"No. About…the tumor."

"And that you're pregnant. Anything else?"

"I'm glad you know. I'm not sad. Really."

Brian got out of his chair and knelt on one knee. He looked up at Portia, and the way her bandage was lit by the moonlight made it look like the kind of halo that circles the paintings of the Virgin Mary. A cool salty breeze blew in through the small opening in the window, and both he and Portia took in deep breaths. He took both her hands. "Will…you…marry…me?"

"Don't…"

"I wanted to ask you that all those years ago in this very spot and I didn't. I should have. I shouldn't have left."

"I left. Not you," Portia said, sliding down in her bed placing her face inches from Brian's. "I didn't ever want to burden anyone. Mother told me my first words were *me do self.* That's how I lived my life. That's how I *live* my life. Yes I will marry you Brain Da Lousy."

Portia and Brian's lips touched ever so slightly at first, then became a strong, passionate French kiss that surprised both of them. Portia motioned for Brian to join her on the narrow bed, and they somehow managed to sleep together in peace all night long.

Morning sunlight never appeared slowly in Portia's bedroom. With no window coverings, the bright light burst in and awakened Brian from his sleep. Portia seemed to be resting soundly, so he didn't wake her as he arose and headed back to his room.

As he let the hot water from the shower blast the sleep from his eyes, he tried to imagine Juliette's reaction to the news of marriage. After visualizing several violent outbursts from her, he worked hard to put it out of his mind by going through the White Sox lineup when they won the Series in '05.

"Are you two out of your fucking minds?" Juliette yelled at the foot of Portia's bed, about as loud as Brian had ever heard a female scream in person.

"You're hurting my ears in more ways than you know," Portia said calmly. Brian sat, shocked and awed, next to the window. He had never seen Juliette *this* crazed.

"This is not the time for marriage! No! I won't have you…taken from me…twice!" Juliette seethed at first, but melted into little girl trembles by the end of her plea. "I don't want some…stranger…to come in here and take over," she said as she stormed out slamming the heavy door behind her, which made the picture on the wall go crooked.

Portia held her hands to her face with palms together as if in prayer for a few seconds, then covered her face with her hands momentarily. She lowered her hands and shook her head slightly as if she had just finished washing her face and was refreshed.

"Brian, see that picture on the wall?"

Brian instinctively went to the picture and straightened it. The picture was a framed, enlarged black-and-white photo of Juliette angelically sleeping in her baby bed.

"Hand it to me."

Brian lifted it off the nail and gave it to Portia.

She turned it over and began twisting the little nails that held the photo in its frame. Brian watched as Portia carefully removed the cardboard backing and placed it on her lap. She retrieved an Exacto knife from the end table drawer and placed the tip underneath a corner of the photo. As she lifted it, Brian noticed that in fact the photo which was on display in the frame was still in place. Portia was lifting a second photo that was hidden behind the first. She raised it up with the photo image facing her.

Brian was stumped. He stood there in dumb anticipation. The way Portia held the large photo with only the white backing facing him, reminded him of how the contestants used to hold their "questions" for final Jeopardy, waiting for Art Fleming or Alex Trebek to give them the signal to reveal their "question." *So*, Brian wondered, *would it be an answer or a question?*

Portia tried hard to keep a neutral expression on her face as she held the photo. She alternated looking at Brian and at the picture, but that morphed into an almost comical succession of smiles, frowns, stressful contortions and eyes filled with total terror. She turned the photo to Brian.

"Come closer."

From across the room Brian could see that it was another enlarged black-and-white baby photo, more than likely taken at the same session as the one that was on display in the frame. But as he tentatively inched forward, he could see that baby Juliette was in a different position and the blanket that was covering her in the other photo was off of her in this one.

"Take a good look," Portia said, her face having settled on a sweet smile.

He leaned over, wondering if this was like one of those *what's wrong with this picture?* puzzles. He started at Juliette's face and worked his way around the baby toys, blanket, and her…feet!

"Holy jumpin' shit!" Brian said dropping to his knees, which hurt, but he didn't even notice. His index finger shook slightly as he counted her tiny baby toes, "One, two, three, four, five, six, one, two three, four, five, six," his voice a raspy whisper by the last *six*. "I'm…I…she's…is it true? Brian managed to ask as he brain swirled in a hallucinatory whirlpool of emotion, hormones, adrenaline, and images of DNA helix ladders. "This is Juliette?" he asked, now as composed as one could be on one's cranky knees. Portia nodded. "She has twelve toes?" Portia nodded again. "Juliette is my…daughter?" he asked, almost falling as he stood up.

"Yes," Portia said, smiling broadly.

Brian walked to the window and blankly stared out to the very spot where they made love and probably conceived Juliette. "It's strange, but I haven't felt anything like this since my father died." He turned quickly to Portia, worried that she took it the wrong way, which he knew was easy to do. "I know that sounds wrong. But when I found out my father had died, I wasn't there, at his side. I got a phone call. I remember visualizing the words coming through the phone, then into my ear, then traveling to my brain, and sending out an alarm to the rest of my body, until my entire being, every bone, organ, hair follicle, absorbed the reality of it. And that's sort of what I'm feeling now. Juliette is *my* daughter. Oh my God! Does she know?"

"Not yet. I'm going to tell her right after this."

"Should I be there?"

"No!" Portia said abruptly. She caught herself and added, "I really think it's better that I tell her…alone."

Brian turned to the window again, and noticed Juliette walking down the beach. "I suppose I should feel elated," he said, watching Juliette avoiding the ocean's water lapping on the sand. "Having a…daughter. A beautiful, wonderful human being daughter..." He turned to Portia and resembled a third grader who couldn't understand why his parents were divorcing. "But I did the math. It doesn't add up."

"She was late. Very late. They had to induce the birth. It wasn't an easy one."

"But why? Why the deception? Why didn't you let me…in?"

"Me…do…self. That's all. I didn't want to burden a young man with my decision," Portia said, not knowing what else to say, except the things she had been telling herself since she was a toddler.

"What about this middle-aged man standing in front of you?"

"There's a house full of burdens here."

Brian turned to watch Juliette disappearing in the distance. "Not true."

"I tortured myself for years over keeping Juliette without a father. But I didn't want to take that chance. She was so wonderful, such a joy, and I didn't want to risk losing her. She was my life."

"I don't think I can screw up her too bad now."

Portia put both hands on her belly, which still didn't show her pregnancy. "I trust you'll try to protect us. All of us."

Brian sat on the bed next to Portia and placed one had on her abdomen, and stroked her bandaged head. "This is a lot for Juliette to take in."

"She can handle it. It's genetic, you know," Portia said smiling.

Brian thought he felt something stir in Portia's belly, but he said nothing. He turned his head and could still see Juliette walking far down the beach. Brian hadn't been to a wedding or a funeral in a while. Not even for an acquaintance. And now he was facing life events at breakneck speed. A ship passed beyond the lighthouse and as his mind raced with possibilities, eventualities, realities, and fatalities, he knew he wouldn't jump the next tramp steamer to somewhere far from here. He knew it was time to drop anchor right where he was.

Brian liked cooking for the house. Timing the burgers, the mashed potatoes, and the broccoli so they were finished cooking simultaneously was a challenge he enjoyed. He only hoped Juliette would return soon and help in the cleanup and preparation for dinner. He concentrated on pouring the perfect amount of lactose-free milk into the large bowl of boiled, peeled potatoes, trying hard not to contemplate what it would be like if Juliette left him alone to care for Smart House. He carefully removed any bit of potato peels, knowing what a stickler Mr. Dawson was for ultra-white mashed potatoes. Mr. Dawson said potatoes were "abused" by illegal aliens in fields and factories and that the skins were the thin membrane that protected the food supply. Brian didn't dare ask Mr. Dawson exactly how they were "abused."

After Brian served Mr. Dawson, Mrs. Pangborne, and Portia, he watched Reyna feed Beatrice her bag of liquid food through the tube that connected to a shunt. She actually seemed to look healthier since the shunt was inserted, and he wondered how long Beatrice could continue in this state. As he watched the milky fluid flow through the tube into Beatrice, he realized it could be many months or even years.

"Do you need any help?" Juliette asked, surprising Brian.

In that instant, Brian forgot that Juliette was his daughter. But only for an instant.

"Nothing has changed," Juliette said sternly. "Biology doesn't mean shit. You know that, right?"

"Is that what you've decided?" Brian asked, thinking to himself that he sounded fatherly in a way he didn't want.

"Yes. That is the way it will be. I'm sorry," she said walking over to the other side of the bed.

Brian went to the kitchen and turned on the hot water tap. It came out cool at first, and he kept his finger in the stream of water until it scalded him. He didn't notice how hot it had become until it was too late, he thought to himself, as he balanced the faucet taps to make the temperature easier to handle. It would take time to have the daughter he didn't know he had. Time and who knows what else.

Pregnancy, marriage, divorce, disease, potato peels all competed for space in Brian's brain as he washed the dishes and placed them in the drying rack. *One at a time,* he thought as he scrubbed one mucky plate after another until it was squeaky clean and moved on to the next.

"I'll dry," Juliette said as she entered the kitchen. "Mom and Grandma are resting."

Brian made the water a little hotter as he picked up a greasy frying pan. "I hope you'll give our marriage your blessing," he said scrubbing the pan.

"Why do you need my blessing?"

"You're…" Brian said, then stopped, to edit his words. "It's important to your mom. And to me."

"As far as marriage, yes, I won't stop you. Mom loves you and I know you love her. I guess that is what marriage is supposed to be, isn't it?"

Brian just smiled and nodded his head. "Ouch," he said getting scalded again. Then an awful realization shot into his brain; his divorce isn't official yet. "Yes, marriage is all about love," he said, and dreaded the fact that he'd have to call Frances to find out where the divorce papers were.

Brian switched on an extra light in the kitchen as the sun set beyond the sun porch windows. As Juliette and he shared kitchen duties he would steal secret glimpses of her, trying to discover traces of himself in her. *That mole on the side of her neck? Her hairline? Maybe the way she sniffles a lot?* It was no use. He decided the two connections he and Juliette shared, in the form of two extra little piggies on her feet, were snipped off by a doctor before she had a full head of hair. As far as he could tell, Juliette was all Portia.

After this day of epiphanies and revelations, the evening was awash in mundane trivialities as if their nervous systems knew it was time to shut down or risk overload. Juliette sat by her grandmother's bedside and played along vocally with *Wheel of Fortune*, *Jeopardy*, and even switched over to the Game Show Channel, where reruns of game shows from the seventies still lived on with the likes of Soupy Sales and Nipsy Russell.

Brian brought a stack of mail that had piled up for the past few days into Portia's room. She had her magnifying glass and enjoyed browsing through the many catalogues.

"Look at this contraption!" she exclaimed, pointing to a page in a catalogue that featured products for the elderly and infirmed. "How does this device function?"

Brian glanced over at the picture of the long, clear cylinder connected to tubes and assorted pumps. He read from the ad in his best TV infomercial announcer's voice, *"Simply place the cylinder over the penis and pump the handle on the manual unit, or press the 'ON' button on the battery-powered unit.*

Portia began giggling uncontrollably.

Brian read louder and began laughing, *"The vacuum will cause the penis to become erect. The soft, comfortable silicone ring, placed around the base of the penis, will aid in maintaining the erection and will not inhibit sexual pleasure. Kit includes vacuum cylinder, four comfort rings in assorted sizes, lubricant and easy-to-follow instruction manual. You must be twenty-one years or older to order sexual aids.* I can't help visualizing Mr. Dawson fumbling with this thing in the dark..."

The door opened and Juliette peeked in, causing Brian and Portia to stop dead.

"What's so funny?" Juliette smiled.

"You won't believe this, honey!" Portia said, grabbing the catalogue back Brian. "*Simply place the cylinder over the penis*...Look at this crazy contraption!"

"Hey, don't show her that!" Brian said, obviously upset.

Portia's giggling eased down then stopped. "Why not?"

"I don't know, it's...inappropriate." Brian said firmly.

"It is gross. Funny but gross," Juliette deadpanned as she left the room.

Portia put the catalogue down and motioned for Brian to get closer. "That was amazing."

"What?"

"You just became a dad."

"I did?" Brian said perplexed. His expression switched from befuddled to enlightened. "Holy crap." Brian leaned over and kissed Portia lightly on the lips.

Brian handed Portia a *New Yorker* and continued going through the foot-high stack of mail. He was tossing envelope after envelope into the trash can when he stopped and opened one that looked like it might be of interest. He read from a letter, "*Dear Beatrice Smart, Your payment for your Personal Post Box Express is due.* Did you now your mother had a personal post box?"

"At the post office?"

"No, this is one of those private businesses that offer a post box."

"No, I didn't. That's surprising," Portia said, putting her magnifying glass down.

Juliette, who was standing just outside the slightly ajar door eavesdropping, headed back to her room and began plotting to make sure she got to the secret post office box before anyone else did.

CHAPTER FIFTEEN

Frances was shocked beyond words when she opened the refrigerator door for some half-and-half for her first cup of coffee that morning. Taped to the carton was a note from Raul. "That weasel," she said aloud, hiking her pantyhose up under her skirt. "Like I need this shit first thing in the morning." Her scheme of selling the house, putting all the money in the bank until the final numbers were settled upon when the divorce was finalized, and collecting interest was starting to wear on her. Living in Raul's small, one-bedroom condo to save even more money didn't seem worth it anymore. She hadn't heard him complain to her face but pulled her lips tight as she read the Post-it, *Frances, in the future please try to put away your dirty late-night dinner and cocktail messes. I found roaches this morning for the first time.*

"So I gave him roaches, huh? That fat pussy, I'll give him crabs next time. I can't wait to get out off this dump of his," she said menacingly as she tossed the note into the trash. She pulled her cell out of her handbag and pushed a stored number. Her divorce lawyer's voice mail activated after a few rings. "Kimberly! It's time to tighten the screws. Let's go nuclear now! I have to make my move! Call me at the office in a half hour." She snapped the phone shut and put it back in her handbag. "I'll have to straighten out Raul at the office," she said, putting the half-and-half on the granite counter and exiting the condo for work.

With morning rush hour just about over, Francis enjoyed speeding faster than usual on the two-lane highway that wound through the wooded suburbs of Virginia. She felt confident that within a day or two she'd finally nail Brian. She knew he was starting a new life wherever the hell he was hiding on Cape Cod, and she figured he assumed everything was going along just peachy-keen. She smiled as she accelerated and maneuvered around a slow moving mini-van and felt deliciously confident that her nuclear attack would work.

She sashayed through the office hallway and poked her head into Raul's office, where he was busy on his computer. "I read your note," she said with faux joviality. "Let's talk," she said, blowing him kiss.

Raul froze in terror momentarily, shook his head, and got back to his computer keyboard.

Frances closed her office door, sat at her desk, pushed the speaker phone button, and dialed her lawyer's number.

"Kimberly Cunningham."

"Don't give me that Kimberly Cunningham shit. The Enola Gay is enroute," Francis said into the phone while she turned on her computer.

"I got your message. You're sure you want to do this?"

"I've got Raul up my ass. I've got to get moving. Brian wants out, so I'll give him an out."

"Just to confirm, we're telling Brian we've changed our mind; we want 95 percent of everything or the deal's off and we'll drag it through the courts for the next several years," Kimberly said flatly. "I'll overnight it to the address you gave me."

"You bet! I just Google-Earthed the address he gave me, and it's a fucking mansion right on the goddammed beach! He's got something going on there that he does not want to lose! I know I wouldn't want to lose that!"

"All right, but you know you won't get anything near 95 percent. And if this goes to court you'll be lucky to get 51 percent."

"This is *not* going to court."

"I'll send it right now. I'll call you later."

Frances deactivated the speaker phone and typed in the address of the Smart house into Google-Earth again. "How did that fucker pull this off?" She zoomed in as far as the program would allow, and took a simulated tour of the homes and estates surrounding Smart House. Imagining she was in her private helicopter and taking hefty bites from the jelly donut with increasing ferocity, she became enraged that Brian had somehow maneuvered himself into to exactly the lifestyle she longed for and felt she deserved. The Cape was where hordes of Kennedys lived for chrissake! That was real prestige. Not like the faux new money of East Hampton, where any schmuck could plop down thirty grand for a summer rental and have the privilege of giving Barbra Streisand the finger after she cuts you off in a crowded parking lot. The Cape was old money. They got it the old-fashioned way; they inherited it.

Frances pushed the speaker phone button and dialed another number.

"Prestige Properties," a high pitched child like voice announced.

"Beth, please," Francis said as she exited Google-Earth and typed in the website.

"Beth here," a perky southern-accented female voice chirped.

"Beth! Frances here. Good news! We're upping our search. Start sending me anything in the low to mid one million range."

"Mah goodness, Frances! Did you win the lotto?"

"You got it, darlin'!" Frances said, affecting a strong southern accent herself. "We're all going to cash in on this one!"

"I'll start a search and email you the latest properties."

"One more thing; it's *got* to be Georgetown!"

"Georgetown it is, sweetie! Bah-bye!"

Frances shoved the last bit of donut into her gob and felt good about herself. Everything was falling into place exactly as she had planned. She timed it perfectly! She was certain that Brian was deep into something on the Cape and desperate for the divorce to come through at the exact time that she was getting ready to dump Raul, although he thought that he was dumping her.

Ding her computer chimed, as it announced she had received a new email.

"Goody!" she said opening the email from Beth. "Damn! One point two mill' for that piece of crap! Wait a minute…oh my God, it's on the same street as Hillary! I've got to see this one," she said to herself as she replied to the email anxiously.

She then clicked on her mortgage loan calculator and began entering numbers; o*ne point two million with a down payment of seven hundred thousand for thirty years with an adjustable rate…shoot! I can afford that! That fucker just better not mess with me.*

Just across town from Hillary's street in Georgetown, George sat alone at the Taystee Diner counter after his last graveyard shift ever. With twenty years under his belt, he was ready to get out. He figured that with his pension he could live anywhere in the country on four grand a month. Even though his official retirement date was almost two months away, he could cash in enough vacation and comp days to make this his last day on the job.

"Where's your buddy been at?" Bob X said as he plopped a plate of *S.O.S.* in front of him. The Taystee diner was probably the last place in Washington that kept that item on the menu; it was a World War II army grunt term for *shit on a shingle*, which was corned beef hash served on toast swimming in gravy.

"He's hanging out with the hoi poloi up on Cape Cod," George said dumping copious amounts of salt onto his steaming platter.

"Is he coming back?"

"Good question," George said, as he shoveled the first morsel into his mouth. "You'll be the first to know after I find out. Hey, did I tell you I'm retiring?"

"How old are you anyway? You don't look *that* old!"

"I'm getting out after twenty-five years of service," George said as he sipped from his chipped coffee mug with decades of coffee turning it a shade of light brown. "Believe me. I'm younger than this coffee mug."

"Shit, I've been waitin' tables for twenty years and I ain't thinking about retiring!"

"That because you love your work."

"What are you gonna do?"

"I might buy this place just so I can be your boss and fire your ass," George threatened.

Bob X caught a fit of the giggles and went into the kitchen. George wished he knew what he was going to do upon retirement. Hell, he didn't know what he was doing after breakfast. But he did know he had it with being a G-man. He was considering three options: become a mail order preacher; open a batting cage in Hawaii; or, he feared, do like a lot of ex-law enforcement guys do…drink himself to death.

Bob X came out of the kitchen again, arms loaded with hot breakfast plates and said as he whizzed by, "If I were you I'd be hanging with Brian on the Cape."

George scraped up the last bits of corned beef hash and gravy with his fork and thought that was probably a better option than the first three. Who knows, maybe a batting cage on the Cape would be almost as good as Hawaii.

It really wasn't that hard a decision for George to go for a long drive after handing in his final retirement papers. He didn't have any family, friends, or even pets to stop him. And he figured it would be a gas to drop in on Brian and present him with the plaque for his crime stopper stunt. It was beyond irony that Brian's bold move to prevent a mugging sent his whole life reeling, and also got him a commendation from the Capitol Police. So after signing the papers at HQ, he didn't even bother going back to his apartment. He just headed for the Beltway without a map; just an address on the Cape written on a piece of scrap paper.

Frances knew Raul was tired of sharing his condo with her, but she also knew that all she had to do was maybe blow him four or five more times, and screw him maybe two or three to buy another month at his place. She didn't feel one bit guilty about it either. He was damn lucky to get it as far as she was concerned. And besides, she liked how it felt. Not the brief sex part. That was terrible. But the before and after when she knew she was getting what she wanted. That made her feel really good about herself.

Kimberly told her the package with the new terms of the divorce settlement was over-nighted and would arrive by ten a.m. that morning, so she got to work by nine just in case it got there early.

Raul was already at his desk, so she stopped in his office, closed the door, locked it, went over to him, and grabbed his cock while he sat in front of his computer. He shook like a girl getting goosed on the cookie line in eighth grade. Frances was wearing as revealing a blouse as she thought she could get away with at the office and shoved her tits in his face.

"Good morning, Raul," Frances said, backing off and straightening her top and bra.

She knew she still had it. And him. Now it was time to wait for Brian's call, which would get her out of Raul's and onto Hillary's street once and for all. She worked hard for what she had so far, and she wasn't about to stop now. She sat across the room from Raul and observed him. She enjoyed watching him recover from her sudden crotch attacks. "After all this time you still get surprised by my cock and awe attacks?" she asked coyly.

"It's more the pain than the surprise. You may not know this, but getting whacked in the nuts can hurt," Raul said sounding pissed off and threatening for the first time ever.

"Oh really," Frances said, acting insulted that her jab in the zipper could be anything other than pure joy. "Maybe I'll just have to curtail my amorous adventures in your nether regions. I'll talk at you later," she said rushing out of his office.

As she walked down the hall toward her office she smiled broadly soaking in the brilliance of her strategy. Raul was a perfect stop gap between breaking up and getting paid off from the divorce, and the next step would set her endgame in motion.

She sat in her ergonomic black leather chair, switched her TV to *The View,* and entered the tracking number of the newly constructed divorce paper package onto the FedEx website.

"Bingo! Package delivered and signed for at 8:59 a.m. by *Brain DeLousie*. I'll bet his brain is feeling a tad worse than lousy right now," she said with devious pleasure. "Damn, he's had it for a half hour already," she said as she picked up her phone and speed dialed her lawyer.

"Kimberly! Mr. Bad Brain has had the package for a half hour! Did he call you? No. Alright, I'll call you when I hear anything."

Frances hung up and unwrapped a chocolate croissant just as Hillary Clinton appeared in an interview on *The View.*

"My new neighbor! Hillary, I'll be there soon!" she shouted at the muted TV screen.

Brian was numb as he scrambled a half dozen eggs in a large bowl. He didn't get a chance to scan the documents in the FedEx envelope, but the cover letter from Frances' lawyer friend Kimberly laid everything out plainly. The new terms were brutal; 95% of the entire escrow account went to Frances and 5% to Brian. Of course, they played up the fact that no alimony would be required and he could keep the mini-van, but that left Brian with about $40,000 cash out of the $850,000 or more profit they made by selling the house. As he poured the eggs into a large cast iron frying pan, the olive oil sizzled and splattered some hot oil onto his wrist. He pulled his hand back and ran it under some cold water. As the pain dissipated, he thought nothing would make him happier than cutting Frances loose once and for all no matter what the price. He hurried back to the scrambled eggs before they turned into a flattened, thick omelet and began mixing furiously.

After Mr. Dawson was served, Brian checked on Beatrice. There was a note pinned to her shirt from Juliette saying Reyna stepped out for just a minute and she was headed for town. He carried the breakfast tray with his and Portia's meal into her room. She had dozed back to sleep, but just as he entered the room the classical radio station played what they called their "SoozAlarm" and John Phillip Sousa's "Stars and Stripes Forever" woke her from her light slumber.

Portia smiled as she recognized Brian standing next to her with her breakfast. "Is it the fourth of July?" she asked softly.

"Kind of," he said, bending over and lightly kissing her on the lips. "It could be my independence day."

"Do tell," Portia said, sitting up in her bed and looking forward to her breakfast in bed.

"I got my final divorce terms from Frances. I'll officially be a free man shortly if I can just work out a few details."

"You can remain a free man, Brian," Portia said solemnly as she put some jam on her toast.

"I've never felt freeer."

Portia managed a smile and nibbled on her toast. "Is Juliette around?"

"She left a note saying Reyna would be right back and she had a few things to do in town," Brian said as he began to eat his breakfast. He didn't want Portia to know he had no intention of fighting Frances for the money and delaying their marriage. Knowing Portia she'd demand that he fight Frances and put her on hold instead. As he looked at Portia delicately savoring her tea, he knew time was more precious than money.

They ate their breakfasts, although Portia left quite a bit, which Brian finished off for her. The window was open, and Portia asked Brian to describe everything he could see.

Portia laid there with her eyes closed as Brian described the sea, the young couple on the beach, the gulls, the ships, and the female kayaker taking her morning spin around the lighthouse with hair flowing in the ocean wind.

Portia dozed off, but Brian still described the scene outside her window down to the minutest details. As he narrowed in on the differentiating colors on the sea gulls, and the varying shades of green and blue in the ocean, and the shapes of clouds he realized how little he normally saw with his eyes; but becoming Portia's eyes allowed him to see so much more. He suddenly remembered that he was supposed to go to the private post office box store to find out if it was possible to retrieve the mail, but he didn't wake Portia. He'd just let her nap, do the dishes, and then later on have Portia call and hopefully get permission to open the box. He gathered up the tray, headed back to the kitchen, and began his morning clean up.

Juliette was nervous. She knew that Portia's attempt to gain entry to the safety deposit box at the bank resulted in disaster. She wasn't quite sure how she would try to persuade the store manager to allow her access to her grandmother's post office box, but she had the letter from the doctor saying Beatrice was incapacitated, and plenty of ID.

She entered the *Mail Boxes 'N Stuff* store and approached the front counter, which was empty. A young man appeared from a doorway at the end of the counter and several steps before reaching Juliette a wide grin beamed across his peach-fuzzed face.

"Juliette Smart!" he said excitedly. "It's me, Mike Fraser. From The Tent!"

Juliette wanted to jump in the air with glee, knowing that Mike had the hots for her all summer at The Tent last summer.

"Hi, Mike! Nice to see you!" she said, shaking his hand.

"Wow! Great to see you! What brings you here?"

"Um, actually, I'm running an errand for my grandma. She's really ill."

"Oh, I'm so sorry to hear that. What do you need?" Mike said earnestly.

"Grandma got this notice to pay for her mail box, so I have the payment...but she also wanted me to pick up her mail for her. But I forget the combination."

"No worries, come on back here," he said, immediately raising a part of the counter for her. He led her to the back of the mail boxes, which was a narrow aisle. "You can get the mail from the rear of the box and read the combination on the back of the door from there, too."

Juliette went to the mail box and shuffled through the mail, retrieving whatever could be important, and leaving several pieces of junk mail there. She walked back to the counter and was led to the customer side by Mike. "Here's the money for the next six months," she said handing it to him.

He took it from her and began twitching the way young men do when they fear a female might be leaving them forever. "Uh, do you think, um, I could call you sometime for maybe, lunch or something?"

"Sure," Juliette said politely. She wrote her number on a scrap of paper and handed it to him.

Mike look stunned as he held the piece of paper up and gazed at the magic number that would reconnect him with Juliette. "I'll call you, uh, later, or tomorrow at the latest," he said excitedly.

"Okay. Bye."

Juliette thought that she actually did like Mike Fraser and couldn't really remember why she didn't date him last summer. Or anyone else for that matter. But now she thought going to lunch with a nice guy might be a good idea. She sat in the car and opened the first piece of mail. And as she read the contents of that statement from Astor Brokerage she almost screamed at the top of her lungs but instead she whispered to herself, "Holy jumpin' shit. I'm rich."

After she calmed herself down, Juliette pointed the car back home and wondered if there's a way that she misinterpreted the financial statement, which was an update on the trust fund, established in her name, to the tune of $250,000. Maybe it was some kind of tax dodge for her grandmother. But if it was real…wow!

She turned on the car's CD player, pumped up the volume to the *Rent* soundtrack. The excitement was too much for her, so she pulled over at an overlook facing the coastline. She pulled the statement out again to study it a little more carefully in case she read it wrong. Nope. A trust fund in her name…and as she inspected the back of the second page…another trust fund in Portia's name for the exact same amount of $250,000.

"Oh my God," she said softly, stunned by the magnitude of the figures. She grabbed the rest of the mail she had absconded and pored over them, to see if perhaps Uncle Richard was also a beneficiary of Beatrice's wealth.

She couldn't find anything that mentioned Richard, which made her relieved at first, but soon turned to terror as she imagined what Richard might do with this kind of money involved.

Driving back onto the road, another thought crossed her mind that prompted her to white knuckle onto the steering wheel. What about Brian? What if he knew about Portia's riches and that was the only reason he wanted to marry her…in her current condition. Juliette tried to stop her mind from thinking such an awful thing about her own biological father…but if her own uncle could be plotting such menacing deeds, why not a father who suddenly appeared from out of nowhere? Or maybe that's why Portia wanted to get married; so that Brian, the penis carrier, could take care of her estate and have control of his daughter.

As her mind raced she looked at the speedometer and noticed she was speeding. She tapped on the brake pedal, which seemed to also calm her down. This wasn't the time for jumping to conclusions. It was a time for careful, measured, thoughtful, spying.

Brian dreaded making this phone call almost as much as the time he had to call his mother from the hospital to inform her that her husband, his dad, had died. In fact, it was that thought that made him feel a little better about calling Frances to tell her that she won. She could have the money if it meant he could have his life back. *Nobody's dead,* he thought to himself, trying to put a positive spin on it. But he thought of Portia lying upstairs with her head still bandaged and a heavy sadness crept back into his heart. He knew why there was a rush to independence, and it was time to make it happen.

He went out to his mini-van for privacy and dialed Frances at the office from his cell.

"It's about time," she said, sounding annoyed.

"I can't wait another six months. What can I do?" Brian asked, his words drenched in total defeat.

Frances knew she had him by the short and curlies. She twisted her face in absolute glorious glee and pulled the chain repeatedly like Kirk Gibson after his World Series home run. She composed herself and licked her lips. "Well, there is a way to expedite the whole process."

"I'm listening."

"If we both tell a little white lie and say we haven't lived together for six months and put some phony dates on some papers and go into court, the judge can waive a waiting period and have the divorce granted immediately."

"How much will that cost me?" Brian asked without hesitation.

"Just agree to the 95 percent, that's all," Frances said as matter-of-factly. "Deal or no deal?"

"Deal. Take the money. And I hope someday, you'll find happiness. Let me know how to make it happen. Bye." Brian said, as he punched the red button terminating the call.

Frances punched her mini tape recorder, turning it off. "That prick! I knew he'd pull some shit like that! What the fuck makes him think I'm not happy?" she screamed to the phone. But her hissy fit was short lived as a wave of euphoria took over her being as she contemplated the victory at hand.

"I wonnnnnnn!" she shouted so fiercely she sounded like a mother bear caught in a leg trap.

Juliette pulled into the driveway and Brian went over to greet her.

"Get everything done?" he said cheerfully, trying to mask his distress.

"Is everything okay?" Juliette asked getting out of her car.

"Oh, yeah. Just got off the phone with my ex."

"'Nuff said. How's everybody?" Juliette asked, pushing the envelopes and papers a little bit further down into her bag.

"Everybody's resting. I think I'll start lunch."

"I'll help," Juliette said, as she began to contemplate exactly how she would begin her covert investigation. Or at least, have a heart to heart with her mom.

CHAPTER SIXTEEN

Brian felt both overjoyed and incredibly stupid. How could he possibly have let Frances get away with her stunt that scammed him out of hundreds of thousands of dollars? But he also realized that it was Frances who wanted to buy instead of rent and picked a townhouse in Adams Morgan instead of the outlying suburbs. It was Frances who made all the financial decisions that led to acquiring massive profits from the sale of their house in the super-heated, now gentrified, Adams Morgan area. He figured he was buying his life back with money he wouldn't have had anyway. He was back where he started before he met her, and closed his eyes and smiled with great satisfaction as he sat with his first cup of coffee alone at the kitchen table.

"What put a smile on your face this rainy morning?" Portia asked, standing in the kitchen unannounced and unescorted for the first time since her fall.

"You're up!" Brian said, excited and surprised.

"I'm feeling pretty good. Fine, in fact."

Juliette rushed in the kitchen, robe flying. "Mom! Are you okay?"

"Yes, yes, let's have some breakfast," she said in the strongest voice she could muster. "I want to get this damn bandage off today."

"I'll call the doctor and take you," Juliette quickly responded.

Portia looked at Brian for his approval, and he nodded in agreement.

"Great! Right after a little breakfast," Portia said, sounding almost chipper.

Juliette knew this was her perfect opportunity to be alone with her mom and get to the bottom of the trust fund mystery. She was not going to let the men outsmart them; not Richard and not Brian. As she showered, she went over in her mind exactly how she would set up her mother to gauge how much she knew about the funds and how much Brian knew. She would make it clear to Portia that she would fiercely protect her and Grandma. She might let her know that there was no need to worry about Richard coming over and ever threatening them again. She might even tell her the secret why: She has a gun hidden in her room.

Portia wore a beret that almost completely hid her bandage, and she looked better than she had since before her fall. Brian kissed her good-bye, and she gingerly got into the car next to Juliette. Brian waved as they headed for the doctor.

Reyna was tending to Beatrice, Mr. Dawson was deep into a legal pad of mathematics, and Brian tried not to think too far into the future as he ground coffee beans in the kitchen sink, since it was such a messy proposition, and suddenly out the window he saw a car. The shrubs were getting thick so he couldn't really see if it was perhaps Juliette and Portia returning, or a visitor.

He placed the lid on the coffee can he was filing with newly ground beans and opened the front door. There wasn't a car directly in front of the house, but he walked to end of the tunnel of shrubs to the curb and to the right, there he was...George!

"What the hell are you doing here?" he shouted to George, enthralled at the sight of his buddy, standing next to his station wagon holding a flat package in his hand.

"Special delivery from the United States Government," he declared officiously, standing erect and saluting.

"What's this?"

George knelt on one knee, presented the package to Brian with both hands, and bowed his head in mock reverence. After Brian took it from him, George stood up, pulled out a pack of Marlboros, and lit one up. "I already checked it out. It's pretty cool," he said, dragging on the cigarette as Brian pulled apart the box. "I still think you were an asshole to do it, but hey, it's your life."

"Wow. Look at all the Whereases! I like this part, *with clear-headed thinking he verbally disarmed an armed attacker.* They left out the juicy stuff I learned from you."

"Congratulations to you. That really is an honor," George said extending his arm to shake Brian's hand. Upon clasping his hand he added, "You could have been killed, you know."

"Come on inside," Brian said, ignoring George's concern. "Wait'll you see the view."

"Do I get to meet the family?" George asked, locking his car with his remote and following Brian to the tunnel of shrubs. "Ever hear of a weed whacker? By the way, what's going on with Frances? Did you manage to get out of that life sentence okay?"

"I'm out, but it cost me," Brian said opening the front door.

George stood in the doorway and stared in disbelief at the panoramic ocean view that was laid out in front of him. "Yeah, but it looks like it was worth it, pal. Sweet!"

"I'm just a boarder," Brian said, leading George through the kitchen and walking into the sun-room where Mr. Dawson sat upright in his wooden chair, snoring rhythmically as he dozed. "That's Mr. Dawson. His great-great-great grandfather was one of the leaders at the Boston Tea Party."

"He looks old enough to have been there himself. Got an ashtray?"

"Let's go out to the veranda," Brian said, motioning for George to follow through the large sliding glass door.

"Veranda? We call them decks in Chicago," George said, snuffing his smoke out on his shoe bottom. "Who's the old man?"

"He's the boarder. Portia's mother is with the aide upstairs."

"How's she doing?"

"Well, she's breathing on her own."

"How's Portia?"

Brian looked at George and realized he hadn't told George anything about Portia's tumor, pregnancy, the insane brother trying to steal her mother's money, or the fact that they were soon getting married. "Let's go for a walk," Brian said, walking down the steps to the beach.

Brian and George had spent many a warm day by the water when they were kids in Chicago, but not walking on sand. The "beach" where they spent most of their time at the edge of Lake Michigan on Chicago's north side at Diversey Street was a few yards of grass that led to a wide concrete walkway that was ideal for long walks and bike rides. As kids they would defy their parents' rules and secretly ride their bikes all the way downtown to the Oak Street beach, where the city created an actual sandy beach with volleyball nets right under Chicago skyscrapers. It was on those secret trips that they would smoke cigarettes and somehow obtain copies of *Playboy* and ogle at the bikini-clad coeds playing volleyball.

On the white sands of Cape Cod Brian confided in George, telling him every detail of his situation at Smart House as George chain smoked and listened intently. No details were too intimate or embarrassing for Brian to divulge as he emptied his brain to a soul other than Portia for the first time since he arrived at Smart House. Even between the most intimate of lovers, there's a secret place to keep the deepest emotions, not for selfish motives, but to protect a loved one. There's a reason a man always answers *no* when the wife asks if her ass looks big in those jeans. And for that same reason a loved one can't show fear when confronted with the harsh realities of life and death. Brian could tell George his fears and the secret emotions he hid from the Smarts, out of the unconditional love he had for Portia and her family.

George listened without saying a word for nearly half a pack of cigarettes. After hearing the entire timeline for Brian's new life, he put out his smoke and buried the butt in the sand. "Do you feel any different being a dad?" George asked looking out toward a fishing boat on the horizon.

"Not really. Maybe that's because Juliette isn't exactly pre-ordering my Father's Day gifts."

"What are you and the rest of the clan going to do about psycho sibling?"

Brian realized there was one secret he hadn't shared with George or anyone else; Juliette's gun. He picked up a piece of green worn sea glass and skipped it into a wave. "Actually, there's something you should know. You know the *F* in ATF?"

"I don't want to hear about it," George said, abruptly rising from the rock.

Brian caught up with him. "It's not me. It's Juliette."

"The kid has a gun?"

"I found it hidden in her room."

"That's bad. Where'd she get it?"

"I have no idea. I haven't told her I found it yet."

"Not good. Never, ever, ever, have a gun in your possession unless you bought it brand new and saw it come out of the box. That gun could have shot JFK from the grassy knoll and been involved in five drive-bys for all she knows."

"I didn't think of that. What should we do?"

"I'll think of something," he said, lighting up another smoke. Okay, we've discussed the *T* and the *F* now how about a little *A* as in alcohol?"

"I've got some beers back at the house," Brian said putting his arm around George and steering him back home.

As Juliette sat in the waiting room at the hospital absentmindedly turning the pages of *People* magazine, she still wasn't 100 percent convinced that her mom was unaware of the fortune they both had already inherited. She was certain of the love Portia had for Brian, but how much did she really know about Brian? Her attention was drawn to a photograph of a teenaged movie starlet with huge implants on the arm of a middle-aged Hollywood director when a nurse who looked younger than the teenager in the magazine appeared from out of nowhere.

"Are you with Portia Smart?"

"Yes. Is there a problem?"

"Come with me, please," the nurse said, leading her down a hall following signs toward the emergency room.

Juliette was stunned to be back in the exact area where they waited to hear about Portia's condition just days ago.

"Wait here," the nurse said, pointing toward a folding chair outside a double door that had a sign that said *Authorized Personnel Only.*

Juliette sat and wondered if her mom had put that sign there and if she had any idea that one day that sign would be keeping her daughter sitting staring at it from a folding metal chair.

The same doctor who saw Portia after her fall pushed the swinging door open and approached her. "You're her daughter?"

"Yes."

"Did you know your mother decided against treatment?"

"Oh my God, no. Why?"

"She believes it might kill the fetus. I don't usually interfere in personal matters but I thought you should know. There's no guarantee that the tumor's growth will be arrested with treatment but there's a chance. If she doesn't take it, there's no chance. I'm sorry I… had to tell you that."

Juliette was stunned as she sat in her folding metal chair next to the double swinging doors. She wondered if she should call Brian right away, but decided to wait until she could sort out her own feelings. She knew that chemo wasn't a be-all, end-all, cure-all. Many articles she read said that many aggressive cancer fighting-agents kill their victims along with the cancer by destroying immune systems. She also knew why hair fell out with treatment; the drugs kill the fastest growing cells first, and hair probably grows slower than a human being in a uterus.

The doors slowly swung open revealing Portia, minus her bandage with a glorious smile on her face.

"Are you okay? You look…well." Juliette said as she rose from her chair and reached out for Portia's arm.

"I'm wonderful. Everything is fine," Portia said emphatically, punctuating *fine* so there was no mistaking.

Juliette pondered yet another round of cat and mouse on the car ride home attempting to ascertain the hidden life of her mom. She silently escorted Portia to the car and after sitting at the very first red light, blurted out, "You've got to tell me the truth! Why didn't you tell me you decided to refuse treatment?"

Portia smiled and a whimper leaked from her lips. Her head jerked back slightly when the light turned green and Juliette accelerated a little too abruptly, giving her a jolt of head and neck pain. "I don't expect you to understand everything in my life or about my life. Just know how much I love you and life itself."

"You're killing yourself!" Juliette screamed, clenching the steering wheel.

"I'm not killing me. There are two things growing in me. One is a lump of cancer that grows and one is a life that grows. That's a pretty simple choice for me."

Portia's words blunted Juliette's rage. Could it be as simple as that when faced with one's imminent demise?

"Could you please drive a little slower, sweetie?"

Juliette realized she had been swerving around corners and slowed to the speed limit. "I'm sorry."

"No need to apologize," Portia said, patting her on the thigh.

Brian didn't usually drink before six p.m., but an early afternoon beer on the deck with George seemed too good to pass up.

"Remember the Snowflake?" Brian asked George with a Cheshire cat smile.

George closed his eyes and began laughing heartily.

Brian joined in the giggles and was reminded how much history the two shared before they parted ways for a decade or so. The Snowflake was a lakefront motel on the Michigan side of Lake Michigan where Brian, George, and hordes of teenagers from Chicago would rent rooms for weekends during the summer before the drinking age was raised to twenty-one.

"If that place wasn't made of cinder block it would have burnt down every summer," George said once his guffaws subsided. "You know, with all the shit I've been through in my life-- busting mafia motherfuckers with battering rams, undercover drug buys in crack houses-- my favorite memories are from before I moved out of my parents' basement. I wish I could go back." George took a sip from his bottle of beer. "Is that what brought you back here?"

Brian put his bottle on the glass tabletop and looked out to the lighthouse. "I think so. I mean, it was a long time ago. This was the first place I lived other than my parents' house. And as insane as this whole thing seems, I've never felt so, I don't know, *needed* in my life."

"I've had it with being needed. I've been so *kneaded*, I'm flattened, ready for the sauce and cheese and to be put in the oven," George said, lighting up another cigarette.

"Hey, that's a good idea. I could use a hot *peez* for lunch. What should we do about the gun?"

"Nice segue," George said sarcastically. "Talk to Juliette. Find out where she got it, but no matter what she says, the only safe thing to do is just bring it to the local police station and tell them you found a gun and you want to turn it in. That's all. We'll visit Andy and Barney down at the local station house, drop it off, and we're done. No worries."

"No worries," Brian said, clinking bottles with George. "Here they are now," Brian said noticing the car arriving on the street in front of the home.

George began preparing himself on how to react to Portia. He was used to working undercover and hiding his true feelings, which most of the time involved nearly browning his pants in abject terror. But upon meeting his best friend's finance, who could be racked with brain cancer, he wasn't so sure he would be able to hide emotions like pity or sorrow.

Brian and George went inside and stood next to the kitchen, by the front door, and waited for it to open.

Juliette pushed the door open slowly with Portia two steps behind. "Oh, hello," Juliette said warily.

"This is my good buddy George," Brian said, stalling a little bit to make sure Portia could hear him.

Portia entered looking amazing. A strange and unusual reflection from a glass table in the sun room shined a golden shard of light across her face exactly where she decided to stop. Brian hadn't seen her without some kind of bandage across her hair for weeks and she had a different hairstyle than before.

"How do you like it? My hair, I mean. We stopped at the hair salon in town," Portia said, nervously feeling the tips of her shoulder-length hair cut in a trendy swoop. "I haven't had hair this short since grammar school. Hello George," Portia said as she extended her hand, pulled George in closer, and gave him a peck on the cheek.

"It's a pleasure to finally meet you," George said joyfully. He was shocked at how beautiful Portia was, with no sign of her cancer apparent. "Brian hasn't had so little hair since grammar school either," he said pointing to Brian's receding hair line.

Brian stepped toward Portia and gave her a tender kiss on the lips as he touched her bare neck, now exposed by the new hairstyle. "You look fantastic!" he whispered in her ear.

"I'm Juliette," Juliette said flatly, extending her arm to shake hands with George.

"We were just going into town to get some pizza for lunch; is that okay with the both of you?" Brian said, as Portia and Juliette entered the kitchen.

"That's good. Just plain cheese for me, please," Portia said, sitting at the kitchen table.

"Extra cheese and sausage on mine," Juliette added.

Brian blew Portia a kiss, and they headed for George's car.

"She is gorgeous," George said and quickly added, "Portia, I mean."

"They're both gorgeous, I know."

"Juliette seems like a tough cookie. Are you sure you're her father? I mean, she is a looker. No offense…" George said, driving his car out of the parking spot.

"No offense my ass, turn left up here. Yeah, a tough cookie all right. Even a tougher cookie when she's packing," Brian said exasperated.

"We're taking care of that after lunch."

"Are you sure? Maybe we should wait?"

"Never waste time when there's a bullet in the chamber, my friend."

"Turn right over there, and go straight into town," Brian said, beginning to lose his appetite.

Portia walked slowly up the stairs and paused at the top, breathing heavier than usual. She saw Reyna, sitting in a chair next to Beatrice, through the slightly ajar door doing her embroidery. Portia knew she didn't feel right, but attributed it to her day at the hospital and the ride to and from with Juliette prodding her for all kinds of information like a little prosecutor. She wondered if one day she might be lying in a bed right next to her own mother, with Reyna tending to both of them.

"Hello Reyna," Portia said, pushing the door fully open.

"Portia! How was it? Are you okay? What did they tell you?" Reyna said greatly concerned, putting her embroidery into her canvas bag and standing to greet her.

"Oh, everything's stable. No news, really."

"I love your hair! Don't lie to me! Is everything okay?" Reyna demanded.

"Yes, I'm okay. How's Mother?"

"She was smiling a lot today. I gave her a bath and massaged her."

Portia bent over to get within inches of her mother's face. "Her skin looks so beautiful."

"I gave her some nice moisturizer."

"You're so good, Reyna. I hope you'll take care of me some day."

"Stop that talk! You have to take care of all of us! We're not letting you off the hook, so easy!"

Portia smiled and went to her room to take a little nap, feeling drained from the day's excitement. She propped up her pillows so she could look out the window. Once she settled in to a comfortable position, she realized that her head hadn't stop hurting and thought perhaps the pain was increasing. Attributing it to the day's events, she thought about hot summer afternoons on the beach with Juliette as a toddler, bucket and spade in hand. She felt the warmth of the sun, the uneven sand under her blanket, the sounds of the gulls, the crashing of the waves, the oceans spray on her skin...but the room started to spin and become dark. She felt nauseous and feared the act of vomiting would make her head explode as the pain increased with each breath. Her pulse increased, and it was as though the blood pounding and pulsing through body was trying to burst her veins and arteries. Her eyes sucked in the swirling darkness of the room like a black hole making her deathly afraid she was going to die. She knew Reyna was right next door, but each time she tried to make a sound she just choked.

Then as quickly as it descended on her, the blackness of her attack began to dissipate, draining from her head down to her chest, abdomen, legs, and through her feet. She felt more alone than she ever had in her life. Even more alone than when she gave birth to Juliette in a room that was carved out of the side of a mountain and surely was once simply called a cave. A midwife who spoke no English was present, but didn't do much other than pat her forehead with a cool cloth and help guide the baby out of her. Like then, she knew she had to suffer in secret. But she also knew heaven was knocking at the door with more frequency and getting things in order was an immediate priority.

"Are you okay?" Reyna said poking her head into the room.

"Yes, fine, thank you…just resting," Portia said, composing herself.

"Just let me know if you need anything."

"Yes, thank you." Portia said, managing to wave to Reyna. She thought to herself that yes, she did need something. And Brian having his best friend there was a perfect excuse to go ahead with an impromptu wedding.

CHAPTER SEVENTEEN

Frances set everything up like clockwork. She arranged for Brian's flight to DC, had a limo at the airport waiting, and he was hurried into the kitchen of his former residence like the president signing a bill that's been sitting on his desk for a week. After documents were signed, they were rushed to a DC courtroom where all Brian had to do was be told when to enter, sit, stand, and speak his lines, which he mostly accomplished by uttering a single syllable. They stretched the truth where necessary, then waited outside the courtroom for just enough time to read the *Washington Post* sports section. After another appearance in front of the judge for about ninety seconds, their uncontested divorce was granted. The judge didn't even look up from his papers when he closed their file and rushed his clerk for the next batch of paperwork.

It was over. Frances took the limo home and Brian watched the car fade in the distance before he hailed a cab back to the airport. He sat in stunned silence as the cab whizzed past the BMW dealership where he used to take Frances' car. He couldn't believe that twenty years of a relationship were undone in less than twenty minutes. And in about twenty seconds after takeoff, he was completely over it and anxious to get back to the Cape to begin his life anew.

Juliette volunteered to make all the wedding arrangements, thinking that tending to so many details would keep her mind focused on the event rather than the absurdity of it all. The ratcheting-up of the time frame for the marriage also made Juliette face the reality no one seemed to be facing; Portia's pregnancy. Juliette surmised that Brian and probably even Portia had the same outlook that she did, basically that they'd jump off that bridge when came to it. Since Portia's health was in such dire straits, Juliette secretly assumed that the pregnancy would somehow be terminated, whether anyone wanted to face it or not. She found a Unitarian minister that was willing to show up on a day's notice to perform the ceremony. No guests would be invited, and it would take place on the veranda. The only logistical problem would be to get Beatrice out there comfortably for the ceremony.

The plans seemed to be falling into place easily, but at the same time, she knew she and her mom had to have at least one heart to heart before it all became 'til death do us part. It was time to reveal the fact that they were both rich. And if Portia wanted her new husband to inherit that small fortune it was fine with her. Juliette refused to think that Brian could have somehow found out and was nothing more than a male Anna Nicole Smith plotting marriage with someone facing imminent death. She'd leave that ugly conspiracy theory up to her mother to ponder without any help from her.

After booking the minister in less than a half hour, Juliette went back down to the kitchen where Brian, George, and Portia hadn't even started cleaning up after the meal yet.

"All systems go!" she announced proudly.

"No way," Portia said stunned.

"It's a go. I've got a Unitarian minister who does this all the time. He's available."

Brian rose from his chair and went down on one knee. "Will you marry me, tomorrow or whenever?"

Portia looked over to Juliette, who had just sniffled, and thought maybe she was trying to stifle a sob. "Are you crying, Juliette?"

"No. Yes," Juliette said as she burst into tears and hugged Portia and Brian, who were all crying in one big lump of emotion.

George looked at them in silence and finished the last bit of beer from his bottle. As he crossed his legs, the gun in his ankle holster bumped into his calf, which reminded him that a trip to the police station should be next on the wedding planning agenda. "I'll start to clean up," he said rising.

"Let's you and I go over the arrangements," Portia said to Juliette as they composed themselves. "We'll be upstairs if you need us," Portia said softly to Brian, as she kissed his hand and left the room.

George thought to himself that it was very, very weird that the term *arrangements* was used primarily for weddings and funerals. "We are still going to have that talk with Juliette, right?" George asked as Brian cleaned up looking like he was in some kind of robotic clean-up trance.

"Huh, what talk?" Brian said, scraping food from a paper plate into the trash and then running hot water on it.

"You realize you're washing a paper plate," George said in amazement.

"Oh," Brian replied matter-of-factly, and then tossed it into the garbage. "Oh, the gun, right?" Brian said, snapping out of his daze. "Do you think it's a good time for that? I mean, with the fact that she's planning a wedding tomorrow and all."

George chuckled at the ridiculousness of it all. "Can you get me the gun?"

"I could ask."

"Get it and we'll take care of it."

"As soon as I finish cleaning up," Brian said as he squirted some dish detergent onto a sponge and began scrubbing a small plastic fork. He stopped himself and looked at George. "We save these. Really."

"I'll be in my car," George said, smiling.

The Red Sox were playing the Nationals in a spring training game and it was being broadcast on the radio. Unlike Brian, George grew up a Cubs fan, so he was glad when the Expos moved to DC and became the Nationals, of course a National League team, which meant the Cubbies would be visiting DC several times a year. He thought about driving out to Arizona and catching the Cubs in spring training upon retiring, but the trip to visit Brian would be easier. At least it seemed easier when he decided to make the much shorter trip north.

Brian knocked on the window with a brown paper bag under his arm. George motioned for him to go around and come into the car on the passenger side.

"Here it is," Brian said nervously as he handed the bag to George.

George lifted a Ziploc baggie out of the brown bag, which contained a small pistol. "Beretta semi-automatic 22 caliber. The preferred weapon of hit men. Does damage at close range and harder to trace the round."

"What are you going to tell them?"

"I'm not telling them anything. Your daughter is."

Brian was briefly stunned when he heard Juliette referred to as his daughter. "She has to go with you?"

"Of course she does. She found the gun, and she has to turn it in. I'm just the middle man here."

Brian closed his eyes and shook his head slowly as he listened to his the air rush through his nostrils and into his lungs. *Focus,* he thought to himself. "I don't want to risk you getting blamed for anything, George. I'm going to get Juliette and have her present the gun. She needs to take responsibility."

"You're opening a Pandora's box," George said, grabbing Brian's arm.

"That box was opened a long time ago. I'm getting her."

Juliette and Portia were sitting on the bed in Portia's bedroom. Portia had several books on her lap and Juliette had a yellow pad. Brian stood in the doorway, knowing the next words he spoke could change everything. He knew he had betrayed Juliette's secret and to an ATF agent yet. "What are you doing?"

"Writing vows," Portia said, smiling.

Brian flashed on the definition of the word *vow* and considered turning around, but instead said, "Juliette, can I talk to you in private?"

Juliette and Portia looked quizzically at each other. "In private?" Juliette asked. "I'll be right back," she said to her mom good naturedly, thinking it probably had something to do with a surprise wedding gift.

"You what?" Juliette screeched through clenched teeth, trying not to shout while standing next to the front door. "What the fuck were you doing in my room?"

"I was searching for things that your grandma might have stashed, like we were all doing, and don't use that language with me!"

"I can't believe this. That gun is my business!"

"Where did you get it?" Brian said slowly and forcefully, trying to will Juliette into telling the truth.

"Somebody gave it to me," Juliette said, and gauged what she would say next based on Brian's reaction. "Okay, I found it. I was hiding by the side of the house when I noticed Uncle Richard's car drive up. He went over to our mail box, pulled out an envelope which fell to the ground, and when he bent over, the gun fell out of his jacket pocket and into the tall grass. It didn't make any sound when it fell. He pulled away, and I grabbed the gun. I was worried he'd come back for it, but he never did as far as I could tell."

"Just tell the police you found the gun and you want to hand it in."

"And who's going to protect us?"

Brian looked ashamed as he gazed into Juliette's eyes. Her question had obvious implications, and he was the one implicated.

"Me," he said, steely eyed. He braced himself for an outburst of laughter but there wasn't one. "George's outside to take you there. I'll meet you at the police station."

"I'll go," Juliette said, softening but not weakening. "Tell my mom I'll be right back."

Brian leaned against the door after closing it behind her and breathed so deeply that it made him cough.

"What's going on around here?" Mr. Dawson asked angrily.

"Oh, nothing. Do you need anything, Mr. Dawson?"

"A hard-on would do nicely," he mumbled from his chair in the sun room.

Brian wasn't quite sure what he would tell Portia, but he headed up to her room and peered in from the doorway. She had her magnifying glass at the ready with a huge tome of at least five hundred pages on her lap.

"What is that monstrosity? It looks like a law school textbook."

Portia smiled. "It's a book of quotations. I'm trying to find the perfect Shakespearean one for our vows."

"How about, *All's well that end's well*," Brian said plopping next to her.

"That's sweet, but I was hoping for something a little more romantic."

"I think it's more to the point," Brian said, stroking her cheek, gently.

"Where's Juliette?"

"Oh, I had to have her…take care of a wedding-related errand."

"No need to say more, I understand," Portia said holding his hand. "Do you still want to go through with this?"

"Of course I do," Brian said, his voice raspy with intensity, which was unusual for him.

"Why?"

"Huh?" he said, snapping back to reality.

"Why get married?"

"I love you. I want to be with you. I want to help…you… and your family. Our family. My family."

Portia sat up straight and got up from the bed. She walked over to the window where the twilight had turned to darkness and lights from the boats bounced on the water. It was the window next to the desk where her computer was, and she switched it on and sat at the chair in front of the monitor.

"Before we go any further in this, I have to tell you something. Or rather, show you something. If after seeing it, you don't want to go through with it, I'll understand."

Brian was stunned as the computer hard drive whirled as it booted up. He flashed back on the time Frances busted him at his computer while he was watching porn, with the porn star who resembled Portia and actually started this entire karmic journey. Shit! Could it be true? Could she actually be the porn star from the orgy video? Would that change things for him? Brian struggled with his moral compass while Portia calmly moved a large magnifying glass on an arm in front of the screen and began clicking on icons and typing in passwords.

Brian was tense as he stood erect directly behind Portia and studied the screen. Portia clicked on Photoshop, a professional photo and graphics program.

"I use Photoshop to design my signs for work. It's amazing what you can do," Portia said as she searched through photo files. "Here it is," Portia said as she turned to Brian. Her eyes were moist, as fear spread across her face. "I was going to destroy this, but I didn't. I should have. But now, it's important that you see it," Portia said with her voice trembling.

"You don't have to show me. Really. I don't need to know everything about your past. I have a past, too. It's the future that's important. I don't care about porn."

"This involves the *future*...porn? What the hell are you talking about?" Portia said, giggling through her tears.

"You're *not* going to show me you in a porno movie?" Brian said embarrassed. "I'm beet red right now, aren't I?"

"Yes, you are and no, I'm not a porn star! That is hilarious!" Portia said, putting her arms around his waist and hugging him tight. "I wish that was all there was to it." She turned back to the monitor, but laughing uncontrollably at the thought that she would be in porn incapacitated her. "I'm sorry, I just can't do it," she said, gasping for breath from laughing. "I was going to show you a doctored picture of Juliette with ten toes."

"Why?"

"I thought that maybe if you were convinced that Juliette wasn't your biological daughter it would give you an easy out."

"I'm marrying you, not Juliette."

Brian took her by the hand and led her over to the bed, where they spooned in silence.

George was sure he felt more awkward than Juliette as the stared numbly straight ahead. She exuded such a bold self-confidence that he assumed it was a front. He was used to dealing with bad-ass dope fiends and gun runners, so he wasn't intimidated. But they had already gone a mile or so and she hadn't said a word after telling him to *go straight.*

"Brian and I go way back," George said glancing at her.

"We go back for *weeks*," she said sarcastically.

George didn't want to bring up the fact that she was talking about her father, so he didn't.

"Make a right, then a quick left, and why exactly do I have to do this?"

"The first rule of gun ownership is never possess one unless you bought it from a licensed dealer and saw it come out of the box brand new. You have a gun and you don't know where it came from; it could have been stolen from Al Capone."

Juliette shook her head slowly and sighed. "So what's the plan Mr. G-man?"

"I'll go in with you, introduce myself, show my identification, and we'll hand the gun over. They'll take it, you'll sign something, and we leave."

"And what if the gun is dirty?"

George shot her a suspicious glance.

"I watch CSI once in a while," she said coyly.

"If it is dirty, then at least you're on record as having found it and voluntarily handing it in. Wait a minute, are you not telling me something? Because if you know something about that weapon and you're not telling me, that could get me into world of hurt," George said doing a not-too-good job of hiding his anxiety.

"How would I know if it's clean?" she confessed. "All I know is, I haven't shot anybody…yet."

George smirked and drove into the parking lot of the Hampton North Police Department. "Just follow my lead. Give me the gun."

"This is a joke, right?"

"What's that supposed to mean?" George said dead serious.

"You're joking. You have the gun, right?"

George's head fell limp. "I thought he gave it to you. Oh, shit. Call Brian and tell him to bring the gun. We'll go in and get started on the forms."

Juliette called Brian on her phone and told Brian to bring the gun to the station. George stepped outside the car and lit up a smoke.

"What have I gotten myself into?" he muttered.

They entered the boxy, modern police station and walked up to thick Plexiglass window with a female police officer behind it. George pulled out a small black leather folder, which contained his badge and ID card, and held it right up against the window.

"George Maldonado, ATF Special Agent, can I see the watch commander, please?"

"Hold on," the officer said and pushed the button on an intercom. "Sergeant Callahan, front desk, please."

A large, Irish-looking man looking a little too young for the shock of white hair that swept across his forehead approached the window from behind the female officer.

"This gentleman's with ATF and requested to see you," the female officer said while monitoring her computer screen.

"Come through here," the sergeant said, opening the latch on the door and then leading them to his tiny cluttered office. "Have a seat. What can I do for you?"

"I'm staying with a friend in Hampton North, and it's come to may attention that my friend's, uh, daughter,"-- as soon as the word *daughter* came out of his mouth he noticed a perturbed look on Juliette's face-- "is in the possession of a gun, which she found a few weeks ago. And I thought it best that she hand it over for obvious reasons. Actually, the gun is on the way over. We, er, forgot it," George said, embarrassed.

"How old are you, young lady?" the cop asked.

"Twenty."

"Is that the whole story?"

"Sort of," she said flippantly, causing George to clench his teeth. "I found it in front of our house in the bushes."

George relaxed slightly.

"And why didn't you call us as soon as you found it?"

"I was afraid. And I knew that my dad's friend was an ATF agent and I would ask him what to do when he arrived, which is what I did."

"Okay, let me just get some forms and you'll be on your way," the sergeant said flatly as he walked over to a large file cabinet.

After several minutes of signing on a few dotted lines, George and Juliette sat in awkward silence waiting for the sergeant to return.

"All the i's dotted and t's crossed?" Callahan asked, wiping his lips with a napkin and taking a seat across from them. "So when will the gun get here?"

"We don't want to waste any more of your time, so we'll go into the lobby and make a call. It'll only be a minute or two, I'm sure," George said, as he backed out of the office with Juliette in tow.

As George and Juliette passed the front desk, Juliette tugged on George's arm, "I have to use the ladies room before

I call," and asked the officer at the front desk where the ladies room was. She walked down a hall to find it while George waited in the front. He was wondering if there could be more to the missing gun story.

"George! Come can you come over here?" Juliette said in a loud whisper.

George followed her down the bright hallway, which was lined with bulletin boards on both sides. She stood at the end of one of the bulletin boards and pointed at a flyer.

"I was standing here waiting because the bathroom was occupied and I noticed this," she said, putting her finger on the female's face on the missing person flyer. "I think I know who this is."

"Who is she?"

"I think it's my Uncle Richard's mail order bride."

"Are you positive?"

"Not 100 percent, but pretty sure."

George led Juliette back to the front desk and approached the officer. His mind was flashing with electrodes and adrenaline like back in the day when he had a hunch about some undercover job about to go bad. He wondered if Brian had already gone there with the gun. He hurried back to the front desk.

"Excuse me, but was a man here looking for us?"

"Uh, why yes. A man did ask for you. Didn't he find you?"

"Did he say anything else?"

"No. Except he asked where the men's room was."

"Thanks," George said with a sense of controlled panic in his voice. "Come on, Juliette."

"Who was looking for us? Uncle Richard?" Juliette asked, being dragged quickly to the car by George.

"Get in!" he said, jumping behind the wheel and swiftly taking off. "It wasn't Uncle Richard. It was Brian. What did you see when you went to use the bathroom?"

"I don't know."

"What got your attention?"

"Uncle Richards's wife on the missing persons poster?"

"Bingo. Now tell me all about the gun. Everything!"

"I found the gun in the bushes after Uncle Richard dropped it by accident. It fell out of his pocket into some soft shrubs. He was snooping outside our house and going through our mail. I was hiding by the garbage cans. I saw his wife, in the car waiting. I saw something fall out of his pocket, and waited. He heard a noise or something and fled the scene, and I searched for it and found the gun in some tall, dry weeds. I thought it might come in handy."

"Okay, so the baggie we had with the gun…what was in the bag with the gun? Exactly."

"The gun was in a Ziploc bag. And there was…a scrap of paper in there."

"I'm listening."

"It had an address written on it with the last address I knew of where Uncle Richard lived. Just in case the police asked."

George jammed on the brakes and pulled to the right, which terrified Juliette.

"Are you insane?" Juliette screamed.

"Can you take us to that address?" George pleaded.

"What? Yes."

"Brian has the gun and the address. He saw the poster with the missing woman. And now he's on the way there to do what, God only knows. We've got to get there quick!"

"Make a u-ey."

George whipped the car around, squealing the whole way, and tore ass down the road.

"Who's back at your house?" George asked, his face eerily illuminated by the green dashboard instrument lights.

"Just Reyna, the nurse's aide."

"Call her and ask her if she knows where Brian is."

Juliette fumbled for her phone and dialed. "Reyna. Hi, Juliette. Do you know where Brian is? Okay. Hold on," she said as she cupped the phone and turned to George. "She said he left just after we left."

"Ask her if he was carrying anything."

"Was he carrying anything? Okay. Hold on."

"A brown paper bag. That's what I put the Ziploc bag with the gun in," Juliette repeated to George.

"How long will it take us to get to Richard's?"

"I don't know, ten minutes."

"Tell her to call if Brian shows up."

"Call me if you see or hear from Brian, okay?" She put the phone on the car seat between her legs so she could feel it vibrate if she received a call.

"When we get there, we have to act fast. And no matter what you see or hear, you have to do whatever I tell you to do. Everything. Promise?"

"I don't know. What if I don't promise?"

"I turn around. And Brian could either be dead or spend the rest of his life in jail if my hunch is correct."

"I promise," Juliette said as if she were an Army Ranger accepting an order for a suicide mission. "Turn right, then the next left, then it should be on the left."

George slowed down after he made the left, onto the dark rural street with only one street lamp per block.

"There's Brian's Quest," Juliette whispered.

George turned off the car's lights and parked a few car lengths behind it. "Listen and listen carefully. Look at the time on your phone. In five minutes call 911 and then stand by the curb in front of the house. Give them this address. Tell them you think there's a fight or something. Then when the police arrive, you just tell them you came here with me to look for Brian. I'm an ATF agent. That's it. That's all you know. And whatever you do, don't come into the house, no matter what you hear or see."

"I understand," Juliette said solemnly as she looked at the time on her phone.

George reached down to his ankle, retrieved his revolver from the holster, and slowly walked toward the driveway, with a hunch Brian was already inside.

Yes, Brian was indeed inside the house. His blood was still boiling from the moment he saw Richard's wife on the poster at the police station. He rubbed his palms together but it only smeared the sweat around. His jacket was lopsided with the gun in the right side pocket. He started to think about where he was, what he was doing, and he stopped himself. It was not a time for thinking, but for doing. He wasn't going to allow himself to think, reflect, ponder, prognosticate, pontificate, or anything other than do what he had to do here and now. He had it with allowing people and things to dictate how he lived his life.

The house was pitch black. Not even a hint of light from any window of the two-story Victorian home that even in the dark looked neglected and foreboding. Each window had a shade down or a sheet over it. He pulled out his keys and activated a red diode light that allowed him to make his way to a door that led to a basement. He thought to himself that he was making too much noise on the ancient wooden staircase but went quickly anyway, and at the bottom he heard whimpering. A child's whimpering. He shined his light in the direction of the sound, revealing what appeared to be a small boy tied to a chair with a hood over his head. He barely caught himself before he nearly fell into a trench. When he looked down into the hole there was a bloodied, naked, lifeless female at the bottom of it. The mail order bride. Next to the trench, a pile of dirt and about a dozen bags of Quikrete concrete. Instant tomb, just add water.

Paralysis by analysis. He had heard that term used often when describing a batter thinking too much about what a pitcher might be planning three pitches ahead and getting called looking on strike three. But most Hall of Famers ascribe to the axiom, see ball, hit ball. The woman was dead. The kid was tied to a chair but Brian somehow sensed the child was safe for the moment. Don't think. Find Richard. Deal with Richard.

As Brian entered an upstairs room, he immediately recognized the overwhelming odor of cheap cologne mixed with vomit and a steamy haze of stale alcohol breath. Richard was face down on a mattress on the floor. The room was eerily illuminated by a large round Elvis clock on the wall that was lined with pink neon. Filthy clothes, trash, pizza boxes, and porno DVDs and magazines were strewn everywhere. As Richard began to stir, Brian reached into his pocket and desperately tried to open the Ziploc bag for the gun. He couldn't believe what he was doing. He didn't really believe he was actually trying to pull a gun out of a bag. He couldn't believe he actually came to this house to see if it really was Richard's and that he had his mail order bride held captive. He felt as though he was in a bad *Friday the 13th* sequel number 12 when he saw the dead woman, shot in the head in the freshly dug grave in the cellar with a little boy tied to a chair, who was assuredly next in line for a dirt nap. He didn't understand why he was there, getting ready to pull out a gun on this monster, but he knew he had to do it.

Richard woozily opened his eyes and began feeling around under the mess of soiled blankets and sheets next to his head. Brian's hands were beyond clammy. He was dripping wet from nerves and rage. He grabbed the baggie with both hands, and he cursed as he slipped and slided along the top of the bag, but couldn't retrieve the gun because of a fifteen-cent Ziploc that wouldn't zip open.

Richard's eyes bugged out as he felt what he was looking for under the coverless pillow. He extended his arm, holding an identical Beretta .22 caliber semi automatic to the one in the baggie.

"I know you. You're the one fucking my sister," he said, releasing more poisonous fumes into the air as he spoke. "I'll bet her cunt is hairy and wider than a sewer pipe."

Brian fumbled with the bag, still unable to slide the Ziploc open.

"When I fucked her when she was a kid, her cunt was tight. She hadn't even grown pussy hair yet. I wouldn't even want to fuck her now. But wait'll I get my hands on Juliette. I'm gonna get her, you know. Some day. I'll bet her pussy is still tight and juicy," he said, his voice thick with mucus, spewing molecules of bile and evil from deep inside him.

Brian dropped the baggie behind him. He never in his life thought such an internal rage was possible. It was as though his blood was boiling in his veins and his head was going to explode. He quickly hopped forward, landing directly on Richard's hand that held the gun. He easily pried it from his greasy fingers and pointed it at Richard's face. Point blank. He had no idea what would happen next as his fingers trembled and his spinal cord felt like it was winding tighter and tighter.

"Look at me! I said look at me!" Brian screeched in a blind rage. The pink neon glistened in Richard's eyes and he seemed for the first time to look like he knew what was going on. "You're not going to fuck with anyone. Ever." Brian suddenly squeezed the trigger once. With barely a report, Richard's head jerked slightly and for a spit second, Brian wondered what exactly happened. He realized he shot the gun but wondered if he missed him. As though in a dream, in slow motion, a stream of thick goo started pouring out of Richard's left eye and his head contorted downward.

George tore ass into the room led by a small flashlight in his left hand and his revolver in his right. He saw Brian standing there with a gun at his side. The room reeked of cheap cologne and gun powder, and on a mattress on the floor was a shirtless man, belly-down, with blood streaming out of his left eye.

Brian stood there in the dark silently, dazed, watching as the blood formed a small puddle in the carpeting.

"Brian! Listen to me! Listen!" George said, shaking Brian's shoulders. "Whose gun is that you're holding?"

"What? George! Oh my God, George!" Brian said, as though he suddenly woke up from a nightmare.

"Whose gun is that in your hand?"

"It's his. He pointed it at me, and I stomped on his hand and took it from him. What's going on?"

"Listen to me carefully! Where's the gun you came here with? Juliette's gun."

"It's right there on the floor. I dropped it because I couldn't get the Ziploc bag open."

"Pick it up! Now!" George screamed, shining the red light on the bag.

George took out a handkerchief, grabbed the gun from Brian, wiped it thoroughly, and placed it back into Richard's right hand.

"Take the gun out of the bag. Then point it at the wall just above him."

"What?"

"Just do it. Now!" A siren could be heard in the distance. "Shoot at the wall one time. Do it!"

A shot rang out and the bullet went into the wall about a foot above where Richard was laid out on the floor.

"Now listen. Here's what happened. You get me?" George said, shining the light into his own face.

"Okay. Tell me what happened."

"You came here, to this house, to see if this was where Richard was holding his mail order bride captive. You thought you were going to call the police but you heard a kid scream and came into the house instead. You went to the basement where you found the kid alive and the woman dead in the pit."

"That is what happened…"

"Listen to me. Then you came up here, you took the gun out of the Ziploc bag and entered the room. Richard was on the mattress, he pointed the gun at you. You fired a shot and missed. Then he turned the gun on himself and shot himself in the eye."

"But I shot him…"

"I'm telling you! This is your decision. You can tell them whatever the fuck you want, okay? But I'm telling you, your name ain't Kennedy and this ain't Chappaquiddik. You're a nobody and nobodies go to jail. You admit you shot this guy, even if he's fuckin' Adolph Hitler, and all it takes is one media whore lawyer looking for headlines and they'll nail you to the cross faster than Pontius Pilate."

The siren stopped and tires squealed in front of the house. Brian stood in a dream world stuck in the cheap after shave soaked room mixed with blood, sweat and death.

"It's your choice. Don't take a chance. Tell them what I told you and there ain't a jury in the world that'll give you jail time. Convince them you're a hero and they won't even press charges. But tell them you shot him, and there's a chance you could be Bubba's bee-atch for a decade or two. Believe me, you just saved the Commonwealth of Massachusetts about a million bucks by offing that evil motherfucker."

George reached up and pulled on a string that turned on a ceiling light fixture. He put his gun in his ankle holster and took out his badge and ID. Then he led Brian out to the hall just outside the room. The front door pushed open as other police cars screeched to a halt in front of the house.

"Police! Police!" they shouted.

"Come up here!" George said holding his badge up. "I'm a special agent for the ATF. Everything's under control. Send for an ambulance. And tell the coroner he's got two to-go."

"The kid!" Brian shouted, which made the first young officer jump back. Brian ran out the door, "Come on!"

Brian, George, and the second officer, a young African American female, ran to the basement. There wasn't any whimpering. The hooded child was slumped forward, tied in his child-sized chair. The female officer shined her long black flashlight into the pit where the naked Filipina woman lay, next to her bloodied underwear. The light from the flashlight was like an intense spotlight that clearly showed a bullet hole in the middle of her forehead.

"What the fuck is this?" she screamed to Brian and George. She shouted into her two-way radio, "Send a lot of back up. Now! Victim, DOA in basement," she pointed the flashlight onto the hood of the child. "Possibly two."

George pulled out a pocket knife and carefully cut the black canvas sack off the child's head. His eyes shot open, and he began screaming uncontrollably in Tagalog.

The female officer knelt next to the child as George undid the ropes that bound him to the Sesame Street chair. She stroked his face and his hair with tears in her eyes. "You're going to be all right little baby. Don't you worry. We're here to help you."

The boy began to hyperventilate and jerk suddenly.

"He's in shock," George said calmly. "Put this on him," he said, handing his blazer to the officer.

"Don't let him see that!" the female office whispered loudly as they moved the boy a few feet further away from the pit where his mother lay twisted and dead.

A water hose and a large black plastic bin used to mix cement were next to the bags of Quikrete.

"I'd check all the prior addresses for this monster and start digging up the basements," George said to the officer as she held the boy in her arms and rushed him upstairs shielding his eyes.

"Jesus H. Fucking Christ!" a male voice bellowed from the top of the stairs. A portly man in a black windbreaker that read POLICE over his heart stood as he surveyed the scene. "Get Willets in here!" A moment later a diminutive young man wearing a similar windbreaker appeared with a camera and a bag of equipment that weighed down his shoulder and began flitting around taking photos.

"I'm George Maldonado, ATF. This is my buddy, Brian DeLouise, who's...an involved witness. Where can we talk?"

Three more windbreakered men entered carrying bags. "I'm Lieutenant Detective Morrisey. Come with me," the large red-faced cop said, waving them up the stairs.

"What's going to happen to the kid?" George asked the detective as they walked out the front door.

"He'll be examined for abuse. Sexual and otherwise. Then turned over to CPS," he said while he lit a cigarette. "It'll be easier if we go to the station for a statement."

Brian was impervious to the chaos around him. He didn't really hear the sirens still arriving, squad car and ambulance doors slamming, commands being yelled, radios blaring. He scanned the scene looking for Juliette. He spotted her leaning against George's car arms folded high, almost to her throat.

"Can I just see my...daughter?" he asked George and the detective.

George looked to the detective and the detective nodded affirmatively.

Brian had no idea what he would say to Juliette as he crossed the street dodging vehicles, emergency personnel, and equipment. He stood in front of her in silence. Juliette nervously fingered the seashell necklace. She looked at him with tear-soaked eyes and rushed into his arms. Brian didn't think he ever felt someone hug him so tight.

"I heard the gunshot. I thought maybe...you were killed," she whispered into his ear.

"No. Your Uncle Richard was killed."

Brian waited for a response, but there wasn't one.

"His wife is dead. Murdered."

Juliette pushed back and looked, panic stricken, into Brian's face. "What about the child?"

"He's okay." Brian said, stroking Juliette's hair. She touched her necklace and faced him.

"Okay. Thank you," she said smiling, and then kissed him softly on the cheek. "I called Reyna to come, and she just got here. She'll drive me home."

"Reyna! Wait. She might be able to help. The child is Filipino!" Brian shouted.

Juliette watched as Brian ran to the van where the officer had taken the kid, poked his head in, and then ran back to Reyna and escorted her to the van. As soon as Reyna started saying, "Huwag kang mag-alala aking munti" which translates to "Don't worry little one," over and over, the boy gradually stopped crying and almost smiled.

It was that moment, just as Juliette arrived at the van and Reyna hugged the boy and spoke to him loving words in his native language, that Brian knew everything would be okay. He did what he was meant to do.

CHAPTER EIGHTEEN

As the days and weeks passed, Brian was nervously waiting for something to happen. He wasn't sure what that something was but it had to be something. After all, he had just killed someone. He told his story to the cops and that was it. He felt as though he was walking through a mine field, going about his normal activities of daily living and at any moment, it would be KABLOOEY! But it didn't happen. Nothing exploded. He just chalked it up to denial. He didn't know when the inner workings of his brain would release the chemicals that would trigger some kind of overwhelming wave of emotions that would change his very existence, and he waited patiently for it to come.

The one thing that did weigh on his mind was telling Portia the truth. Lying to the police as he did was one thing. Lying to Portia wasn't even an issue. If he were to tell her anything, it would have to be the truth, the whole truth, and nothing but the truth. He didn't know what her reaction would be. She could tell the police, for all he knew. But at this point it made no difference.

The weather was definitely changing. George was sunning on the veranda in a tee shirt and shorts as if it was in the eighties, not in the sixties like it actually was. Brian dragged over a folding chair and tapped him on the shoulder.

"I'm going to tell Portia what I did."

"Why?" George asked without opening his eyes.

"I feel like it's the right thing to do," Brian said, his voice cracking.

"You already did the right thing."

"Did I?" Brian asked curtly. Maybe it would be George who would trigger everything, Brian thought.

George quickly sat up straight and looked Brian dead in the eye. "I'm glad you finally fucking asked."

Brian's head jerked back in surprise.

"You go sit in front of your computer, alone or with Portia or with the entire fucking Smart household gathered around and Google this: Richard Speck Sex Drugs Video. Then click on any of the links and ask me if you did the right fucking thing. Do I need to remind you who Richard Speck is?"

"No need. My mother shuddered in fear whenever that name was on the news. She was a nurse in Chicago."

"Yeah. Eight nurses tortured and murdered. I remember the story. You remember the story. But unfortunately not everybody remembers the fucking story," George said, catching himself as he started to raise his voice. "You Google that. And see the video of that fucking animal, in jail, with tits he grew on taxpayers money, doing coke with his fuck buddy in jail and laughing about it. That motherfucker admitted on camera that if they knew how much fun he was having in jail they'd set him loose. It took a jury forty-nine minutes to find him guilty and give him the death penalty. And the courts overturned his execution so he could spend the rest of his life in jail, having the fucking time of his life getting his tits sucked and getting fucked by a parade of murderers until he died of a heart attack. Massafuckingchussetts doesn't have the death penalty. You watch that video and then ask me if you did the right thing. You know they found another body, right?"

"From Speck?" Brian asked, confused.

"Uncle Richard. In his last house. A missing Russian mail order bride was found when they dug up the basement."

Brian reached out with his right hand.

"Thank you, brother," George said solemnly as he spat in his right hand. George spat in his right hand, and they shook hands.

"One other thing," George said leaning back into his recliner. It was Benjamin Franklin who said, "The only way three people can keep a secret is if two of them are dead."

"Thanks. I am going to tell Portia. Some day," Brian said, as he stood and breathed in the salty spring ocean air. He bounded down the steps and walked straight to the water's edge and turned left for a long walk up the coast. Maybe regret and remorse and fear would one day explode inside his soul, he thought to himself. In the meantime, he'd live his life.

It was decided there would be no guests for the wedding that had already been delayed for weeks. Just Portia, Brian, Juliette, George, Beatrice in her wheelchair, Reyna, Mr. Dawson, Mrs. Pangborne and a minister would be present for the late afternoon outdoor ceremony. The food would be take-out from The Laughing Gull and the music would be provided by Juliette's iPod, which consisted almost entirely of opera, classical music, and show tunes, connected to a boom box.

The Unitarian minister at the Smart front door was a thin man around forty, with wild, frizzy hair, an ill-fitting brown suit with a flowered tie, round John Lennon glasses, and a permanent toothy, goofy smile.

Juliette opened the door and assumed he was the minister. "I'm Juliette, thanks for coming on such short notice," she said politely.

"I'm Reverend Mooney, always thrilled when love calls!" he said, bouncing on his white Converse hi-tops that had a peace sign where the Chuck Taylor circular emblem usually is. "I just have a few papers to sign, and then we can rock and roll. I have to be at a drum circle in a couple of hours, but no rush," he said, handing Juliette two envelopes. "One is for the donation," he whispered.

"Have a seat in the kitchen, and I'll get the bride and groom," Juliette said as she pointed to the kitchen table.

Juliette knocked on Portia's door.

"Come in."

Juliette gasped softly after she opened the door and took in the splendor of her mother standing backlit against the ocean view, gloriously resplendent in her simple beige cotton dress that was pulled snug under her breasts and flowed outward. She wore a wreath of yellow daisies that looked like a halo with the glistening golden sunlight shining through them.

"You look amazing," Juliette said, enthralled.

"Is it too hippie-ish?"

"Not at all. It's beautiful in its simplicity. Classic."

"You have to sign some things in the kitchen with the minister. He's waiting downstairs. I'll go get Brian. Magnificent," she said, exiting the room.

Brian and George were at the top of the stairs preparing to lift Beatrice in her wheelchair and take her downstairs to the veranda for the ceremony. She was in a dress and even had makeup on for the first time since she fell ill.

"Be careful! Don't make her nervous!" Reyna shouted at the men as she supervised them negotiating the stairs.

After they reached bottom, Reyna took control of the wheelchair and wheeled it into the sun room

"Brian, you need to sign something in the kitchen, after Reyna releases you," Juliette said as she headed for the kitchen.

The minister sat at the table with his papers laid out in front of him, next to a copy of a leather-bound, beaten-up book with no title on the cover.

Brian quietly sat next to him and said quietly, "I'm the groom."

"I'm Reverend Mooney. Congratulations," he said handing him a small business card with the yin-yang symbol on it.

"Do you have any quotes or sayings or anything that you want me to include in the ceremony?" the reverend asked with a huge grin.

"Let's wait for the bride," Brian said uncomfortably, then did a double take as Portia entered the doorway and paused. He hadn't seen her in her wedding gown until this moment as he was flush with emotion; he flashed on his serpentine journey that brought him to this place and wondered what might have been if only he had not left that summer, or had talked himself into joining her on her trip to Europe. He could barely get out the words, "You…look…gorgeous."

"My, oh my!" the minister proclaimed loudly. "Angelic!"

Portia looked at the minister and knew he was the wrong person to ask on whether or not she looked too hippie-ish. "I dug this out of an old trunk in the attic. I'm amazed it still fits," she said, flattening the dress down. She wondered if her pregnancy was showing but didn't bring it up.

"All I need is your signatures and the two witnesses," he said, laying out the form. Brian nodded and left the room to get Juliette and George.

"Is there anything you'd like me to include in the ceremony, Portia?"

"Yes, it's a quote from Shakespeare," she said, handing him a small card.

"Oh, that is lovely," he said glancing at it. "Is this your first marriage?"

"Yes. And my last," she said laughing.

"That's the attitude!" The minister sang.

Brian, Juliette, and George appeared in the kitchen and stood behind Portia. "Here we are," Brian said joyfully with arms around Juliette and George, who both appeared less-than-joyous.

"Usually it's the bride and groom who look nervous, not the witnesses."

They spent the next few minutes signing forms, and the reverend notarized the signatures. "I hate to rush anything, but I have to be at a drum circle in an hour and a half. Is there any reason we can't do the ceremony in a few minutes?"

Brian and Portia exchanged *what the heck* glances and said, "No."

"Well, let's do it!" the reverend said, bounding out of his chair.

Brian snuck up behind Juliette and whispered in her ear, “Can I talk to you for a minute?” and then said aloud, “We’ll be right there!” to the others.

He took her by the arm and out the front door.

“You look terrified. What is it?” Juliette asked.

“If you don’t want me to go through with the wedding, I’ll understand, but I’m doing this because of my love for your mother and for no other reason,” Brian said shaking. “You’re right about me being your biological father. It doesn’t mean shi... anything. But if you have any doubt that the only reason I want to marry your mother is my undying love for her, we can call it off.”

Juliette grabbed her ever-present seashell necklace and pulled it outside of her blouse. “You see this? I’m never without it.” She fingered each of the many small seashells that made up the necklace and came to a stop on two of them. “Look at these. Notice how they’re different from the rest? When I was in kindergarten, everything was going fine until one day when we all took our shoes and socks off. That was the day I was mortified when everyone made fun of my…” She held up the two little sea shells, that weren’t sea shells after all, but looked like two shriveled up tiny white peas, and added, “...two extra toes.”

Brian reached out to touch them with his shaking index finger.

“Mom put them on this necklace. I know it sounds gross, but after I forced her to have them removed I didn’t want to part with them. There wasn’t any bone in them; they were really just oversized skin tags. But she told me why I had them. I knew you were my biological father since the day after you first arrived. If you loved Mom, I knew you’d be back.”

It crossed Juliette’s mind that this would be a good moment to tell Brian about Portia’s trust fund, but she figured, why not wait until after the ceremony. She no longer had any doubts about what was deep in Brian’s heart.

They walked onto the veranda arm in arm to the waiting group.

"I'm getting married!" Brian said triumphantly, twirling Juliette like a ballerina.

Reyna wheeled Beatrice to the center of the veranda, and the group gathered around her facing the ocean. Brian and Portia stepped forward with Juliette, George, Reyna standing behind with Beatrice in her wheelchair and Mr. Dawson in a white resin deck chair. The sparkling scenery and sea spray air charged each of them with a feeling of pure bliss. Perhaps even Beatrice comprehended the moment since she had an expression on her face that could either be joy, or perhaps just gas. The Unitarian minister, battered book in hand, faced them and began the ceremony.

"If anyone knows for any reason why this joining should not take place, please speak now or forever hold your peace," the reverend implored, looking directly at the group.

Portia looked at Juliette, who appeared to be fidgeting and then suddenly spoke up. "I have something to say," Juliette announced, startling even Mr. Dawson. "I want to bring up something that could have an effect on this marriage."

"Juliette, I'm going to…" Portia seethed, but stopped when Brian tugged on her arm.

"I think Brian and Portia should know that I've done some covert surveillance and made a discovery that may change things. Mom, I found out that you and I each have a trust fund worth almost a half million dollars set up by Grandma. That's it," she concluded sharply.

"What?!" Portia asked, as though she just found out she was sentenced to life in prison. "Are you sure?"

"Positive. I can fill in the blanks later, if you still want to go ahead with the ceremony," Juliette said apologetically.

Portia turned to Brian and smiled a crooked, slightly embarrassed smile. "I guess that means we can go on a honeymoon now."

"This is a first!" the minister said. "I now pronounce you husband and wife!"

Reyna pushed the button on a boom box and the choral climax to Beethoven's Ninth, the *Ode to Joy,* began to play, as Brian and Portia embraced and kissed passionately to applause.

After a champagne toast, the minister left for his drum circle and everyone went to the sun room for food laid out on tables.

Brian and Portia sat next to each other on the very same rattan sofa where twenty years ago they first made out and made love. Brian watched Juliette talking to George and wondered if perhaps she was conceived on that very sofa. But even more perplexing was that the beautiful, graceful, brilliant, talented creature on the other side of the room causing his buddy George to laugh hysterically was actually somehow brought into this world with his biological help.

Brian got up from his end of the couch and knelt in front of Portia. "I think we should get some rest. Let's go upstairs," he said, helping her to get up.

CHAPTER NINETEEN

There was no honeymoon. Portia didn't feel well the next morning. In fact, the day after the wedding Portia couldn't get out of bed, slurred her speech, and couldn't hold a cup of tea. The ambulance was called, and Brian sat in back holding her hand along the way, praying silently as he watched her fade away until she was barely conscious.

Brain and Juliette sat next to each other holding hands in the waiting room, neither wanting to express their dread. The doctor approached wearing casual clothes one might wear if one were having a barbeque.

"Have you decided?" the doctor said, file in hand.

"Yes. Do whatever you can," Brian said looking at Juliette, thinking he had to look strong and brave. "What about the…baby?"

"We're in uncharted territory here really. We just have no way of knowing," the doctor said glumly. "I'm glad you and Portia agreed on surgery, but time is of the essence. We should start right away," he said, leading them to a small cubicle. "Armando will have you fill out some forms."

Brian was in a daze signing the forms and wanting to scream at the irony of his lifelong nickname, Bad Brain. There wasn't a time in the past thirty years when the word *brain* didn't jump out at his on form letters, jury duty notices, junk mail, and from the lips of old friends.

Juliette and Brian sat together and passed the time reading magazines, talking on the phone, and trying to visualize a happy, 100 percent healthy Portia emerging smiling from the operating room.

Six hours later the doctor appeared looking exhausted and nervous, still in his goofy blue slippers and surgery gear. "We just won't know for a while. We removed a benign tumour that what was wound around her optic nerves; it's called an optic nerve neural sheath meningioma. Unfortunately, we had to remove the left eye. We didn't have to touch the brain at all.

We think we got it all. But it's not an exact science. We just have to wait."

"So...there's hope...with the exception of the eye, she could make a full recovery? Brian said, unconsciously squeezing Juliette's hand tighter and tighter.

"I would think so."

"And what about the baby?"

"So far so good," the doctor said brightly. "It was all local anesthesia and we believe Portia should deliver normally, naturally or with a Cesarean."

Juliette squeezed back just as hard, they turned toward each other, and both bowed their heads in silence as the top of their foreheads gently came together.

CHAPTER TWENTY

A few weeks later there wasn't just *a* miracle; there were *two*. A Cesarean birth of a preemie, weighing only a little more than four pounds, and an excellent prognosis for Portia. Brian hadn't slept in thirty-six hours, yet he bounded up the four flights of stairs when the nurses station called him on his cell while eating a jumbo black-and-white cookie and downing his fourth straight cup of stale cafeteria coffee. He hit the landing and as he turned the corner there was a loud *bing* and the elevator door opened, with a jubilant Juliette.

"Wait for me!" she said, calling after Brian as he zipped past, clapping her hands lightly in celebration.

Brian prayed a continuous loop of Hail Marys just under his breath.

They stopped at the door to Portia's room and peeked in. Portia was sitting up, her right eye closed, her left eye covered with a black eyepatch that had an eyeball drawn in the middle of it with a silver pen.

They softly knocked on the door frame and rushed to Portia's bedside. She opened her eye and beamed a smile that told them both all they needed to know.

"Go look! Go look! Go look! She's gorgeous!" Portia said, slobbering kisses on whatever hand, cheek, pair of lips, or body part she could grab. "Go!"

A nurse brought them next door, and there she was; Baby Portia, in an incubator. She was pink and tiny but looking as healthy and perfect as a newborn could be.

"My eyesight's not so good, you count them," Brian said to Juliette, stroking her shoulder.

"The kid got cheated. Only ten toes."

The circle was complete when Beatrice passed away in her sleep the day after Portia arrived home with the baby. Baby Portia grew stronger as the days and weeks passed and the cold northern winds gave way to warm ocean breezes.

Beatrice's room was converted into a nursery. The walls were filled with photos and paintings of her. Brian sat in a rocking chair with Baby Portia in his arms, feeding her from a bottle as he gazed out at the ocean view. He heard one short, one long, and one short blast from a hand-held foghorn in the distance and knew what it meant; George and Kate would be stopping by within the half hour. It just cracked him up that those two quickly became an item, and George had stopped drinking and was getting back to the form he had when he led the north side of Chicago in schoolyard basketball. He could see them in their two-person kayak rounding the lighthouse island. Brian laughed to himself all the times he saw the female kayaker out there and didn't know it was Kate from The Laughing Gull restaurant. And laughed even harder that she and George hit it off famously, culminating with them moving in together and Kate convincing George to escort her to her AA meetings every day.

Portia tiptoed into the nursery with her hand covering her left eye. "Ta da!" she shouted revealing her gleaming new prosthetic eyeball.

"It's beautiful! My God, it looks so real."

"You've got to see it up close," Portia said as she bent over and began to kiss him tenderly.

"Get a room!" Juliette whispered through cupped hands. "I'm all packed," she said tiptoeing over and kissing both the baby and Brian on the forehead.

Portia beamed. "That's great. Who's driving you to the airport?"

"George and Kate."

"They just gave me the signal they are on the way over," Brian said, still feeding the sleeping baby.

"I can still cancel."

"No, go. You need it. Do it now or you might never get the opportunity again. I sure wish I had gone to Europe with your mom. I'm glad you're not going alone. He's a good guy that Mike Fraser. It's a good thing he let you raid that post office box."

"Some things are just meant to be," Juliette said softly. "I'll bring my bags downstairs."

After George and Kate arrived and took showers, they went into the nursery where Brian was rocking Baby Portia to sleep in her crib with Portia and Juliette looking on.

"How is she doing?" Kate said lovingly as she peered through the crib's vertical bars. "She looks so healthy! Ten fingers, ten toes, right?" Kate said, causing smiles around the room.

"We're ready to go," Juliette announced. "Oh, I almost forgot to tell you. Margaret from The Tent called. She wants to know if you can put up a few people from the summer's first show. She said to call her."

"Sure! That'll help the cash flow. What show is it?"

"NY Shakespeare touring company. They're doing *Macbeth*."

Brian and Portia gasped in mock horror.

"Whaaaa?" Juliette asked.

Brian explained to Juliette the ancient superstitious rite of the *Macbeth* mention. Juliette happily complied; spinning, spitting, knocking, asking to enter the room, and laughing hysterically as Portia tickled her ferociously during the ritual. When it was finally completed and the laughter stopped, George entered the room. All were there, in Beatrice's room suddenly so quiet the only sound that could be heard was Baby Portia's breathing.

"What's going on in here? George asked.

"Oh, nothing," Portia said, gently stroking the baby's heard. "Just putting the end to an ancient curse."

Just then, Baby Portia opened her eyes and let out with a loud "Googahhgahahhggoag".

"You're welcome!" Brian said. "You better get going. I'll be right down."

Everyone exited, except for Brian and Baby Portia. He sat gazing out on the coast, the lighthouse, the rocks, the waves, the marbled sky, and felt that distinct, indescribable comforting pleasure one can only feel when one is totally safe at home.